THE LOITERERS

ELLY ~~ELLIOTT~~

BANGS

Revision 3.2 – First CreateSpace edition

ISBN: 1466310545
ISBN-13: 978-1466310544

For K,
for L,
for A,
and for M.

Prologue

The heart of the machine is pounding, and Shayna is a part of it. Her body is incorporated into its rhythm. Its gears turn with the twisting of her arms and her feet rise and fall with its pistons. Its oil and corrosion pool with her sweat. In time with her pulse and her breath, the stencil cage swings down, the dye spreads, and a fine mist of fixer solution sprays over one more in an infinite series of branded shirts for the Power Elite. The steady flow of identical movements and moments seems to dissolve the passing of time. Somewhere in her clattering memory of motors and pipes she's a twelve year old girl, first learning to pull these levers. In a blink she is eighteen, expecting to blink one more time and be old – but for a moment her mind wanders. The gray steel unexpectedly parts into a field of vibrant blue, and the drone of the machinery is suddenly shot through with a resonant sound. She's only remembering a dream, she realizes, but for one second the memory is so sharp and real that it shuts her eyes and sends a weird shiver down her neck. For a second, the color and the sound breathe through her. Then the pounding metal roars back with a snap of explosive pain.

"Mind if I smoke?" the nurse asks, though she's already lighting up.

Shayna looks up from her damaged hand. She takes her half-burnt lunch cigarette from behind her ear and leans over the metal desk to share the flame. Then she sits back anxiously while the nurse takes a long, dejected pull and looks her patient over before finally saying "All right, let me see it."

Shayna lays her hand on the desk, wincing as the stranger's fingers prod the skin around the gash, left of the palm, cut deep along the heart line. When she diverts her gaze from the blood her attention lands on a machine too clean and new to belong here: a tall thing with enclosing arms, like a man-sized centipede standing erect with its back to the wall.

"Now how did you do this to yourself?" the nurse asks.

"I got it stuck under the stencil cage when it pressed down."

"Now why did you do that?"

"I just got distracted, I guess. I had this weird..." She feels a flush of panic the moment the careless words have left her mouth. She knows what the consequences will be if factory administration decides the injury was her own fault.

"This weird what?"

"I just suddenly remembered this dream that I had last night. That I'd forgotten."

The nurse glances up and then continues wiping the blood and mechanical grease out of the wound. Eventually she mutters "Must've been some dream. All right, step into that scanner there."

Shayna glances uncertainly back and forth between her and the nightmare metal centipede.

"It's standard procedure. Everyone who comes in here gets a full-body scan. It's for the population forecast. It's painless. It'll give me a look at your hand."

Shayna snuffs out her cigarette and does as she's told, standing still in the center of the enfolding arms. An eerie warmth passes through her. Her teeth vibrate in their sockets. Then it's over and she slumps back into the folding chair.

The nurse only stares into the computer screen while her cigarette burns down to its end and the air turns more opaque. Shayna sits in anxious silence, trying to read this woman, trying to see the verdict coming, but her eyes are as lifeless as polished stones in the screen's blue glow.

She must be a Greentowner, Shayna decides. Her labcoat is too clean to belong this far out in the Tropolis. She's very old, maybe forty or more, but her teeth are natural teeth, yellowed in between. Her blond hair is white at the roots. She probably lives in one of the Inner Rings, but not in the Cology itself; she may be wealthy, but she's still mortal and it shows.

Just once the nurse looks up to pass Shayna a glance almost too quick to register. She seems to stifle a sigh. Then she picks up a syringe full of orange goo and says "It's not too deep. This sealant will close it up and sterilize it. It turns flesh-tone in ten minutes. It'll sting like hell while it sets, but you can go back to work. Just don't pick at it. You'll get the feeling back in those fingers pretty soon. The numbness you mentioned is only a pinched nerve."

"I can't afford this," Shayna interrupts, pulling her hand back before the goo can reach it.

"It's on me," the nurse responds. "No charge."

"What—? Why?"

"Because I say so."

Shayna puts her hand back on the desk. The goo burns in the gash and sets in a silence she's is afraid to break, even to say thanks. She waits for a cue to be dismissed, but the nurse's eyes go straight from the wound back to the screen. Eventually Shayna rises, but the moment she touches the handle on the door she hears the woman say:

"Wait. You... care to sit down?"

The folding chair screeches when Shayna pulls it back again.

"You're eighteen years old, you said," says the nurse.

Shayna nods silently.

"Born the second of April. So you just turned eighteen. Just recently."

"Yesterday."

The nurse sighs slowly, sadly. Then she rubs her hand over her face and laughs – a hollow, sickly effigy of laughter. Her voice is a rasp just loud enough to make out when she says: "The bastards I work for and all their damned customer service protocols. I'm not supposed to share the test results with the sample group, no, *that's* against the rules. But it's instantaneous, you understand? The results process right away. I see everything. Like it's all for my own amusement. Day after day they send me down to this shithole—" she coughs "—as if it matters. As if we're all dumb enough to think they give a rat's ass about this place, about you, about me, about anyone out here. And, hell. You probably can't even follow a word I'm rambling at you. You're just more empty-headed trash from the outer rings. Another *Outsider*. That's what you're supposed to be to me. But it's a big sick joke when we actually have everything in common, isn't it?" She pauses a moment and then repeats her own words to herself with a trace of awe: "We have everything in common."

Shayna squints uncertainly.

The nurse says: "Forget it. This is all. One last question for the paperwork. You've heard that old proverb, 'ignorance is bliss.' What do you think? Do you believe that?"

The words hang ominously in the smoky air. Shayna looks uneasily at her hands on her knees and feels her palms suddenly sweating. She can sense it coming, whatever it is. She can feel the weight hiding behind the words.

"Think it over. Take your time. Don't answer l-lightly." A moment later the nurse abruptly collapses into a violent fit of hacking. She pulls a white handkerchief from her pocket and clamps it over her mouth.

Shayna watches anxiously, but the coughing finishes. The old woman in white hurriedly wipes her lips, wads up the handkerchief and tosses it into the plastic wastebasket by the door.

"Well?"

"No. It's not."

The nurse's cold gaze slowly scans her patient, appraising her. Finally she nods and says: "Then you have between fifteen and twenty-three days to live."

In the time that follows, Shayna will revise her memory of this moment. She'll remember that her pulse was hammering while the details were laid out to her, that her thoughts were fluttering in panic, that her entire corrupted body was coursing with what seemed like a tangible liquid terror. She'll remember that her silence is the result of shock, but it be an invention of hindsight. The truth is that her silence now is honest and clear. In the first moments in the wake of the prognosis, she feels perfectly numb.

"Time for you to go back to work I think," the nurse finishes, emotionlessly.

Shayna stands from the chair and drifts hesitantly toward the door. She looks back many times, but the nurse's eyes are fastened to her paperwork. As she turns the steel handle, she glances down into the wastebasket. The wadded-up handkerchief is full of blood.

PART 1:

RUST

21

The bus hummed past the last of the powered streetlamps along Galt Avenue and seemed to hesitate a moment before lurching ahead into the total night. It descended after the protective white flames of its rain-speckled headlights, down into one of the dead neighborhoods to the South of Angelis, where blackened bricks loomed against the dirty red sky. Glass shards and sagging storefronts glittered like eyes in the concrete jungle and were snuffed out in the bus's diesel wake. When the last fiery aura of sodium bulbs dissolved into the unmarked cross-streets behind, the wilderness of the dead city was all-surrounding.

Shayna stirred from her half-sleep and leaned her head against the rumbling glass. Her reflection looked back through red-framed eyes; its off-blond hair was still darkened with soot from work, and its body looked even smaller and frailer than usual. Looking through that dim image, she watched the nothingness slide past. In those waves of invisible motion, she thought to herself that it might have been the bottom of the ocean she was staring into. It could've been deep space.

Her lungs drew in and expelled the sweaty atmosphere, and when she opened her eyes everything had jumped into strange focus. She felt the air pressing on the smoke-stained walls of her chest; the throbbing stabs of faint but permanent migraine behind her eyes; the shirt bunched and sweaty in her armpits and the oversized army coat that hangs from her shoulders to her knees; the dull pain in the roots of her tight-clenched teeth, the clammy restlessness of clenched fists in lint-filled pockets and clenched toes in soggy boots; the noise of whining motor and turning wheel and splashing pothole; the smell of damp and sick humanity; the creamy fluorescence of flickering advertisements shining across the ink-smeared and ass-polished vinyl. For the tenth time since the prognosis, something had switched in her mind, and it made everything seem suddenly unreal – or too real. One way or another, it was suffocating.

This deep in the dead city, the route grew twisted and erratic to avoid the streets that were too weathered or full of debris to drive. The motors grunted as the bus started up a long hill, and through the wiper blades the fiery glow of civilization was staining the cloud bottoms again. Soon the first streetlamp peaked above the crest like a breaking dawn.

Her hand rooted through her coat pocket and closed around her phone. She hesitated in aimless thought before pulling it out and dialing the same number she'd already dialed three times that night, and this time he finally answered.

"Hello?" Tom's voice crackled and stuttered. "Shay?"

The words caught in her throat.

"Hello," he repeated.

"Can I stay at your place tonight?" she heard herself finally say.

The static yawned.

"Shay? What's— Is something wrong?"

"Nothing's wrong. I just want to stay at your place. I can't sleep at mine. Is that okay with you?"

An uneasy pause.

"Sure. Sure, yes."

"I'm almost there," she said. "I'll be there soon."

She dropped the phone back into her pocket and sighed. A perverse and involuntary smile crossed her face, and she felt her fingernails stabbing into her palms, and she laughed at herself as she wondered just how she would tell him. How she would tell anyone. How do you tell someone you'll be dead in three weeks?

In that moment the neon of civilization rushed in and burned her eyes until she shut them. The black chaos of pothole splashes faded into echoes of the empty-headed soundtracks of holographic ads and gas bars. The brakes screamed and the doors opened with a hydraulic hiss.

Distorted signage and luminous Company logos were melted all over the sidewalks, dripping from plastic facades into gutters. Televised eyes in billboards tracked her as she walked. Displays in storefronts barked commands to attention – ragged urchins in muddy soda-ad shirts pleaded for change – and she passed them all by, gliding in oblivion over the sparkling tiles as if practicing for ghosthood.

She turned down a side street that shot out into a desert of parking lots and warehouse loading docks, where red-hot bulbs looked down from their looming poles onto flaking yellow paint and rusty chains. On the near edge of this expanse one apartment building stood, and at its doorstep perched the last three prostitutes of Friday night: one in leopard-print, one with a catlike tail and a long mane of glittering golden hair, the third with grotesque plastic wolf mask. Shayna hurried past, reflexively averting her gaze, but it wasn't because of the mask or the darkness that her heart was hammering in her face as she mashed the rusty buzzer by the door. There was something else, a less tangible pressure, that made her bound fast up the steps even though she was already out of breath. When she saw Tom Nice the garbageman squinting sheepishly past the edge of his door, she did not say hello. She just ran to him, wrapped her arms around his wiry frame and squeezed until he suppressed a groan.

"Are you okay?" he asked. His warm hands settled cautiously on her shoulders and did not move.

"Yeah," she said, feeling even more uncomfortably short than she usually did.

She let go. Their eyes met for a brief moment and then both looked quickly away.

The apartment was heavy with memory. Her first panting breath of air hypnotized her with nostalgia: the faint odor of rancid garbage and the sulfuric yellow pages of old paperback books, the bitter aroma of clove cigarettes. There were lines of glittering trinkets and plastic knickknacks, blinking Christmas lights and kitschy lamps and everything else he'd salvaged from the Heaps.

"I need water. Want some water?"

Sinking down into a moth-eaten pink armchair, she nodded and accepted the cup he handed her. It was small, delicate, very pale. Something was inscribed in thin golden letters on the side. She read the mysterious words, slowly and stutteringly, sounding out the syllables to herself. She looked to Tom for help, but he just smiled faintly and waited for her to go on.

"By... appoint-ment to His Majesty, the King of.... Sweden?"

"I dug that out last week. Nice, right?"

"Where's Sweden?"

"Somewhere in China. Somewhere with Kings, anyway. Which makes that a royal cup!"

Shayna examined it in quiet awe and asked, as if too loud a voice might damage it, "Should I be drinking out of this?"

"Go ahead." He smiled proudly.

Ignoring her own thirst, she sipped with reverence. The water was clean, faintly sweet, exquisitely clear. It didn't really wash away everything that had happened, but she visualized it doing so anyway.

"I'm going to see how much I get for it tomorrow," he said, carefully taking the cup back and setting it on the counter. Then he stood in uneasy silence.

She found his collection of dolls and action figures in a cardboard box at her feet and started sorting through them.

"I was just going to bed," Tom muttered quietly. "It's late. You kind of missed everything."

She knew he really wanted some kind of explanation. He meant to ask what had happened and whether she was actually all right – and having come here in this state, at this time of night, suddenly asking for the intimacy of a place to sleep after having been so distant for so long, could she really tell him nothing? It didn't matter. No words would come to her except "Sorry. I didn't realize."

Against her protests he gave her the bottom bunk, even though it was by far the better of the two. Only when the springs creaked under her did she realize how exhausted she was. She never knew whether her thanks had been aloud or only a first passing dream as she lost consciousness – and when she faded out completely, she reached out instinctively for the same bright blue and loud sound, but it was not there.

20

Sunlight burned in the yellow curtains.

She found herself wrapped up in his bed, the covers sun-warmed and sweaty around her. Her feet were soggy, still tied up in heavy black boots. Objects in her coat pockets were stabbing into her hips. Thankfully her switchblade had been locked. When she rubbed her eyes, yesterday's unwanted memory washed back over her. She closed her eyes.

When she stirred again, the light in the blurry window had turned from the dim orange color of sun shooting through the smog at angles, to the solid tan light of midday. She squinted at the clock above the stove and read three-fifteen in the afternoon. The shock pushed away the tangled sheets and sat her up on the sweaty bed.

"Is ignorance bliss?" she whispered to herself.

Hauling herself onto her feet, she found the top bunk empty. She was alone.

"Yes," she answered. "Yes it is. Definitely."

A note stuck to the front door read:

Shay. lock up when you leav, key is in mouce hole in halway. im off work at 8. gowing to be at the grean room? have a good day. Tom.

She sighed.

Looking around the apartment, she had forgotten just how well Tom's work paid – both his official Company job and the illegal salvage it enabled. His legally rented apartment had its own bathroom, complete with a shower stall and running water. *Heated* running water, she discovered in a wave of envy, having found herself unable to resist testing the shiny chrome knobs. For a moment she only stood watching it drip and steam, anxiously weighing whether to take advantage of this. It felt so unlike herself to steal water. That was the first thing they taught you in school. Respect property. Don't steal water. But, *well, fuck*, she thought, and fought her way out of these sooty, sweat-stained clothes. Standing there under the oblivionizing hot rain, fully nude for what she realized could have been the first time in weeks, she felt even more naked inwardly than outwardly. She stood there exposed in a bathroom that was not hers. The water and heat were not hers. The abrasively ginger-flavored Garbageman soap was not hers either – but as it started to loosen all the caked grime and dead skin, the human odors and layers of deodorant residue, the knot in her stomach loosened too. She took her time.

She scrubbed as hard as she had to feel like a slightly different person than the one she'd been yesterday.

She'd pay Tom back, she resolved. However much the landlords charged per shower, she could afford it now that her life savings was just another thing she couldn't take with her. She briefly remembered the small wad of cash stuck up behind the wall of her own living space, another thing she'd forgotten to pack. The thought of going back there made her sigh as she rinsed off the last suds and killed the water.

Standing still, dripping dry behind the textured plastic glass while the steam swirled, she thought the unthinkable thought of going back to work on Monday. There was no way. Going to the plant every morning had been hard enough even before she'd known her days were numbered.

The lacquered floorboards were cool and smooth under her bare feet while she washed her clothes in the sink and strung them out along the line outside the window. She looked for something to cover herself with in until they dried, and found Tom's clothes neatly stacked and reeking of ginger and clove smoke. She pulled a shirt over her head, and somewhere between the hem and the neck a memory cell fired.

It's three Winters before, on a cold night under a heavy maroon sky, empty of clouds, dusted with sparse stars. She and Tom are looking down from a high place somewhere and all the others have wandered off. Below them and past a broken concrete railing, a steep slope of dirt and weeds runs far down to meet the roaring flyway. The cars down there all look like steel sparks or shooting stars, nearly too fast and bright to see.

"Wow," she hears the alcohol mutter for her.

He responds to the shiver in her voice by unzipping his army coat. It's big even on him, and when he wraps it around her shoulders for the first time she feels it hanging like a curtain.

"For keeps," Tom says with slurred words.

"What? No."

"Take it."

"No!"

"Take it. You're cold."

"Are you sure?"

He reaches into the coat's inside pocket to take his flask out, his cold fingers fumbling across her left breast. Blushing his embarrassment, he takes a swig and nods with certainty.

She pulls the coat tightly around herself. She ducks her head into the folds of muddy-green twill, warm and worn, and fills up her lungs with its spice. She peeks out and looks at her friend. His eyes are staring down into the rapids of white and red sparks, his gaunt shoulders somehow not minding the cold. A strange feeling washes over her.

I really care about him, she thinks to herself through the booze haze, too unsure of the weight of these words to speak them. *Yes, I... care about him.*

The night's memory turned dim. She'd expected the shirt to be way too big on her, but it fit well. Tom's broad but thin chest turned out to have a similar circumference to her own.

She leaned out the window and smoked. Down in the soot-blackened alleyway, waist-high kids were tromping through puddles, laughing and shouting incoherently to each other. She took a drag as she watched one of them trip in a pothole and then pull himself back up, briefly showing his stunted arm.

She opened the fridge, already knowing that the bounty within would burn her with envy. Her empty stomach yearned to mooch just a little cheese from him, but she already felt guilty for using the shower, his bed, his apartment, his kindness. Still wearing his shirt, she pulled on a soggy change of other clothes and draped the old coat over herself as she left. She kept the key.

She thought again of her own place, the bare room she had left last night with not much more than the clothes on her back, resigned to the loss of everything that wouldn't fit in the suitcase: a few last trinkets, mementos of her mother, her bass, her bicycle. Those were things she could probably do without for a few weeks, but she'd forgotten the money in the wall, and what was left in her pocket wouldn't cover much more than the ride back to get it.

The late Saturday afternoon air was hot, damp, and more than averagely perfumed with methane. Small gusts of wind blew in rhythm with the passing cars or the blocks flitting by the bus window. They felt like the labored, musty exhale of the whole city, the whole Tropolis, as if the streets and the buildings were all breathing down her neck. While stopped at a crosswalk she watched the red signal beating. She waited for it to turn still and solid.

She stepped out onto the outskirts of one of the Unfinished districts, the cleanest section of the Tropolis outside of Greentowne. There was no broken glass here: the windows here had never held any glass. The doorways had never had doors and the floors had never had carpets. The buildings all glowered down with hollow eye-sockets of unadorned cubic concrete, edges that could almost break skin, skeletal walls that had been raised up and abandoned before they could be given flesh. Only the snowy traces of concrete dust, gradually accumulating everywhere, hinted that anything here wouldn't last forever.

Drops of rainwater were still filtering down through the empty elevator shaft, drumming a pulse regular and slow. The stairs were pitch black but she knew them by heart. Five floors up, breathless, she pulled back a plywood sheet and squintingly stepped into her room.

A sudden earsplitting shriek hit her, then a frenzy of wind. She screamed and darted backward, hitting her shoulder on the sharp concrete wall, stabbing splinters into her hand as she shoved the plywood back against the opening and plunged herself into total darkness. Her back braced against the sheet, her hands shaking, she stood in fearful paralysis.

Behind her she heard the flapping of wings and then nothing but the usual distant mutterings of television. Still, she let the seconds turn to minutes before she dared to peek into the room again. Squinting through a hole in the sheet, she looked over every inch of the space until she was sure the bird was gone.

Faint breeze was drifting through the glassless window, and the giant TV billboard across the street cast its noise and light straight through. The plastic curtain had slipped sometime in the night. She rushed to re-hang it before doing anything else, even knowing she'd only spend a few more minutes here.

What had it been? A seagull? But bigger. Grotesquely large. All she could remember was the rabid fluttering of its wings, filling up the whole room. Somewhere in the middle of that vortex of feathers had been a beak, hooked and razor-sharp, open and screaming – and eyes, like human eyes, but larger. Wide and white hot. In that shadow of memory, it was like no bird she had ever seen or heard of.

It had probably looked nothing like that, she decided. With her eyes closed, waiting for the heat to drain out of her heart, she thought: *probably just a pigeon.* Transformed by her stupid phobic imagination into something that could never really exist. She remembered the day Carl had found out about her fear of birds, and how he'd made it his new running gag. He'd found a rubber seagull somewhere and for days made a prank of throwing it at her, until she chucked it into an open sewer. Carl, the first kiss she'd always regret. Carl. The jerk.

She contorted her arm to reach through the hole in the wall where a vent would have run, and her fingers returned with a wadded-up plastic bag. She brushed the spiders off and looked instinctively over her shoulder before leafing through the bills, counting twice to be sure.

It seemed enough to survive for a month. Anyway, she thought, did she really care if it wasn't? How much worse could starvation be than the blight?

With the cash in her coat pocket and the old pink electric bass slung over her shoulder (if only to pawn it), there was nothing left worth taking with her. Only a few photographs she'd stuck to the concrete walls with chewing gum. Some last scraps of clothes. She picked among the candles and other things placed around the head of her mattress: a lighter and Balmic-brand cigarettes, a towel, a roll of toilet paper. In the corner was the clean skull of a cat. Everything else she stuffed into the pockets of her coat and started back down.

But she paused. Something buzzed in her head and kept making her look back. She took a last uncertain look around the room.

There it was. She returned to the cat skull and lifted it up. Underneath it was a silver ring, tarnished black. It had been her mother's final gift to her.

Rolling down the lonely gray street on her squeaking bicycle, she glanced over her shoulder only once. Up there, the sheet plastic curtain rattled uncertainly in its empty concrete socket.

"Three years," she whispered to herself, and felt an unexpected mix of emotion tightening in her throat. A day ago these dead blocks had felt enough like a home. Today one glance around was enough to make her pedal desperately harder until she was out of breath. She added up all the solitary days and nights, all the weekends she'd slept straight through, all the weekdays she'd come straight home from her shift at the plant only to perch on the sill and watch the TV billboard until she faded out. Now that those burnt-up days added up to the final three years of her time on Earth, she felt her wrists tighten around the handlebars until they ached. She was angry. So angry.

So this is it, she thought to the streets that spread out before her now, endless and empty: *the last two or three weeks in the whole shitty life of Shayna Newman.*

The hot wind howled through the ruins, the plastic wrappers scratched softly along the pavement, and the wheel spokes beneath her rattled and squeaked, all as if to echo back: *this is it.* Even the solvent fumes wafting on the air here had the taste of finality. The yellowish sky was streaked with long, thin clouds – like the credits of a movie, she thought. The stupidest movie ever made.

She began to picture them now, the whole group – Tom and Carl and Balboa and Katja – strewn around the Green Room's couches, just as she'd left them. She'd have to tell them sooner or later. Wouldn't she? They were her friends, after all, as sparsely as she'd seen them lately.

"Hey, everybody," she rehearsed. "So it turns out I'm fucking dying."

No.

"We better hang out while we can, because...."

She cleared her throat and spat into a passing gutter.

"Hi everyone. Yes, that *is* an expiration date stamped on my forehead. What does it mean? Well, funny you should...."

She lowered her head until it rested against her knuckles on the handlebars. Between her squinted eyelids, past the line of the bike frame now distorted by the first tears, the pavement rushed along like television static.

Between fifteen and twenty-three days, she remembered. Fifteen. Twenty-three. Two weeks. Three weeks. She repeated these numbers to herself with every wave of passing streets and every squeak of the pedals. She counted up and then down again to zero. She tried to picture oblivion but it wouldn't come. There was no feeling except the dread and frustration of expecting to feel something more. There was no sense to make of all this yet – except to think, in wry passing, that the timing had been perfect: even if she lived all twenty-three days, she wouldn't live to have another period.

The laughter came on unexpectedly. It was as compulsive as it was upsetting. The sound ricocheted between the concrete walls and chainlink fences, and the echoes were cruel and mocking and sharp, until she bit her tongue to snuff them out.

She felt herself blushing even though she knew these blocks were deserted for miles, and under her breath she cursed herself for it. *No time for that*, she thought, angrily wiping the water out of her eyes. *No time left to be embarrassed. Or bored. There's nothing left to do now but enjoy the time I have, for all it's worth, no matter what. Back with my friends.*

The wheels rattled hard across the gaps in the steel as she crossed an old bridge. The canal below was dry down to its last few inches of iridescent pollution, creeping patiently out toward the sea.

And for the sake of that, she further realized, *there's no time to dwell on this. No time to sulk or sink into myself. No time to count the days or think about what happens at the end of them. I have to forget what I know. Forget it all and just live. That's my mission now.*

Just live, the bridge seemed to echo back at her with its rattle.

It was the smallest and most obscure in a long series of sleazy hangouts, set between a mosquito-filled canal and an avenue of mottled neon that eventually stretched Inward all the way to the Cology – a spoke in the rusty wheel of the Tropolis. The building in which the Green Room was buried still resembled the majesty of its long-derelict self. A mammoth domed ceiling was still mostly intact. Flecks of gold leaf still glittered up there in the day's dying light, and a few of the old seats still wore weathered scraps of velvet and foam. If not for the missing floorboards and ominous sag in the balcony, the big theatre might even have been usable. As it was, the only life in the building was behind and beneath the splintering stage: a series of stuffy lounges collectively known as the Green Room.

In the alley, above the entrance, somebody had cut some words into the crumbling brickwork. They looked ancient, but Shayna could not remember ever noticing them before now.

"Abandon all hope," she read to herself before descending the stairs.

It was early. The smoke layer was only faintly visible, like the surface of a monochrome ocean, swirling in her wake and rising over her head as she slinked uncertainly down the last steps.

There she was, exactly as Shayna had imagined, exactly as she'd last seen her. Katja was reclining on ratty velvet pillows in her usual corner, a smoldering joint resting between finger and thumb, one unfamiliar boy perched attentively at each of her elbows. Her clothes were a second skin, worn-out not by use but by design, as fine and fashionable as anything this far outward. A halo of pink neon incidentally ringed her pale face and short obsidian hair.

"I don't believe it!" Katja called when their eyes met. "Is it really you?"

The elbow boys regarded the intruder uncertainly until Katja whispered something which caused them to evaporate into the haze. There was a rising heat in Shayna's sternum, something old and familiar that she snuffed out on reflex as she settled into the booth and accepted to hug she was given. She knew better than to stoke that fire by thinking about what it was.

"I haven't seen you in ages! What has it been? Six months? A year?"

"It hasn't been that long, has it?" Shayna took off her bass. "I do come here sometimes."

"I don't even know when the last time was that I saw you. Or you returned my calls."

"I…. Sorry."

"Well, where have you been all that time? What have you been doing? I thought maybe you'd found some new friends or something. Or hooked up with somebody."

Shayna gritted her teeth and half-rolled her eyes before she hid it. What could she say? Sitting around, bored? Watching the TV billboard? Sleeping? Avoiding everyone?

"Playing?" Katja asked, eyeing the bass.

Shayna took it off the seat and slid it into the dirty space behind the booth. The strings squeaked against the concrete wall, making her wince. "No, nothing. Nothing at all." She struggled to think of an answer that didn't sound pathetic, and decided on: "I've been in exile."

"Interesting." Katja tilted her head as if rolling the words around inside. The she drew a breath through her joint and wheezed: "Well, how long are you staying exiled? Will I ever see you again?"

"I'm done, I'm back. And I'm—" The words stuck. Soon she would be drunk – soon she'd have all the excuse she needed to say something like this without calling so much attention to it – but her impatience was welling up again. "I'm sorry I've been so distant all this time."

This seemed to catch Katja off guard, more even than Shayna had expected, but she only swallowed a sigh and said "Well I'm glad you're back. We'll celebrate that properly tonight."

"Is everyone coming? Like usual?"

"Who?"

"You know, the whole group. You. Tom. Balboa and Carl."

Katja seemed to count back over the names until one of them exploded in front of her with an almost audible pop. "Dear God. Have you really been gone that long? You don't know? Nobody told you?"

"Told me what?

"About Balboa."

"I guess he hasn't been around the last few times I was here, but I didn't think.... What is it?" Death was on the tip of her tongue.

Katja leaned close and said through incredulous laughter: "He joined the comps! He's at security academy!"

"What?!"

"True story. He told us himself. We tried to talk him out of it, or maybe we just shouted with him a lot, but he wouldn't have it. Just ran out. Nobody's talked to him since. It must have been right after you, you know, went into hiding or whatever. But that was at least a year ago, Shay. Seriously."

A twinge of lightheadedness hit Shayna as her incredulity finally lapsed into belief. "What the hell could he be thinking?"

"Who knows? I guess he decided he'd rather stomp on faces all night than kick around with the likes of us anymore. I wouldn't have figured him for one of *them*, but maybe we never really knew the kid. So quiet all the time." She added: "Except when he was behind his drums, I mean."

"He was quiet," Shayna distantly agreed.

"But Tom and Carl still hang out here, sure. They'll probably be around in few hours. And some other people you probably don't know at all. I'll introduce you."

Fluorescent lights buzzed against the green walls. The music pumps exhaled only faint idle static. Shayna picked idly at the hard orange crust on her hand.

"What's the hell is that?" Katja asked.

"I hurt my hand really bad at work. They put this goo on it, like a bandage." She held it out and Katja grabbed it to inspect it closely.

"How'd you hurt it?"

"It was really stupid of me – I wasn't looking and I put my hand right into the machine. I was distracted. I had this dream last night. Or maybe it was a long time ago, or maybe I've had it many times, I don't know. It was really weird. Like I'd forgotten it, but it just suddenly just came back to me in a flash. Has that ever happened to you?"

"Sure, but I've tried acid. You haven't done anything like that, have you?"

"No."

"Of course. Well, what was the dream?"

Shayna hesitated. "It was just… this color. This bright blue. And there was this loud ringing sound. They were both really familiar. But somehow I can't remember them specifically now. I can't describe them."

"That's it? That's the whole dream?"

Shayna only shrugged uneasily and stared away into the slit windows along the ceiling.

"What's wrong?"

"I guess I'm kind of anxious today for some reason. No reason. Just anxious."

"I can tell. I know you're kind of straight-edge, Shay, more than the rest of us, but this is good for that." Katja's pale fingers offered the glowing joint.

The exile sighed pensively for a moment, then sighed and accepted it. She thought she saw her friend grinning in the corner of her vision as she shut her eyes and took a single long pull, down to the bottom of her lungs, and held it.

She exhaled slowly and opened her eyes she to peer around the crowded space, the heavy layers of smoke swarming the neon, the spires of stacked dirty glasses looming over every table. The music pumps were blasting heavy bass against a raging ocean of voices. Saturday night was in full swing and everyone was stuffed into that booth just as she'd left them. In fact –

"A baby with a black eye!" Carl yelled. A punch line.

Tom rubbed his forehead. Katja rolled her eyes and grimaced. Carl's smile died and he looked at Shayna and then at his hands – and right there, in that scene, the déjà vu was so overpowering that she wondered whether she had not been hurled back in time. Nothing had changed between them. The green neon ambience gave them all the look of being preserved in formaldehyde, pickled in alcohol.

"Good one, Carl," said an alien voice, breaking the hypnosis of the moment. Shayna looked to her left and found him right there: a pasty man with buzzed head and sharp gray eyes, an undersized nose and mouth. Noticing her noticing him, he returned his cigarette to his lips and raised his hand to shake hers.

"You probably haven't met Fish," Katja said from her other side.

Shayna accepted the hand and found its grip clammy. "Fish?"

Katja drunkenly whispered: "Fish has everything. He's a genius. An artist, really."

"You mean a dealer?"

Fish smiled. He picked up a half-empty shot glass and made a toasting motion with it. Somehow this simple act was deeply ominous. Then he got up and disappeared.

"It's always good to be close to someone like Fish," Katja said in Shayna's ear. "First, because –"

Something distracted Katja mid-sentence, making a smile spread across her glossy lips, becoming a laugh. Shayna looked at her – and in that moment, lost in the burn of the neon on Katja's silvered eyelids, her magazine-cover figure, her clean bare shoulders, the spark that Shayna had snuffed out earlier roared back to full life. Envy. Seething and bottomless. Those extra six inches of height, even without heels. Those shoulders that drew boys like flies to raw meat. Those Company-certified contours that meant she sold the T-shirts instead of stamping them. That carefree smile that could only belong to someone who still had the love and security of not just one but two living parents. There were so many flavors of happiness in that smile, and Shayna was so sure she'd die only ever imagining them. Even before, when she'd given herself decades left to live, she'd been exactly as sure.

The distraction ended. Shayna wiped the burning emotion out of her face just in time for Katja to turn back and continue "What was I saying? Oh, right. First, so they can get you things. Second, so they won't deal roofies to somebody they know is stalking you."

Shayna rallied her self-control, but some contempt escaped into her voice when she asked "He deals *roofies?*"

Katja shifted uncomfortably and failed to speak before Carl yelled over the noise.

"Shay! Shay! Welcome back from exile!"

"Hear, hear!" Tom yelled, entirely too loud, and everyone toasted. Cheap booze sprayed down onto the table where the glasses crashed. Shayna smiled and swallowed the last of the shot that was apparently hers. She couldn't tell what it was, besides dread.

"I need air," she said.

"Me too," Katja squeaked.

Carl opened his mouth and shut it, and his eyes sank back into his drink as they left him behind with the other guys.

There was something weird about him tonight, Shayna thought, glancing over her shoulder at him on her stumbling way to the stairs – even weirder than usual. This intuition was already dissolving into the scalding warmth now spreading down from her throat.

Climbing the last of those stairs was like removing a gag. The moon hung between the rooftops directly above, the yellowish crescent only just beginning to turn into the red and white Company logo drawn by laser onto the dark part. A cool breeze was blowing through the alley, carrying away the smoke, leaving only a faint flavor of diesel exhaust. Breathing felt beautiful.

Katja squinted through her intoxication and said "I forgot how short you are."

"So?" Shayna responded bitterly.

"No, I didn't mean— There's nothing wrong with that."

"Easy for you to say."

"I just mean I always remember you as my height. You're taller on the inside. That's what I meant." She winced. "That's just how it is these days. My parents were telling me. Their generation was full of medium-height people.

It seems like everyone our age either stopped growing really young or they never stop at all, like Tom. You ever notice that?"

Shayna bit her tongue.

From the smoking stairs two young men emerged: the anonymous elbow boys who had roosted on Katja's shoulders earlier. Shayna had assumed they were suitors. One was short and skinny and maybe sixteen years old, a mouse of a human being. The other was heavier-set and wore a wispy brown beard.

"You know *them*, don't you?" Katja asked.

Shayna shook her head and killed the last of the fire in her belly.

"Damn have been gone a long time. These are Float and Becker."

"I'm Shayna."

"You should join our team," Katja added.

"You have a team? What kind?"

"We're into some really extreme shit," said Becker, trying pointlessly to curl the thin ends of his adolescent moustache. "It's ultra hardcore. You'd love it."

Shayna stared at him.

"It's hard to explain," said Float. "You can't really understand until you do it. You should."

"You definitely should," Katja said.

"Drugs?"

"No, no. Better than that." She leaned drunkenly against the brick wall and shut her eyes tightly, struggling for words. "It's the new fun. It's kind of a sport. But not really."

Shayna raised an eyebrow.

"We're going on a run tomorrow," Katja said, returning to full wakefulness and focusing her gaze tightly on Shayna. "You should come. Tomorrow, at two. Just trust me about this."

"...Okay."

Becker and Float smiled contentedly and looked on. Everyone shared a reflexive sigh of general, objectless appreciation and leaned back into the brick wall.

Shayna's thoughts puddled on the edges of awareness, soon trailing off into a pristine meditative haze. Her brain felt heavy, gelatinous, silent – except for the recurring realization that this was good, that it was good to be among friends, that she had almost forgotten how good it felt. To talk to someone besides herself. *Maybe Katja's right,* she thought. *How long have I been gone? Long enough to not even know anymore.*

Carl was standing at the top of the stairs, leaning his head meekly out into the alley. Noticing that Shayna had noticed him, he resumed his normal air of overacted masculinity and stepped forward into the scorching orange light, scratching at the hair under his lip. He walked as if massive weights were fixed to his feet, or directly under his belt, but all she saw was his gut, his head of unkempt sand-colored hair, the hairless legs extending from his torn-off khaki shorts. He settled into a pose he liked. Then he stared at her.

"You're drunk," Shayna observed, pointlessly.

Carl shrugged drunkenly. He opened his mouth as if to say something, but Katja interrupted:

"Oh, God. He's calling again."

"Do you want me to—?" Float and Becker said, almost in unison.

Katja held out the phone and Becker took it. He marched away to the street, whispering "No, you can't. It's— Because she told me to, that's why. She doesn't want to talk to you herself."

"Are you okay?" Float asked, guiding her back down into the smoke, leaving only Shayna and Carl in the alley.

Shayna threw a confused look in no particular direction.

"She dumped one of her boy-toys today," Carl explained coldly.

"You're so mean," Shayna said. "Why you have to be mean to everyone?"

"Boy-*friend*," he muttered. "Whatever. One of the random guys she screws around with when she's–"

"So mean, all the time."

Carl hovered on the edge of snapping back with something, but finally settled into an uncharacteristic defeated sigh.

They stood in silence under the pale caged light. Something filled up the space between them that was more choking than the smoke had been down below, so Shayna started back down.

Carl didn't move from his leaning spot against the bricks, but just as she was about to go back under she heard him call down the creaking stairs:

"Wait. Could you come back up here a second?"

She gave him a weird look that was lost in the shadows, but did as he asked. She gazed expectantly at him as he scratched his face and bit his lower lip in thought.

"I just wanted to tell you," he began. It seemed like he had rehearsed this, to no avail. "I mean, I wanted you to know that, um."

Shayna looked around uncomfortably.

"I haven't seen you in a long time," he said. "Am I going to see you again after this? Soon?"

"I'm out of exile."

"So I'll see you around. I'll see you again."

"Well, yeah."

"Then I want you to know that, um. What I said the last time I talked to you, before your exile. It's okay. I didn't really mean it. Like that. I didn't mean it like it probably sounded. I'm not really..." he paused to sling some invisible weight off each shoulder "in love with you."

The pale light flickered in its cage.

"Oh," Shayna said. Then half-lied: "I didn't realize you meant that."

"No, I didn't mean it. That's what I mean. And I want us to be friends. It doesn't have to be... weird... between us. Or anything. Right?"

"Weird," Shayna echoed. "Right."

Carl's face twitched momentarily into something like a smile, and then he turned his back on her and trudged away toward the street.

"Where are you going?"

"I work Sundays," he said over his shoulder. Then he was gone.

"It's been forever since I drank," she found herself saying, back at the table. This made her pause to try to think of anything to say that wasn't completely pointless and self-evident, but she failed.

"A toast," said Tom. "To Shay's triumphant return from exile. To many more."

She picked up the shot in front of her, and made a fatal mistake: she let herself realize that there were only three Saturday nights left. Her alcoholic euphoria died like an unplugged machine.

Her brow was furrowed, her eyes staring bitterly into the oily shot in her hand. Everyone was watching her expectantly before she noticed.

"Yeah," she said hurriedly, forced a smile, and drank.

She waited for it to sink in. She tried to absorb herself back into the conversation. Nothing happened. She felt dimmer than before, but the euphoria had not returned.

As it always did in the Green Room, the alcohol kept coming, inexplicably, invisibly. Whenever she slammed her empty glass down on the scuffed and scribbled tabletop, it was full again in a blink. Meanwhile the slurred conversation ebbed and flowed. In a moment it steered away from her, into subjects she couldn't add anything to. She waited for what became a long time.

Then Katja's voice was suddenly in her ear, saying: "Hey. Why so glum?"

Shayna looked up and knitted her brow.

Katja said "I wanted to ask you. Why did you go into exile, anyway?"

"Because I only feel lonely when I'm surrounded by my friends," she mumbled, before she thought to lie.

"What?" Katja asked, cupping her ear against the music.

"Fuck, nothing."

The conversation steered away again.

Unthinkingly trying to show self-sufficiency, she rooted through her pockets. Her hands found the silver ring. She stared at it fondly in her palm, studying the glittering reflections of the few edges that still glittered.

"What's that?" Tom asked.

"*Memento Mori*," she said with a smile.

"What?"

"That's Latin. It means memory of the dead. It's what my mother said to me when she left - she gave me this ring. You can see inside it says *Memento Mori*. A memento of her."

"No."

"No? What do you mean no?"

"That's not what Memento Mori means. It means: 'Remember That You Must Die.'"

"That's true," said Fish. "Remember that you must die."

Shayna stared bitterly. She traced the edges of that memory, over and over.

"Fuck," she groaned, and dropped the ring on the table in disgust.

"What's wrong?"

"I don't want it anymore. Somebody, anybody, you can have it. For keeps. Take it." She pushed it around the table, but Katja grabbed her hands and held them tightly, shoving the ring hard into her palm.

Leaning very close, she said: "No. This is yours. Your mother gave it to you. It's your memento of her."

"I don't want it anymore. I don't need any memento."

"No. It's yours."

Shayna sighed.

"Fine." She watched Katja nod and withdraw. But she promised herself she would pawn it. Tomorrow. As soon as possible.

Euphoria had suffered another setback. This demanded a shot.

And two more.

Or five.

She remembered sickness.

Stumbling up the stairs, holding onto two people.

Dry heaving. The rusty lip of a trash can.

Her voice wailing: "I'm fucking *dying!*"

Katja saying: "No you're not! We're here. We won't let you."

Her lips replying: "Pffft."

Orange lights spinning.

Yellow sunlight dripping down the stairs.

Tom at the top, about to leave.

Her voice was shouting something even she didn't understand. Then she was falling down again into strange and unsettling half-dreams.

19

The green ceiling was there when she opened her eyes and the pink electric bass was laying heavily across her lap. When she sat up, the throbbing rush of blood to her head knocked her back down into the ratty booth seat.

Her fingers dug her phone out of her coat pocket and held the screen to her face. It took a long, groaning moment to read the digits and decide that it was something like one in the afternoon.

"Groan?" Katja asked, from somewhere else. "Was that a groan I heard?"

"What? Yeah," Shayna groaned.

Katja drifted in from an adjoining room, bearing a cracked plastic cup of water.

"What do you remember from last night?" she asked.

"Most of it, I think."

"I mean, do you remembered this morning when Tom left."

"What about it?"

"You didn't want him to leave. You kind of went into a panic when he was heading out. We had to hold you back."

"No," Shayna grunted, unsettled. "I don't remember that. Nothing."

"Thought maybe you might know what that was all about."

"No."

"Hmm," Katja said, letting a faint smirk cross her lips. "Well, do you feel okay? We've got to catch the bus pretty soon if we want to go on that run. With Becker and Float. Remember?"

She fought to push herself up against the gravity in her head. "I still don't know what you were talking about. It sounds dangerous."

"Well, sure. But it's fun, too."

Shayna replayed these words in her head. Dangerous – *like it matters in my case.* Fun?

Katja relented and said "It's okay if you're not up to it right now. We'll just—"

"No. I'm ready. Let's go."

Katja raised an eyebrow.

The bus let them off at the 900th street flyway interchange ten minutes before the agreed meeting time, but Becker and Float were there, ready and waiting: two boney boys standing triumphantly in the middle of a vast lot of pulverized concrete, projecting a sense of being its own private kings. As the two girls hiked out toward them, a hot wind picked up and tore charismatically at Becker's flowing trenchcoat. The weather-scorched grain silos behind him looked on.

"Have we got a plan?" Katja asked them.

"The Beast," Float announced.

"The Beast," Katja echoed with a smile. "Have we got flashlights then?"

Becker slung a frayed knapsack from his shoulder, reached in and produced a single rusty antique. He switched it on for a moment as proof that it worked. "We're ready to rock," he said, stroking his thin facial hair.

"You figured out where it is?" Katja asked.

"What's *the Beast?*" Shayna whispered.

"This way," Becker said, trotting away through the rubble field with Float following eagerly in his footsteps.

"This lot where we're standing right now," Katja narrated, confidentially, "There used to be a factory here. A special chemical factory. Can you smell that?"

Shayna sniffed the air. She hadn't noticed it before, but it was there – a faint unfamiliar aroma. Chemical, but not merely chemical. Strange. Haunting. Warm. "Yeah."

"It's not good for you," said Float. "They say it makes you start to see things if you breathe it too long."

"What is it?"

"Depends who you ask," said Katja. "Everyone who lives around here has a different story about the Beast and where it came from, and what made it. But it was ten years ago, whatever happened. The factory was here. I heard it was a factory for making steroids, which explains it. You know. Drugs that make your muscles grow huge. It's what the comps all take. They're required to take them."

"Right."

"But they say there was a spill one day. They spilled a whole vat of the stuff down into the sewers, and the story I heard is that it all spilled down into a big nest of rats that no one knew was there. And most of them died, except there was one rat who survived, and it started growing. It started growing muscles, like human muscles, except even bigger, much bigger. And it started standing up and walking on its hind legs. And it was hungry, from all the growing. Pretty soon there wasn't enough food in the sewers, even after eating all the other rats, so it chewed a hole up through the basement of the factory and it started eating the workers, one by one. They say that after a while they closed the plant down and sent comps in to kill the Beast, but they couldn't find it."

Shayna shivered unexpectedly.

"So they just demolished the factory," Katja said. "They blew it all up with dynamite and sealed up all the sewer entrances and assumed that it was dead.

But the people around here, who live in this neighborhood, they know better. They say they still see it sometimes for just a moment. At night. On rainy nights, because it likes the dark and damp. Scratching along under the street lamps. Then a dog will disappear. Eaten. But if anyone's dog gets eaten, they're always sure to find another one as soon as they can, because they know that the dogs are all that keeps it away. They keep its hunger down so that it never comes looking for kids or full-grown adults, though some people say that still happens too."

The two kings of nowhere had stopped. They were searching through the rubble now, hands in their pockets, upturning cinderblocks with their feet.

"And the Beast is still....?" Shayna murmured. "It's down in the sewers?"

"Where it's always lived. The Company blew up their factory and sealed off parts of the sewers, but they couldn't seal them all off. Water still has to flow through here. And anyway the Beast can chew through any wall it wants. They say it has its own tunnels down there, and it's been building itself a whole nest. That it guards, killing and eating anyone who sees it."

"Who says that?"

"The neighbors."

"How do they know it's building a nest? If it kills anyone who sees the nest."

"It's what everyone says."

"Don't you think they just made it up?"

"You don't know that. How do you know?"

"Because everyone knows there's no such thing as monsters." The memory of the bird shuddered briefly through her mind, forcefully enough to make her add: "Except in nightmares."

"Found it," said Float. He yanked upward on a seemingly random piece of frayed rope and a sheet of rotten, dust-caked wood came up with it. A slow belch of rancid steam howled out of a pitch black circle in the ground.

"The neighbors told us the entrance would be here," Katja said. "The rest of the story must also be true." With the tip of her shoe she pushed a cinderblock shard over the lip, and they all counted off the time before it splashed against the theoretical bottom.

"Sounds like about ten feet deep," Becker said.

"Twelve," Float said.

Shayna thought it sounded like thirty.

"You brought the rope?" Katja asked.

Becker produced the rope from his knapsack. It wasn't actually rope; it looked more like a large amount of thin white string that had been braided over and over again by hand until it was passably thick.

"Did you make that yourself?" Shayna asked him.

"It's good rope," Becker protested.

"It'll do," Katja said. She helped Float tie it to the base of a little rusty pipe nearby, and then they dropped what was left of it down into the hole. "All right. Let's do it."

"You're just going down there?" Shayna asked incredulously. "Down into the sewers? Why?"

"You won't understand until you do it," Becker barked. "Are you in, or are you gonna wimp out on us?"

Wind howled around the opening. Tiny concrete chips rattled across the edge and down into the void.

Katja was already on her way down. She knitted her hands around the rope, put her feet against a wall past the lip, and walked backwards down it. In only a few steps she was submerged completely in the dark. An anxiously long time later, they all heard Katja's oof and a watery splash.

"You okay?" Shayna shouted down.

"Fine. It's not far. I can still reach the end of the rope. No problem. But I can't see a thing. Toss the flashlight down, will you?"

Becker threw it down the hole like trash into a can. They all heard it crack loudly against the concrete floor. Something rattled.

"Dumbass," Katja said.

"Still work?" Float asked.

A few weak sparks of light glittered down there and then winked out. More rattling. Crunching glass. Finally the light held steady, but it didn't look much brighter than a candle flame.

"Come on," Katja said.

Becker and Float in turn took the rope and started down. Shayna peered apprehensively after them. The little spark of rusty light shone up at her. *Shit*, she thought, and did as it asked.

The weight of the three of them before her seemed to have pulled the braid noticeably tighter and thinner. She heard it squeaking as it bit into her fingers. As soon as she'd reached the knotted end her grip gave out and she dropped with a yelp into the formless black, her feet hitting muddy concrete bottom, the rest of her stopped by a pair of invisible hands.

"Thanks," she whispered to Becker. She tried to meet his eyes, but all she could make out were the stony edges of his face, glowing ominously in what little gray daylight still shone from above. She could hear their feet scraping along, but the flashlight was too dim to notice if it was working at all.

"I can't see a thing."

"Get farther from the daylight and your eyes'll work better."

"I'm leading," Katja said. "Just follow the sound of my feet."

The scraping continued. Shayna made out its direction and crept after it. Her outreached fingers contacted frayed wool and she followed its motion.

"Stop poking me," Becker said.

"Sorry."

The scraping moved in and out of invisible puddles. Shayna strained her ears to scrutinize it while shadowy static washed across her vision. From somewhere up ahead came the sound of running water, getting louder with every step. An underground river?

Now there was another sound, this time from behind. Rattling. Splashing. Shayna reeled around and saw dust falling through the entrance hole while the dangling braid whipped out of sight and a shadow crossed the milky trace of daylight. The four darted blindly for the entrance.

Katja shouted upward: "What the hell do you think you're doing?"

Something tiny and round peeked over the lip at the top of the hole and stayed there, unmoving, making no sound. Shayna realized it was the silhouette of a child's head.

"Let the fucking rope back down and leave it alone!" Becker yelled.

A tiny voice echoed meekly down at him, speaking Spanish.

He whispered "Does anybody speak—?"

"I do," Katja said. "She told you to stop using bad words."

Becker stomped his foot and pursed his lips.

Katja replied something Shayna couldn't understand. The little girl took a while to respond. Then the argument erupted, Katja shouting, the kid's voice whining and screaming and her tiny feet stomping in the dust above.

"What's going on?" Becker demanded. "What's she saying?"

Katja just kept shouting.

The kid's head disappeared from view. Silence fell. Shayna held her breath.

"Is she gone?" Float whispered.

The kid's head reappeared along the concrete lip, and with her tiny outstretched hand she started letting the rope down by the handful. Then it all fell, slapping against the muddy concrete in a big wad.

Katja kept shouting, but it was no good. The plywood sheet started its inch-by-inch struggle to cover the hole back up amid a hail of concrete dust.

"Chica mala!" Katja roared as the last light died.

"What the hell happened?" Becker yelled in the pitch black.

Katja said "She said she's supposed to keep the hole closed up and never let anyone go down it. When I told her we weren't coming back up yet, she just flipped out."

"It's okay," said Float. "This is all right! Is your heart beating? Can't you feel it?"

Everyone paused.

"Yeah," said Katja, through an invisible smile. "You're right. This is perfect."

"What are you people talking about?" Shayna asked.

Katja sighed and said "Relax, Shay. You'll feel it too."

"Feel what?"

"Life! If you just *trust* me, you'll realize that all of this is making you feel more alive than you've probably felt in years. That's what you came here for. And it's just getting started."

Becker chuckled. Shayna could smell his sour milk breath.

"I don't feel anything," she said. "I just want to get out of here."

"That's just fine," Katja said, "Because the only way out of here now is to go deeper in."

"Let's go!" Float proclaimed. "Into the depths of the labyrinth!" His words echoed under their footsteps in the puddles.

Her eyes finally adjusted. The faint glow from their rusty light grew into something just bright enough to barely see by as it played across the wet concrete walls and the puddles under their feet. Everything here was greased with trickling yellowish water – and blackened underneath that, as if concrete could be infected and rotting, more rotten the deeper they went. With every half-petrified step the smell was thickening too. It was the same smell Shayna had detected on the barren lot above them, warm and chemical, though down here it wasn't even a smell so much as the raw sensation of having a bloody nose. It made her eyes water. She tried to breathe through her coat but it didn't help, so she breathed shallowly despite her racing pulse. She didn't dare to look outside the safety of Katja's dim and narrow beam. She followed Becker by the inexplicable sloshing sound she heard coming from his backpack.

The tunnels were less intact the further they went along. They backtracked from dead ends where the ceiling bent tiredly down into the floor. Where the walls still stood they were riddled with fissures and holes, some bleeding rust like half-open wounds, some peeking into other dark chambers where the flashlight's beam didn't dare to reach. Some were big enough to climb through, so they did.

Katja trained the light on the lip of a hole in the floor and Float knelt to inspect it. No words were exchanged or needed. It didn't look as if the otherwise level ground had caved into the space beneath; it looked as if something had carved the concrete out from where they stood. There were marks of long, ragged scrapes. Rusty splinters of rebar stuck out around the edges like red ribs from gray flesh.

"Jackhammer," Shayna muttered. "That's what did that."

No one responded.

As soon as Katja's light confirmed that there was a solid floor at the bottom, she and the boys started down.

"You're just–?" Shayna blurted.

"So stay up there alone," said the rusty flashlight beam.

She descended.

The sparkling static she saw in the pitch black was getting brighter. Small things moved in the corners of her vision and were gone when she turned, but she told herself they were just reflections from the flashlight – or maybe the side effect of holding her breath against the thickeningly acid atmosphere, or of the atmosphere itself.

"You don't seriously think the Beast is real," Shayna said to the shadows. "It can't be real."

Katja's silhouette glanced over its shoulder and kept creeping along the dingy wall.

"There's nothing alive down here," Shayna said.

Something crunched underfoot.

"Exactly," Katja answered. She had stopped. The flashlight was pointed at the ground.

The other three gathered wordlessly around where she had knelt. She picked something out of the puddle at her feet and held it to the light.

A hooked bone. Snapped off at the end.

"Human?" Becker whispered.

"Look how small it is," Shayna stammered. "Fast food. Fried chicken."

"Child," said Float.

"*Dog*," whispered Katja.

Everyone looked at her and at each other in turn. Only the trickling water spoke until Katja stopped dead at another fork in the tunnel.

"What is it?" Becker asked.

"There," she said, pointing down the left. "Another bone."

It lay just at the edge of the light's reach. This one was whole, each end still padded with rubbery connective tissue that glowed as if from its own residual life energy when Katja held the flashlight to it.

"I'm telling you, it's just more stupid f-fried chicken," Shayna said.

Becker whispered: "Shut up. Do you hear that?"

Shayna scoured the dripping silence. Her blood ran cold. Some sound came from down there, and it wasn't like dripping water. It clicked and snapped in random patterns. There was a smell here too, strong enough to overlay the hot chemical atmosphere. Something rancid and sour. Another step in they saw the smears on the ground, reddish-black, forming a trail that glistened in the yellowish light – curving around the dimly-visible corner just ahead.

The light from Katja's silhouette quivered faintly. Then she advanced on silent feet. The boys followed. Shayna followed. The adrenaline was doing things to her. Every sound echoing through the void had turned deafeningly loud. The tips of her fingers were freezing.

Stepping over the bloody smears, they looked down the tunnel.

They sighed.

It was a dead end, piled to the ceiling with black plastic trash bags, some torn, some gnawed by rats, some hanging open and gushing their contents onto the muddy floor. One sitting near the foot of the little heap, where the trail of supposed blood ended, was overflowing with leaky bottles of spent motor oil. Katja tested the smears on the tip of her finger and confirmed her disappointment.

The sound they'd heard had just been another stream of rusty water through the ceiling, drumming on a bag that had been tied air-tight and then inflated by decomposition. A lot of bones hung out of another bag, along with some stacks of greasy paper buckets.

"Smarty's Chicken Stop," Shayna read aloud.

"Damn," Katja said, reading a bootprint that was stamped clearly in the oily smears. "I guess some garbageman found this place and started using it as an extra dump. Tom said they do that if it shortens their route, or something."

"There's probably a way out of here pretty close by, then," Shayna said, letting out a slow breath. "However the garbageman got in here."

"Probably," Becker muttered.

So they followed the trail of oil smears back the way they'd come and down the other fork. After only a few more turns they found themselves peering down a long straight passage. There at the distant end, through a forest of the black outlines of rusty pipes, across the sound of rushing underground rivers, they made out a faint dusting of gray daylight on a wall with a rebar ladder.

"Thank God," Shayna said.

"Sucks," said Becker. "Mission failed."

"But you felt it, right?" Float asked. "I felt it."

The four of them came to the slimy brick edge of a rushing flow of brownish water. There was a horrendous smell there, much worse the rotting trash.

"Feel anything, Shay?" Katja asked, stepping up onto the narrow ledge that crossed the water.

She joined her and the boys on the ledge, using a rust-flaking valve as a hand hold, and for a moment it genuinely crossed her mind that—

"Wait," Katja said, pointing the flashlight down the side-tunnel. Her voice called down: "Hello?"

The yellowish beam played over a corpse in coveralls and the long-fingernailed thing that chewed on it. The light splashed in the river. Something howled. Something scratched the rust from the metal.

Becker's fingers dug into Shayna forearm and pulled her out of her trance as they bolted for the light in the distance, tripping over pipes, hitting their heads on the valves, scraping their hands and knees on the rust and bricks and the bones of dogs that clattered above the howling and scraping on the pipes behind her – the scraping of claws that knew those pipes by heart or could somehow see clearly in the pitch black – and then she was choking on the dirty water rushing over her head and being pulled hard up by the others, and her soaked boots kept slipping in the mud and slime and her eyes burned from the water and her fingers ached but it was the rebar ladder that was cutting into them, and it was daylight burning her eyes, and it was Float gripping her shoulder and pulling her out and away from the manhole, wheezing, spitting foulness, deafened by her own heart, lying on her back in the dust. The howl was still rising from the depths and still coming closer.

"It's going to climb up," Float said.

Becker hurriedly slung his knapsack from his shoulders and produced a jug of gasoline, which he poured down the hole while Float lit a match. Shayna didn't dare look down. When the fire exploded to life, the four of them fled the smoke in a hurry. It had that same chemical smell. The roaring grew louder, more panicked, and then ceased.

"You had that gas with you the whole time?" Katja panted.

"For making a torch or something if the flashlight gave out," he coughed.

"Holy shit!" Shayna yelled between breaths. "Holy *Shit!*"

It was then that she realized that Float was laughing – and suddenly she was laughing too. All of them were. They collapsed in the rubble and propped their backs against a half-demolished wall. They looked back at the billows of black smoke streaming from the shaft entrance and made a chorus of laughs and heavy exhales until Shayna thought she'd faint from lack of air.

"We did it," Float said. "We killed the Beast."

"It wasn't a myth," Katja gasped.

"I *do* feel it!" Shayna's mouth shouted for her, drunkenly, ecstatically. "I'm alive! I'm *alive!* You were right!" She stood up and spun in place, arms outstretched. She couldn't remember ever feeling so vitally happy in her life as the deathtrippers laughed. "You were right about *everything!*" she shouted as she passed out.

She woke up on the bus, a pair of ring-laden hands clasped around her head. She felt dizzy.

"You okay?" Katja asked.

Shayna swallowed, cleared her throat and sat up.

"We both smell like hell," Katja said. "There's a pay-shower on 719th. One of the less sleazy ones. You want to come?"

"My bass. My bike. They're still at the Green Room."

"It's not far out of the way."

"Actually, I think I have some errands to run."

"Covered in sewer water?"

Shayna said nothing. She couldn't explain why she didn't want to go with Katja – why she suddenly found herself not wanting to be near Katja at all. It was something in the smell that hung between them. Not the sewage, but underlying it, the chemical. The memory of her own laughter had turned strange. The memory of blood-soaked blue coveralls.

She only wanted to find Tom. There wasn't room in her head to ask why.

Pedaling back to Tom's place on legs clad in muck-encrusted pants, the bass strapped again across her back, her mind settled into a total blankness. Her hands shivered in the warm air. The bad taste in her mouth wouldn't leave.

On an empty street she was attacked by a strange gravity. The bike wobbled beneath her. She dismounted, tried to lean it against a dead brick wall, let it tip over and clatter against the sidewalk. She sank to the ground, breathless, lungs heaving, thoughtless tears pouring over her mud-caked face. She didn't move for a long time.

Tom rolled along on his own bike. He found her sitting against the wall and smoking with her pink bass in her lap. Her scuffed hands rested along its strings and her salt-stained eyes were lost in the gutter. When he skidded up to her she greeted him by raising her eyebrows in surprise and letting out a breath of smoke.

"What are you doing?" he asked. "Playing?"

She shook her head, took her hands off the strings, put them back.

"Did... something happen to you?" he asked.

She merely sighed and squinted on down the street.

"Is that my shirt?" he asked.

She looked at him.

"Whoops," she said through the cigarette.

Back at his apartment, she reeled the last of her clothes in through the window and considered them in her soiled hands.

"Can I use your shower?" she asked hesitantly.

"Yeah, um. Sure."

"I used it this morning too. I can pay you back for it if the landlord charges by the shower."

"By the quart, actually. And by the watt for heat. Comes to about two hundred per hot shower for me."

"Oh."

"But, um, don't worry about it. On me."

"No, really, I'm—"

"Forget it. It's on me."

She was too dazed to argue. She closed the bathroom door behind her, stripped out of his clothes and went to work laboriously scrubbing the warm chemical stench off of herself with hands that burned in the gingery suds. There was no pleasure to take in it this time. With hesitant desperation she stuck out her tongue and lathered it up, swished the ginger suds around her teeth, then spat and stood propped up against the glass door, coughing and sputtering.

"Are you okay in there?" Tom's voice asked through the sweating door. The sound of a second faucet underlied his words.

"Are you washing those clothes? Don't do that!"

"It's my shirt," he protested.

"But I got it dirty."

He didn't respond. She dried and dressed in time to help him scrub the last of the sewage out.

"Smells as bad as me on a weekday," he said, playfully. "Gracious."

"You should have let me wash these. You're too damned nice."

"That's my name. So what happened to you?"

She found herself saying "This world is pretty screwed up, isn't it?"

"Well, yeah."

"But still, there are some things you always put past it. Like, you go through your whole life knowing for certain that there's no such thing as monsters. And then—"

"Monsters?"

She hesitated. Half an hour ago she'd needed more than anything to confide in someone, but here in the moment, leaning in shell-shock over the sink, she couldn't find it in herself. As if he'd believe it anyway. As if she could even bring herself to go back over it in her own mind, let alone in words.

"I don't really want to talk about it."

Her blank eyes stared deep into his weirded-out ones. His enormous hands brushed against her scuffed ones in the scalding suds. Something had changed about the air moving through her lungs. It was as if—

But then he was wringing the water out of her clothes and leaning out the window to put them on the line. She shook her head back to normal and dried her hands off.

Everything she'd had in her coat pockets lay sprawled out on the counter, including the wad of cash that she was thankful to have kept in its plastic bag. The Memento Mori was there too. When he wasn't looking, she took a few bills from the cash wad and hid the rest in the back of his fridge.

"Hey, did you take that royal mug to your connection already?" she asked him, snapping the fridge door shut.

"Oh, yeah. He wasn't that impressed for some reason. Only offered me ten bucks for it."

"Well, can you connect me to him? I want to try to get some money for something."

Tom shrugged. "Sure, I guess. He's just the guy who runs the pawn shop two blocks up Deckard. Not really a special connection or anything. But he probably won't try to screw you if you tell him you're a friend of mine."

"Got it. I'll be back here in ten minutes." She hung the bass back on her shoulder.

"Huh?"

Her boots were still a little soggy and foul as she trudged hurriedly toward the main drag with a fresh cigarette between her lips. The bass strap cut into her shoulder. The black-tarnished silver ring felt burning hot and impossibly heavy in her palm. Its memory kept washing over her, uninvited:

"No point in fearing what you can't do anything about," Ruth Newman tells her daughter one day. She says this constantly in the last days, always too clearly trying to convince herself. Her face clenches slightly in a characteristic way whenever she tries to well up some new paraphrasing of the way she wants her daughter to feel about what they both know is coming; anything better than the ways that come naturally. "Think of it just like I'm making room for something new to come into the world."

Nothing works. The daughter sleeps less every night. She lays awake in waves of phantom heat, staring across the narrow gap between their couches. She knows that some day soon that other couch will be empty. She prepares herself as well as any twelve-year-old can, but she always braces for a spoken goodbye. She doesn't prepare to simply wake up in that room alone and see those other cushions as empty and neat as if nothing had ever laid there – or to find the tarnished ring clenched in her palm, like something stolen out of a dream, crudely etched with two words in a dead language – and know it for the only remaining evidence of the hand that used to wear it.

Shayna snuffed out her half-burnt cigarette out and returned it to her pocket as she pushed through the heavy black-iron-barred door. The shop swirled thickly with yet another bad smell: tobacco smoke of a different kind.

The windows were small and tinted, and the bars cut the light down even further. It was dim everywhere outside of the fluorescent display cases, but one corner of the room was pitch black. Inside it was the faint outline of a short pudgy bald man silhouetted against a gray stack of bibles. A piece of red hot fire wavered in the middle of his face.

"Can help you?" said the flame, dimming momentarily.

"Tom Nice is a friend of mine," Shayna told it.

The shadow shifted in its chair, making the wood ache. He leaned forward and brought his face and his cigarillo into the light. "Yeah? And you are?"

"Shayna."

He looked her up and down through squinting eyes. A puff of smoke blew at her, smelling of brimstone.

"The name's Nemo to you," he grunted. "What you want, toots?"

Her hand slapped the ring down on the glass counter and flicked it toward him.

A fat-fingered hand pulled it back into the darkness and held it for the shadow's appraisal.

"It's tarnished, but it's pure silver," she said. "I promise. Tom can vouch for me."

"You looking to get cash for it?"

Shayna glanced into one of the glowing cases behind her.

"Actually I want to trade."

"For what, hon?"

She stepped backward and looked over her shoulder into the case. She placed her hand on the warm glass and watched it draw a foggy outline.

The broker leaned up out of his squeaking chair and hobbled around behind the cases to the one she was looking at. He unlocked it at the back and reached his stubby fingers out across the landscape of dusty wine-colored velvet.

"For that ring – and only because you're a friend of an important associate, you understand – the best I'll trade is this one," he grunted through his cigarillo. "Snubnose thirty-eight."

The revolver clanked heavily against the glass. Shayna picked it up experimentally, holding it with both hands and aiming it around the room with the length of her arm and the barrel perfectly rigid and parallel, the way she'd seen done on TV.

"I reckon you can't aim worth dick anyway. Any of the fancier stuff'd be wasted on you."

"Bullets," she growled nervously.

"I'll throw in five. Final offer."

"Fine. Done."

"Need a receipt? Or you just wanna take it and go?"

"Isn't there a waiting period? Papers to fill out? Stuff like that?"

He smiled. "Not in this part of town, sweetheart."

It had all happened much more abruptly than she'd imagined. She peered down at the hunk of dirty chrome in her hand and the five fat tubes of brass and lead clinking across the glowing glass.

"Just keep it out of sight," said Nemo. "Till you want to kill somebody."

His eye continued to scrutinize her down the length of the smoldering cigarillo while she figured out by trial and error how to open it for loading. Then she chambered each of the five bullets, snapped the thing shut and slid it into her right coat pocket.

"You bring that electric bass in to pawn as well, or do you just carry it around with you everywhere?" he asked.

She hesitated. Her hand reached automatically for the strap.

He stared expectantly.

"Everywhere," something inside her blurted out suddenly.

"Suit yourself, hon."

She moved to leave. When she paused in the open door and looked back, some light from outside reflected off the bass's silver parts and shone around the room. Nemo grunted, shielded his eyes and sank back into the dark.

Feet planted on the sidewalk, she stared across the street and read the glowing neon rising up above the concrete.

"Smarty's Chicken Stop," she muttered through her cigarette as she reignited it.

It dawned on her that it had been more than thirty hours since she'd eaten. Even the aftertaste of soap and sewage and adrenaline and the queasiness of last night's undying hangover couldn't hold back the ravenous surge of appetite that hit her now.

She crossed the street and got in line. For half an hour she sat down at the curb and gorged herself on three consecutive orders of deep-fried birdflesh, mechanized dinner rolls and soda.

As she sat there amid a mountain of greasy paper bags and buckets, waiting to burp, she tried to figure out what it was she was really feeling. She wrapped her fingers around the gun's rough handle in her pocket and knew that she had become starkly unfamiliar to herself now. That couldn't be helped, she figured. Given that her days were numbered. Given that she'd seen her first dead body and witnessed the gruesome death of... something. But the electric bass slung there behind her, hard against the edges of her spine, was still at least familiar. And the damp green army coat hung over her shoulders. And the soggy black boots on her feet. These things that had no memory of today.

What a strange fucking world this is, she said silently to the chicken bones scattered at her feet. *Strange fucking world.*

She pressed back through Tom's door to find him sunk down in the pink armchair, watching cartoons with an open can of soup stuck between his thighs. Cold clam chowder.

"How'd it go?" he asked without looking up.

"Fine." She sank down unthinkingly onto the bed.

"I'm probably heading to the Green Room. Soon as Megaduck is over."

Shayna rubbed her eyes. "Aren't you afraid of having to get up and go to the Heaps with a hangover tomorrow morning?"

"I just drink a lot of cups of coffee on Mondays," he said, lifting the chowder to his lips and taking a long slurp. When he'd downed the last of it and finished chewing, he took a clove cigarette from behind his ear and used the can for an ashtray.

"You know those make your lungs bleed, right?" she asked him.

"Which, the cloves?"

"Yeah. I heard they kill you."

"So? They cover the garbage smell. Anyway, you smoke all the time. Regular cigarettes kill you too, you know."

"No, I smoke Balmic brand. They're good for you."

"Oh, Shay. You really believe that?"

"It says so right on the box," she said, offering him the pack. "They make your lungs cleaner. They clean the smog out."

"It's a lie. They're exactly like the other brands except for the package. You can't trust that stuff."

Frustrated, she said "Well if you can't trust the packaging, how can you know anything at all?"

Tom just stared into the cartoons and shrugged.

"Anyway, count me out of the Green Room. I think I'm still hungover from last night. I think I'm just going to go ahead and crash."

"All right," he said, eyes fixed on the TV. His foot pushed her suitcase along the floor toward her.

"No, I mean...."

Tom glanced up from the commercial.

"Here," she said. "Crash here."

"You want to spend the night here again?"

"Is – is that okay?"

His brow furrowed for a moment and then he hurriedly said "Yeah. Yes, that's okay."

"If it's not okay, I won't."

He shrugged. "It's fine."

"There are just some complicated sorts of things," she muttered half-consciously as she collapsed, "that I really have to, I mean I can't.... I don't want to be alone. Anymore."

A moment later she felt a blanket being draped over her.

She listened to the noise of the cartoons for a vague space of time, and then the sound of his feet on the floorboards and the ruffling of his coat, and the clicking of his door.

In her last stir of consciousness she took the gun out of her pocket and slipped it under the corner of the mattress.

18

Shayna started awake at dawn with the memory of that dream of noisy blue just out of reach again. She lay back down and shut her eyes, but her tiredness snuffed out as soon as she remembered herself. She shouted silently:

No more sleep. No time left to waste on sleep.

But...

Now what.

She lay still and deep in thought. Minutes ticked by on the clock above the stove.

Tom's arm slipped off the top bunk and dangled at her side. She stared into the dirty lines of his palm and watched the fingers brush against the edge of consciousness.

Monday morning. She realized distantly that work at the shirt factory started in an hour.

Not going back. Definitely not going back to work today.

But they still hadn't given her last month's paycheck, she remembered. Might as well go in and get it, she decided. She could officially quit at the same time. Maybe the ride to the factory would give her time to think and draw up a real list. *Yes*, she thought, *a list. That's what I need. A list of everything I need to do and try before I die.*

An hour later, stowing her bike in the alley behind the plant as the throngs of her former co-workers fell into line at the rolling doors of peeling wood, having added nothing to the list, she sighed pathetically. There was only one thought that kept circling the drain: *lose virginity*. Wasn't everyone supposed to want that? Wasn't dying a virgin supposed to be the worst of all fates? But no matter how she turned it over in her mind, she couldn't make it into something worth putting on that list.

"I want to talk to the manager," she said when she passed the attendance officer.

"What section do you work in," he grumbled distractedly.

"Printing Station 117."

"What about."

"Getting my last paycheck and quitting."

The officer gave her a weird look. "Sign in then," he said. "Go past your station, up the stairs to the office. Talk to Larry. Next!"

She initialed the sheet uncertainly; the same sheet she'd initialed every weekday morning for the past four years.

The conveyors were groaning awake as she pushed past their operators and down along the line – past the vats filling up with boiling color and harsh-smelling steam – past the corroded pipes that always smelled heavily of bleach – past those valves, in the usual carefully-timed way, that spewed rhythmic bursts of steam that were known to leave permanent scars – along the catwalk with the loose bolts, edging along the squealing railing with everyone else, until she finally arrived at her seat in the nest of blackened pipe. The magnetism of habit pulled on her, but she just stood there in the corridor, looking down. The timeless outlines of her own two feet were stenciled in the pale gray fixer residue on the floor grating. The rhythmic music of the factory was rising to its morning roar.

It felt unreal to continue down the line instead, past other women and girls in their own identical pipe nests: all the other versions of herself, taking their bug-eyed goggles from the hooks on the wall and glancing only briefly up at this alien creature that could ignore the buzzer. It felt dreamlike to walk all the way through to the stairs marked "off limits", and all the way up to the windows – the white-glowing slit windows that looked down in perpetual vigilance – the windows whose gaze she'd never dared to meet.

Inside there were desks drowning in paper. Between the mildewy spires of pulp hunched a stocky man in a shirt that had buttons. His hands were kneading hard into his face.

"Hello?" she asked.

"What are you doing up here? This office is off limits. Get out of here."

"I need to speak with Larry."

"I'm Larry," he barked. "Get out of here."

"I need last month's paycheck—"

"Get out of here."

"I'm quitting. And you owe me a paycheck. I wasn't paid on the first."

Larry shut up and sighed. His body looked well-fed but his eyes looked sick. The hairs of his unkempt moustache stuck out of his upper lip like feathers from a roadkill bird.

He rolled himself over to a tall gray filing cabinet. His slouching back turned to her, he grunted "Name."

"Shayna."

"*Last* name. Idiot."

"Newman."

He rifled through the files, then said "First name."

"Shayna?" she repeated uncertainly.

"Is that your name or not?" he shouted.

"Is."

"Printing station 117," he mumbled, half-audibly.

"Yes."

"And you're quitting."

"Yes."

"I don't have a replacement for that station. I'm withholding your paycheck until I do. Go back to your station."

"What?"

"Go back to your station. I'm withholding your paycheck."

"No. I'm quitting."

"Go back to your station."

"I'm quitting."

"Go back to your station."

She stared in disbelief at his still-turned back.

"Go back to your station," Larry repeated. "Get out of here."

One foot started to obey, but she stopped it. Breathing hard, fists quivering, she said "I'm not going anywhere until you pay me for last month!"

"Fine. Go back to your station and I'll have your check by C-O-B. Get out of here."

Without even knowing it she had stepped back out onto the metal stairs, and she hated herself for it. Her curses were muted by the gushing of the vats below. Then she sighed.

Would one more day of work really hurt? she thought. *One day of work for a month's paycheck.*

From the office door's God's-eye-view, she could see the lines of conveyor belts rattling along above the fields of cubicles like hers. She could see her own would-be workload of blank shirts piling up to a critical mass above the one empty seat amid all those pipes. It made her queasy. Her fingernails picked at the rust on the railing.

She clambered down the metal stairs, took her goggles from the hook on the wall and put them on. She took the levers and fell into the rhythm, and the motors and cogs went to work, stringing identical seconds into a seamless blur of hours.

A deafening buzzer sounded throughout the factory. The music of the machines ground to a halt. Shayna took a deep breath and hung her goggles on the wall hook, then followed the throngs to the nearest exit.

Two hundred people lit two hundred cigarettes and smoked them hungrily in two minutes. Another buzzer sounded. Two hundred smoldering butts snuffed out under feet.

Shayna went back and took her goggles from the wall hook. The shirts came and went. The logo of the Power Elite burned itself into her eyes.

The lunch buzzer rang. Ten minutes.

She took a deep breath and became one of two hundred people waiting in line behind ten vending machines. As always, she was all but last. Two hundred wrappers of joyless candy littered the ground outside the big rolling doors and were left to blow along in a mighty flock when the buzzer rang and four hundred feet stumbled hurriedly back to their posts.

Goggles. Rhythm. Shirt. Logo.
Buzzer. Halt. Goggles. Stand.
Cigarettes. Buzzer. Snuffed out. Sit. Goggles.
Buzzer. Closing time. Six PM.

She reflexively started to leave the factory before she remembered. In a wash of rage she ran back and jumped up the metal stairs and pushed against the office door, but it was locked. Larry was hobbling through another door on the far side of the scuffed soundproof glass.

She flew back down the stairs and tried to push through the crowd fast enough to catch him on the other side of whatever door that was, but the throngs budged for no one. When she finally squeezed back into daylight she found only chainlink fences and empty parking spaces.

Suddenly she wanted to drink.

Waves of smoke breathed through beams of green light. They washed over Shayna's third empty glass, slid along the sharp and luminous outline of Katja's neck and blew through the dim spaces between her and the regular compliment of whispering men who eyed her from the adjoining booth. The smoke's pale tendrils seemed to floss Tom's yellow teeth as he leaned back and let a hammered bolt of laughter rumble out of the depths of his angular chest. They entered into the small nostrils of Carl's stubby nose and blew out between his chubby cheeks when he puffed a sigh of some emotionally fatigued kind.

"How many nights a week do you guys come here?" Shayna asked over an overflowing glass and the trash blasting through the overhead speakers.

"Most of them," Carl replied.

"Since when?"

"How long have you been in exile?" Katja asked.

"Yeah, that's exactly it," Tom said. "It was about that same time. That we started coming here every night, and you kind of vanished. Both of those two things happened around that time. The same one, time. When they both... happened." He burped loudly.

"What changed then?" Shayna asked. "What did—?" But before anyone gave her the answer, she remembered it and muttered "Oh. Never mind."

Carl rubbed his eyes and pursed his lips tightly. His free hand dropped his glass onto the table, either clumsily or angrily, making Shayna remember a particular argument and a particular shattering mirror.

Katja was eyeing her from across the table and looking away when Shayna turned. The tension between them had been thickening since she arrived, until she could feel it tangibly in the air. The pressure around that table built and built until she unthinkingly stood and stumbled upward for the alley.

The corners of the cool bricks stabbed into her shoulderblades. She closed her eyes and took a long breath. When she looked again, Katja had appeared at her side, her head cocked to the side.

"Are you all right?" she asked. "I mean, I can tell you aren't. So what is it?"

"Nothing."

"That was an intense experience we shared yesterday."

"Yeah, and I—" She trailed off and rubbed her eyes.

"You what?"

"I can't believe it happened. *Did* it happen? Were we just hallucinating from the fumes in those tunnels? What did *you* see down there?"

Katja paused. "I don't know, exactly."

"You don't know? How can you not know? Did we kill it?"

"That doesn't matter."

"How can you say—?"

"What matters is how it made you feel. That's why we went down there."

"I don't even know what I was feeling anym—"

"We're going on another run and you should come with us," Katja interrupted. "Don't look at me that way. Don't look like you're surprised that I'd ever want to do it again. You're not surprised. Don't you remember the way you felt when we were all running away from there? When we knew for sure that we'd survived? You were dancing on air."

"I was high on the fumes. That's all."

"You were scared shitless like the rest of us. Maybe a little confused. But you felt alive. In every cell. Alive in your blood. You were one of us."

"And what if I did hallucinate the whole thing? Maybe it never happened."

"Then the *feeling* was real, and I saw it in you! You felt more alive than you ever had before. And don't you tell me you don't know what I'm talking about!" She had drunkenly grabbed Shayna's arm and was digging her nails in deep.

Shayna wrenched herself free. There was a heat spreading in her chest, flowing into her clenched fists. A fight? Was this a fight? She shouted: "Why? Why do you think I felt that? Why should I have felt alive? We could've died!"

"Exactly," Katja said, her voice suddenly placid. "Exactly."

Shayna wavered in the night air, dumbfounded.

Katja sank into herself, deflated. "I'm sorry," she said. "I'm... drunk. I mean, you don't have to come with us. I'm sorry. Never mind. But you should still come with us."

Shayna bit her tongue until Katja had drifted out of sight, safely back underground. The stub of her cigarette lay dying on the cracked mud.

When she locked the bathroom stall and sat down, she was stared down by a photocopied flier pasted to the inside of the door. It said BLACK FACTION in block letters, followed by a long quote. Due to boredom and overhydration, she read it all:

> "We now recognize that in historical times, the human world was divided into public nations, which were considered to occupy either the 'first' or the 'third' world. Respectively: one world for wealthy consumers of produced goods, and a separate world for the impoverished and exploited producers of those goods. The Company improved upon the geographical inefficiency of this model by eliminating all national boundaries and re-configuring humanity around centralized hubs of consumption, closely encircled by the sites of production. Today you may walk into the third world from any point in the first, simply by pointing "outward". Likewise, to travel "inward" from the outer rings of any sector of the Tropolis, toward the nearest Cology, is to trace the flow of economic activity: up the food chain, so to speak, from the assembly of raw goods, into progressively more abstract forms of consumption and re-consumption."
>
> –*Rokosz*

A second author had added the words "EAT ME ROCOX."

Shayna slumped back down into the booth just as the music pumps finished out their current song and a started a new rhythm, rough and upbeat, making her wince when she recognized it. "Oh God."

"What's wrong now?" Katja asked.

"I can't stand this song. I hate this song."

Carl rolled his eyes and nodded in agreement.

Katja looked at the ceiling for a moment and said "Oh, this one. It plays so often at the store that I don't even hear it anymore."

"What song?" Tom asked.

"It's called '*Not That Bad*,'" Carl said. "By those talentless shitheads the *Power Elite*."

The guitars had started up. Shayna tried to focus elsewhere, or think of something else to talk about, but now everyone was shutting up and listening.

"You have to admit it's pretty catchy," Tom said.

"Oh, it's *catchy* all right," Carl said.

"Why do you guys hate it so much?"

"Are you not hearing this shit, Tom? Are you not hearing these lyrics?"

"*You have it good, you have it good,*" the speakers yelled down.

Tom shrugged.

Carl stared gravely into his drink and said "To think of these assholes topping the charts. To think *this* shit is what filled the vacuum left by *the Smurge.*"

"At least you don't have to print their T-shirts," Shayna groaned. "Or – oh, God, here it comes."

"What?" Tom asked.

As the song climbed to its ragged crescendo, the singer's voice declared:

Your friend's been wailing day and night
The 'sembly line took off his hand
But he's still got his balls all right
Why can't he take it like a man
It's not that ba-ad
It's not that ba-ad

A glass exploded against the wall by an empty booth. Shayna didn't even realize she'd thrown it until she noticed the shocked looks everyone was giving her.

"Sorry," she said, lowering her head and looking away. She felt Carl watching her with a particular kind of interest.

The speakers moved on in the playlist. More Power Elite.

"Over my dead body," Carl said. He raised himself up to stand on the seat, knocking the table with his knees, tipping over the glasses.

"What the hell are you doing?" Katja protested.

His belly hung out from under his shirt as he stretched his arms to the ceiling, pulling the speaker wires down from their hooks. The nasal voices died with a pop except for the echoes from other rooms – and then, plugging his phone into that hanging mess of plugs, a different beat started up. He almost fell as he climbed down.

"That's better," he said. He looked straight at Shayna.

Everyone listened uncertainly until the beats cohered. The recognition came over them in a wave of nods.

"Now there's a song I haven't heard in a while," Fish observed. "This is *Machinery Anthem*, right?" He snapped his fingers several times. "By the Smudge."

"The *Smurge,*" Carl hissed. He turned to everyone else and said "This was the song. This was the first one."

Everyone gave him a questioning look.

"Where it all began," he said.

"What are you talking about?" Katja asked.

"When we met, stupid! When we all met. This was playing."

"You remember what song was playing when we met?" Shayna asked in faint awe.

Katja said "What, back in school? I don't even remember what grade we were in."

"No." Carl's every slurred word was dripping with a rising intensity. His forefinger pointed into the table like a knife. "No, we didn't meet in school. It was after our allocations. Right after."

"Are you sure?"

"I didn't have friends when I was in school. You were my first real friends. I was fourteen. You, me, Shay, Balboa, Tom. It was the Smurge's last concert ever."

"Yeah," said Tom. "Yeah, yeah, of course. I kind of remember now."

"Remember the grass. The rainy night and the grass."

Katja snickered.

"Not the drug," Carl growled. "I mean the ground under us. The hill. We were sitting on a hill, the four of us, trying to see over the wall into the stadium."

Shayna stared into her glass and tried to remember.

He continued: "That was the Smurge's last show. None of us had enough money for the tickets. So we climbed that hill. *Machinery Anthem*. The song we heard rising up over the bleachers and the street and the hill. The last song in their set. The last music they ever played for any audience, anywhere, ever."

"Right, before they split up," Tom said.

"Before they were *assassinated*," Carl corrected.

Tom looked away, knowing better than to get into that argument again.

Carl continued: "That was when we met. The first words we ever shared. The moment that song ended."

Shayna drifted on the edge of the memory. The grass smell seemed to waft in her nose.

"*Remember?*" he demanded.

Shayna nodded.

"Jesus, Carl," Katja said. "Why are you talking in that voice? You sound homicidal."

He gradually sank back into his seat, tossing a faint shrug off each shoulder. "It's important. To me."

"No. You're just drunk. And it's messing with your meds again."

He seemed to bite his tongue.

"That's where all your bad poetry comes from too," she added off-handedly.

Carl turned a deeper red and miraculously managed to contain himself.

"But that's true, though, about the song," Tom said, his cool voice breaking Shayna's hypnotic trance. "That is when we met. I didn't even go to school with you guys, remember. I was four years ahead of all of you. Yeah, we all met on that hill and became friends right after, right? That weekend. And we then decided to – hah! – we decided to, you know. Form our *tribute band*." By now he was convulsing with laughter, smacking his heavy palm against the table.

"It's not funny," Carl said.

"Fish, whatever your name is, you should have seen it. Remember, Katja? How we shoplifted all our outfits from the thrift store? And my guitar was the only real instrument in the band at first. Remember we made Balboa's drums out of gas jugs, and Carl just played air guitar until he got that real one from the pawn shop?"

"It's coming back to me," Katja said. "It feels like forever ago."

"I was the only one with any actual musical skill," he laughed. "Carl, our *lead guitar*, had never pulled on a string in his life."

"I sold my bone marrow to buy that electric guitar," Carl said solemnly, though it only provoked another round of explosive laughter.

"And you were only fourteen so you had to borrow my ID to get the meat shop to take you! That was great!"

"Yes. It was."

"So you were all in a Smurge cover band or something?" Fish asked, half-interestedly.

Tom said "Not just a cover band, a *tribute* band. We didn't just play the songs. We pretended to actually *be* the Smurge, and we never did anything else. We had costumes and everything. I was Jon Manderlay, Carl was Bruce Fain, and Balboa was the Bomber," Tom continued. He turned to Katja. "And you—"

"I was Clara Ruthless! I was so obsessed with her."

"And I just did backup," Shayna murmured. No one heard her.

"It was so crazy it almost worked," Tom said. "Man oh man. Those were the days. We were out of our minds."

Carl took his shot bitterly.

Fish scratched his head and eyed the stairs. "Big fans, huh."

"You have no idea," Tom said.

"Wait, wasn't Smurge the band that put out that career-killing single with all the political jargon right before they broke up?"

"Before they were *assassinated*," Carl corrected.

Tom motioned for the speakers. "Right, that's this song. If you can make out the lyrics, it talks about public government, anti-corporatism, unionism, stuff like that."

"It's why they were killed," Carl said, smoldering.

Tom continued to Fish: "I mean, I guess *Machinery Anthem* wasn't their biggest hit, no, but we lived for that stuff. It was all we ever talked about. We used to hang out in Beau's – I mean Balboa's basement every single night and weekend just listening to the Smurge and pretending to be them and screwing around with instruments we didn't have a clue how to actually play."

"Well, right on," Fish said and yawned.

"It was nuts," Katja said.

"Nuts," Tom said. "And then after a while we mainly started hanging out here instead."

"Right," Fish said.

"And everything went straight to hell, happily fucking ever after!" Carl yelled. He jumped out of the booth, knocking the table one more time, and stormed off into the luminous smoke.

He came back to rip his phone out of the dangling wires. Then he stormed off again.

"Meds and booze don't mix, sleazebag," Katja said. "I've always hated that guy."

"Always? Why?" Tom asked.

"Creeps me out."

"I guess I see that."

Shayna listened absently to this exchange. She knew she'd heard it before, almost word for word, but something made it stick in her mind this time. She looked back and forth between her friends in the booth beside her, and suddenly thought: *Wait. Do we* all *hate each other? Are we friends? What are we?*

She thought: *Yes. One way or another, we hate each other, and we always have. But maybe we hate each other less than we hate everyone else in the entire world.*

At this thought she sighed and slouched. She threw back another shot – and as the alcohol's cool melodic tentacles trickled into the caverns of her brain, she looked at Tom, bobbing his head into a cloud of yellow neon.

But I care about him, she thought distantly. *Yeah. That's what this feeling is.*

She kept herself sober enough for the bike ride back to his apartment. She forgot everything else.

Except the song.

It haunted her dreams.

17

One day everything is simple, and this simplicity is a secret they share as siblings. One day the five of them live to tug at the loose threads of all the rotten oppression in the universe, trusting that the right tug in the right place could unravel the whole thing.

On a different day they're only getting stoned again in Balboa's basement.

The drummer slumps on his plastic crate and lands one more unsteady barrage on his snare, like somebody dipping his toes into a pool too cold to ever swim in.

The noise stirs Tom out of a sleep he hasn't really been getting. He squints around and says, two days late and to no one in particular, "I still can't believe nobody showed. After I made posters and everything."

Katja responds by snuffing her cigarette out and glancing faintly at the TV. Balboa responds by accidentally dropping his stick and only staring at it on the floor. Shayna responds by nodding distantly.

Carl responds loudly: "I can."

They all ignore him. Lately ignoring Carl has become reflexive, Shayna realizes. Soon their minds will automatically filter him out of every conversation, but until that time—

"Fudge," his shrill, accusing voice calls out. "Did you do it?"

"Stop calling me that," Balboa hisses. "I told you never to call me that!"

"Did you do it or not?"

The drummer glares bitterly and says "No. I didn't."

"Damnit, Fudge!"

"Fucking cut it out!" Katja and at least one other person yell at him. "Stop calling him that."

"I'll stop calling Fudge Fudge when he goes on his diet."

"I'm not going on your stupid diet," Balboa shouts, reddening. "One meal a day? Nobody can do that."

"You better do it anyway."

"You don't own me."

"I've told you before and I'll keep on telling you, *Fudge*." Carl pauses to proudly ignore everyone's protests, then continues: "You're not the Bomber. You're never going to be him until you loose the weight. Eighty pounds. You're eighty pounds fatter than Beau was. And frankly, Fudge, it's hurting the band. You're holding us all back."

"*You* loose eighty pounds!" Balboa yells. "There's eighty pounds of fat in your head!"

"I'm telling you now. For your own good. Do it or you're out."

"Out? Out of what?"

"Out of the band."

Balboa sneers incredulously. A nervous silence descends over the room. Shayna scrutinizes everyone in turn, wondering if the group is going to let Carl get away with that.

"Who made you king?" Katja says. "You can't just kick people out."

"I started this band and I hold it together," Carl declares, ridiculously. "It's obvious why no one came to the show. We suck."

No one responds.

"So lets get some fucking practice," he persists. "Let's all jam or something. Right now. And on Friday night we'll play another one."

More than one groan is heard.

"Come on," Balboa murmurs.

Katja says "We're not going to be ready by then and you know it."

"Better start right now," Carl says.

"No," she insists acidly. "My throat hurts. I won't sing."

"Fine. Then let's do something else. I got it. You know how I've been telling you about my big plan? With the lunar logo projector? It's almost a new moon and the Company logo is on full. It's the perfect time, and I found out where the projector is. We could go there, break in, change the logo."

"Not this again," Katja whispers to Shayna, too low for Carl to hear.

Still, he sees it. He turns to Shayna and says "We'll need those bombs you keep saying you have. Get through the fences and doors. Create a diversion."

"Bombs?" Shayna stammers. She feels herself blush. "I never— I never said I had them. I said my friend, he— I said he knew how to make them."

"Then let's go talk to him. Right now. All of us."

The basement stands still.

"Why not?" Carl spits. "I'm only saying we should do what we've been talking about doing all along. Put into practice what the music is all about. I'm only saying we should get up off our lazy asses and do something!"

"Sit down, Carl," Katja says.

They all stare wordlessly as Carl picks up his guitar and turns all the knobs to their maximum. He forms a chord and then hits it so hard that it sounds like a car crash, and Shayna feels it in her entrails when she covers her ears in shock. Two of the strings snap before Carl finally drops the instrument, rips it from its plugs and starts dragging it by its neck toward the stairs.

Shayna sees him pass a mirror. He looks into it long enough to notice that he's still wearing the wig with which he pretends to be Bruce Fain. He nods to his reflection, then punches it with the force of his whole body. She thinks she sees a piece of mirror still embedded between his knuckles as he vanishes into the daylight.

"You're all shit to me," they hear his voice thundering. "You all suck Company dick."

"Don't come back here!" Katja shouts after him, needlessly.

For a while they sit, waiting for their hearts to slow down, the heat to lessen. Only when the last shard of silvered glass clinks on the floor do they all look up. They each meet eyes in turn, and something passes between them. The old unspoken clarity dissolves and a new one enters. Just like that, they pass between two ages.

The song was still drumming in her head when she woke up. As the new dawn set fire to Tom's window, the grating twang of Clara Ruthless's voice was repeating the lyrics at the bridge:

Make black waves break
Against the white walls
Make the waves break

Make the waves, she sang to herself in her mind, as she drew in and released a long, exhausted breath through a rotten throat. Her hangover made her touch her forehead, checking a suspicion that part of it had caved in during the night. She was hungry but her stomach hurt too much to want to eat. It was the same way with sleep.

Nothing to do but get my damn paycheck, she thought as she leaned upright and edged around Tom's dangling arm.

She rolled up to the giant rolling doors to grudgingly join the throng and the motions it was going through. She signed in with the attendance officer and pushed among the conveyor operators, past the vats of boiling liquid color, through the jungle of bleach-smelling pipes and rhythmically hissing valves of searing steam, along the railing of the catwalk that was always about to break and plunge into the mechanical abyss below, past the cramped nest of blackened pipes where the outlines of her feet on the metal grating. She hurried up the winding steel steps to the eternally vigilant slit windows and pressed through the door.

Her angry words died in her throat. Larry was there. So was a comp.

"That's her," said Larry, eyes glowing with spiteful triumph.

"This area is off limits," the comp told her. "I need you to step outside right now."

Shayna froze. The comp's thick-soled boots squealed on the plastic floor. His black armored vest hung heavily on his inhumanly muscular frame. His hand, encased in a glove of dark metal, planted itself on the handle of a stun baton the color of crude oil. The red and white company logo burned like a hot brand on his broad, padded shoulder.

"Are you deaf, little girl? Outside. Now."

She found herself backing involuntarily through the door. Through the slit window she watched the comp share a few more words with Larry, then the lines of overhead fluorescence reflected in splinters of white hot light over the dome of his polished ebony helmet as he trudged heavily between the desks toward the door. He seemed to grow taller with every step, until he clanked out onto the catwalk as a giant. She couldn't meet his eyes.

"I understand you verbally assaulted your supervising officer yesterday," the comp told Shayna.

"No," she said to his chest. "I just want my—"

"Did you or did you not verbally assault your supervising officer yesterday?" the comp demanded.

"No," she said.

"Did you or did you not?"

"I didn't!"

"He says you did."

"I just want my last paycheck."

"That's not permissible," said the comp. "For you to assault him verbally."

"I'm quitting," she said. "I just came to ask for the paycheck. I was never paid for last month."

"I understand that, but it's not permissible for you to assault him verbally."

Larry appeared at the slit window with a mug in his hand. His stony eyes watched the conversation hungrily.

Shayna took a breath, shook her head and said evenly: "I'm sorry, officer. If I can just get my paycheck, I will never come back here. There will never be a problem again."

"I understand that he politely asked you to continue working until a replacement worker is hired. A few short days of your time. That's a reasonable request."

Shayna said nothing.

"Is there going to be a problem with that?" the comp asked.

"Yes," she said forcibly. "I have to quit."

"Is there going to be a problem with that?"

"I quit. Something personal. I can't go on working here."

"Is there going to be a problem with that?"

Shayna said nothing.

"Go back to your station," the comp said. As he moved back through the door, he added: "If I have to come back here again, there will be physical consequences. Is that understood?"

She didn't give him the answer he wasn't waiting for – but he followed her back down the steel stairs to Printing Station 117, glowering down on her as she hesitated. She thought of running, but she could hear his breath. She could see his fingers ticking on the handle of the shiny black baton.

She ripped her goggles from the wall hook and sat down. She took the levers and fell into the rhythm. The shirts rolled along. The fixer residue splattered onto the floor.

"So why can't he take it like a man," one of the other Printing Station women sang, mumbling as if in sleep. Shayna cringed. The wall of black body armor was still there in her peripheral vision and the flow of time was already mechanically accelerating.

Shirt. Logo. Dye. Splatter. Seconds. Minutes. Hours.

The lever groaned to a halt in mid-motion. The comp was gone. She got up and started to make a run for the exit, but her feet froze on the clanking floor outside; he was pacing the corridor now, knocking his baton against his armored thigh, watching the monotony. He started to turn. She fell back into the rusty nest.

"Fuck," she said and took back the levers.

Buzzer. Goggles. Stand.

Cigarettes. Buzzer. Snuffed out. Sit. Goggles.

Once she looked up through the labyrinth of corrosion and tried to remember the dream of noise and color – but it still escaped her. The blue in her memory felt dimmer with every stamp of the machine.

Shirt, splatter, seconds.

Buzzer. Lunch. Buzzer. Goggles.

Buzzer. Closing time. Six PM.

The comp was gone. She peered up at the glowing slit window just in time to see the fluorescence wink out line by line. And then there was nothing to do but spit angrily on the fixer-stained floor gratings and make her way back into the daylight, there to sit on the curb and smoke bitterly and let herself remember that she'd just burned off another five percent of all the life she had left. Nine more hours she couldn't even remember. Without the weight of her mental fatigue and the soapy sheen of the fixer on her skin and clothes, she could have convinced herself that it was still morning.

Her head felt a little better, but her guts felt the same as before. She didn't want to drink. She hopped on her bike and pedaled her rage back to Tom's apartment, not even knowing what the hell she'd do when she got there.

The door opened as she was putting the key in the lock.

"Oh, Shay," Tom said, a little surprised. "How are you doing?"

"Are you going to the Green Room?"

"No, actually. I'm going out on business. You know."

Three huge empty sacks were slung over his shoulder and there was a gas mask and a shiny compass in his hands.

"You're going on a Heap raid?" she asked in a whisper. A wave of cool excitement touched the burning pressure behind her ribs.

He looked over his shoulder with cartoonish paranoia.

"Can I come with you?"

"Come with me?" He scratched his fuzzy head. "Well, you, ah. It's really dangerous, Shay. And really illegal. We're dead meat if we get caught."

"I know. Please. I've always wanted to go on a raid with you."

"You know, it's not really a *raid*. It's sort of an expedition."

"Then I want to come on the expedition. Come on. I'll be careful. I do whatever you say. I'll be your best friend."

He sighed and looked anxiously at his boots.

"You really want to come along?"

She smiled and darted back into his apartment, saying "You still keep your spare gas mask under the sink? By the way, you're the greatest, Tom. The greatest!"

"Yeah," he said.

They caught the Metro amid the gathering shadows. When they stepped off, the last embers of sun-streaked clouds were dying on the lip of the dirty sky, and the atmosphere was no longer breathable.

The Heaps were wreathed in the shadows of their own yellow fog and the stench was at its peak. By now Friday's rains had soaked deep into the stratified refuse, making the ground swollen and boiling up with the gasses of its fermentation – and the dry and windless stagnation in the wake of that storm had been near perfect. April's first day of strong Pacific wind would smear those rancid clouds in a wide swath across hundreds of miles of the Tropolis, dropping crows from billboards all the way to the Ford Street; but for now it was all contained here, softly cupped within the towers of trash, held like a breath.

Helped by the lightheadedness of panting strange fumes through the thick mask, the first moments of beholding the landscape of filth were always ones of awe; pure, speechless and unthinking. Clambering down a hill toward the electric fences from the closest stop the Metro dared to make, she could see for herself some of the distance the Heaps had crawled. That unholy ground was alive, she knew: always changing, constantly destroyed and rebuilt, continually following its some mysterious path across the face of the city. Its living flesh poured in scrap by scrap, truckload by truckload, from every corner of the trans-continental sprawl. Sometimes its spires grew hundreds of feet tall before the garbagemen attacked, tearing them down and spreading their mass thin with their dirty yellow dozers, filling up the deep pits while other dozers deepened those pits and carved out new ones, and still other men and machines hauled the uprooted dirt away to some other place. Whenever the diggers couldn't dig the pits any deeper and the dozers couldn't fill them higher, the Heaps simply moved. Another neighboring city block would vanish and another empty grave would appear in its place. Elsewhere, another block-sized plot of the Heaps would be patted down and paved over and given streets, curbs and chain-link fences. In this way, the entire Tropolis was going through a gradual transmutation into pristine and inaccessible vacant lots. Some day every inch of the earth would be skin over a subterranean mountain of trash. Or so Shayna imagined and understood.

She followed Tom into the shadows of the rust-bleeding hulk of a derelict garbage truck, where she followed his example, leaning back into the mottled steel and taking looks both ways down the street. She tried to read his expression through the eyeholes of that pig-snouted rubber mask, but couldn't.

"What are we waiting here for?" she asked.

"My connection. He helps out with the raids – expeditions."

"Who? That guy Nemo?"

"Speak of the devil."

Out there in the dim night, something roared madly. Then they appeared out at the end of that long street bordering the electric-fenced spires of waste: two white hot eyes that burned in the tendrils of yellow gas. The eyes jolted ravenously forward and barreled over the rain-greased pavement for the two huddled pig-faced trespassers. Too fast for Shayna to finish flinching, the old truck screeched to a tire-burning halt at the curb.

"You," yelled the rubber-snouted thing behind the wheel, heaving itself out onto the street. Nemo's well-worn comp boots thudded hard against the pavement and then took up the laborious work of throwing his bulky frame over to Tom and the wrecked truck. He had the gait of somebody who never walked anywhere.

"I brought a friend," Tom told him through the muffling mask.

"You bleeding idiot," Nemo yelled, slinging some sacks over his shoulder. "You sump-sniffing rat-head! What'd you do that for? You want to ruin us? You want to fuck us both?"

"She won't be any trouble. I trust her."

"What if *I* don't trust her?" Nemo pointed his middle finger around like a switchblade. "What if I don't trust her to keep her damn mouth shut to the comps? What if she squeals for the arrest commission? What if she steps knee-deep into a muck hole and we get to yank her out? What if she trips a sensor?"

"She's a friend. She promised to be careful. She'll help carry."

"Then how about you two fucking lovebirds just go in there without me," Nemo said, throwing his sacks down on the ground. "Just go in there and carry your own shit and get your sorry ass a new connection."

"Fine," Tom said. "Find a new garbageman."

Nemo shut up. He took up his sacks again and stood there, tapping his gloved fingers expectantly on his elbows.

"Let's go already," he said.

The mask covered Shayna's grin.

Through a dead spot in the electric fence and up the first rise in the rancid earth, the smell through the filter was already so strong that Shayna knew it could only be lethal. Were she to pull away that heavy, chemical-stinking rubber membrane and its foggy eye lenses for even a moment – if she took even one full breath of the air that already faintly burned on the exposed flesh of her neck and ears and wrists – she knew it would melt her lungs like the rain-fermented sludge squishing beneath her boots.

"You know what the penalty is for getting caught sneaking in here?" Nemo growled between wheezing breaths, trudging close behind her. "Five years. High level. It's funny, you know – they catch you breaking into the Heaps, they figure you belong here. They put you to work here."

"Digging," Tom said. "Mainly the convicts do the digging."

"Because the Company can't afford full-face masks for all of them," Nemo continued. "They just get mouth masks. They'd drop dead if they worked in the raw heaps, so they just dig in the dirt. And get breathing trouble. And grow the pox. The pox, kid."

"Shut up," Shayna said. "It doesn't stop *you* from coming here."

"Just thought you should know what you're in for, toots," Nemo said. "Know what you're laying on the line with us rats."

Sparse orange lights shone down from the indistinct tips of looming poles, lighting up the billowing haze. When the haze cleared for a moment Shayna made out the rows of security cameras.

"What about those things?" she asked. "Can they see us?"

"All blind," Tom said. "Just for show. Regular cameras can't see through the haze, so they put up infra-red ones. But those were all blinded by the fire."

"There was a fire here?" Shayna asked. "When?"

"Always," Tom yelled. "Underground. They catch on their own. Pooled-up organic oils, chemical reactions, high pressure. We used to put them out, but the new manager is stingy with water. He just lets them burn."

"Underground fire," she echoed inaudibly as they started the long trudge up a steep hill.

When they reached the summit and peered down through a break in the gas, she saw it. Blood-red embers glittered in patches at the foot of each hill, peeking out from between sheets of rotten cardboard, burning upward through the depths of ruin. In the muck-ridden valleys they formed glowing veins whose light ebbed and throbbed with the currents of unsteady wind, or they collected in sickly blotches around puddles of whatever volatile stuff had boiled up out of the stewing underground. The yellow breath of the Heaps spewed from every burning crevice.

"So this is where bad people go when they die," She thought aloud between heaved inhales.

Tom gave her a shocked look through the eyeholes of his mask and demanded: "How can you tell? How do you know they were bad?"

She looked quizzically back for a moment before she realized.

"No," she murmured. "I just meant—"

"Oh," he said.

Hot pangs of embarrassment coursed through her. Somehow in the excitement of coming here she had forgotten; but she knew that this twenty-mile swath of refuse, set apart from the five-thousand-mile-wide trash heap that constituted the Tropolis at large, was where everyone – regardless of what they'd done – went when they died. Now it was hard not to make out the unmistakable outlines of what had once been human remains, scorched and scattered among the venomous hillsides, and it was hard not to choke on the thought that her own inevitable grave waited somewhere out here within the stewing ground.

Her throat tightened suddenly. Her knees felt as stiff as solid bone.

Nemo climbed up behind them and stood wheezing in his place. As soon as he had half-caught his breath he started clambering down the other side.

Shayna didn't move. Tom hesitated. The gas blew in thick and turned acidly opaque in the space between them.

"You all right, Shay?"

Consciousness waned. Her gloved and burning fingers reached blindly into the cloud and found him. They took hold of the side of his coat, pulling herself closer to him, and her arms wrapped themselves around his abdomen. Eyes shut tight behind the foggy lenses, she held on tight and waited for her throat to open again.

"What are you kids waiting for?" Nemo grumbled from somewhere below. "We don't got all night."

"It's, uh, it's going to be all right," Tom said. He looked around and repeated stupidly "You all right?"

"Yeah, yes," she managed. She let go hurriedly, composed herself and started in the direction of Nemo's stumbling boot-thuds in the gathering murk.

They climbed down the lip of a caldera of trash, deeper into the blackened and smoking heart of the Heaps. They stepped carefully now, searching out pieces of metal or concrete to use as stepping stones where everything else slid away underfoot. Nemo tripped and plunged his knee into a whole crate of bad apples. His muffled profanity mingled with the bitter atmosphere.

"What should I be looking for?" Shayna asked. Her eyes had been scanning every passing inch of the squishing, gurgling ground for a trace of something valuable.

"Not here," Tom said. "We're still in the brown plots. This trash came straight from the Tropolis. All pretty much worthless."

"Then where are we going?"

"It's not much farther."

They started their trudging, slippery ascent of the next mountain of sludge and twisted debris. The cloud was still thick around them. The stinging smoke hung in layered curtains, drifting on the thin wind, turning everything in sight into shadow and the glow of cinders and looming lamps.

Something changed. The higher they climbed up the side of that spire, the more the uniform sludge gave way to hard and dry ground. The wrappers and paper and scrap metal gave way to other things. Strange things. Pale things. Things that collected with ever greater density as the climb went on.

Shayna paused when something seemed to shine up at her through her foggy and breathless eyes: something purely white. She knelt down and found a tiny porcelain angel staring up from the palm of her hand, miraculously and perfectly clean amid this world of shit. Shaking off a moment of mesmerism, she quickly stuffed it into her pocket and hurried to catch up – but Tom and Nemo had stopped dead in their tracks only a few yards further. There they stood at the crest of the trash spire, smoke swirling around them, Tom in his towering skeletal lankiness and Nemo in his obesity, silhouetted against a colorless ambience from the other side. When she finally reached that high point, she saw the yellow gas curling along the lip of the next caldera but drifting no further down, as if magically repulsed by what they touched. The air was almost clear down there, all but for the luminous aura that left burning afterimages across her foggy vision.

Everything was pure white.

"This is it," Tom said. "The white plots."

Shayna gaped and murmured: "You mean this is—?"

"Yep. The Cology's garbage. Straight from Angelis. Or at least the Inner Ring."

There was something both deeply exciting and disconcertingly sacrilegious about trudging onward. Her boots painted a trail of muck across the virgin trash. She followed after Tom and Nemo's hasty march, but the urge to stop and examine every passing weird trinket and discarded shard of glamour was unbearable. She looked down and tried to imagine what sort of world these things had come from – the world of white teeth and clean things and new things and plastic things – the world of the movie actors, the glossy magazine covers, the saintly Company heads and their families – the world she could never see or touch or know. Not her world, where there were only varying shades of gray, all fading eventually to black; the world of Outsiders.

She saw white scraps of paper. White broken shards of plates and dishes. Huge bunches of brilliant white clothes, bedsheets, pillows, curtains. Uneaten loaves of pristine white bread wrapped up in clean plastic. Trash that was nicer and cleaner than brand new things in the Tropolis. Piled up under one of the lamp poles was a minor mountain of shiny porcelain toilets – dozens, perhaps hundreds of toilets. Not one of them looked as if it had ever been used. She tried to picture a world with too many clean toilets to even know what to do with them all, and her imagination danced there within the electric drone of a forest of harsh white-hot lights and trip-lasers, all humming together like a choir of industrial ghosts.

"Hold a moment," Tom said, stepping up to one of the lighted poles towering above the saintly slopes. Shayna watched him fiddle with an electronic keypad.

"Security stuff actually works in this part," Nemo told her. "This is the part they actually give a crap about. And they give a *huge* crap while they're at it, toots. Always the first stuff they bury, and the deepest too. *Five years* for getting caught rooting around in here. Five years, I'm telling you. Serious business."

"Why?" she asked. "Why do they protect it so hard if it's just going to be buried? If it's all just trash to them?"

Nemo laughed through his snout. "Think about it, kiddo. What do you think would happen to the Company if rats like us could run free in here? Carry out all we like? Sell it for our own profit? They'd go bust overnight. The whole wide Company. Bust overnight!"

"Why don't they sell it for their own profit?"

"And shut down all those factories that make the crappy Outsider stuff?"

"Done," Tom yelled.

They marched on between the dead lasers and started over the next rise. Looking back, the smoldering excretions of the Tropolis were just a dark band separating the luminous ground from the dull orange night.

Awe and exhaustion and raw surreality washed over Shayna and she shouted out between panting breaths: "You know what this reminds me of? Tom? It's like... like what it must be like to stand on the surface of the full moon. But not the regular moon. I mean the moon the way it is sometimes, out by the water, the ocean. Have you ever been to Bessemer Park?"

"What are you talking about?" Tom called back.

"Bessemer Park. On a tall bluff, jutting out. I was there once, one night, when there was a big wind blowing in from the ocean. It would hold you up if you leaned back into it. It must have blown all the haze out of the sky. The stars were so... so clear, and so many of them, like I'd never seen before. And you could see that the full moon isn't really that color, that red color. It's white, burning white. The whitest color you could ever see!"

"I don't know what you're talking about," Tom said.

She looked up the slope at him, his bony ass, his stick legs still climbing fast when she stopped breathless and aching. God damn he was far away, she thought, as she picked up a porcelain doorknob from a pile the size of a house and threw it as hard as she could. She thought she saw it drifting down in slow motion through the perfect silence.

"There it is!" Tom shouted. "It's still here!" He disappeared over the edge of the spire.

"Hot damn!" Nemo yelled, doubling his lumbering pace.

Shayna followed tiredly after them. Finally, crossing over the lip of that crater of wasted riches, she beheld the two men ravenously filling up their sacks with the treasure they had come for: a gigantic mound of small rattling plastic bottles.

"What is that?" she asked in a daze.

Tom tossed one of the bottles at her. She caught it, held it up to her eye-windows and squinted into a fistful of multicolor pills.

"Get your ass over here and start packing!" Nemo yelled. "Sweet Christ! It's the motherload! We'll be rich, Tommy boy, rich!"

"They'll bury all of this first thing tomorrow morning," Tom said through his snout. "First thing. Soon as they start up."

"Bet your ass," Nemo panted.

"I hope they're still good like that source of yours said. The labels all say they're expired."

"Don't worry," explained Nemo. "Trust me. I know the way it works with drugs. Clinics in the Cology toss their whole inventory every two months. To keep the industry fresh. Keep their labs pumping this shit out. My source, I'm telling you – my source is rock solid. A friggin' genius. He knows these things."

"Drugs?" Shayna asked.

Tom said "Medicine for every disease there is."

Hypnotized, she watched their hands scoop the bottles hurriedly into their massive bags.

"The blight?" she asked suddenly. "Cures for the blight?"

"Who knows, maybe."

"Maybe?" she demanded. "Is there...? Can you find out? How would we find out for sure?"

"Well," he panted, "I guess I'll ask the source about it when we take this stuff to him tomorrow. I dunno."

Her stared into the bluish depths of the vial in her hand. She read the label a few times, mutely, not understanding the words. Then she rushed to join the men, picking up handfuls of bottles and stuffing them into their sacks, or into her oversized pockets when the sacks were full.

"Some of these things you can't get in the Tropolis at all," Tom told her. "This'll save lives, Shay."

"And make a shit ton of money for us rats," Nemo laughed.

When every sack and pocket and armpit was full, they started the long and much harder walk back. Every heavy step sounded like a chorus of maracas, and when they crossed out of the light and back into the burning lands and the curtains of stinging smoke, their feet seemed to sink deeper than before. Her exhaustion was crushing now, the sack's rattling weight slicing hard into her fingers, and she kept wondering how long it was before dawn, and whether those cameras and trip lasers were really blind after all, and whether the comps might appear any moment, screaming down out of their black helicopters amid a flurry of spotlights and megaphones and sparking stun prods – but the heat in her coat had become warmth. The ache in her chest had become life. *I've felt this way before,* she thought to herself. *But it was years ago. I don't even remember what made me feel this way before.*

They rode the truck with all the windows rolled down, faces finally unmasked, without a thought for the stench or the cold. Nemo shifted stiffly into overdrive and they roared through the empty pre-dawn streets at breakneck speed. The engine noise made any conversation impossible, but it seemed to Shayna that the racket of those rusty pistons pretty eloquently expressed what they all must have been feeling.

There behind the wheel, cloaked again in shadow, Nemo had turned back into nothing but a flaming cigarillo stuck between hugely smiling teeth. Every once in a while Shayna thought she heard a dry chuckle leak out of him, and every time it sounded like a summative declaration of everything he was. This must have been his perfect moment, she thought: freshly victorious, burning fumes on empty streets in the dead of night with a fortune in trash behind him.

She watched Tom sitting there beside her in the passenger seat, sucking contemplatively on a clove cigarette and staring down the black road ahead. The orange glow of the fleeting street lamps lapped over his face in waves. He didn't seem to notice her staring so intently at him, or he didn't care; he let her watch him for a long time.

As for Shayna, there was no thought in her head. She just leaned back into the springs and savored the smell that followed his slow exhale.

16

At first light she was still breathing the bittersweet aftertaste of clove smoke. Pink pre-dawn was burning on the fissures in the taped-up window, through the jagged teeth of the Tropolitan skyline. She felt unnaturally alert and awake.

The angel she'd taken from the white heaps felt cool in her palm. Tom's forearm hung over the edge of the top bunk as always, its dirty creases outlined in the rising yellow sun.

She leaned upright and started lacing up her boots. She studied the pile of vial-stuffed sacks lying in the corner by the door. Somewhere in there might be a cure for blight, she remembered. Somewhere in that overstuffed bag was the hope of her salvation. Nemo's source would know.

Yes, she thought – everything had changed. Relief was washing through her like the clear ocean air breathing over the Tropolis at Bessemer Park. There was something else, too. Some pristine light-heartedness lay deeper within that feeling, more tangible the more she questioned it, but still inexplicable. Whatever it was, she stowed it with the angel in her pocket as she draped the army coat over herself and slipped through the door. It was time to get her damn paycheck.

Even if there was a chance now that she wouldn't be dead in a month, she wasn't turning back. She was getting out of there. This was what she repeated to herself in her mind with every revolution of her rusty pedals. Getting out of there. Getting out of there today.

Let the comps come, she thought. *Just let them come and threaten me again. I'm getting what I'm owed and then I'm getting out of there.*

The crowds of workers were just assembling that morning as she stowed her bike behind a dumpster. She was one of the first in line.

"I only need to speak to Larry," she told the attendance officer.

"Executive consultations are on Wednesday mornings," the officer said. "Larry won't be in his office until noon. Talk to him then."

She handed back the clipboard unsigned and backed out of the line.

"This is a closed facility after nine AM, kid," the officer told her with a roll of his eyes. "If you want to talk to Larry, you need to sign in now."

"What am I supposed to do for the next four hours?"

"Work." He shoved the clipboard hard into her stomach and said "Last chance."

She signed with a sweaty hand and walked inside with gritting teeth.

"Getting out of here," she muttered as she took her goggles from the wall and bitterly wrapped her fingers around the lever. "Getting out of here," she hissed with every wave of fixer mist that spit out from the machine. "Getting out of here," she chanted rhythmically under her breath when the buzzer sounded and she joined the hordes of smokers on the fence-enclosed pavement outside, only to follow them back in. Hunched over between the pipes, she only glared straight through the swinging stencil cage, past the overhead conveyors and lines of rusty cable and blinking lights. She looked straight through all of it and up at the lifeless windows of the soundproof office.

The buzzer sounded again, but unexpectedly. Off schedule. Not a single angry burst, but a repetition of three, warning, mournful chords. She pushed her goggles onto her forehead and stood amid a sudden and eerie silence. All the machines had stopped.

Feet clanked on the rusty plates. One of the administrative officers was walking down the line, shouting: "Break, twenty minutes. Accident. Break. Twenty minutes."

Shayna drifted in a trance with the rest of the workers, back toward the daylight. Halfway down the line she noticed everyone taking the long way around vat 19, and a small crowd was gathered there on the corroded steps leading up to the catwalk. Something made her pause. She broke from the herd and stepped up to the gathered workers.

"What happened?" she asked. "Anybody see?"

"Catwalk gave out," rasped a woman in black coveralls. She had a light case of the pox.

"Was anyone hurt?"

"Both killed."

"What?" Shayna asked in shock.

"I said *both of 'em were killed*," the woman shouted indifferently over the drone of the machines.

Shayna instinctively raised herself onto her toes to get a better look.

"Nothing to see," the woman said. "They fished 'em out already."

"Now they'll finally replace that catwalk," said another onlooker, a girl of maybe thirteen years. "Two of us will get those jobs. They had walking jobs, too. Quality control. I'd kill for a job where I got to walk."

The rest of the crowd bled away and left Shayna standing alone. She stepped up to the torn-off edge of the metal plating that hung above the sloshing, steaming vat – the same squeaking, precarious railing she had inched along every workday for four years. She braced herself for some horrible sight below, but there was no trace of anything. The broken section of catwalk hung solidly in its place. The darkly boiling depths of liquid orange were pure and featureless, waiting to be piped down into the Printing Stations. An ancient sign on the wall above them read: INDUSTRIAL SAFETY - IT'S UP TO YOU!

Back in the light of day, unable to decide whether or not she was rattled, she found all the workers falling into lines leading up to collapsible tables.

"What's going on now?"

"They're giving out paychecks," somebody said. "About damn time."

"I love it when they think they need to boost our morale," said somebody else.

Shayna sighed and joined the crowds.

The twenty minutes was almost up when she finally stepped up to the table and told her name to the officer with the box of stacked checks. But she already sensed what was coming, even before the first weird look from that clean-clothed man. She could smell it.

Instead of a check, his stubby fingers produced a yellow slip of paper from the box. The officer hid its scrawled words from her by cupping it in his hands.

"Your paycheck has had a two-week hold placed on it," he said.

The return-to-work buzzer sounded.

"On account of the labor shortage," the officer added.

The buzzer repeated, full of angry authority.

"And you have two citations for gross insubordination. I should warn you that three citations adds up to a jailable offense."

The buzzer lashed out a third time in sound and fury. The crowds had all dissolved into the waiting dark of the plant's rolling wooden doors.

"You have to return to your station now."

Shayna found herself laughing quietly, then loudly. She shut up and turned automatically to face the plant's open mouth. Its faintly glowing roof, the cranes and cables and chugging machinery all loomed over her. She heard the vats boiling to life.

She turned away and started for the curb.

"You can't do that," the officer shouted. "You can't leave without permission."

"Sure I can."

"That's a third citation," he said. "Your paycheck will be permanently frozen. Three citations adds up to a jailable offense. You're breaking Company law."

"I'm getting out of here," she said, pausing to pick a cigarette out of her pocket. "I quit."

"And those goggles are Company property! That's a felony!" To someone other than her he shouted out at the top of his lungs: "CSS! *C-S-S!*"

She didn't wait to find out what those letters stood for. She bolted for the alley, mounted her bike and rolled, not knowing whether anyone was following. She swerved right instead of left at the end of the line, shooting fast down into the roaring commotion of freight trucks and loading docks around the back side of the plant, squeezing through any gap in the stacked boxes or heaving workers or robotic lifts that looked too narrow for the broad and armored shoulders of the comps she imagined bounding after her as fast as the bike. Finally she pedaled hard over a half-sunken line of train tracks, missing the grille of a slow-moving diesel engine by an arm's length, and glided out of reach of the fabric plant and on down a line of soot-blackened ruins. When she finally dared to look back over her shoulder, the bike rolled over an empty liquor bottle and threw her hard onto the cracked cement.

Miraculously, the unlit cigarette was still stuck between her lips. She flicked her lighter with a badly scraped hand and took a short pull. Then she finished the laughter where she'd left off.

Here in shadows of abandoned industry, something mixed with her anxiety. It was that invincibility again. The same thing she'd felt on the Heaps. It swirled in her shaken mind like the smoke mixing with the kicked-up soot under her bruised left hip.

That makes two felonies I'm guilty of now, she thought as she peeled the fixer-stained goggles off her forehead and twisted them hard in her hands. She'd have to be careful now. They would have her name on file. Shayna Newman. Person of interest. Crimes against industrial efficiency. Theft of one pair of crappy old goggles. Evasion of CSS. Gross insubordination. *Fuck them*, she thought - but that would be it for her. If she ever swiped her ID card at the wrong terminal. If she ever tried to apply for another job without getting a fake card made. They'd send her to the community service camps – maybe the poisoned pits at the end of the Heaps. They'd put her among the lowest of the low, the institutionalized, the Thirty Percent. All the convicts who shoveled shit at the end of a stun prod so long and so hard that it darkened their flesh from head to toe, or so it was rumored.

And still somehow she could only laugh. She smiled. She picked herself up and walked her bike along that gritty path, back to the nearest main drag. *What is this invincibility?* she thought. *What's wrong with me?*

She headed cautiously for the alley where she'd hidden her bike, thereby to roll back to Tom's apartment.

Tom.

I love Tom, she thought.

Her feet and wheels ground to a slow halt in the black dust.

In the passenger seat of Nemo's pickup, the orange glow of streetlamps laps over his stoic face in waves, bitter clove smoke spewing from his nostrils.

In his bright kitchen her tired eyes stare deep into his weirded-out ones, and his giant hands brush against her scuffed and bleeding ones in the scalding soapy water.

"For keeps," he says with slurred words, his gigantic army coat draped over her shivering shoulders on the hill above the rushing sparks of the flyway.

I'm in *love with Tom*, she thought.

Hot anxiety pounded on her eardrums now. Her invincibility waned into nothing. An ecstasy of panic rose to a roar in her head as she realized with gut-wrenching suddenness that she had always, from nearly the first moment she met him on that grassy hill by the stadium, been in love with Tom Nice the garbageman.

And only now, after three and a half years, had it dawned on her.

His apartment was empty. The rusty clock above the stove told her it wasn't even noon yet. Out of breath, still descending from the adrenaline of her resignation, not really knowing how she felt about anything at all now, she pulled the window open and perched on the sill. She stared up into the oily smoke from the stovepipes across the alley until some pigeons began to cooh somewhere and electric chills moved through her spine. She checked the wad of bills in its hiding place in the back of the fridge, and checked it a second time when the number came up much smaller than she'd hoped. She lay down on the bottom bunk, stared at the square of sky between the toes of her boots, and tried to untangle her thoughts.

She glanced at the corner by the door and noticed the giant sacks missing.

"Damnit," she told the ceiling as she whipped out her phone and called him, but when his voicemail picked up she had no words. She'd wanted to go with him to ask the source in person, but she could already hear him trying to talk her out of it.

Her sleep was unintentional and too continuous with reality even to notice. The clock hands turned unsteadily. The window light shifted in angle and hue. The fridge held and released its rattling breath. She slept out of not knowing what else to do. All she wanted was to advance the flow of time – but when the her phone's irritable buzzing stirred her awake at five, she groaned and clenched her fists at the waste.

"Hi," she said dizzily.

"Did you call me earlier?" Tom asked. The unmistakable sound of the Metro's squeaky gears underlied his words.

She rubbed her eyes hard and held the phone away from her face while she sighed deeply.

"Yeah. I just...."

"Just what?"

"What did Nemo's source say about the pills?"

"We haven't done that yet. I'm on my way to do it now."

"But what about the sacks? What happened to them?"

The static paused.

"Are you at my place?"

"Yes," she said, feeling her face redden. "Is that all right?"

"Y-yeah. Right. The sacks. I had to leave them in trash bags this morning at a drop point. Still haven't met this source Nemo keeps raving about. Very anonymous. Very secret. We have to cover our asses more carefully than with regular Heap salvage."

"But you're going back to meet the source now?"

"Yeah."

"I'm on my way," she said, leaping out of the bunk fast enough to make her eyes swim. "I'll be there as fast as I can. Just tell me where it is."

"Uh, sure. It's just business, but I guess you can come. It's that old playground. On 743rd street. By your old school, right?"

"I'll be there," she said, and hung up. She slammed his door behind her and bounded down the creaky stairs. The bus she needed was just pulling up to the stop two blocks away. Climbing up into its sweaty interior, she silently blessed the old man in the rusty wheelchair who'd been ahead of her, holding everything up, needing the ramp. But when she got a good look at him, she flinched. The blight on his neck was already half the size of her head. He couldn't have much time left. She silently blessed him a second time and wondered,

If this doesn't work, will I be like you in two and a half weeks? Will I be the one breathing heavily in the front of the bus – the one everyone else tries not to stare at? And where will mine grow? On the neck? In the guts? Inside the head?

No, she remembered, *the blood. That's where the nurse said mine was.*

She wondered: *And if this* does *work, will I be able to save you too?*

With this thought her mind stopped. She stared out the window.

The area wasn't fully dead yet, but it couldn't have long. The playground neighbored the faded remains of a playfield that was overgrown in blackberries and surrounded by chainlink and razor wire. Another fenced-off section already bore the fresh dusty scars of dozer treads and the ghostly outlines of rooms on the smooth foundation. The last accessible section wasn't much more than a dry fountain smelling faintly of urine, and some elderly plastic benches facing a young concrete wall.

She found Tom perched on the edge of the bench. For a moment she stood watching him from a distance, trying to figure out whether there was anything to brace herself for. Then she hurried up to him and asked:

"I'm not too late, am I?"

"No," he said, taking a yawning look around the scene. "Nemo's late. So is the source."

She forced herself to look away from his eyes and the cool yellow light tracing the curves of his fuzzy head. She scanned the playground. There was no one else around but a solitary bum, perched on the edge of the shadows by the fountain. He wore a poncho with the patterns of a Persian rug, and every inch of his face was covered either by mazelike tufts of sandy gray hair or by a pair of scuffed sunglasses. There was something unthinkable about the possibility of real eyes hiding behind those mirrored lenses – lenses that seemed to be staring intently at the two of them, never turning.

"Is that guy...?" Shayna began.

Tom looked up and returned the bum's stare, a little uneasily, and the bum took his cue to hover forward on rag-curtained feet. He stopped with anxious casualness a few feet away.

Shayna watched the mouth under that mud-matted beard open and close and exhale a low growl, but she couldn't make out any words. The silver lenses stayed pointed at some invisible thing down the street, making her wonder faintly whether he was addressing them at all.

"Sorry?" Tom asked carefully, cupping his hand to his ear.

The stranger cocked his head to glance at him and Shayna in turn, then stared back at the thing in the distance. He repeated the low growl, but this time she could make it into two words.

"Mister Nice," the bum said.

Tom nodded. "You're the source?"

A soot-blackened hand emerged from the folds of his poncho and extended toward Tom. The fingers were bony, the nails long and mottled. Tom took the hand and shook it. Then the bum, never looking at the two of them, turned and hobbled toward the near alley. They watched him ooze along the pavement for a while before they rose up to follow.

Between mountains of plastic bags and towering stacks of rotten newspapers, the bum paused and glanced back to see if they were still there. He nodded once and then started down a series of sunken steps, caked with bird shit, leading to a wrought-iron door. Tom and Shayna stood at the top, looking down on the bum's hands fussing with a rusty padlock and chains. The caws of crows echoed through the alley.

Shayna shivered and scanned the empty rooftops. Tom must have noticed.

"This is just business," he whispered. "You don't have to—"

"I'm fine."

He placed his hand limply on her shoulder and squeezed once. She sighed.

The padlock surrendered to the bum's key and the iron hinges squealed grudgingly open. She watched the shadows swallow up the ratty wool poncho and the long tendrils of matted hair. Then they waded in after him.

It was cool in there and too dark to see anything. She found herself choking on the memory of the last labyrinth she'd been in, as she remembered how to follow footsteps through a lightless void. She heard hinges, and somewhere in the pitch ahead of her she made out a tiny glimmer of faintly bluish light. She followed it through a door and to the top of a set of old wooden steps.

"Shut the door," the bum's voice murmured. "And lock it." She complied, sliding a heavy bolt into place as soon as she found it in the blind dark. Then she turned and stepped down into the alien space. It was a laboratory.

The rattle of pill bottles startled her as she scanned her surroundings. She saw work tables made of steel, maybe a dozen in all, in neat rows. Along each one lay beautiful pieces of glass of every size and shape, connected by snaking networks of tubes. There were machines of all kinds, some ancient and corroded, others pristine and polished. Notebooks full of illegible handwriting lay open by a stack of small plastic dishes. A grid of dim fluorescent bulbs hung above each table, but most of the light in the room came from a flickering screen.

A bright yellow work lamp clicked on to her left. Tom and the bum were there, sorting through the ocean of bottles that consumed the whole surface of the table in front of them.

"I would appreciate it… if you didn't touch anything, my dear," the bum murmured. His appearance struck her. His eyes, now naked of their scuffed mirrors, were truly ancient. In Shayna's whole life she was sure she had never seen wrinkles like that. He must have been more than forty years old. Fifty. Sixty? Could a human being live to be that old?

He looked up briefly, annoyed by her staring, and she looked away.

The bum's sooty hands picked up one of the bottles and turned it slowly around while his antique eyes appraised the tiny words and numbers on the label. He had a lamp with a magnifying glass inside it.

"Is this all yours?" Shayna asked the old man, motioning for the wonderland of instruments.

"Mm-hmm," he confirmed quietly. He grunted something inaudible, then turned to Tom and muttered: "Gamma pentothal. You have a lot of gamma pentothal here."

"What's that?"

"It's..." the old man began, then trailed off. He took a long blink and heaved a shallow sigh, as if his mind was an antique quill pen he was dipping into the ink of his memory. "Analgesic. Opiate. It would be more useful if it were made into an intravenous general anesthetic. Of use in surgery."

"I'm really only here to sell this stuff."

"I see," the old man mumbled.

Shayna studied his voice like she had studied his eyes. Everything he said was hushed to a low rumble, but every small sound carried an enormous weight. Maybe it was the same weight that pulled down the bags under his eyes and made him walk so slowly. He had an accent, too. It was hard to pick up, but it was there: clean, deliberate, purely enunciated. She couldn't remember where she'd heard words pronounced that way before.

"Antibiotics," he said, pointing to another group of bottles he had set aside. "And antivirals. Very strong ones. They should be used sparingly. Only when an illness is very serious. Close to death."

"What illnesses?" Tom asked, passing a glance at Shayna.

The old man combed his beard idly with his fingers. He said: "These antibiotics will cure Plague. Tuberculosis. Blackpox. Strep throat. Syphilis. And Leprosy. The antivirals will cure ebola and meningitis. Redpox. AIDS. Rabies. Hepatitis."

"Blight?" Shayna whispered, too quietly.

"I've never even heard of some of those," Tom said.

The bum sighed and fixed his eyes on the garbageman. "These should be administered by a doctor. An expert. In the correct dosage, for the correct disease. Otherwise they could be dangerous."

"Right. I'm really just here to sell. So how will this work? Are you taking this stuff off our hands? Is it still good?"

"It is good. I do not have money. I can locate the sick, the buyers, within the week. I can transact on your behalf."

"Blight?" Shayna asked, louder. "What about the blight?"

The old man fixed his eyes on her and she felt herself shiver. "Mm-mm. Blight. Not cured by a pill."

"Then how?"

"Injection," he mumbled, shook his head and said nothing more.

Tom cleared his throat and asked Shayna, "Do you know someone who's got—?"

Somebody knocked on the door. Tom went to answer it.

"Get the password," croaked the ancient.

Tom climbed up the stairs to the door and said, "What's the password?"

A pause.

Nemo's muffled voice said: "Meff— Messif— Meffisti— Shit, man."

The ancient shook his head pathetically and made an inward waving motion. Tom unbolted the door and swung it open, and Nemo bounded down the steps. Tom locked up again.

"Hey, Doc, sorry I'm late," he said, and coughed.

"Mephistopheles," the old man enunciated.

"Right. My fault. How could I forget." He took a lighter out of his pocket and flicked it.

"Don't smoke in here."

Nemo looked gravely at the ancient, then grudgingly let the flame die and stuck his cigarette above his ear. He came forward and examined the mass of pill bottles. "We got anything good here?"

"Yeah," Tom said. "Plenty."

The old man sighed and went about re-straightening the groups of bottles. He named the piles aloud: "Analgesics, antipathogens, OTC's, psychiatric medications, and synthetic hormones."

"How much?"

Tom peered questioningly at Nemo. "How much of which one?"

"How much is it all *worth*, stupid. How much money?"

The old man drew a long breath and answered quietly, "That depends."

"On what?" Nemo chuckled.

"The patient. You may decide the prices for yourself, but the people who need these drugs will not be rich. Nor can I provide a down payment, as I have told your associate."

"Well, damn, but—" Nemo scratched his head in thought. "Need. So you're saying some people need these pills to live, right? So, they're desperate. You're saying we can sell as high as we want."

"Nemo," Tom started.

The old man murmured, "You can."

"I bet we could top a hundred thousand bucks if we try. One fifty? You think?"

"No," Tom said, wincing. "Listen to yourself." His bland expression had broken down. He was angrier now than Shayna could remember ever seeing him – though that wasn't saying much.

"Who else would I listen to?"

"I'm not going to auction people's lives to them."

"Fine. Then I'll do it."

"No!"

"Well, damnit, Nice! You gonna stop me? I'm entitled to half of that goddamn pile. Even Steven. Our deal. And I'll be damned if I don't do whatever I want with what I'm fairly entitled to. Half the pile."

A third, Shayna thought, but said nothing.

"The hell you—" Tom stammered.

A rattle sounded: one of the bottles in the old man's sooty hands.

"If you like," he muttered, "These medications... behavioral drugs, psychedelics, recreational hormonal libido enhancers, will save no lives, but are expensive as contraband. You might claim this half of the pile as your own."

Shayna watched Nemo try to think of a reason to reject the offer. His mouth opened once or twice to sneer a word, but eventually it shut.

The old man sorted the bottles for him and helped pour his share of the loot back into his duffle bag. Shayna and Tom watched in bitter silence.

Finally Nemo slung the bag over his shoulder and headed for the door. At the top of the steps he paused to light his cigarette and examine the label on one of his bottles. His smug voice echoed down: "Libido enhancer! Damn, kids. Way to lose."

The door slammed. Tom went and bolted it again.

"Why are you working with him?" Shayna asked.

"He's got a truck," Tom said bitterly.

The old man said "If you like, I might recommend the highest realistic prices at which these products might be sold. It would still amount to a sizable revenue. In total."

"No. No pay. Take them."

The ancient regarded the garbageman with his cavernous eyes. "No pay?"

"You know how to use them, right?"

The ancient nodded.

Without another word, Tom collected his empty bag and started out the door.

"I'll catch up with you," Shayna said to him.

"Catch up?"

"Just wait for me out there. Give me a minute. Is that okay?"

He gave her a weird look and did as she asked. The door closed.

Shayna turned shakily toward the old man. The two stood stone still, looking at nothing. Then his eyes and hands turned to the bottles on the table. Ignoring her, he picked up a notebook and pen and went to work scribbling a list.

"Injection," she said. "You said the blight is cured by an injection."

He nodded solemnly.

"Is there some way to—? Can you get it somehow? Is it something else we might find on the Heaps?"

"No. It must be specifically adapted. For each patient."

"Can you make it?" Her heart was pounding.

"I lack... the necessary equipment. It is extensive. Only in the Cology. Or the Charity Center."

She released a slow breath that became a muffled, unintentional laugh. Then she turned and stared emptily into the darkness of the long basement.

"Someone close to you is affected," said the ancient's voice. "Or yourself."

She nodded.

"Too old," the ancient said.

"Yes."

After a pause, he whispered: "I am sorry."

"I'm Shayna," she said, turning around and forcing a placid smile to appear beneath her damp eyes.

He continued peering down through his magnifying lamp. His voice grumbled: "Doctor Virgil Kingsford."

"You're very old." As it left her lips she realized it sounded rude, but she couldn't help herself. She'd never seen anyone like him.

The old eyes regarded her briefly and he grunted "Yes." He didn't sound annoyed or upset. Somehow he sounded guilty. His old hands kept scribbling notes in the silence.

With a defeated sigh she went to the door and opened it, but when she looked over her shoulder she saw him staring back at her with one hand raised and open.

"Give Nice my gratitude," he said.

She nodded and was gone.

He stood in the alley, surrounded by the light at the end of that tunnel. His face bore a bitter look for the world in general, and a half-spent cigarette.

I'm going to have to tell him, she realized. *I have to tell him. How much longer can I keep this feeling to myself? Can I?*

They walked side by side, and his eyes stared coldly ahead.

Can't I? she thought. *It doesn't matter.*

"I thought we were splitting it all into thirds," she said as they waited at the curb. "Since there were three of us."

"Oh," he said. "Well, but, we didn't bring back any more than we would've without you."

"So?"

"So we didn't bring any extra sacks for you. Nemo and me would've carried your share if you hadn't been there. So I figure it was still only split two ways." He bit his lip and gave her a sidelong glance.

"Never mind," she sighed as they boarded the bus. He took the window seat.

Not now, she thought to herself. *I don't want to tell him now.*

They went back to Tom's apartment and rolled their bikes in circles through his neighborhood – rolling off the tension. Kids playing kickball in intersections parted for them and shouted interference. Lonely-looking men in tank tops leaned out of broken windows and watched them enter and exit their ruined lives. Washed-out pedestrians made fleeting eye contact and focused again at the ground in front of them. Somebody recognized Tom and waved. Nobody waved to Shayna.

"You could have made a lot of money back there," she told him.

A yellow stoplight passed them by.

"No I couldn't," he said.

I have to tell him, she thought.

"Tomorrow," said Katja.

"Tomorrow," said Becker.

"Yeah," said Float with a wide grin.

"What *about* tomorrow?" Shayna asked, coughing in the wake of the night's first shot.

"You know what," Katja said. "Our next trip."

"Have you decided what it'll be yet?"

"The White Line," Float said.

"You mean that train? The one that follows Reagan Avenue? Up on those stilts? What are you going to do? Climb up?"

"More," Katja said, interrupting the other two. "I won't ruin it. You should come and see. It'll be the most exciting thing you've ever done, I promise. Not exciting like last time. A different kind of exciting. A really good kind. Tomorrow at six at Reagan and 211th street. Look. Be there. That's all I'm gonna say."

"It'll be dangerous," Float squeaked enthusiastically before Katja could shush him.

"That a good thing?" Shayna asked.

Katja cleared her throat and said: "There's no life without death. You can't know one without getting to know the other."

It was bullshit - but something still stuck when Shayna tried to wash it out of her mind. She sighed.

"Shay?" Carl kept asking. "Shay, there's something I, um. I have an idea I want to share with you. Maybe we could—?"

She stopped hearing him when the stairs thudded with a rhythm she knew.

"Never mind," Carl said.

She watched the garbageman step down into the swirling green-neon haze, all the day's bad news finally washed out of his face by the booze and company. Now he was strutting across the room, half-dancing, turning himself around in mid-step and catching himself mid-fall but with a catlike grace all his own.

I'm in love with you, she thought, repeatedly, preparing the words in the back of her throat. She watched him fall down into the seat across from her, and there came the lull in conversation and her chance to pull him aside.

But in that moment her eyes unfocused. She found herself looking past him, into the mirrored column behind him and past the back of his head – she found herself looking at the other girl next to Katja. The one who stopped growing at age twelve. The one hunched over there in the ratty olive drab, with the uneven cigarette-stained teeth, unkempt hazel hair, pimples on her temples. The frail girl who had never been interested in anybody before; who no one had ever been interested in. No one. Never.

"Will you tell me what's on your mind?" Katja yelled, smacking Shayna's arm in playful drunken rage.

"Nothing." Emotionlessly, she added "I had a kind of crazy day" and then burst into a fit of weird laughter when she realized the magnitude of her understatement. *I had a crazy day. That's what I'll tell the comps when they come to take me away*, she thought. *If I live that long.* She reached for the second shot.

"Crazy day?" Carl said. "Yeah. Just wait till Saturday."

"For what?" Katja asked.

"You know where I work, right? I work at the regulator plant."

"So what?"

"*So* I hear the whitecoats talking sometimes. They talk about the weather. They know about the superstorms before they hit. They have to know about them, so they know how much S-O-2 to send up that day. And there's one coming, a superstorm. The big part of it will hit here on Saturday. I'd dress warm if I were you."

"That's crazy," Shayna said. "Nobody knows when superstorms are going to hit. That's the point. That's why they're called—"

"If they already know, then why hasn't it been on the TV?" Katja interrupted.

"Why would it be?" Carl said with a sneer. "What's in it for the Company if we prepare for it? Storm damage stimulates consumer spending."

"Bullshit."

"Fine. Don't believe me. See if I give a crap."

"I like the storms," Tom said drunkenly. "I think they're fun. Watching everything go crazy out there while you're tucked safe inside."

"Attaboy," said Fish, rousing from some stupor. "Always on the bright side."

"Yeah," Shayna muttered blissfully.

For that matter, she thought, *has Tom ever had a girlfriend?* She couldn't think of one. Not one, in the whole four years she'd known him. *But he wasn't gay. Right? Shit. How do I find out?*

"Oh hell," Katja said. "I have to get out of here ten minutes ago. I have to go pick up my kid sister from the monastery before they lock up. She's always hanging out with those whacky monks."

"Whacky monks?" Tom asked, chuckling.

"Those whacky monks, yeah. The Urbanologers. Or whatever. Cass thinks she can see the future now, did I tell you that? They have her totally convinced. Now every time I come home she pulls on my knee and whispers '*four up, three down, floating down, floating down.*' But our parents don't mind them. Somebody has to take her during the day I guess. If she can't go to regular school."

"Tell me if she foretells the next lottery numbers," Carl said.

"Uh huh," Katja said on her way to the stairs.

Without thinking, Shayna got up and followed her up into the alley. "Hi," she called drunkenly. Her ears were ringing musically over the drumbeat of her pulse when she finally said "Listen. You know Tom?"

Katja smiled. "Yes, dear, I know Tom."

What the hell am I doing? she thought. "Never mind."

"Come on, what about him?" Katja demanded. She checked her watch again.

"Nothing, nothing," Shayna insisted. "Nothing."

"We'll finish this conversation later," Katja said forcefully and ran for the bus.

So Shayna stumbled back down into the smoky lair and returned to her place across from the face she had even dared now to think of kissing – across from the column where the small, ragged girl she was stared in tragic euphoria from behind the silvered glass. She drank like someone who had no job to go to tomorrow, though she somehow kept the fact to herself, knowing it would only invite questions. She didn't want questions. She just wanted to ride the drunk bus home with the guy twice her height who smelled like clove smoke and trash, who scraped his gigantic boots against the pavement in the warm grassy night, who was cool and meek whenever he was sober but electrified with crazy joy when he wasn't. She wasn't going to save herself. There was nothing left to do but try to be happy in the time she had left, and he was it. He was all she wanted.

15

Morning lapped at the edges of the bed. She lay there being hungry and thinking. She examined the scrapes on her hands. She rolled over, reached under the bed and picked up her stolen goggles. Staring into the two circular bug-eye lenses, she thought of the squeaky catwalk she had crossed every weekday for four years and wondered:

What if it had been me whose weight finally broke that old beam? She sat up and instinctively picked up her old pink electric bass from its leaning spot in the corner. A song was stuck in her head: the only love song the Smurge ever made. A true oddity. She had known how to play it once, but how long ago was that? She counted off the months in the tries it took her to get the first measure right. Then she was bored, and the scrapes on her hands were sore.

She remembered: The White Line. 6pm. Reagan and 211.

She needed to find Katja. Then she could talk to Tom, she promised herself – only after she talked to Katja. After she found out whether it was wise to say anything to Tom at all. She wanted to tell him everything. She needed to. Still, he meant so much to her as a friend. She couldn't stand the thought of ruining that now.

Yes. Katja.

But was she really going on the run with them?

She lay back down.

When she leaned back upright another hour was gone, the scabs on her hands itched, and she knew what she had to do.

With a deep breath, she reached under the corner of the mattress and found the gun's cold crosshatched metal with her fingers. She flipped it open and shut, then slid it cautiously into the wool-lined pocket of her army coat. She laced up her boots and mounted her bike.

The memory of the smell made her shiver as she passed under the rushing white noise of the flyway onramp and on down among the shadows of the silos. The chemical scent. The bleachy aroma, burning her nose and eyes. The great wide lifeless desert of pulverized concrete. She stopped, caught her breath, then rode in fearful circles around the place.

Just when she was sure she'd never find it, it appeared, half-hidden by the low remains of a demolished wall. The manhole lay in empty wait.

Shayna pushed her goggles up onto her forehead and stood there for a minor eternity, watching it from a distance, making no sound. The day was warm and there was no wind. She sat down on the broken wall and smoked, never taking her eyes from the black hole.

When the cigarette was spent she stood up, put her hand on the handle of the gun in her pocket and hovered closer.

She thought: *What the hell was I feeling in that moment?*

She stood at the lip of the open hole and stared straight down.

No sunlight fell down there. She could see nothing. Just something dangling on a string. She knelt and reached her quivering free hand down into the void, and it returned with a six-inch wooden crucifix.

Something squeaked from behind. She turned away from the cross and stood up quickly.

The little girl was there. Dusty white bows glowed among her black braids. She wore a rough pink dress, and the shoes peeking out from beneath it were ridiculously large.

Shayna released her grip on the gun in her pocket and let herself breathe.

The girl said something in Spanish.

"I don't understand," Shayna said, though it was clear enough she'd been told not to mess with the crucifix.

The girl waved for Shayna to follow her.

"No, I was just about to leave. Sorry. I know I shouldn't be here."

The little girl just kept walking and waving.

Giant yellow clouds crept across the dusty sun-filled sky as they walked out of the rubble and far down the street, along rows of broken-down houses, yards enclosed in short chainlinks, windows with bars, small dogs that did not bark.

At the end of the line there was a tall, narrow house. The windows were all dark beneath the sagging roof.

"Espere," the girl said, and vanished inside.

Shayna echoed the mysterious word and stared up at the battered spire looming over her. Two crows perched on the weathervane, still and featureless, like holes in the sky.

The girl reappeared on the broken walkway. With one hand she carried something unidentifiable. With the other she held the hand of another child, a boy even younger than herself. The children spoke quietly among themselves. Then the boy said:

"You are stupid."

Somewhere a dog barked.

"Says who?" Shayna asked.

The boy asked the girl, then translated her answer: "Our parents. People in the neighborhood. Said for us to tell that to you. You went into the nest."

Shayna said nothing.

The little girl whispered something else, and the boy said: "Eat many dogs. Parents afraid for the children. Neighborhood men go down in with guns, but they never found. But you killed."

"It's dead? You're sure it's dead?"

"Dead, yes," the boy responded, without words from the girl.

The girl whispered something else.

"You take something from us," said the boy.

"Take what?"

"For thank you."

The little girl very slowly held out the thing she carried in the other hand. It was a fine gold necklace chain, glittering wildly in the sun, to which some things dangled by steel wire – slightly burned, barely identifiable, but... teeth. *Its* teeth.

"Oh God," Shayna said, taking back the hand with which she had almost touched the thing.

"Yours," the boy insisted. "For thank you."

"For thank you," the girl echoed.

"I don't want it. I mean, I can't. Thanks, really, but I can't accept it."

The girl screamed something angrily, and the boy said: "This is strong magic. Very strongest. For protection. It will keep you safe. It protects you against devils and evil ghosts."

"I wasn't even the one who did it. It's not mine. It belongs to Float and Becker."

The children spoke quietly to each other. The boy sighed and folded his arms in frustration. Then the girl whispered something into his ear and he said:

"The people in the neighborhood said. You do us evil unless you take it. It is yours."

The girl glared hard and held it out farther.

Shayna reached out and hesitantly took the tooth necklace. She held it by the far end of the chain, never touching the teeth. An electric shiver ran through her as she dropped it softly into the empty breast pocket of her coat.

"Strong magic," she sighed.

The children in turn nodded seriously.

"You saved us," the boy said. "He ate many dogs."

Shayna froze.

"*He?*" she demanded. "'It' or *'he'?*"

The boy stared quizzically.

"Was it... human?" she clarified fearfully.

The children consulted in a whisper.

"Before," the boy said.

Then the two of them retreated quickly into the darkness of the house. She saw their four eyes peeking out at her from between the crooked blinds.

Shayna shook her head and started back for her bike.

"Strong magic," she whispered to herself. "Protect me from evil ghosts."

She felt its indistinct shape there against her chest, close to her heart, bouncing with her stride.

"Gross," she whispered, and met the disconcerting watchful gazes of the dogs that did not bark as she passed.

She rolled along. With each passing block her chain squeaked louder and her muscles burned brighter. She couldn't remember the last time she'd taken such a long ride, and out of nothing except not knowing what else to do. Nothing but some half-baked thought about wanting to live the last of her life to its fullest, soak up the world while it lasted; some notion that wasn't coming that easily now. Still, there was something here. Some unknown force propelled her along no matter how deep her fatigue ran, and some inexhaustible energy coursed through her to the tune of the song stuck in her head, making her forget the teeth in her pocket or the scrapes on her hands or the doom in her blood. She thought: *So this is what it's like to be in love. This is what the movies were all trying to tell me about. Suddenly I understand. Suddenly everything makes sense.*

She rolled past schoolyards in the throes of recess. All those kids killing time before going back to their law obeyance classes and industrial safety training. All the boys getting sorted by mathematical aptitude, the girls getting sorted by beauty grade. All those eighth-graders about to be allocated and sent out to face completely different forms of brutality than the one's they'd learned about in their locker rooms and detention cells.

From the top of a low hill of one-story flats and convenience marts she squinted out across the long urban plane as it stretched out to meet the just-visible dark sliver of the ocean to the South. She could see the regulator plant down there, its towering spires running full-blast, its gigantic jets of pale gas firing madly upward into the creamy sun. She could faintly smell the sulfur from where she stood.

She rolled on down that long hill, under rail bridges whose yellow skin bled rivers of rust onto the sidewalk, along lines of utility poles where ponds of congealed tar waited for the next heat wave, past the fence-enclosed hordes of assembly-line people all taking their fleeting smoke breaks.

No more smoke breaks for me, she thought. *No more lunches at the vending machine. No more buzzers.*

I'm free, she thought, and inhaled a deep breath of the warm wind rushing through her hair.

She skidded to a halt and took a long look around.

I'm lost, she thought.

The tracks of the White Line stood tall above the city on pairs of straight legs of pipe, a series of inverted V's straddling twenty miles of Tropolis. The intersection Katja had named was next to a massive concrete block at the foot of one leg.

Shayna rolled up to the curb on the edge of six in the evening with a stomach full of MegaMeal and a head full of anxiety. She was still rehearsing the words in her head – whatever words she hoped to use to ask Katja about Tom – even though she knew that rehearsing was all only going to make it harder when she finally got her chance. *Hurry up already,* she muttered through her cigarettes, one after another. There was nothing worse than waiting.

The sky was overcast and thick with water, turning prematurely dark. Whether or not Carl had been telling one of his characteristic lies, something was definitely brewing up there, and the White Line slashed against it, sharp and pale. Shayna peered out in either direction along its path between the smokestacks and radio towers and what tall buildings stood in this part of town. Somewhere out of sight southward it bent down from its hazy heights to meet the cruise ships and orbijets crowding the port's asphalt planes; somewhere to the north it met the Cology and passed through those mammoth slopes of cloudy glass, into the unknowable interior. The White Line ran nowhere else.

"You couldn't," Becker's voice finally said, echoing from down the street.

"But what if you *could*," Float said.

"You just couldn't. It would never work."

"There's always a way. Anything is possible."

"Not anything," Katja said disinterestedly.

"What's not possible?" Shayna called to them.

"Float was saying you could use the White Line to sneak into the Cology," Becker said.

"If you climbed up by the docks, where the train starts off slow, you could grab onto it and ride it all the way – if you did it right," Float insisted.

"That thing goes supersonic," Becker said. "The wind shear. Megaduck couldn't do it. It's insane. And they comps would just shoot you once you got inside anyway. Even if you didn't die first."

Float stroked his chin and postulated: "Who knows. Maybe it would be worth it. Just to see what's inside."

"You showed after all," Katja said. Her eyes beamed triumph.

"Actually I'm not doing it," Shayna said. "I just want to ask you something."

Katja slumped into herself and stared coldly. "You're not coming with us?" She pointed upward and said "Come on. It's only eighty feet! A hundred, tops!"

Shayna glanced up and shook her head.

"Well, what do you want to ask me?" Katja muttered.

Shayna glanced at the boys and said "Alone."

Katja checked the clock in her phone and said "We don't have time for this. We're behind schedule. You'll have to ask me later, okay?"

"Later? When?"

"Tomorrow I guess. I've got to deal with my sister again after this."

Shayna threw down the butt of her last cigarette and mashed it under her shoe.

"Got the rope?" Katja asked the boys.

Becker slung his sack down and pulled out the same rope as before.

"Got the thing?" he said.

She opened up her own bag and reverently removed something she had apparently fashioned out of a massive number of coat-hangers and tape. A grappling hook.

Together they struggled to tie a knot that satisfied them all.

"Do you know what you're doing with that thing?" Shayna asked.

"I saw it on TV," Katja asked, stepping back from the concrete block and swinging the thing in a rapid and wide circle.

It shot straight into the ground on her first two casts, but on the third it flew a perfect arc, scraped against the concrete metal somewhere up there, and did not come back. The rope held strong in the air when she tugged on it.

"Piece of cake," she said.

One after the other the boys followed her up the rope, with great effort walking vertically up the side of the concrete block and disappearing over the edge.

"Hey!" Shayna yelled. "What are you guys doing?"

Amid the sound of Becker and Float's excitement, Katja's head peeked out over the edge and looked down. A piece of charcoal sky passed behind her as she said "That's a secret. If you want to know, you have to get your butt up here!"

"Fine!" Shayna yelled angrily and obeyed.

Not one more day, she told herself. *I can't wait one more goddamned day.*

There was barely enough room for the four of them to stand on the top of the block at once. There in the middle, the pigeon-stained gray concrete met the shiny white metal of the leg that held up the Line. It was only a couple of feet thick. Looking up its length toward the tracks, it seemed to stretch into infinity.

"Why does the track have to be so high up?" Shayna asked.

"So the passengers can't see down to our level," Becker said. "Duh."

Meanwhile, Katja had already started climbing, using the raised bolts as footholds.

Shayna groaned and yelled "I just need to ask you something in private!"

"Ask me at the top!"

Becker grabbed the pipe, but Shayna pushed ahead of him, thinking that if Becker lagged behind she'd have a moment alone with Katja at the top. She lifted herself up on the first bolt and grabbed the next. *I must be insane*, she thought, and felt the warm wind rise.

"Don't look down," Katja called from above. "Don't think about it. Just focus on the bolts and on me."

"I *know,*" Shayna yelled back bitterly and kept up her hurrying pace.

Soon she had closed the distance between herself and Katja. The girl's ankles were close enough to grab. She wondered whether Becker were far enough behind, and without thinking she looked down over her shoulder only to freeze, gripping the metal tightly, wondering how in the hell she had let herself climb up this far already. The ground must have been six stories down. How much farther up was the track?

"Keep going!" Becker yelled from below.

"*Katja*," Shayna yelled, and kept going.

"What is it?"

"This is the last time! I'm not doing this stupid shit with you anymore! This is insane!"

"Whatever you say. Wimp."

The Line was getting closer. The wind felt colder up here.

Suddenly the pipe was buzzing, shaking, vibrating so rapidly as to seem electrified. She felt her fingers begin to slip and then there was a noise, humming, resonating in her guts and unbearably loud. She opened her mouth and couldn't hear her own scream. Then in a blink it was all gone. Her ears rang in the calm silence.

"What the *fuck* was that?" she yelled.

"The train passing," Becker yelled. "It's okay. Everybody okay?"

"We better hurry up," Katja said. "We've got to make it over before the next one."

"When does the next one come?" Shayna yelled.

Nobody answered.

"We're almost there," Katja yelled. "This is great!"

Only because she was too scared to even think about going back down now, Shayna climbed onward amid the whistling wind and her own aching fingertips and total breathlessness.

Then it was there. Katja dug her feet into a narrow foothold along the side of the Line, grabbed hold of the shiny white lip of the track and heaved herself over it. She gave a little yelp and disappeared completely over the other side.

"Katja!" Shayna shouted desperately. Was there even something solid up there to hold onto? Were there empty gaps between the tracks? Could she have fallen? Shayna let herself glance down over the edge of the pipe.

A couple of cars circled the parking lot twelve stories below like hungry mice.

"Oh God," she hissed, shut her eyes and pressed her face to the cold metal. "Oh God."

"Come on!" Katja yelled from above. "Grab my hand!"

"Fuck you," Shayna responded. In a jolt of adrenaline she grabbed the lip and hauled herself over without help. She found herself rolling down into a tubular space made of gleaming spools of wire. There behind the edge of the lip, she could imagine she was at ground level if she ignored the tops of the buildings and smokestacks and radio towers that peeked into view. Or she could accidentally imagine that the ground had ceased to exist altogether – that an infinite abyss of stormy sky spanned out on the other side of the coiled metal floor. The tube stretched into infinity in either direction, but looking North she could just make out the luminous angular shape among the clouds where, theoretically, the Cology's crystal walls parted.

"You did it!" Katja yelled. "Way to go, Shay!"

Shayna glared hard and lay back into the wire, waiting for her breath.

"Anybody ever tell you you're cute when you're hopping mad?" Katja said. Suddenly she grabbed Shayna's face and kissed her forehead. Then she said: "Now what did you want to ask me?"

Becker's fat fingers appeared above the lip.

"Help!" he shouted.

"Ask me at the bottom," Katja said and hurried to pull Becker and then Float up and over.

When Becker had half caught his breath he grinned and said "Now comes the fun part." He unzipped his backpack again. This time he took out four lengths of steel cable, about five feet in length, each with a wide leather strap at each end.

Shayna stared blankly.

"It's easy," Becker said, grabbing the lip opposite where they'd climbed up, heaving himself up a bit and looking over. He took one of the cables and did something with it on the other side of the lip while Katja and Float watched, and continued: "They're pretty stiff, and the pipe on this side is a lot narrower, see? You can just reach down, hook it around. The hard part is just stepping off the foothold. It's kind of a little leap you have to take."

"What insane thing are you doing now?" Shayna asked, stumbling fearfully to join them in looking over the edge.

"Sliding down," Becker said.

Shayna laughed sharply.

"The pipe on this side is smaller around, see?" he said. "And smooth. No bolts. And in this particular place it's not so steep an angle. Right here they had to build it over that building down there, so the foot is farther out. Shallower slope."

"You're insane," Shayna said. "That's insane. You're going to kill yourself."

Katja sighed and said, not with frustration so much as embarrassment: "This isn't actually an original idea. We didn't think it up. People have been doing it since the White Line was built. See?"

She indicated something Shayna hadn't noticed before: an array of colors, symbols, knitted lines sprawled across the shiny white metal. Strange writing. Small scrawls of graffiti. Katja took a pen from her inside pocket and added a design of her own as Shayna watched in wordless awe.

"I didn't make these," Becker said, indicating the cables. "I borrowed them from a guy who's done this a lot of times."

"We need to go," Float said.

"How long before the train smashes us?" Shayna asked ruefully.

"It's not the smashing that gets you. It's a mag-lev train. All these wires go super-electrified when the train even starts up. We have to get off the track before it even starts up at the far end."

"All right," Katja said, addressing the boys. "You guys go first. To prove it to Shay here. I'll stay up here to make sure she follows, then I'll go last. Now go! Chop-chop!"

"Loop it like this," Becker explained hurriedly, demonstrating how he tangled his wrists up in the leather loops and locked his grip around the slack. He said: "So even if you accidentally let go, it still holds onto your wrists. You won't drop."

"I can't do this," Shayna said. "I'm climbing back down the way I came up." She grabbed the lip and peeked down that edge again, but as her stomach churned she felt Katja's hard grip on her shoulder, pulling her back down.

"You will not," Katja said. "No one goes alone. That's the rules of our team."

"I'm not part of your team. I'm going down."

"Don't make me kick your ass."

"I'm going," Becker said, and did.

Everyone clung to the edge and looked over, watching him move his feet unsteadily along the razor-thin edge down there by the pipe. He hesitated.

"Electricity," Float said.

Becker nodded. He checked the leather that bound each wrist to the steel cable looped under the pipe before him. Then, visibly bracing himself, he rocked forward on his boots just a little and fell off.

"Oh shit! I did it wrong!" he yelled out.

Shayna opened her eyes to see him flapping in the chilly night, turned around backwards and looking back up at the track as he slid along the pipe, hung by his arms. Amid a blood-curdling screeching of metal and the excited screams of Float and Katja he was rapidly gaining speed, while his eyes were fixed in sheer terror and amazement on everything flying by between his dangling shoes. An eternal screeching moment later he had crashed into the dirt all the way down there, on the other side of a chainlink fence. They saw him struggling to free his hands.

"He's alive," Katja said. "Go."

"Going," Float said, lowering himself onto the tiny ledge. "Watch how I do it," he said.

Instead of looping the steel cable as Becker had, he carefully turned himself around, facing the tracks, straddling the pipe on shaky legs as he hooked it under and secured the loop on his wrist. He pulled it tight with his teeth. Then, giving it no second thought, he stepped off the ledge. This time Shayna managed to keep her eyes open to see him slide around the pipe and flop down into hanging position as he slid, facing forward.

"Now you," Katja said before Float had even touched down. Her hands pressed on Shayna's back.

"*I can't*, goddamnit. You know I can't."

Katja's voice turned cool. "Shay. You're my friend, and I'm your friend. What does that mean to you?"

Shayna gulped.

"To me," Katja continued, "it means that either neither of us get electrocuted to death up here, or we both do. So think of it as *my* ass you're saving."

"Oh God," Shayna said.

"Go! *Now!*" Katja screamed.

She did. She wasn't clearly aware of herself as she slid her feet down onto the narrow ledge and did as Float had just done. She woke from her trance exactly one moment too soon. Her feet were still clinging to the ledge, the loop fastened around the pipe beneath her. She looked in terror up into Katja's eyes peeking above that lip of shiny white metal.

Her feet slipped. She plunged straight down into dark empty air

I'm going to die, she thought – *right now. I'm going to drop straight down. The end.* The leather bit hard into her wrists. Metal screeched above her. The air began to fly, and then it sang against her, howling through her coat and hair. Rooftops and stovepipes and an abyss of empty air flew past the tips of her boots. She hadn't realized she'd been screaming until her screaming became laughing, and she laughed until she was breathless. Things flew faster down there. Cars and bicycles. Unconscious bums and restless scavengers. Comp cars gathered at the donut front. Fires in trash cans. And then so suddenly up flew a loop of razor-wire at the top of a chainlink fence, and then two sets of adolescent boys' arms grabbed her and failed to take the force of her impact with the ground. The crash was still hard enough to stun her and leave her reeling and speechless while Becker and Float freed her wrists and readied themselves for Katja.

Shayna gathered herself up in the dust. Her mind was rushing. Epiphany washed electrically into her brain as Katja came crashing down, and as soon as the last leather strap was undone the four of them squeezed through a gap in the fence and took off running – and there it was, radiant in her every muscle fiber, dazzling in her head, euphoric in her heaving breath: the same feeling that had come over her in the aftermath of the Beast. Unthinkable. Indescribable. Making her drunk.

"Katja!" she yelled ahead as the ran through the dancing shadows.

"Wait till we're out of sight," Katja yelled back.

"I *do* feel it!" Shayna shouted. "I understand! I feel everything!"

"Life!" Katja cried back ecstatically, "That's *life*, Shay! *Life!*" And when they darted off down a narrow alley and huddled blindly in the darkness, waiting to know there were no comps coming, her hand found Shayna's neck and held her close to confide in a whisper:

"The secret is that death stalks us. It never just comes and strikes. It looms. It hovers. You turn your head for a heartbeat and it's already come and gone. You hear about it. You don't see it. You only see it on TV, like it's not even real."

Shayna huddled there, trembling and dazed and drunk. The adrenaline rush buzzed like good music in the tips of her fingers.

"But without it, life isn't real either," Katja whispered. "Nothing is real. Everything fades and loses all its color, and nobody lives anymore. Except us, Shay. We live. Because we seek it out. We go out looking for death. To get close to it and look straight into its eyes. Because that's the only way we have – there is. To bring yourself to life."

Becker and float giggled in quiet awe. Their faces were invisible in the dark, but the passing light of comp car lights glittered in the line of a tear.

"*Nobody lives anymore,*" Katja whispered. "*But* we *live.*"

The red and blue flashes passed and never returned, and the air in the alley turned thinner. Katja's shadow checked the time in the dull glow of her phone.

"I've got to catch a bus," she said, and started immediately for the light at the end of the narrow alley.

"See you Saturday night," Becker's shadow said.

"Wait," Shayna stammered, shaking herself from some kind trance.

"Hurry up," Katja said. "Ask me on the way to the stop."

Shayna followed the order, though her lungs were still out of breath and the leap to her feet filled her vision up with sparks. The euphoric surge she'd felt moments before was creepily evaporating, replaced by a sickness in the pit of her stomach, like an uncomfortable nakedness. Although—

"You wanted to know something about Tom."

"Right," Shayna said as she hurried to catch up, "Is Tom...?" But then, again, she hesitated.

Their half-running feet were quickly coming up on a Metro signpost. From behind came the distant grunt of hydraulic brakes and the guttural hum of the motors. Finally, summoning all that was left of her rapidly-fading near-death spiritual intoxication, she said: "Does Tom have anyone?"

Katja passed her a backward glance peppered with a smirk. "*Have* anyone?"

"Is he with anyone?"

Katja stopped abruptly, turned straight around and faced Shayna on the sidewalk under the rushing charcoal sky. On her lips glowed a smile that made Shayna turn redder than she already was.

"Tom has never had anyone. That's what he told me."

"You've...?" Shayna stuttered. "You've talked to him about—? I mean you've discussed—"

"Love?" Katja said with a small snorting laugh. "Sure. One night in the Green Room. We somehow got talking about his love life, or lack of one I guess. Kind of." She seemed to pause in thought.

"And?" Shayna asked impatiently. "What did he say?"

"He was completely sloshed. So was I, and that was months ago. I mean I don't remember all the details. I just know there weren't many details. He's pretty much a loner. Maybe even a virgin. I was even into him myself back then, but I guess he wasn't interested." She studied Shayna closely and said: "Am I to understand that Shay has developed a crush on Tomcat?"

"I'm in love with him," Shayna replied silently in her head, but nothing left her throat. She nodded limply.

"Since when?" Katja asked excitedly.

"A little while."

The Metro hummed closer and began to groan on its brakes.

"It never would've crossed my mind – but you would be cute together," Katja appraised as a bus-side deodorant ad jerked to a halt behind her. Doors hissed open and an unearthly light spilled from within.

"What should I do?" Shayna demanded in unthinking panic.

"You're asking me what to do?" Over the whir of the change-slot she shouted down: "Tell him! Do you want me to tell him for you? I'll tell him if you won't. If you want."

"But he means so much to me as a friend," Shayna mumbled in the cooling wind.

"Tell him!" Katja shouted as the plastic panes hissed shut between them.

Diesel soot swirled warmly in the bus's wake.

Shayna's mind gradually cohered again. She floated backward, leaned into a line of chainlinks and just stayed put there, staring out into the blotches of evening light traveling furiously among the smokestacks in the West. She patiently waited for deep breathing to quiet down the roaring of her heart. She held her hands out in front of her, fingers spread, and laughed inwardly at their shaking – laughing at herself – at the wimp she felt like. Having flown by her fists a dozen blocks through the rushing sky. Having looked death in the face twice now. To think that this trivial thing could make her quiver now.

I'm telling him, she thought. *I'm dying and I'm telling him.*

She walked for her bike with this promise echoing in her mind, as a sudden chill washed through the sidewalk labyrinth, making the pedestrians and bum-lined bricks all shiver in a wave. She walked faster for warmth until her breath was running out all over again – and when the electrical fuzz began to seep back into the edges of her vision, she searched again in her throbbing chest for that inexhaustible reserve of strength she'd felt in the biking afternoon, and tapped it. The sparks receded, and the pain in every joint turned into pride, and the naked sickness in her entrails unfolded into ridiculous buoyancy. It made her pause, made her laugh at herself, this bizarre thing coming over her. It was in the way she could see everything's color visibly brightening; it was in the way the cold felt like energy instead of its absence; it was in the way the dead cinderblocks had all started oozing the sense of secretly being alive, their graffiti no longer manmade but manifested from within as it could be their own impassioned message to mostly ignorant passers-by, their globs of stray mortar revealed as the afterbirth of a new world that was not really rotten and doomed at all but glowing internally with endless possibilities for everything to suddenly click, to work, to wake up. It was in the total absurdity that anything could the whole wide gruesome Tropolis look beautiful. As if this feeling was the only thing it had ever lacked.

I'm high, she thought as she picked her bike up from the dust and straddled it motionlessly, too absorbed into the straight infinite distance of the road to know about pedaling. She thought: *I'm high, or dreaming. Or else this is the first moment in my entire life in which I'm neither.*

The rear tire badly needed air, but she whispered to it: "Just to the Green Room. Just get me that far. Just one more time. That's all I ask. All I need."

She confided in the rusted-through bicycle, the rushing pavement, her own burning calves: I'm dying. And I'm in love with him and I'm telling him. No matter what.

The high dwindled eerily when Shayna plunged back into the murky social depths, though it didn't die – now that she wished it would a little, now that there was nothing to do but sit and wait. Now that inexhaustible strength had no outlet but in the nervous tapping of toes and the stuttering tides of caustic liquid through a glass, burning its lip-stains radioactive green under the neon, quivering in her hands whenever anyone thudded down the stairs.

Carl stumbled back from the bathroom, apparently not noticing the piece of paper stuck to his heel. Shayna nudged it free with her foot. It was another flyer titled BLACK FACTION. Underneath a scribbled phallus were the words:

> "The first sine qua non of any mass political movement is dissatisfaction. If revolution is to be paraphrased as a sort of combustion, then misery is the fuel. The igniting heat, furthermore, is the ability of individuals to recognize that their misery is not solely their own, but rather held in common with their peers, and therefore a possible basis for organization. Any cursory assessment of the outer Tropolis and its conditions will lead us to conclude that there has been no shortage of our combustible fuel - and yet we have seen no significant ignition occur for more than a century. [...] We may surmise that he Company has leveraged its monopoly over the organs of culture so fully that countless would-be explosive reactions have been near-totally inhibited; individuals, though collectively miserable as a direct consequence of Corporate policy, have been convinced that their miseries are sole and unique, and to attribute these miseries either to irrelevant or illusionary sources; or worse, to themselves and to each other."
>
> –*Rokosz*

She leaned back and rubbed her eyes.

"Tom is coming tonight, right?" she asked Carl.

"I told you. He's here every fucking night. Like the rest of us."

"But *tonight?*" she asked drunkenly, and regretted it.

"Fuck if I know," he responded. He was as pissed off as he always was, possibly and then some.

"You okay?" she asked.

He muttered something about the Company automating his job at the Regulator plant and reassigning him, and the new job involved working with people. People he hated. She was too distracted to make out the details, even if they'd mattered. Carl hated all other people. It was enough.

Fish kept leaning over and drunkenly saying something like "I've got a new thing I think you'll be into. People like you, they like this thing, this thing I'm talking about, see?"

"What is it?" Shayna asked.

Fish answered extensively, but she didn't listen to much of it. "So yeah," he finished. "And remember, the first hit of anything is on the house. Anything you want, I'm your travel agent, see?"

"I see," Shayna murmured, her eyes stuck on the stairs – though secretly she knew to herself that she was done with Fish, him and whatever monstrous thing he had to offer her. Done with every high but this one, she thought, and a shallow sigh escaped her.

"Remember the Professor's got you covered," he said as he drank with a roll of his eyes.

"Who's the professor?"

"Me."

"Professor Fish."

"No. I'm not Fish anymore. Just the Professor."

"Whatever," said Carl, who had been silently perched on the edge of the conversation like a gargoyle. He was already too drunk for the good of anything, but he threw back another shot and inexplicably hissed "Damn it all to Hell!"

"Kat said you were on some meds, Carl," the Professor noted coolly. "What meds are you on?"

"Fuck you care."

"Maybe I can help."

Carl shrugged and muttered "Felicidrine. Fifty units a day."

"Pitch that Unified-Company-Health shit, my friend. Pretty weak, isn't it? And ethanol antagonizes the hell out of it too. I've got something for you. Better. Stronger. Binds to different receptors and won't be affected by blood alcohol. Give it a spin?"

Carl just shook his head and looked on.

Shayna's phone lay heavy in her palm with time's digits burning on its face. It was late. *Maybe he wasn't coming,* she thought. *Maybe I should call him. Maybe I should just go back to his apartment. Maybe he's already asleep there.* At this thought she swore under her breath and moved her cigarette from above her ear to her mouth. There was too much urgency now. Years of folded-up urgency were unfolding with every passing disjointed moment and gulp of sickening time-killing liquor. The smell of clove smoke was getting stronger here – a phantom smell, coming from nobody in that cluttered room but somehow welling hazardously up from within. Something in her guts had gone from warmth to burning.

Carl's face hit the table.

"You all right?" said the Professor, slapping his back.

There was no answer – nothing but a low gurgling, turning into a muffled growl, drunkenly evolving into a slow trickle of mangled Smurge lyrics that wedged themselves into a tangled dissonance with whatever Power Elite tune was ringing through the room.

Shayna shook her head and sighed.

"I've got to get out of here," she said, and, in standing up, accidentally realized roughly how much she'd had to drink that stupid night.

"Don't worry, I'll keep him upright," the Professor yawned.

She was already hauling herself up the stairs – but just then a shadow eclipsed the searing light of caged bulbs on bricks up there; a cool silhouette spilled down and held her within itself. The phantom clove smoke billowed heavily, and peering groggily up through it she saw her friend.

"Uh, hi," Tom said as he stumbled down.

As he hesitated meekly there before her, her mind was trying and failing to race. She could not think or move or utter a damned word. *Something's wrong,* she thought. *I've had too much. It's all kicking in at once. Something's burst inside my head.*

Tom slinked into the luminous haze and took her seat next to the ruined Carl and the wryly smiling Professor Fish.

Fucking melodrama, she thought as she snapped herself back awake and started drifting on counted steps through the crowd. *It's time. You promised. You bitch.*

Ten steps. Tom was scribbling something on a scrap of paper under Nemo's eager gaze. She stood at the edge of the table looking silently down. She thought: *In three weeks I'll be dead.* She thought: *Three and a half years.*

The Professor tucked the scrap into his coat and Tom stood up again and started for the stairs.

"You're leaving?" Shayna asked.

"Oh, yeah," he muttered. "Just giving Nemo's number to Fish. Tomorrow's the big drunkfest, you know. Friday night always is. I'm saving up my tolerance tonight. I guess."

"R-right."

Smoke swarmed the neon. Somewhere a stack of glass cups fell over.

"Well, uh, good night," Tom said and turned.

"Wait," yelled the phantom clove smoke and the liquor and the pounding of her heart. "Wait," she yelled to him, and it was finally too late to turn back.

"What's up?"

"I'll come with you."

Together they climbed out of the hazy depths and into the cool night din and diesel. They drifted toward the Metro.

"You, uh, planning to stay at my place again tonight?"

She sighed and said, as soberly as she could, "If you don't want me to stay there, really, just say I shouldn't, and I'll leave. Really."

"No, it's okay."

"You really don't have to. I mean I can— I don't want to—"

"You're in trouble of some kind?"

"Not for much longer."

"I don't mind," he said emotionlessly. "If you really need to stay for a while. I mean—"

"I love you," she interrupted.

Tom hesitated on the sidewalk, peered both ways down the long empty street, and glanced emptily down at her. He didn't try to meet her eyes, nor her his. They just stood. The windows stayed dark. The moths kept smashing themselves to death in the street lamps.

"Oh." He added simply "Well, I love you too."

She stared at his chest and felt her alcoholic breath enter and exit.

"We've been friends for a long time," he said.

"Not just that," she whispered as drowsiness hit her in a wave. "No."

"No?"

"I mean I'm in love with you."

The insides of her hands felt suddenly warm, and when she looked at them she saw they had taken hold of his.

"I'm in love with you, Tom. I've always, I think, been. I have. I *have*."

"Oh."

The Metro wheezed to a hydraulic halt at the curb. Shayna followed him into the pale inner light of the last bus home. Sitting next to him on the lacerated vinyl, she tried to read his expression in the corner of her eye, not daring to risk a direct look. She weighed whether to let her knee touch his, or whether even to reach out and try to hold his hand. Alcohol was already closing like a curtain on the night and on everything and on her, and the mad backbeat of her heart and the shaking of her hands and the racing of what few thoughts she had was making her drunk all over again. Time wouldn't work properly.

She was short of breath on the stairs to his door. She was drinking water from the King of Sweden's coffee cup. She was lying on the bottom bunk and all the lights were dead, and sleep was right there waiting.

"No," she hissed, and heaved herself sickly upright. Breathing deep and slow from the suffocating television-static darkness, she got up and looked over the edge of the top bunk. Tom's eyes were open and looking back at her.

"You're kind of drunk," he whispered.

"It doesn't change this."

He was silent.

She stepped up onto the bottom mattress and wrapped her fingers around the cold steel bars at the top. She pulled herself precariously up until she could feel the warmth of his face crossing the gap to her own – and held herself there, staring at the shadows of his mouth, only breathing, until the smell of exhaled cloves dissolved the last traces of her writhing anxiety. The throbbing passage of time finally held its breath.

"Okay," he whispered, as their lips softly lay down against each other.

At first they kissed barely – like clouds brushing against each other in the dirty reddish night. It became more like booze flowing in slow motion into the parabolic depths of a shot glass under green neon. Finally it was like another drug, nothing even in the Professor's repertoire. Nothing Shayna had ever quite allowed herself to imagine.

The kiss ended. Tom rolled over and lay on his back, staring blankly at the ceiling.

"I— I like you," he whispered. "I mean, but. I don't know exactly. How I feel. About this. Yet."

"That's okay."

"I don't have very much experience."

"I don't care."

"I have a thing," he stuttered quietly. "Where I just don't really like being very physical. With anyone. No one I know. Except... yeah."

She answered with a shrug that was lost in the darkness, a sigh that was lost when the fridge whirred to life again.

"I mean you shouldn't expect too much from me."

"That's okay. I just want to be with you. Any way I can."

His silhouette nodded and said "Okay."

She held his hand and kissed the palm through a wide smile.

Then she was tired and woozy again, lying on the bottom bunk, her mind gone back to racing. Staring at the half-logo half moon that shone brightly in the window at her feet. Thinking: *My first kiss. The most perfect three seconds of my entire life.*

Yes. Everything is right.

Nothing is wrong.

Nothing.

14

Conscious reality first disentangled itself from her dreams around ten that morning, and Tom was already gone. She crept barefoot to the window and squinted up above the lip of the opposite roof, into distant billows of gathering thunderheads, and watched the rain come and go through the brilliant yellow sun.

Her memory of the prognosis was there as always like an aftertaste or a hangover – but she thought now about Tom. She tried to pit these two thoughts against each other, and she found to her surprise that it was the hangover that died down to nothing. Time wasn't slipping away anymore. Time had only just begun. So she climbed up to the top bunk – where the phantom cloves were stronger – and lay down and kept sleeping in without a twinge of regret, like she hadn't since the God-damned diagnosis.

What have I done? she thought as she rose to consciousness for good. Sleeping within his scent had worked on her like a drug, and now the room was painted in weird colors. The sun in the dust motes ebbed and flowed in fast and unsteady rhythms; gliding back to the window, she saw that the sky up there was still rising into the full throes of its chaos, but it was beautiful chaos, full of light. The luminous damp wind howled between the clotheslines. Bits of trash shot through the alley like mad birds, but she had no fear. The storm was clearing out the Tropolis's sickened haze too fast for smokestacks and underground fires to replace it.

For no reason she went outside. There she found the vacant lots transformed, silvered with water, laced with gigantic puddles that the sky turned into luminous rivers of liquid gold. Flocking plastic bags caught themselves in the chainlinks and turned the fences into giant sails, until the wind began to pry the poles up from even the solid concrete. The stoplights were all swinging in their places and their bulbs were flickering unsteadily. Broken doors were flapping on their hinges. All these barriers, one by one, coming down.

She leaned into the wind and let it hold her up, and in one hard gust she was sure that if she leaned another degree it could take her all the way off her feet and carry her up into the billowing fiery sky, never to fall back down. It was something she'd imagined many times, in many storms – but now, for what she knew was the first time in her entire life, she didn't want it to. *What a feeling is this that could actually make me want to stay here in this screwed-up world.*

This time it was with a passion that she lifted her pink electric bass out of the crevice between the bed and the wall, it was with more than dull curiosity that she lay her fingers on the strings and struggled to get the chords right. As she perched there on the sunlit wind-howling steps of the building, her ears encased in a pair of headphones borrowed from Tom's stuff, re-teaching herself note-by-agonizing-note to play the same song that had been stuck in her head for the second day straight, she felt not merely inspired but possessed. *Because I can't speak*, she thought. *I'm mute except for this song. It can speak for me.* She thought: *It* has *to. It's important. There's nothing more important.*

She paused only to smoke and crack her aching knuckles. Her ass went completely numb against the concrete slab and her tailbone began to make her cringe. The weather came and went. The sun peeked between different clouds. The wind swept the sidewalk slate clean of her lifeless butts.

At some point it dawned on her that she couldn't remember the last time she'd eaten. By then her fingers were too sore to go on anyway; the scabs from the rebar fleeing the Beast had started to loosen, and the joints cracked a little too loud when pressed. Better to fill her stomach before the drinking to come, she realized, and so strapped the bass against her back and set off.

At first the wind blinded her, but her stolen goggles gave her clear sight.

The gun was still there in her coat pocket when she buried her hands against the cold. Her fingers recoiled. That metal felt as alien to her now as it had when she'd held it for the first time, and in this she felt a great wave of unexpected relief. She had lost its black metal instincts. Here among the empty-eyed derelicts, the dark scuttling alleyways, the huddled masses of sharp-beaked birds, she already had all the invincibility she needed.

She found the streets all lifeless on the way there – but the waiting line at Smarty's Chicken Stop had grown out longer than she'd ever seen it. The obese and the skeletal alike were huddling there together in a vast throng, their legs spread a little to brace themselves against the apocalyptic wind.

"What's all this?" Shayna yelled to a gaunt man whose coat hung horizontally from his leaning shoulders.

"Somebody said a superstorm's coming!" he yelled back.

"So?"

"Don't you remember the last superstorm, kid? Shut down all the Smarty's in town for a whole week! This could be your last chance to get a MegaBreast Muncher Meal till God only knows!"

"If I don't get my chicken fix I'll fucking lose it," somebody agreed.

A hundred other people squinted their eyes against the wind and looked on.

She found the nearest corner store already well-raided and lifeless. All the fizz bottles and individually wrapped snacks had been swept clean, leaving only a solitary box of particle bread. It would do.

"And a pack of Balmic," she added when she passed the bills through the bars to the clerk. "Wait. Actually? Make it cloves."

Back in the day's unsteady golden light, huddling in a brick alcove as she lit the first one, she remembered why Tom stuck to them, and why she'd never been able to stand them herself. The bitter, overbearing flavor coated the inside of her face like utility pole tar. Supposedly it weakened the gag reflex too: a true garbageman's cigarette. But it was a taste she could acquire quickly. If she only had two weeks to live, she never wanted to live another second without it.

Leaning back in the stillness of the brick alcove, she remembered the kiss. She stood there and remembered it for half an hour before she walked on.

Now she felt her invincibility begin to waver. The harder she thought back on those moments of the past night, the more this inner warmth became a dry heat, tinged with sharpness. She replayed his words in her head and started to realize that she wasn't completely sure what he'd meant when he'd told her not to expect too much. That could mean multiple things, she thought. She stopped and stared down the dead street in thought, and started to wish for something to wash out the aftertaste of the cloves. Something to keep this force under control.

The sound of distant shouting made her turn. Across the street, through a bulldozed gap in the buildings, a freight train was rolling slowly by. A few people were running at its side, clutching plastic bags. One man stood there in the dust, watching.

The Shayna she had been until yesterday – like any good Outsider, especially a girl of her size – would have left the strangers alone. But she was curious, and she was still invincible. Like the person she wanted to be, she crept over the rubble and joined the standing man. The two exchanged a brief glance. Together they watched the runners struggle to grab at the rusty metal and haul themselves aboard.

"Everybody knows somebody who's died in a superstorm," he explained with a ruined voice. "They think they'll be safer farther East and inland when it comes."

"Not you?"

He didn't answer at first. In the corner of her eye she studied the deep scar that stood out from the dirt in his face; the pale spot where his beard no longer grew right.

"Hope is a boxcar," he said. "If you can get on, it might take you somewhere beautiful. Somewhere you'd never get to by other ways. Or it might take you somewhere evil, or it might suffocate you with the diesel fumes going through a tunnel. But once you're aboard, you're stuck going all the way to the end of the line, or else you're going to break both your legs trying to jump off early."

With this, he hobbled away and left her there. The last of the runners hauled themselves up and disappeared around a bend in the tracks.

Hope is a boxcar, she thought as she walked back to the street. The soft warmth and sharp heat stirred together in her stomach. She thought back one more time on the kiss, and made her choice. *I'm going all the way*, she resolved – and the heat vanished, the warmth resurged, and everything became clear again.

I'm losing myself again, she thought – *but in the opposite direction. I'm unfamiliar to myself, to anything I've ever been, but this time it makes me want to laugh. To shout. To dance in the street.* And she leapt without warning into the middle of the abandoned intersection and spun on her thick-soled black boots, looking around at the rocking stoplights, the rolling trashcans, the flocks of paper and plastic all shining furiously in the lengthening shadows. She thought: *Clearly I have gone insane. I'm taking this all too far, too fast, but it's the only way now.* Dancing in the ruins, she thought: *I, the ugly one, the small one, the quiet girl who always hung around the edges of the room, no nearer – I've turned visible. I could burn brighter even than Katja. I am everything I've never been, my own exact opposite. Beautiful and alive.*

The wind raced against her goggled eyes, under the lifted heels of her boots, between the wide-spread fingers of her open arms, through her unkempt hair and the howling strings of her bass and out along the great madly flapping length of her army coat. That coat she'd depended on to conceal her from the world, to protect her from all the ways she'd always felt frail and vulnerable. Now it was lifted high behind her like a spread of olive drab wings.

She thought: *I am everything.*

Six hours later, the rain-scarred brickwork flickered darkly in the rushing night alley. It said, and she said, both in voices too broken to be made out: *I am nothing.* The storm hissed it. The black-on-olive stain of a spilled shot wafted it. Shayna chanted it with her every heaving breath: *I am nothing. I am nothing. I am nothing.*

Katja's voice ran after her: "Shay! Don't leave! It's not safe!" Somewhere back down there in the echoes of the Green Room stairs she thought she even heard Tom himself cry out to her: "Come back!" But she wouldn't. She shouted over her shoulder with a garbled stream of whatever obscenities came to mind.

Wait, she wondered – *what has happened? Why am I running?* Then she remembered: the red bulb hanging over the couch in the back room.

Her stomach spasmed and she felt the puke rising again. *Stay down*, she willed. *Stay down in the stairwell, Katja.* The bicycle was so close. Almost there. If she could only reach it. Liquored stupor and thudding heart. Wailing wind and buzzing bulbs in cages. They all whispered: *nothing.*

"But the storm!" Katja yelled, clearing the stairs. "The storm!"

"Fuck the storm!" Shayna thought she replied, though she doubted whether any of the words made it. She whipped the bike into position, hooked her leg over the top bar, and in a blaze of drunken motion was gone.

"Fuck the storm," she mumbled into the dark shapes flowing liquidly around her – and when she rolled into the intersection a gust came up so strong that it pushed her to the rain-slick ground.

Wait, she wondered – *what has happened? Why am I doubled over and dry heaving on the curb?* Then she remembered. Tom reclines. Carl says: "Yeah, back there." The red bulb shines through the bare threads of the crummy curtain. Katja doesn't get her warning out in time.

Back in the present, the bike's water bottle got caught in the gutter against the roaring wind. Shayna found it full and sucked every drop down into the fray of her stomach, and the next hurl washed out clean, so she lifted up her bruises from the pavement and mounted again. She didn't care if she didn't feel well enough. Something in her sputtered hot and still heating against the liquor-numbed freezing wind. The storm was still getting colder. Every burning exhale was whiter against the black night; each one muttering: *I am nothing.*

It was so black up there. It was like nothing she had ever seen. At first she couldn't understand. *Something in my goggles*, she thought, but they were still up on her forehead. *Something in my eyes*, she thought. But in the sparse light of the surviving streetlamps she could make out her breath, the bike, the streets and fallen stoplights and broken glass outlines spilling along in waves of intoxicated motion. The sky was actually black – shockingly, unnaturally black, deeper than the darkest color. Staring upward in gasping awe, she thought: *What could do that?* The city was powerless for miles around. Maybe the whole Tropolis was powerless. All but for the continual pale sparks of lightning too distant to make out.

She thought about making it to higher ground. Some place from which to get a look at the skyline. Maybe she could see the funnels and the sheer howling wind grinding all the rotten brickwork down into dust. She thought: *let it take the whole city this time. Let it take me. I've changed my mind. Take me anywhere but here.*

She pushed the goggles back down over her eyes and pedaled harder. She felt another wet gust hit like a slap in the face and the temperature took another sudden dive. The gale turned head-on and her pedals jolted dead against her weight. The shriek of the wheels, the roar of thunder, the mad howling of the black sky, each chanted with her: *I am nothing. I am nothing. I am nothing.*

Her clenched teeth began to ache from the wind chill. Now her peeled-back lips formed a perverse grin against the thickening rain. With all her free breath she began to laugh madly.

Everyone must be worried, she thought. *Back at the Green Room. I could die in this storm. Let them worry. That's all I want now. God damn them. God damn him. He must want me dead anyway.*

She thought: *But it's not really that bad, is it? Just to find out that I'm just what I always thought I was? Familiar to myself. I've got to calm down. Holy God I'm hammered. It's just the booze. All just the booze.*

This feeling will be gone tomorrow, she thought, but the thought rang false, dimmed, vanished.

She thought: *And what is this on my goggles?* It was frost.

The murky, liquor-blurred distance before her molded itself into a railing. A bridge. She turned her head to the overpowering gusts and looked over, trying to see how far the bottom was, but there was nothing to see. Abruptly she noticed the bike wobbling differently, jerking weirdly even when the wind slowed down.

She stopped. She squinted down past her leg. The rear tire was completely flat.

Another frigid gust smashed against her in time with the metal-tasting heat rising in her veins. She let loose an animal scream as her freezing fists lifted the bicycle high above her head – some of the crank's teeth sliced her in the ribs – and then, blind with rage, hurled it straight down into the abyss.

When the adrenaline faded, her mind was blank. She lay her hands on the frost-biting railing and squinted down while the wind took on an eerie stillness. A blink of lightning traced the rushing canal far below.

"Fuck," she breathed emotionlessly. The liquor resurged a third time and she found herself asking:

Wait – what has happened? What am I doing here? Alone and sick and dripping wet in the middle of the pitch black storm. Lost. Now on foot for good.

The gusts picked up again. Hailstones nipped at her fingers and face. The lightning was closer now and the thunder had started to rattle the bridge, and in one frost-blurred glance over her shoulder she thought for a moment that the lightning traced the featureless gray spike of a funnel cloud making its first stabs at the ground. It was much too close. Mere blocks. From here she could already feel it. She braced herself against the railing and with all her might pulled herself into the face of the gale, thinking only of the far side of the bridge.

This can't be real, she thought. *This can't have happened.* She remembered:

She waits for hours on the apartment steps. She practices the song until she can't stand to. Night arrives before he does and his phone doesn't answer, so the bus takes her to the door that leads her down into the folds of luminous green smoke. Her friends are perched there at the table as always – all except Tom. Everyone is already drunk. Katja walks up to her.

"Tom hasn't come by yet, has he?" Shayna asks.

"No, he's not here," Katja answers. The shadow of something odd is in her voice.

"I guess I've got catching up to do."

Shots are set out and taken between breaths of burning cloves. A shot for passing time. A shot to slow down the ecstatic throbbing of an impatient heart. A shot for feeding the same fires with the undoubted promise of what could be to come. Shots too fast and many. The muffled storm begins to leak through the ceiling.

"Hope he's not out in that stuff," Shayna says drunkenly to herself as her fingers turn her phone in her palm. "I hope he's okay."

"Who?" says Carl, bitterly.

"Tom," Shayna says, and smiles.

"He's been here for hours."

Shayna looks to Katja but finds her buried in Float's awkward kisses. She turns back to Carl and says: "He's here? Where is he?"

Carl sips and points indistinctly into the crowded murk. "The back room. That curtained-off part."

"What, that storage room?"

"It's not for storage."

She gets up and follows uncertainly after his pointing. She hesitates before the moth-eaten curtain, squinting at the holes where a solitary ruby-colored lightbulb shines through.

"Yeah," Carl says dimly, answering her questioning look. "Back there."

"Wait!" Katja shouts, too late.

Paralytic disbelief and a girl's sweat-greased flesh. Heaving lungs and open jeans. The dim red light on his fuzzy scalp and the bright white flash in Shayna's vision when she cracks her forehead against the concrete wall. Then the crunch of a porcelain angel under her boot, the lunatic wind above, the commands not to enter it, the pounding of the wooden stairs – all whisper:

Nothing.

13

She squeezed through the hole in the boards and confronted the source of the unsteady yellow light: a roaring fire in an oil drum, attended by half a dozen derelicts, all men. They stood up from their crates and stared as she peeled off her goggles. The faces under mottled beard and layered soot showed no trace of intention, but the soot-framed eyes spoke clearly enough. They could see the youth in her shivering, clammy face – and the army coat that usually obscured her sex was now drenched and form-fitting.

The men kept staring; no one moved. She folded her arms tightly before her and shivered and wondered anxiously what now. But she felt a weight against her hip and remembered the gun. A few hours ago she'd thought of chucking into the nearest canal, and now that her invincibility was gone for good, her frozen fingers clamped with gratitude around the handle. There was still an icy puddle in the bottom of the pocket. She couldn't tell if the chamber was full of water or just damp on the outside. Would it still work? *Fuck it*, she thought. She was freezing. She curved her numb finger around the trigger and stepped forward.

The derelicts silently parted as she stepped up to the flaming drum, never taking their eyes off her, and she didn't look up from the fire. Fear tightened in her chest. The air in here was so still. The wind kept screaming just outside. The fire blasted warmth in her face, but she was still shivering uncontrollably.

"You shouldn't be here," someone said, with a voice like an old diesel engine.

She couldn't tell whose beard had moved.

"No place for a young lady," the bum said. "You should be at home. With mama and papa. They must be worried half to death."

Shayna said nothing. Her teeth were chattering.

"Didn't you hear me, little girl?"

"My mother is dead," she said, unthinkingly.

"Father?"

"Never met him."

"Still shouldn't be here. You should be more careful. Watch out for yourself." She could tell which one was speaking now. His only identifying feature was a soiled piece of gauze tied about his neck.

"I know," she stuttered. "I got lost. I'm fucking... freezing."

The bums stood like statues in the flickering light. The one who had spoken moved silently among them and approached her. Standing close, he started to unwrap the dirty pink blanket that covered him. *The gun*, she thought. *The gun* – but he only held the blanket out to her.

"Take it," he said.

She shook her head.

"I said take it," he said hoarsely. The fire reflected in his bloodshot eyes.

She hesitantly obeyed, awkwardly struggling to drape it over both shoulders with one hand still stuffed into her pocket. The bum scrutinized her coldly. Only when she had finished wrapping herself up in it did the eyes gradually return to watching the sparks rising from the fire. One by one the bums sat back down.

"You should watch out for yourself," the bum growled again.

The blanket was warmer and drier than it had looked. Finally she felt the shivering begin to subside, and the ice started to melt out of her hair. She hunched over and lay her forearms on her knees.

It was there almost the moment she closed her eyes, before she even knew she was asleep – and it wasn't a memory this time, as it had been that day in the factory, when all this started. It was the same dream, recurring exactly. At first there was nothing but a formless white void.

Then there was the sound.

She felt it shuddering in her bones before it reached her ears, like an quake welled up out of the earth; rough, grating, and yet somehow musical. It was overwhelmingly familiar even though she couldn't tie it to any memory. It rose in volume until it seemed to paralyze her, blotting out her consciousness – and when it rose to its peak, the white backdrop suddenly split wide open, as if torn or burned. Behind it was the blue. It was like no real color. It was as familiar as the sound, but she knew with certainty that she had never seen it outside of this recurring dream. Though she had no clear sense of a body, she felt movement - the brutal acceleration as she seemed to fall upward into it.

She jolted awake to find herself laying flat on a foam pad, uncomfortably warm under three more blankets, still soggy from head to toe. Her hand was still planted on the grip of the gun. Nothing was missing from her pockets. Every zipper was in place.

The bum with the neck gauze was perched close by on a crate, poking at what was left of the fire with a broken antenna. No one else was there. Sensing her wakefulness, he glanced briefly over his shoulder at her.

"I had a daughter of my own," said his diesel voice.

Dim gray light was peeking through the crosshatched glass. The wind had died down.

"What happened to her?" Shayna asked carefully.

The broken antenna paused in its stirrings.

"You should watch out for yourself," he said.

She lay flat in the uneasy silence for a long time. Then she peeled away the sopping blankets, stood, and exited without a word.

The sky was spread a heavy gray-brown from horizon to horizon, featureless and smooth. The sun inside it was only an ambiguous patch of lighter color, like a spider's egg on a featureless ceiling. Shayna watched it a long time before she could tell that it was closer to dusk than dawn, and that she was headed West and not East. With the networks still apparently down, her phone had no clock – and somehow that was the most apocalyptic sign she'd seen through the entire storm, as if she'd found herself outside of time. At least the wind now breathing among the timeless buildings, though humid, was soft and warm. The sound from her dream seemed to echo between the walls of the alleys.

The Metro signposts still stood, but she didn't recognize the route numbers, and the schedules had all blown away. Not that the busses would be running anyway. There was nothing to do but keep walking and hope she crossed a street she knew.

It could have been an hour later that she reached the avenue on which the Green Room lay. There was a lot of broken glass along that street, and an impressive number of people in Company Works coveralls swarming over the damage. She looked through them all and ten blocks down, to the visible spire of the old theatre sign that marked her hangout. Her emotions had felt scabbed-over enough when she'd first stumbled awake. Time and walking thought had irritated the wound. Standing here now, glass crunching under her boots, she felt it bleed as fresh as the moment it was cut. She searched her pockets for a cigarette, but all she had were the cloves.

She threw the pack down on the street and raised her foot to smash it, but the foot wavered. The inside of her face turned sour and tight. She knew as she stomped that she would feel the treads on her own guts, but she ground it hard anyway. Then she walked on through the rotten debris, refusing to dignify the tears with a whimper or a wipe of her hand.

It was only then that she realized she'd still been unthinkingly walking back toward Tom's. She had no home at all now. The memory of the bottom bunk ached like a phantom limb, and she couldn't conceive of returning to her old place either – not that gray citadel in the unfinished district. She closed her eyes as it washed over her: the full crushing clarity with which she understood that she would rather die than go back there to rot alone. There was nothing left to hold back for. She sat down on the curb and cried.

The sun had found the fine sliver of emptiness at the edge of the sky, and beams of platinum light were spilling over the undulating lines of rain-greased rooftops. New clouds were marching out across the deepening charcoal and the wind was building up toward a final whimper.

What's left? she wondered to the sunset. *What's left for me to do?*

She thought: *I already know how this is all going to end. Slow death. It's as good as written. I'm just waiting for it now. But why should I even wait? What's there to be patient for?*

"Not a God damn thing," she said aloud.

The gun lay heavy against her thigh.

The dream sound seemed to pound harder in her mind's ear as if to hold her back as she reached into her pocket and felt the crosshatched metal grip. She was possessed now by the same feeling she'd had that day at the factory, before the diagnosis; the feeling that almost cost her two fingers. That tiny shard of unreal memory somehow seemed so burningly important – but it was meaningless. Just another unintelligible clue for some stupid riddle she wouldn't live to answer. It was nothing that didn't blow away on the thin wind as she put her finger on the trigger and started to lift the weapon out.

The networks chose that moment to resurrect. Neon and windows and streetlamps all burst to life in buzzing unison and the charcoal overhead tinged instantly pink.

Her phone rang. It was Katja. Not knowing what else to do, she let go of the gun, straightened her voice and answered.

"Shay! Thank God. You made it home all right."

Home, Shayna thought. "Yeah."

"How are you? Are you okay?"

"Fine."

"I mean, like, with what happened with Tom and everything."

"Fine." Through a break in her composure spilled the question: "Are you going to tell me who she is?"

"Well, do you actually want to know?"

"No. Fuck. Forget I asked. I don't want to talk about it."

"That's the spirit. I mean, unless you need to talk about it."

Something in Shayna was wearing thin. *Do I hate you, Katja?* she wondered. *How long have I hated you?*

"Did you just call to see if I was still alive, or is there something else?" she growled.

In the pause that followed, she thought she could somehow hear Katja grinning.

The last rays of twilight had just snuffed out when the deathtrippers assembled. Shayna had watched the light disintegrate as she walked all those miles, thinking to herself all the way that she'd have told Katja to fuck off if the invitation had been to anything but this. There was nothing else she wanted more than to do this, she realized as they pried up the nails on a trespassing sign. Now there was nothing else left.

"The old King Television tower," Katja declared, magnanimously.

"You sure we can make it all the way up there?" Becker asked. He sounded almost hesitant. Becker. "It looks like an awfully long climb. Even for us."

"Only one way to find out," Float said. He passed a giddy glance at Katja.

"What about the storm?" Becker said, with some embarrassment.

"The superstorm is over," Float said. "This is just a regular storm now. Nothing we can't handle."

Katja said, as if narrating: "I have to confess, I felt bad about the White Line. I knew even before we started that it just wasn't in the true spirit of our group. It wasn't original. Dozens of people had already tagged the rail up there. We borrowed their cables. I wanted to make it up to you. Give you guys something special this time. Something real."

A distant roll of thunder accompanied the moment she spread her arms to the foot of the dead tower. Twenty stories of rain-blackened bricks and dead-eyed windows rose out of the ragged ground and cut darkly into the reddish sky. Just visible above the end of those bricks, receding into angular infinity, was the radio tower itself: a spire of crisscrossed red and white steel beams, capped with the unlit neon logo of a three-pointed crown. The first speckles of warm rain fell as they stared upward.

"You all saw it on the way here," Katja said. "Make your own guesses, but I'd put money on that little blinking red light on the crown being the highest point in at least thirty miles all around. Maybe even the highest point outward from Angelis itself. The view must be like God."

Becker's brow was knitted in apprehension. Float and Katja smiled their ambition. Shayna showed them no emotion at all; she stood as cold as concrete in the thickening rain and the rising aroma of humid electricity. Her thoughts weren't for them – although she found herself in the middle of Katja's searching gaze in this last moment, as if the decision to begin was somehow hers.

The boys didn't wait. They squeezed through the boarded-up doors and disappeared into the sound of tromping puddles and stone. Through the ruins of a lobby, Shayna and Katja followed them into a stairwell that was wide and walled by empty window frames. The boys were hurrying, shouting incomprehensibly to each other, already a few floors up.

"If you want to say something then say it," Shayna found herself coldly announcing. The searching gaze was still fixed on her, lit up in each passing beam of dim purplish light from outside.

"Oh, Shay. Tomcat meant more to you than you let on, didn't he?"

Shayna said nothing.

"Yeah, well, I'm sorry," Katja said. "Boys are never worth it anyway. Nothing but trouble. Dogs, every one. Though maybe less intelligent."

"That's easy for you to say," Shayna responded.

"Just what do you mean by that?"

"You don't know what loneliness is."

"Hah!" Katja yelled after a moment – a moment that betrayed the sting. "If only that—"

"Not all of us were certified Physical-A in school."

"You're still sore about that after all these years? I know factory work is hell, but you think it's that great being a walking mannequin in retail? The beauty grading system is bullshit!"

"I've seen what bullshit it is. You can have any guy you want. You're that special. Not me. I only wanted one. I only *ever* asked for one. But that was too fucking much to ask."

The sound of Katja's labored breathing echoed in the stairs, but no words. Five floors above, Becker and Float were panting heavily between their indistinct mumblings. The sparks of streetlamps glittered through gaps in the boards.

"Not true," Katja said finally. "Not true."

"I saw you macking on Float last night. When will you get tired of him? Who'll be your next boytoy?"

"He—! It's—!" she stuttered, then said more quietly: "It wasn't my idea. You don't understand at all. He started it."

Right, Shayna thought through a cruel grin in the dark.

"Now he says he loves me. Or he *thinks* he loves me. He barely knows me. He loves his idea of me. I don't know what to do! It's not my fault he feels that way. He's just a kid. I think he might still be in school."

"No one's even ever *thought* they were in love with me," Shayna said.

"Oh yeah? Maybe you were just too dense to notice it! Ever think of that?"

"You mean Carl."

"No."

Shayna hurried on, burying her exhaustion under the force of her resurging rage.

Katja said "You should know, that girl who was with Tom is just some random girl. They never met before as far as I know, and he doesn't have any feelings for her. He just gets that way when he's sloshed. It's the only time he seems to have any interest at all, physical or emotional or otherwise. It puts a kink in the idea of him ever being in a serious relationship. All I'm saying is that you can't take it personally!"

Shayna had run herself completely out of breath. She clung to the railing, lungs heaving, sparkles swimming through her vision.

"He rejected me, too!" Katja shouted. "Remember that!"

"I don't give a rat's ass. The ocean is all full of fish for you. You'll just go out and find some other piece of meat."

"So will you, you dumbass! Wait and see!"

"*Yeah*," Shayna laughed. "*Wait.*"

The purple light shone on Katja squinting upward, not understanding. All the running had stopped. Everyone was waiting to catch their breath. Low thunder mumbled through the walls.

"I've never seen you like this," Katja said, her voice beginning to crack. "Is it really all just Tom? Or is there something you're not telling me?"

Shayna leaned over the railing and looked up into the spiraling flights. The urban sky's dim light glowed at the end, and the rain was starting to trickle down with it. She rubbed the tears out of her eyes and wondered what waited for her up there. She knew that Katja was right; this wouldn't be like the White Line. This was something more than merely dangerous. Something was waiting up there.

A strange instinct crept over her. Her fingers numbly unbuttoned the army coat's breast pocket and found the teeth. Without a thought, without a feeling, simply as if there were nothing more natural to do, she pushed her hair back and fastened the unholy necklace in place.

"*Espere*," she whispered to the dark. Then she stood up and kept going.

"Hey, I was your only best friend in the fucking world, last time I checked," Katja called, shaking her from some trance. "You can tell me. You know you might feel better if you told somebody. Have you told anyone?"

"No."

"So there *is* something!"

Shayna sighed and found herself saying "I just didn't want to die a virgin. That's all." She spat over the railing and watched the wad sink into the spiraling void.

Katja climbed on, rendered conspicuously wordless.

At the final end of all those squishing stairs, Shayna found the boys kneeling and panting in the pounding warm rain, perching as close to the edge of the roof as they could make themselves. A few bicycles and cars crawled like mites among the mazes of glimmering orange roads, and the din was breathing loud and deep. Pink clouds crawled across the water-heavy neon sky. From this height the deathtrippers could already see for miles in every direction, and the tower still loomed behind them.

"Holy," Becker wheezed.

"It didn't look so tall from the ground," Float said to the blinking red light up there in the clouds. "The spire must be twice the height of the building."

"At least," Katja said, squinting in the rain.

"I won't make it to the crown," Becker managed. "I'm... spent. I'm too tired."

"I knew this might happen," Katja said. She was narrating again, but this time it was more forced, and she was avoiding Shayna with her eyes. "I enlisted some help from Fish. I mean the Professor."

From the pocket of her jeans she produced a tiny plastic bag with four green pills inside. She gave the first one to Becker.

"What is it?"

"It's called Swatter. Comps use it on heavy missions. It's smooth. Not harsh. It won't make you feel hyper or jittery or anything. You just won't be able to get exhausted, no matter what you do, for a few hours. I think it's supposed to dull your pain response too."

Becker hesitated.

"I already tried it myself," Katja assured him. "You'll be okay. But if you want to turn back now, that's okay too. Really. No pressure."

Becker swallowed it. Float took his with a triumphant grin. Katja passed her water bottle around while she and Shayna took theirs, stoically.

Float gave Katja a look and a kiss on the cheek. He combed the rain out of his hair. He put his foot on the Tower's first cross-support and started hauling himself up. Becker's lungs appeared miraculously full of breath again, and he quickly followed. Katja pushed her rain-shined black hair over her ears and waited.

"Go ahead," Shayna said, not sure what she herself was waiting for.

"Together," Katja said.

They climbed for the crown.

It was an awkward ascent. Shayna might have worried had she thought about the complications of climbing back down, but in her mind there as no concept of a return trip. There were only the steel beams under her soggy boots or clenched in her aching hands.

"Shay," Katja said, shyly.

The rain made the beams slippery, but the rust helped. The horizontal supports were set too far apart at first to climb from one to the next, but the diagonals running between them were just shallow enough to walk very carefully up. With each successive tier the beams were set slightly closer together and the tower narrowed. With each tier her fear twisted itself more into the shape of sure-footed confidence, and though her breath and heart were still running much too fast, she felt her exhaustion lifting. The drug was working.

"Shay," said Katja.

The rain had soaked her to the bone. This time she knew never to look down. As long as she didn't, she existed in a world in which there was no ground – just an all-surrounding cosmos of rushing purple clouds, whirling sheets of hot rain, and a long steel angular path to a tarnished neon crown and a jewel of pulsating red.

"Shay," Katja said.

"What."

"Shay, you know *I* could love you."

Shayna felt the teeth dangling along her neck. She glanced at Katja hauling herself up onto an adjacent beam. Shayna only smoothed her wet hair back again and responded: "What do you mean?"

"I *mean*," Katja said with a short laugh, against the quivering of her voice. "I mean that you're beautiful! I mean that I... I like you. We could be more than friends. If you wanted that. If you're really in such a big freaking hurry."

Nothing occurred to Shayna to say except: "Since when?"

"Since forever. I thought I was pretty obvious. You never seemed interested. Did you really never see it? Did it never cross your mind at all?"

Shayna kept climbing without a word. Something was happening. The instinct from the stairwell was returning now. A feeling was washing over her in waves, like the rain, and it wasn't the drug. Something was wafting on the warm electric air.

"I'm just saying that if you don't want to be alone, you don't have to be," Katja called up. "You don't have to think so narrowly about love! Just think about it, okay? But, anyway, you're so much more beautiful than I know you give yourself credit for. There are a lot more fish in your sea than you think. I promise! I really wouldn't worry about dying a virgin, if I were you."

She heard herself say simply "I have less than two weeks to live. I have the blight."

A weirdly tranquil moment passed in the thickening rain.

"Blight?" Katja yelled. "How do you know?"

"I was diagnosed a week ago."

"I'm sorry."

"Save your pity," Shayna said, harshly.

Saying it had been easier than she'd imagined. Up here, it seemed like there were no secrets left worth keeping, no costumes left to wear.

"Christ, Shay! Are you—? I mean, can I—? I don't know what to—!"

"Then don't say anything," Shayna snapped. By now it wasn't that Katja annoyed her; it was that the conversation felt like a distraction to the surreal tranquility that was coming over her. The words were as distant as the ground. *Now there's nothing*, she thought or whispered – *now there's nothing but this moment. Nothing outside of this tower. And this is where the story ends. I know it. This is where everything is going to end. It's so close. As if I could just reach out and—*

There by her hand on the next beam, six black talons clutched the steel. They were thicker than her fingers and twice as long. Their razor-sharp points etched loud marks in the rust. The scale-plated flesh of the human-sized feet stood tall and rigid and glistening in the rain, and above them Shayna could not make herself look – but she could feel the hot rapid breath dripping from that monstrous serrated beak. She could feel its huge eyes burning through her paralyzed core. She could not breathe or think. She stayed frozen solid to the beams until there came an earsplitting shriek, the fluttering frenzy of gigantic wings, the flapping down-drafts pounding on her eardrums, and then nothing.

"Shay!" Katja called – and then she was there, just on the other side of her eyelids. "Shay, I'm here. Just breathe. Just breathe and focus on the light up there. Don't look down—"

"Did you see it?" Shayna shouted.

"What?"

"Did you *see* it?" she demanded, opening her eyes to glare.

"See what? I don't know what you're talking about!"

"*It,*" Shayna hissed. "That thing! The horrible bird!"

"I didn't see anything," Katja said. She scanned the empty air around them, even looking down for a moment, and confirmed: "Nothing. No bird."

Shayna looked at the beam where the talons had been. The scratches were still there, but indistinct.

"Shit," she wheezed. "Shit. Shit. It was real. I saw it. It was here."

"There's no bird around here. I'd be able to see it."

Shayna looked around and saw she was right, but she also knew it had been there. She knew it had been the same bird. It had been there that day in her apartment in the unfinished district.

"Could the Swatter be making you hallucinate?" Katja asked.

"You tell me!"

"Professor said it energizes you. Increases your awareness. Dulls pain response. That was it. He said there were no side effects. Not until withdrawal."

Shayna looked up into the red clouds as lightning flashed all the rusty beams a ghostly white. The whole tower seemed to shiver when the thunder finally arrived.

"Fuck it," Shayna said, and continued climbing even more ravenously than before. She could feel the rain soaking her back, dripping down her legs in her sagging pants or pooling in the elbows of her coat. This high up she could feel the faint swaying of the tower in the wind. The dead neon crown. The blinking red warning light. All of it was within her grasp. It was just another fifty vertical feet past the two boys' climbing behinds.

More lightning. This time the thunderclap made her stop and struggle to cover her ears as best she could without letting go. It rattled in her bones. It came rolling a second time and she found herself shouting against it at the top of her lungs what she was not even aware of thinking:

"*What am I worth?*"

Another flash. The thunder was more immediately now, even louder than before.

"What am I worth?" she screamed, and her voice was muted. With each scream she climbed harder. She burned the distance with her rage.

"Shay!" Katja was shouting from below.

Then Becker and Float were shouting from above. Cheering triumph. Float had reached the top to perch on the old neon logo and let his feet dangle.

View like God, Shayna thought, peering up. When the flash came it blinded her. A wave of pure heat washed through her body from where she gripped the beams. Over the ringing in her ears she could still hear the twisting metal, the splintering neon tubes, the chattering of the whole structure beneath her – as the crown, still glowing from the strike, wrenched free of its bolts and went down.

She felt the rush of air as it passed. A few shards of glass touched her back. She turned her head in time to catch one fleeting glimpse of Float, partly engulfed in his own smoke, his arms spread wide like wings and his feet together, clear the edge of the roof and disappear when she shut her eyes.

The sound of the debris finally hitting the ground rang out as loud as the thunder.

The tower stopped rattling.

Step by step, deaf and half-blind, she started the long way down.

PART 2:

ICE

12

The pink glow of dawn was stretching itself across the drying Tropolis. All the soot and garbage and bird shit that the storm had scoured away had finally begun to return to the surfaces and streets and everything felt newly born, though the turbulence of this renewal still rang out across the city in the rackets of the reconstruction crews, the gigantic engines, the robots, the stimmed-up shouting workers. Through nerves and veins now reeling from the unexpected shock of the drug, it was all torture to Shayna. Crashing wreckage, burning light, waves of choking dust. She was exhausted and halfway into the sleep of hypothermia, but each amplified sensation hit like an electric shock and kept her and Katja stumbling blindly onward through the urban wilderness, leaning on each other whenever they started to fall. They looked for a quiet way through the middle of it all.

"Where are we going?" Shayna asked.

"I know. But it's the only place I can think of. We can't make it anywhere farther away."

"Quiet *where?* Where is Becker?" She couldn't remember where they'd lost him.

"Here it is. The whacky monks."

Something cohered in the middle of the whole freezing, shouting mess. The heavy concrete frame of a door came into shocking focus as Shayna steadied herself against it. She found herself staring into the back of her own hand there, and became so deeply involved in every tiny cell that the color of her blood made her gasp when she finally noticed it. It was so bright. Her hands had never hurt as they scraped and blistered on the rusty beams, but now fine tendrils of pain were creeping in.

Katja yanked her inside and they shuffled together through a concrete space, between rows of pillars looming in a sleepy darkness. It was warm in there, and not so blinding or loud. Her senses began to clear, but not soon enough to stop her from tripping and falling against a passing door. It slammed open.

On the other side there were three men whose bald scalps shone in the fiery glow of dawnlight through red stained glass – whose bodies were wrapped in robes so black they could have been woven of pure shadow – whose eyes all turned harshly on the shivering intruders.

"S-sorry," Shayna said.

Katja said "We need help. B-blankets. Freezing. Withdrawal."

One of the sitting men jumped up and started for the door with hands ready for shoving.

"Grant," a voice said. It was like wind in dry grass. Now Shayna saw the fourth man behind the three, lying flat on a wooden slab, surrounded by an array of candles and small glittering objects. His ancient eyes were fixed on her now. A withered husk of a hand lifted up and waved inward, and the standing man reverently approached him and knelt to listen. Shayna's painfully heightened senses let her hear every word.

"Just strays," the man named Grant whispered. "Uninitiates. They're polluted. I'll remove them."

"No," croaked the splayed ancient, and pointed at Shayna. "Tell her to come closer. Look. Her wounds."

Grant turned and looked the intruder icily up and down, hesitating on the half-dried blood painted in aching palms and the old blood stain on her shirt between her ribs, where the teeth of her bike's sprocket had cut deeper than she'd realized the day before. She peeled the goggles from her forehead and felt the marks where the metal rims had been strapped too long against her skin.

Something changed in Grant. The coldness faded slightly.

The splayed old man said "It's a sign. The great order brought her."

"No, no," Shayna murmured. "I'm sorry. I really didn't—"

"Wait here," Grant told the madly shivering Katja as he pushed her outside and bolted the door. As he led Shayna closer to the slab where the old man lay, she kept hearing her watery boots squish against the tiled stones. She felt dirty and strange.

"Don't be afraid, child," whispered the man laying down. "Closer." The flesh was stretched thin over the bones that gazed sleepily up at her. She knew then, if she hadn't already, that these rasping breaths were his last.

"We're sorry we bothered you. It was an accident."

"There's no such thing. Do you know where you are? Do you know us?"

"You're the Urbanologers."

"I am the fifteenth High Lurker of the Urbanological Church of the Tropolis. Ravenly." His bony hand hesitated and reached up to indicate his collarbone.

She uneasily remembered the teeth that still dangled from the chain around her neck. Instantly she felt sick and reached back to undo the clasp. Ravenly seemed to half-protest with his eyes, but he kept staring at the charm until she uncertainly placed it in his hand and helped his emaciated arm to hold it over his sternum. He drew a deep, rasping breath. His lips drew as much of a smile of gratitude as they were capable of.

"Now," he said, "Tell me how I'll repay you for this."

Shayna said nothing. She tried to stop shivering.

"You seek something," he whispered.

"Just blankets. A bed. Shelter."

He shook his head. "More."

"What makes you say that?"

"It tells me. I can see for myself. Many things reveal themselves to me as I get closer to the crossing. Something is following you. Something terrible."

She remembered Float and felt the tears welling up again. "What's following me?"

He lowered his wrinkled eyelids and said: "There is.... a rip, full of music. There is a knight in black. He's both traitor and hero. A sword, pink. A golden circle. I see two transfigurations of the Devil. They are the friends of your friends. No-name and many-names."

There was so much certainty in his thin voice, but she had no idea what he was talking about.

"I see a gigantic bird," whispered his fading voice.

"What?" she gasped. "What did you say?"

He only peered knowingly back at her. She watched him close his eyes and become so still for a moment that she wondered if she'd just heard his dying words – and when she made out the shallow but persistent rise and fall of his chest, she felt something in herself collapse. Even if she'd only met him a moment ago, and only by accident, here in this tomblike space she felt as close to him as to anyone she had left. She lay her forehead down on the slab and stopped trying to hold back the tears. She found herself telling him everything: about the dream of noise and color, about the nightmare bird and the diagnosis and everything that had followed from it. She said it all in an unsteady whisper, without even knowing whether he was still lucid enough to hear a word she said – but when she looked up again, his eyes were open.

"Leave me now," he said.

Shayna wiped her face and backed away from the altar. She watched the dying man call Grant back and whisper something to him while another of the sitting men pushed her through the door and back into the dim hallway.

Katja was sitting there against the wall, hugging her knees for warmth, her eyes swimming in their sockets. "What happened?"

"I don't know."

She didn't know whether to go or stay. She knew they both needed to find some dry warmth, and soon. She could still hear the ear-splitting roar of the sweeping machines out there and her head ached with it, but she already felt the guilt of having tripped over something sacred. She lingered in the shadows, yearning to sleep.

It was just as she was bracing herself to pull Katja up and go back outside that a hand fell on her shoulder. Grant stood there like one of the pillars around him. The eyes under his luminous scalp bore disapprovingly down on her. Finally he said, uneasily: "Our departed High Lurker has given us his final instructions. You are to be taken care of. You'll have bed and food here at the monastery."

"What about Katja?"

"Temporarily," he said with a nod. One of the other bald men appeared and followed Grant's signal to help Katja up and lead her away. When they were out of earshot, Grant continued: "I hope you understand that this is not done. Taking the unclean into our sanctuary. We would never have allowed it if it were not his command."

"Ravenly?"

"Never speak the name of the dead unless you want to unrest his ghost."

"Sorry."

He passed her the necklace of teeth with a reverent hand and said "Consider that the first teaching of several, if you choose."

"What do you mean?" She put the teeth distractedly back in her pocket.

"He commanded us to help you. Share with you. On the strict condition that you reveal it to no one – no one else at all, you understand – we'll share our wisdom with you. Our most solemn secrets. You'll receive however much of our guidance as you ask for, for as long as your quest lasts."

"My quest? My quest for what?"

The robed man said solemnly: "The cure."

11

"There are a lot of things I need to teach you," Ruth Newman tells her daughter one day. She's at the sink, forcefully scrubbing the black stuff off of her hands. For as far back as Shayna can remember, her mother has always come home from the plant with these blackened hands. Blackened by what, she never knows – only that those hands must be scrubbed raw before they're allowed to touch anything. Shayna stares down into the graying water, wondering.

"Are you listening?" Ruth asks with surprising sharpness.

"Yes."

"Listen good, 'cause there's a lot. For the next week or two, I'm going to try to teach you everything I know. As much of it as I can."

Shayna squints up uncertainly. She watches her mother raise her hands up and let them drip. The black stuff is driven all the way down into the fine creases where it never leaves. It clings to a ring that glitters only faintly through its tarnish.

Ruth starts to say something, but only coughs shallowly into her upper arm, as quietly as she can. Every day now that cough is worse, and the weird stain behind her ear peeks out a little more through the hair she combs over it.

Finally she clears her throat and says "Some things I can just show you. Other things you need to memorize, because I know you're not old enough to understand. Just do your best. Just try to hold it all in your mind until you're older."

"That's crazy," Shayna says, rubbing her face.

Her mother kneels to look her in the eye. "It's not crazy. It's important. You need to know about sex, for one thing."

"Ew, mom."

"What, ew? You're twelve years old. You have your cycles. You must be mostly through puberty already, you know. God, I don't know why I didn't bring this up years ago. I mean, you haven't done it yet. Have you?"

"No."

"Listen, I know this is weird to talk about with your mom, but if you don't get it from me, you'll just get it from the vid, and that will fuck you right up. You don't want to end up like me, do you?"

"What do you mean?"

The mother sighs. She doesn't speak again until they're on the bus.

"You remember what you mean to me, right?" she tells her daughter, quietly. "You remember how you changed everything for me?"

"Yes," Shayna answers stoically.

Ruth's voice creaks in places as she says "I know I've told you this all before, but I need to say it one more time. For myself. Because I'd have died a long time ago if you hadn't come along. Those seven months you grew in me were the hardest of my life. I thought about ending myself, you know. I did a lot in those days. Finally I decided I'd wait till you were out – and we almost both died when you did come. You remember how small you were? Remember what the medic said you were the size of? Remember?"

"A tallboy," Shayna answers irritably.

"A tall can of beer, yep. Long and round and kind of yellowish. He said I should name you after the brand. My girl, *Golden Times*. Maybe just G.T. for short. He was already filling out the papers that way when I came to."

"I know."

"But when I held you for the first time, that was it. It all changed. Every last little thing. Because I loved you, and I knew I had to live. Just like that."

Shayna stares at her feet and reddens slightly.

Her mother wraps her arms around her and squeezes briefly. Then she wipes her eyes and says "All right, I'm done. Thanks for letting me tell you all that."

Shayna nods and looks out the window.

"You're glad I didn't name you G.T., right?"

"Yes."

"He was just about to write that in. If I'd taken one more second to wake up, you'd be G.T."

"I know."

"Men can be that awful," Ruth says, dimming her tone. "Most of them are. They'll do worse than name you after bum wine, if you let them. God, if you learn anything from me, make it that. Don't ever think you need anybody. A guy who won't take you straight to hell in a hammock is a rare kind."

Shayna swallows hard.

"If you're into boys, I mean. If not, that's okay too." Ruth pauses her speech, but keeps staring. "Well?"

"Well, what?"

"I'm just curious. Like if, you know, maybe you like girls instead, or both."

"Why do you think I like girls?"

"I don't think anything either way. But you are kind of a tomboy, right? There's nothing wrong with that! I'm just curious, though. We never talk about these things."

"I'm not a tomboy."

"I just mean you don't to dress as, you know, girly as the other girls your age. When we go to the bins you don't like what I pick out. You always go for the loose-fit stuff. You don't wear any makeup."

"I just don't need to get into a beauty contest with everyone, okay?" She thought bitterly: *I could never win.* "I don't *like* anybody, okay?"

"It's nothing to be ashamed of, you know! Liking somebody."

"I'm not ashamed. I just don't get why you're asking me all these questions all of a sudden and telling me all this."

The mother's playful grin drifts away on a slow sigh, and her eyelids lower, braced for some shock to come. In that moment everything darkens and sheds its color. The air congeals and the city past the window becomes a muted void.

"I never think about this moment," Shayna tells her mother, who now turns translucent and blurry before her eyes. "But I did what you said. I waited. I was careful. It didn't help."

"I'm sorry," says the apparition.

"That it didn't help? Or for leaving me?"

The image continues to dim, losing definition. Shayna knows she'll be conscious again soon whether she wants to be or not. She knows she'll probably forget this feverish, drug-addled dream the moment her real eyes open. And yet, as if any of it were really happening, she pauses in thought when the ghost asks her:

"I hope you can forgive me for it some day."

As the last shape bleeds into nothingness, she answers: "Never."

When something latched onto her toe she expected to see a beak – but when she startled awake she found herself alone in the narrow room except for the blurry shape of a young girl standing at the foot of the bed. After a long squinting moment, she recognized her.

"Cass, it's you." Shayna groaned as grogginess hit her in a wave. The light in the window was dim and cool. She peered at it through the water in a clear plastic cup as she struggled to drink.

Cass said nothing. She rocked her head slightly from side to side and bit her lower lip in her characteristic way, her eyes fixed on nothing in particular.

"Do you remember me?" Shayna asked. "Your name is Cass, isn't it? Katja's sister? We met a long time ago. I'm a friend of your big sister."

"Fish," said Cass. "Fish-ish-ish."

"No, I'm Shayna."

Cass said nothing.

"Is she here?" Shayna thought to ask. "Is Katja here? Is she okay?"

Cass seemed to ignore the question. Then suddenly the head-rocking stopped. She looked hard into Shayna's eyes, leaned in close and whispered: "*Fow up, three down, fwoating down, fwoating down.*"

"Four up. Three down. Floating down."

Cass nodded.

"That's what you were trying to tell her," Shayna said. She shuddered and gripped the blankets tighter to herself. "You were trying to warn her that Float would die. You did see the future."

Cass went back to biting her lip.

"Is she okay? Are Katja and Becker okay?"

"Oak hay," Cass said. "Sweep."

Shayna felt small hands softly lay down on her eyelids.

When she woke up again, the only sickness she felt was a crushing hunger for food and nicotine. The light in the window had changed back to how it had been when she'd first lay down in that bed, and she realized just how long she'd been asleep. Her phone's clock confirmed her dread.

"Monday," she groaned as she leaned up.

With the blanket wrapped around herself she went to the window. Her clothes, splayed across the warm rooftop just outside, were all dry. As she pulled the threadbare and still blood-stained old shirt over her head, she uneasily remembered the strange encounter with Cass. As she laced up her boots she remembered what Grant had said. A cure.

She finished dressing and started out, but her hand hesitated on the knob. With a sigh she pulled the gun out of her pocket and contemplated its weight for a moment before sliding it under the foot of the mattress. To the new twinge of nakedness left in her empty pocket, she thought: *enough death for a while.*

This time her senses were much clearer as she stepped out into the monastery's main hall. Huge pillars loomed in the dim light of dirty skylights high above – stepping up to one, she realized that it wasn't a stone column as she'd thought, but instead a section of a plastic utility pole. Its weathered surface was covered in layer after layer of graffiti in spraypaint and black marker and wheat-pasted paper.

Down in the shadows at the end of the line of columns she spied an altar draped in ragged velvet, where one of the monks was dealing with the candles. She went to him.

"Hi," she said awkwardly. "Is Grant around here somewhere?"

The monk turned and began to open his mouth.

"Don't try to talk to him," said Grant. "He's taken a vow of silence."

The silent one sighed as Grant stepped up to them. Grant's robe was no longer that simple black: now it was encircled by a yellow stripe. Another monk was at his side.

"I realize we never properly introduced ourselves," he said. "I am the Sixteenth head of the Urbanological Church of the Tropolis. High Lurker Grant."

"I'm Shayna."

The High Lurker motioned to the monk at his side and said "This is my Vice Lurker, Kelroy. And that there—" he pointed to the silent one "—is Lurker Gomad."

Gomad waved meekly.

"Come with me," the High Lurker said to her. "There's one more thing Our Departed asked of me."

She nodded goodbye to Gomad and followed where Grant and Kelroy walked.

"First," Grant said uneasily, "Tell me. You've heard of the Urbanologers. What do you believe we are?"

"Monks?"

"Scholars. Disciples. Healers. What do you know of our ways? Our teachings?"

Shayna cleared her throat and said "You believe that the city, the Tropolis, is... a living thing, right? You treat it as—"

"Not a living thing," Grant said. "God."

Kelroy made a sweeping motion to indicate the lines of utility poles throughout the space. He said "What do you see?"

She shrugged. "Utility poles."

"Nothing more?"

"Lots of posters and stickers and tags."

"What the uninitiated see as chaos, a jumble of words and symbols, we recognize as a secret and holy language."

"Well, what does it say?"

"It's more than just a written language to be read. It is the emergent divine. These poles are the medium for traces of Its very thought process – transmitted subliminally, through the hands of taggers and the knives of stencillers. We bring the poles here and set ourselves to the work of interpretation."

The three of them descended a flight of worn concrete steps, into a space lit only by sparse lines of candles – though there was an eerie light up ahead.

"So you believe the Tropolis is a God," Shayna echoed meekly. "A God that speaks to you through show bills."

"Not *a* God," Grant corrected reverently. "*The one* God. Perfect and all-surrounding. It is everywhere and everything, and we are all a part of It. Are we not?"

"Hmm."

"We are the cells of its divine body," Kelroy said. "The blood of its astral veins."

"We are all tied into its structure, the Great Order," said the High Lurker. "It gives life to each of us. And far more than that to those who know how to ask for more."

They had arrived at a large double-door of yellowish wood. That eerie light was seeping out from within. Grant placed his hands on the handles, but did not turn them.

"This room has never been looked into by anyone who has not solemnly taken the Tropolis into himself and dedicated life and soul to its sanctity. Have you any faith? Do you believe on the City?"

Something droned in the silence.

"I don't know," she said honestly. "But I, uh, keep an open mind."

Grant sighed and uttered something under his breath, profanity or prayer she couldn't tell. Then he opened the doors onto the gigantic neon altar.

She was too blinded to see much of anything inside, but while the doors were open she made out a number of objects on the blue-burning shelves. A plastic owl. A pair of red sneakers. An ancient dip pen. A croissant. And... was that... a sex toy?

The doors shut. In the squinting candlelight, the High Lurker reverently held out his hand to Shayna, and something shone faintly in his palm. Something rectangular.

"He asked that you have this. But you must take absolute care of it and return it to us when the time comes. It's one of the holiest artifacts known to us. Men have spent their lives seeking it."

Shayna picked it up and inspected it. "A pre-pay Metro pass?" It was a little scuffed.

"Not a Metro pass," Kelroy said. "*The* Metro pass. Blessed by the Hand of the Tropolis. The greatest of the divine powers reside in the most inconspicuous and common of forms."

"I'll take your word for it."

"Don't. See for yourself. Use it."

Shayna nodded meekly and put it in her pocket.

"Now," said the High Lurker, "You must leave, and we must return to the body to continue our vigil. He should be approaching the sidpa bardo."

She followed them back through the dim corridor and up the worn steps. "You talked about a cure. Is there a cure?"

Grant said "For blight? Of course there is. Charity Center has it. The Insiders have it."

"But for me. I'm too old for Charity, and I'm an Outsider."

"Indeed."

"Is there a cure for *me?* Where can I find it? Where do I even look?"

"If Our Departed High Lurker knew the answer, he took that wisdom with him." Grant sighed. "But he seemed to believe you could find it. The Tropolis hides within itself limitless and splendorous secret things. All things comes to those who ask in the proper way."

"Which is?"

They had arrived at the door to the dying room. The High Lurker said quietly "I told you we're bound to help you however we can. We can discuss it later, after the vigil. But for now, nothing."

With overstated silence, he and Kelroy moved through the door and closed it behind them. A bad smell wafted in their wake.

Gomad glanced up from the altar he was attending. He made feeble eye contact with her and then turned back to what he was meditating on. A tiny portable television was sitting on the altar, beaming the ghostly outline of a beer commercial.

"Weird," she whispered as she left.

Cranes had risen. Steel mandibles had come to digest the broken walls. Bodies had been found and burned. In the warm and windless morning, the dissonant music of reconstruction was ringing through the bright yellow sky.

Shayna bought herself a pack of normal cigarettes at the first crummy little shop she stumbled across, then perched on a curb to feed her addiction while she surveyed the area. She memorized the local Metro numbers and tried to get a sense of direction. There to the north she spied the only useful landmark: the uncrowned steel tower, rising like a gash into the sun's corona.

Her hesitant phone call to Katja went unanswered. Busy at work, she guessed, though after a moment she found it hard to imagine working on a day like this. Especially in retail – but Shayna couldn't tell how Float's death had affected even herself. How would Katja be taking it?

Shayna found a secluded spot to count how much money she had left on her. The only thing she really wanted to know was how long she could put off going back to Tom's apartment for the rest of it, and her bass, and the other stuff. It wouldn't be hard to avoid Tom himself – she knew all the times he'd be away at the Heaps – but the smell of cloves alone would be hard enough to deal with.

Her fingers closed idly around the artifact the Urbanologers had given her. She took a closer look at the Metro pass, turning it in the light, holding it against the sun, but still she could find nothing unusual about it at all. The blue-glowing digits on its face read 491 dollars of credit. That much would probably buy a few trips across Angelis. At most it might get her to the next closest sector of the Tropolis, maybe to the outlands of Bay sector, but not nearly as far as the inner circle around Bay Cology.

A bus grunted to a stop at the curb. She didn't recognize its number.

"Blessed by the hand of the Tropolis," the High Lurker had said. What the hell did that mean?

Only one way to find out, she thought, and climbed up through the hissing doors. She and the driver eyed each other distrustfully as she swiped the card through the reader. The machine trilled its satisfaction. She sat down in back and inspected the card again.

No, that couldn't be right. She questioned her memory. She got off at the next stop and sprinted to the next bus, where she squeezed through the door and swiped the card a second time. She hid it under her sleeve until she could huddle in the shadows at the very back and prove her excited suspicion: the blue-glowing digits hadn't gotten any lower. It was stuck at 491.

The Metro pass, she thought, and hid it in her pocket. She laughed to herself as she traced its frayed plastic edges with her fingers, knowing them now as the frayed edges of the power to freely travel to any point in the entire Tropolis. Bay Sector. Coover Sector. Hell, she thought – York Sector. How was this possible? Where in God's name had it come from?

Or, she thought, *where in the Tropolis's name had it come from?* But could she really buy that? It had to be a glitch, no matter how miraculous.

There would be plenty of time for wonder later, anyway. For now all she wanted was to push the pass to its nonexistent limit. *Take me anywhere*, she thought at it. *Take me to the very end of this stupid world. That must be as good a place as any to begin my blind quest for a cure, if it exists.*

The cure.

She leaned her head into the glass and felt it rumble the bones of her head as the sunny Tropolis outside turned more unfamiliar with each fleeting block. She felt the bus climb a flyway onramp and accelerate past 120, and smiled a little as her dream took her.

For a moment she knew it had been there again – the white void, the musical sound, the rip opening into vibrant blue, and finally the first inklings of something more – but before she could make it out she was snapping awake.

The window smacked her in the face as the bus decelerated. On the other side of the glass, the sparse lanes had mutated into a jostling river of cars, and their colored exoskeletons formed an ocean in the streets below. The whole scene was eerily dark even though the sky in all directions was still burning its bright morning yellow. She squinted in disbelief until one look through the opposite window told her where she was. The crystalline facets of the Cology were looming too high to see. All around in their unimaginably vast shadow, in irrigated turf and polished mirror-glass spires spreading out as far as the eye could see, was the fertile Inner Ring. Greentowne.

She groaned and reached instinctively for her cigarettes as she wished she'd been more specific in her wish: *take me anywhere except Greentowne*. But the Urbanologers had said something about listening to the secret and muddled language of the city. *Maybe this is part of it*, she thought. *Maybe there's some divine order to the misfortune of coming here.*

The hissing doors opened onto streets that were unsettlingly clean. Short little cubic bushes were everywhere, brandishing their thorns toward hunched-over passers-by. Everyone moved in a hurry. Everyone was covered in the same shade of light iridescent gray, as if to blend into the walls around them. No Greentowner seemed to ever make eye contact with any other, but Shayna knew they were all watching her, whenever they thought she wasn't watching back. Their eyes in her peripheral vision shone like the tips of small knives from within the furrowed sockets of such well-fed faces. Noses that wrinkled and nostrils that flared. Hands that stuffed into pockets. They were all packed against each other like sardines, but they passed around her with room to spare.

A few of blocks down, just past the edge of the Cology's immense shadow, she found a bus stop that said it would take her back to the outer Tropolis and eventually back out to the coast, near the Regulator plant – not ideal, but it would do. She was squinting as she read the sign in the sudden daylight. It said she had twenty minutes to kill.

So she climbed a series of wide concrete steps, up into the grassy geometry of a high overlook. There were benches up there, and pay-telescopes on poles, all gathered only to stare up into the featureless icy facets looming above. The yellow sun was perched just above the Cology's upper slopes, tracing out the otherwise-invisible crosshatched seams in the crystal. It stood there like a white glass anvil, a mile high, five miles to a side. A squat angular hourglass whose perfect opacity gave no suggestion of how much time was left. She knew she could have stared up at it for a year without ever getting used to it. It wouldn't fit into the imagination. It resembled no earthly thing at all, and surely that had been the first principle of its designers – knowing that, to the people of a world like this one, nothing could be more hypnotic or more desperately alluring than the otherworldly.

What could be inside there? she wondered, pointlessly. The overarching walls betrayed nothing. The pay-telescopes were all worthless. It was the one sacred question for which not even the television had an answer.

She was feeding bills into the insanely expensive pay-fountain when she noticed it, set apart in an adjoining area of the Company plaza: an obelisk, arms' width and twice as tall, made of what could only be the same stuff as those impossible walls. Cology glass. When the water ran out, she went to it in a hypnotic daze. When she touched it, her fingers slid across it without a trace of friction, without the oil of a fingerprint, without anything. When she put it between her and the sun she saw the whole thing glow in a deeply alien way: no discernable point of sun or shadow passed through. Just featureless, perfectly distributed light. It had no shadow.

There was a plaque posted at the foot of the obelisk. The only word she read was "unbreakable." At this she squinted and felt strange in her stomach. The music in her head had dried up.

Some childish but insurmountable instinct made her pick up a stray piece of gravel and try to scuff the Cology glass with it, but it was just as she feared: no matter how hard she pushed, the rock couldn't make one hairline scratch in the icy smooth surface. In fact, there was no trace of imperfection on the entire obelisk, neither scratch nor dent nor dirt, and by the concrete at its base it looked to have been standing there for years. Maybe decades. She shivered.

"Incredible, isn't it?" said a voice from behind.

Shayna jumped a little as she turned. The man who stood there took his eyes off of her and instantly gazed away into the depths of the Cology. His face was old, gaunt, bloodless. The narrow brim of his hat had the look of having once been thicker and straighter, like most of the material of his suit, and the collar was high up and locked tight against his sagging neck.

"Incredible, isn't it, I said," he repeated, and cleared his throat. He still wouldn't meet her eyes directly, but she could see a look in his. He looked as though he felt courageous for speaking to her.

"What, you mean the Cology?"

"But what's most, what's…." He cleared his throat again. "Do you know what's most incredible of all?"

She looked between him and it. She opened her mouth to answer.

"It's open to everyone," the stranger interrupted. "Anyone can live Inside, no matter where he starts out in life, no matter how low and poor. No matter how badly off. If you're smart and sufficiently dedicated, you'll get Inside. It's incredible."

She turned away and sighed. Dim light was radiating from within the icy walls of the Cology, changing the color of the shadows below. The innermost buildings of Greentowne were all painted in eerie monochrome. She stared out into the luminous geometry and told herself it was better to bite her tongue than to start contradicting strangers. His mind was made up. What good would it do to argue? But when the running count of her remaining days flitted through her head, she felt something shift within her. Suddenly she could only think: *What good will it do to stay quiet?*

She turned back to him and asked "Have you ever known an Outsider who got in?"

The stranger looked caught off guard. The question hit him harder than she'd expected.

"Well, I know they do," he said.

"How do you know that? How about you give me the name of any Outsider who's even *seen* Inside. Or one Insider who's ever left."

"You're wrong. Anyone can achieve— become an Insider. All it takes is dedication, and honest hard work, and prudence. It gives us hope— for all, it gives, hope. An example of self-betterment for us all to rise up to, it vitally sustains... it sustains society. It's everything. You see."

Shayna reached for her cigarette and said: "Then why aren't *you* in there?"

"I will be," he said instantly. "I will be before long. Why? Because I work hard. To advance myself. I'm not a slothful runt like you are."

Shayna looked at him.

The stranger glanced shakily around a few times, then walked off in a hurry – and as he did his high-mounted shirt collar slipped down for a moment, revealing a cluster of raised brownish blotches, rising toward his ear like the fingers of a hand. Blight.

When he was gone, the lone ragged girl from the outer Tropolis sighed, re-adjusted the goggles on her forehead, and slumped down on the nearest bench to stare out across the landscape of neat vegetation and painted-over graffiti.

Something landed hard on her shoulder. She half-expected to find the worn stranger perching there again, but the hand she found was encased in a black armored glove. Her blood ran cold in the shadow of the towering wall of ice as she looked up into the face of the comp, and his heavy features glowered wordlessly down.

He pointed in turn to a series of poles. Each one held a camera and a sign that said NO LOITERING. Then he said "Would you mind telling me what you're doing here, miss?"

A cluster of conversing Greentowners on the other side of the plaza had fallen silent and were now watching intently. Shayna had noticed them standing idly around when she entered the plaza, so – ignoring the pounding of her heart – she pointed at them and said "I'm doing what they're doing."

"There's no loitering here."

"Then what are *they* doing?"

She couldn't believe herself as she said it. All he had to do was swipe her ID through his scanner or check the contents of her coat and she'd live out the last few weeks of her miserable life in a community service camp. *What the hell am I doing?* she thought, but there was a heat growing in the pit of her stomach. There was some threshold she'd crossed.

"There's no loitering here," he repeated. He sounded almost surprised.

"Look. Over there. Loitering."

"I have to ask you to leave the premises." His fingers were ticking on his stun baton.

She stood up, but not fast enough. His metallic hand clamped tightly around her arm and maneuvered her down the tripping stairs to the sidewalk. She didn't resist. She kept her hands out of her pockets. She just stared back at the staring Greentowners and went where the comp took her, until she felt the blood rush back into her fingertips when his grip released.

The loiterers in their silvery black and blue clothes stood there at the top of the stairs, smoking and watching suspiciously. The comp stood like a body-armored wall between them and her, towering two feet over her with his arms folded and his various weapons gleaming in the shifting gray shadows of the Cology. His harsh blue eyes watched her every move as she drifted back into the monochromatic crowd.

You got away, she told herself. *You're safe. Get on the bus.* By the time she reached the corner, however, the heat had only grown. She felt it pushing on the walls of her chest as she stood there, trying not to let herself look back. She cleared her throat and some phlegm entered her mouth.

She turned back and walked along as casually as she could, her eyes fixed straight ahead and away from the plaza stairs, although she was watching the watchers in her peripheral vision. She passed the comp without a glance up. Then in a rapid movement she whipped her head to the side, spat straight onto the Company logo on his chest and bolted into the crowd as fast as her legs would carry her. His shouts and the gigantic thudding of his boots followed her as she dove into the thickest part of the crowd, too fast for it to part around her. She swam hard against the swirling morass of silvered silk and plastic briefcases, the men with their harshly cropped hairlines and the women their razor-sharp eyebrows, all of them bracing themselves and working hard to ignore her. She only hoped that, being so small, her inertia would be less than his – and it seemed to work. She darted into the next alley and slid into the narrow chasm between two dumpsters. She knelt with her back pressed against the hard wall and, trying to keep her breath quiet, peeked around the side just in time to watch the comp thunder past.

His gun was drawn.

The concrete at her back was suddenly harder, more real. The now-familiar high of deathtripping surged back over her, but it only made her feel sick. She hadn't meant it like that this time. She'd had no idea.

Her ears were ringing as she lit a fresh cigarette with a wildly shaking pair of hands. After a moment she realized the ringing was only her phone. Carl.

"What do you want," she answered. She mentally noted that the battery was low.

"We have to talk. I need to see you." His voice was unusually soft.

"Can't talk now. I'm in Greentowne."

It had dawned on her that the comp might spot her if she tried to make it back to the bus stop. For that matter, all the comps in the whole area would be looking out for her now. The cameras were everywhere.

"What the hell are you doing in Greentowne?"

"Trying to make it out alive."

"Hold tight then because I want to show you something really wicked."

"I've already seen it," she said through a grimace. "Remember that day at the reservoir."

"No, something else. Tell me exactly where you are."

She wondered why he wanted to know. Could it really hurt to tell him? She kept her head down as she crept to the edge of the alley and read the name of the nearest intersection.

"Hearst and forty. In the alley."

Down the block, floating on the top of the river of gray, the comp's head turned. She darted back between the dumpsters amid a gust of hushed profanity.

"Got it," Carl said. "I'm close. Be there in twenty."

"What—?" she started, but he hung up. "That's great, Carl."

She was as good as trapped here anyway. Nothing to do but stay ducked down between the dumpsters and wait for the shakes to pass. She had some time to try and clear her mind, and no shortage of clearing to do – but the smell only reminded her of the Heaps, and all she could think about from then on was Float. He'd be there by now. Whatever the reconstruction crews had found at the Tower's foot would be scattered into the poisoned hills with all the other undocumented casualties of the superstorm.

Now she remembered what she'd really wanted when this all started, when she'd so desperately caught that bus to Tom's apartment that night. Her real desperation had been to find a distraction from her thoughts. *Clear my head?* she thought. *There's no clearing this. My head was clear all that time before the diagnosis. Fuck. Maybe this is better.*

She thought: *the need to avoid thinking must always rise with the amount of shit there is to think about.* She wanted anything but to think about Float. Tom. Blight. A crack of lightning. The red glitter of open zipper teeth. Blood that turns into poison.

Something shook her from her thoughts, rumbling in the ground beneath her. A burp of diesel perfumed the air and the whole alley outside the dumpster chasm was suddenly throbbing in yellow light. She scrambled fearfully to her feet and got ready to run – but Carl's face was there, squinting through a hexagonal windshield. He swung the van's door half-open, smashing it into the side of the dumpster, and shoved his head awkwardly up to shout at her:

"You can drool over my wicked wheels when we've made it the fuck out of Greentowne. Jump in and buckle up! Chop-chop!"

The passenger-side door opened just wide enough for Shayna to duck underneath and squeeze through. As soon as she had strapped herself into the seat he mashed his foot down on the gas. The machine lurched forward and then instantly choked and died.

"Fucking—!" Carl screamed as he resurrected the engine.

"Calm down!" Shayna yelled as the jolt of acceleration knocked her back into the seat cushion.

The throngs of gray parted in a frightened hurry for the orange siren lights as the van barreled into the busy street and swerved on screaming rubber. Carl cut off three cars and a bus on his rabid way to the flyway onramp. Horns blared. Bumpers crunched. The inertia was like a punch in the face.

"I said calm the fuck down!" Shayna shouted.

"It's okay now," Carl said ruggedly. "We're safe now. We made it out."

Shayna craned her neck to look back and survey the damage – but all she could see was the vast river of rushing concrete, the mirrored spires, the geometry of turf and the looming Cology all mercifully receding.

"Aren't you gonna thank me for saving your butt?" Carl said, taking his eyes well off the road to peer at her. He took one hand off the wheel to scratch at his groin.

"I didn't ask to be saved."

"Well yeah. Girls never do. That's the point."

"The point of what?"

"Being a guy."

Shayna sank uneasily into her seat.

Carl said: "What do you think of my wicked wheels?"

"This what they give you to run errands at the Regulator plant?"

"*No*," Carl said defensively. "No."

"Then what, you're telling me you own this?"

A horn blared somewhere on the roaring flyway. Carl straightened the wheel and bit his lip. "No, it's for my other job. My job as a FIFE."

"A fwhat?"

"Fiber-optics Infrastructure Field Engineer."

"What does that mean?"

He reached under his seat and whipped out a green steel cube with dangling wires. He tossed it into Shayna's lap for her inspection.

"I go around replacing those things. They're everywhere. Buried. They're always wigging out."

"What do they do?"

"No idea," he said, fumbling for a cigarette. "So sometimes I get to drive the Chickmobile."

"The what?"

"You know, for picking up chicks. They – we take it out cruising on Saturday nights. Hot chicks everywhere can't resist the wicked wheels. It's just like flypaper."

"This piece of crap van?" She chuckled.

"Don't laugh. I'm serious." And he was, or he was trying to be. He was disheveled. He mumbled: "They say it's just like fucking f-flypaper."

"Who's 'they'?"

Carl swallowed and hurriedly said "Onlookers."

A voice crackled out of the box on the dashboard, saying: "Yo, Spaz."

Carl twisted his fists on the steering wheel and ignored it. Shayna studied the redness in his furrowed face.

"Come in, Spaz," the radio repeated. "Sir Spaz. Spazmeister. Captain Spazzotron. Answer the damn radio, Carl."

Carl took the receiver down from the ceiling and growled into it "What."

The radio said: "What's the word about that crap node in Greentowne?"

"Just a loose plug. It's good now. But, uh, I'm reading another dead one now. Out on Corson. That's node ID 85-35-Q."

"That one looks just fine on my end," the radio said. "You haven't gone rogue on us, have you? You're not out there... picking up hot chicks, are you?" A chorus of muffled laughter was just audible in the background.

"Fuck off, Gomez. Over and out."

The air in the cab went dead with the radio. Carl pursed and un-pursed his lips in silent pensivity.

Shayna leaned her head into the glass and stared out into the now-comforting dust of Outer Angelis – where things had shadows and nothing was unbreakable, and there were not so many cars. She didn't care, but she asked anyway: "Where are we going?"

"There's something else I want to show you."

They rolled on for half an hour, barely speaking. It was not a normal silence. It congealed between them, tightening the air until both had cracked their windows just to breathe. When Carl finally spoke up again, Shayna could hear the effort in his voice.

"Why'd you go?"

Shayna leaned her head up from the glass and said "Huh?"

"When you went into exile a year ago. Why. I want to know why."

She sighed. "Was it a whole year?" She shrugged.

"No. Tell me. I need to know."

"It wasn't about *you*, okay?" She tasted the words for their truth afterward. "I don't even remember. It was a crazy time. A lot of things changed."

Carl sighed bitterly.

"A lot of things were changing for all of us," Shayna continued. "We stopped going to Balboa's basement. We moved to the Green Room. And then I left. And then Balboa joined the comps, apparently. And Katja invented deathtripping."

"And Tom found his inner slut."

Shayna gritted her teeth and pressed her face back into the glass.

"So a lot of things changed. But why did *you* leave?"

"I can't explain it. I just... lost my taste for people."

Carl looked darkly ahead into the road.

"That's insane," Shayna said. "I know it's insane. That I could do that. Just retreat into that castle of mine. Just work all day and then go home and watch the TV billboard across the street until I fell asleep, never really talking to anybody. For a whole year. For who even knows how long. It makes me sick now just to think about it, but it happened somehow. One day I just..." She sighed. "I just stopped."

Carl uttered nothing as he turned the van down an offramp, and a dead neighborhood rose up around them. The air was heavy with the must of abandonment.

Suddenly he said: "But *what* caused it. What stopped you. What changed everything."

"I told you I don't know. There were a lot of things. I don't remember."

"Nobody does. Except for me."

His nostrils were flared and his knuckles were white along the wheel. He mashed a button on the dashboard and a chain-link gate opened for them just in time. They barreled past it and down into a black mouth in the ground, snuffing out the day, leaving the headlights to play across bare concrete and oily puddles receding into a tunneling void. The phantom smell of warm chemicals and sewage fluttered through Shayna's nose.

Carl killed the engine and plunged them into fizzling darkness until the searing white beam of a huge flashlight exploded in his hand. Their watery footsteps echoed. There was a ladder recessed into the wall.

"It's just up here," Carl said as he started climbing.

Shayna grabbed the rungs and looked up to see his bulbous silhouette cast in that dangling white electric glow. She followed until she was fully out of breath, then farther, until she imagined a hundred vertical feet of shaft behind her now; until she was promising herself that this was the very last enormous height she would ever climb. What was this place?

"What the hell is this place?" she called up.

"Almost there," Carl panted. Then: "Hah!"

A metal hinge creaked up there and then strong yellow light flooded down, making her squint. Carl's outline gave way to daylight and the crazed screeching of seagulls.

"Get off! Bastards."

"Are they gone?"

"Yeah. Come up."

The sloshing of waves echoed down, and a salty wind sang through the mouth of the manhole. Then she was standing there at a broken railing set along a concrete ledge, surrounded on all sides by the surging gray of Corson Bay fifty feet below. Beyond, the sun-drenched Tropolis stretched out its arms, and between the hills of its hands the flat inscrutability of the Pacific stretched into infinity. The afternoon's dirty clouds were curled around the warm disk of the sun like wrinkles around an eye.

"That's some kind of beacon for ocean navigation," Carl said, indicating a little tangle of metal boxes and pipes by planting one foot on them. "That's what this place is. A lot of those fiber-optics nodes I showed you are tied up here."

"Well, it's nice."

"I needed to talk to you."

Shayna waited.

"Katja told me," he said.

"Yeah? Told you what?"

"That you have the blight and you're going to die soon."

For a moment the whole landscape tightened like a vice around her. She turned away from him and let a pressurized sigh out to sea.

"So it's true?" he asked quietly.

"I guess I forgot to tell her to keep her mouth shut about that. Who else knows?"

"But-! Why did you keep it from everyone? How long have you known about this?"

"A week. I just didn't feel like shouting it to the world, okay?"

"Well why the hell not?"

"It's *my* doom, Carl. I'll deal with it how I want to, and I don't need people reminding me about it! Giving me grave looks. Treating me all kinds of special ways. I just don't need to think about it so fucking much. I just wanted to enjoy the time I had left, and talking about it with everybody wasn't going to help that, was it?"

"So you just *lied* to all of us about it? You just told the biggest lie of omission ever told between us?"

"Fuck you!"

Carl stopped. He sank into himself and rubbed his hands over his face and said "This isn't even what I brought you here to talk about."

Shayna hurriedly wiped her eyes before he looked again. The wrinkled sun glowered down. Gulls were circling back. She wanted to leave.

"I just wanted to talk about what happened. Before you went into exile. About how it used to be."

"I don't."

"I mean the music. I wanted to talk about the music."

His mumbling, tortured uncertainty had faded. His voice was suddenly heavy and resigned.

"You mean our tribute band? You mean the Smurge's music."

"Yes."

She shrugged her shoulders. "What about it?"

"I keep thinking about that night in the Green Room, when the Power Elite came on. When we listened to Machinery Anthem together. I saw you. You remember how it used to be, between all of us, when we still had the band. When it fell apart, they forgot everything. Tom. Katja. *Balboa.* They lost it. They lost the music, and now just look at them. But *I* still have it, and I saw it in you that night. We, *we* didn't forget!"

"Yeah? What didn't we forget?"

"You had your bass on your back that night. I still have my guitar, and I've been practicing. I never stopped. Did you?"

Fragments of that stupid love song started to roll through her head again. She grimaced and shook them out and said "If you want to talk to me about how great those days were, you're the one who's forgetting things."

"Like what?"

"Like, the original Smurge was a four-person group. So, you pretended to be Bruce Fain, Katja played Clara Ruthless, Balboa played The Bomber, Tom played Jon. Who did I play, Carl? No one. I was no one."

He shook his head rapidly and corrected "No, you don't understand. God, no, the band was always shit. I mean *us*. We were the only ones who were any good back then anyway. We could start something new, just you and me. We could make our own tribute band, with *you* as Clara Ruthless, like you should have been in the first place."

She hesitated to say "For a week or two, you mean."

"I had this idea before I knew."

"Great."

"But what does it matter. You're the one who didn't want to be treated specially. And if I..." He kept clearing his throat. "If I only had two weeks to live, I know that's how I would want to spend it. I'd want to spend it on the music."

She listened to his voice and knew he was holding something back, something huge, but she'd heard enough already. She stared out to sea and sighed blankly.

"Just think about it," he muttered.

"All right. I'll think about it."

He nodded sadly and stared Eastward to the Cology's faint outline in the haze.

After a while they pried up the metal and went back down into the void.

The ringing of Shayna's phone barely rose above the roar of the engine and the road. The digits burned through the reflection of the dying orange sun, unrecognized. She squinted uncertainly and answered. "Hello?"

The voice on the other end was older. It was male. It was anxious. It said "Is this...? Who is this?"

"You called me. Who are you?"

Carl eyed her curiously while she waited for an answer.

The voice said "You're Katja's best friend, aren't you?"

Best? "Who is this?"

"Her father."

"Oh." She sighed away a ripple of crude envy. "Yes. I'm a friend. Shayna."

"Do you know where she is?"

She hesitated. "No."

"Where and when did you see her last?"

Her mind raced suddenly. *Do they know about the tower? What should I say?* "I'm not sure."

"If you see either of them, Shyla, please call us right away. Call if you hear anything about where they are. We're very worried."

"Them? Wait, who are you talking about?"

"Katja and her sister. They're both missing. Since sometime Saturday night. Since the storm."

Shayna said nothing until after the call died. "Fuck."

"Who was that?" Carl asked.

"Have you seen Katja? I've been trying to call her but she doesn't answer."

She smoggy light traced his pensivity. "She's at the Green Room."

"How do you know that?"

"It's where I saw her last. She's not going anywhere in her condition."

"Carl, what condition?"

He rolled his eyes. "Don't ask me. I'm not a *Professor*."

"Take me there," Shayna said, pulling her seatbelt to its very tightest. "And step on it."

Carl cocked his head to one side. "Whatever you say."

The engine screamed like a deranged animal, and the horns blared in a rising chorus, and the rust and concrete and clouds out there dissolved into a pure horizontal frenzy of metal-tasting inertia.

Twelve minutes and thirty miles later she was jumping down onto the sidewalk and flying through the alley to the door whose inscription again instructed her to Abandon All Hope. She pressed through and hurried down into the suffocating neon.

She swept through room by room (even looking behind the ratty red curtain), but the place appeared empty, the smog layer thin to none. Someone had cleared away all the previous night's trash and ash and vomit and empty glasses. Or maybe they had all cleared themselves away. For the first time, ominously, she wondered: *who runs this place? Does anyone?*

"Carl!" she called up the stairs, where he was still stumbling after her. "Carl, where is she? Where did you see her?"

"Not down there," he panted. "Up in the high section."

"Where is that?"

He pointed between the empty booths and dead green neon to a nearly-invisible door, a slab of plywood flush against the wall at the far end, only visible by its pitch black seams. Beyond it she found herself stumbling through the old backstage. Frayed ropes and sagging matte black walls rose up toward the little glimmers of gray-white daylight in the holey ceiling. In desperation she yelled out Katja's name, and again, louder. As loud as she could.

At first there was nothing. Then there came a distant dry scraping.

"Who's there?" growled a distant male voice. It came from a ghostly trace of yellow electricity, far up there.

"Wait!" Carl yelled, but she ignored him and hurried deeper into the void until she couldn't make out the shape of anything anymore; only that glow on the far side of the blackness and the endless flights of stairs.

It was a small circular balcony overlooking the ruined theatre. It was draped in thin curtains and all the old seats were gone, replaced by mattress pads and colored pillows bleeding their fluff. Katja lay flat by the edge. Her glassy eyes stared upward.

The floor creaked behind her as she entered and she reeled around to find the Professor brandishing a short crowbar. When he recognized her he sighed and let it hang at his side.

"Oh, Shay, it's just you. I'm glad you're here."

She went to Katja, grabbed and shook her shoulders frantically. Nothing. The face among the musty pillows was more vacant than she'd thought a living face could be. Those eyes were like the sea. She shook her again.

"Stop that," said the Professor.

"What the hell did you do to her?" She lunged for the blank-eyed boy and wrapped the front of his shirt around her fingers, but un a flash his hands were locked firmly around her wrists, the crowbar thumping on the pillowed ground, and even her adrenaline couldn't budge him. He was much stronger than he looked.

"No, no," he said, with a voice that was infuriatingly unfazed. She could feel the murder in her glare, but he could have been watching television as he stared calmly back at her and said "No. That's not my name. Call me—"

"I said what did you do!"

"It's not like that at all. She asked for my help, so I helped her. Shhh. It's okay."

His grip lightened for the moment she needed to wrench herself free. She stood still and breathing heavily on the foamy ground, thinking of the crowbar, thinking of the gun knocking against her hip, but inevitably only kneeling by the side of that empty husk among the pillows.

Katja's eyes blinked sluggishly.

Carl finally arrived at the top of the stairs. When he met Shayna's eyes he briefly cocked his head toward the Professor as if to ask *should I kill him?*

"She's fine," the dealer told them both. "She's okay, okay?"

"*This* is fine?"

"She's in an artificial trance. She took a psychiatric medication for acute emotional trauma. It puts you in a different place, where you can process the stress. It works as a cortical zeta-receptor agonist, creating a stable OOB waveform in the frontal—"

"When is she coming out of it? Bring her out of it."

"That's what I'm telling you. I can't. Only she can do that. Any drug's effects are an interaction between the physical and the psychological. This one is heavily psychological, and there's no counter-agent to that. She'll come back when she wants to."

Shayna collapsed against the wall, hands in her face. Carl drifted toward her but stayed a few steps away, too uncertain of himself to touch anyone.

"She asked for my help," said the dealer, meditatively rolling a cigarette. "She was having some kind of anxiety attack because of what happened at the Tower. She felt responsible for Float. What could I do? Refuse to help?"

Weird specks of light were shining through the thin curtain, coming from the cracks in the domed ceiling of the main space. From here they looked like stars that were somehow broken; like a dark night sky that had been made in a bad hurry.

"It's common for these trances last several hours," said the Professor.

"How long has it been for her?"

He scratched his head and said "Fourteen."

"And you just left her here?"

"I've been here taking care of her. Keeping her hydrated. Turning her. Keeping the dust off her eyes. It's how it's done."

"What if she never comes out of it?"

"That rarely happens."

"If she..." Shayna stammered. "If she—"

"I know. If she doesn't wake up, you'll castrate me in an interesting way. Fine. But she will. Just cool it, okay? You can both stay here with me and watch over her if you want to. It can't be that much longer."

So she sat. She did her best to breathe normally again. Carl paced slowly back and forth on the hollow floorboards, uncharacteristically quiet. They waited.

"Fuck this," she said. "We're getting her out of here."

The dealer rubbed his eyes. "And take her where?"

She hesitated. "To her family."

The dealer started to say something, but didn't. After a moment Shayna started to awkwardly lift Katja's catatonic weight by her armpits, and Carl hurried to take up her feet. The dealer stood back and pensively massaged his face for a while before taking Shayna's place, and she guided them back down through the void, the endless flights of stairs, and the darkened chambers of the Green Room. She swung open the doors to the Chickmobile's back compartment and helped load Katja inside. The dealer climbed in after her, and the two of them sat on the spools of wire, hunched over in the cramped space with the empty body lying between them. Carl shut the door and took the wheel.

"Wait, where am I driving?" he shouted through the back wall of the cab.

"Her family lives in Rosewood, don't they?" She turned to the dealer and asked "Near the monastery?"

"How would I know?"

She shouted back through the wall: "Head for Rosewood. I'll call them and find out the exact place." But when the engine roared to life and the compartment began to rattle and thud around her, her thumb wavered over the glowing keypad. She watched Katja's head rocking back and forth against the dirty metal floor. She pressed call and raised the phone to her ear.

The dealer grabbed her arm – this time not with enough force to stop her, but only to warn: "Why are you doing this?"

"Because it's the right thing to do. She's in trouble. She should be home with her family."

"What do you think her family's going to do? They'll probably just take her to the Urbanologers. That's the best treatment they can afford, and you know how much that'll help."

"They asked for my help finding her."

"I know you care about Katja, but there's nothing you can do. You know that if you bring her home like this, they'll ground her as soon as she wakes up. She'll be grounded for weeks." He paused. "A couple of weeks is a long time. Too long. Don't you think?"

She canceled the call and took the phone back down. She looked at him.

"She didn't tell me anything, okay?" he said. "I overheard her talking to Carl about your condition when she thought I was out of the room. Your secret's safe, but I'm telling you this as a friend. You won't help anything by doing this."

Shayna stared down into the glowing screen. "God damn it." The battery icon was blinking red. "It doesn't matter what I want."

"If you say so."

She dialed the number again and raised the phone to her ear, but it only rang once. Silence. She took it back down and stared into the black screen. It was completely drained. She sighed.

She pounded on the wall and yelled to Carl: "Just take us to the monastery so I can plug in my phone. You know where it is?"

"Got it," he yelled back. "But then I have to take this thing back to HQ or they'll have my balls for breakfast. I'm sorry."

Kelroy answered the fat wooden door. His face was stern even before he saw the girl hanging between Shayna and the Professor's shoulders.

"What happened?"

"She's just in an induced therapeutic trance," the Professor said. "She's a little late, that's all."

They pressed forward, but Kelroy just stood in the partly-open door, looking down nervously. "What would you hope for us to do?"

"I just need to plug my phone into the wall," Shayna said – but when she heard herself, the seeming coldness in her own voice, she felt herself crumble further. She cried out "Can't you help her? Aren't you supposed to be healers?"

"At least let us put her down for a second," said the dealer.

Kelroy hesitated and stepped back from the door. They hauled Katja's dead weight between the pillars and finally to the bed Shayna had been sleeping in. When she looked up she saw Grant standing and watching, silently.

"You shouldn't have brought her here," Kelroy repeated. "Take her to a doctor."

"Do we look like we have that kind of cash? They wouldn't let us through the door!"

"Her family may have a savings."

"They don't," said the dealer. "And it won't help anyway."

Now when she thought of the voice on the other end of that phone and shuddered. To think of explaining all this to that voice. She'd have to explain the tower. It would come to her own involvement in all of it. Cass was still missing.

Kelroy said "Our relations with her parents are already strained. You shouldn't have involved us."

Shayna sank brokenly onto the foot of the bed. "I know. I know! But you can't do anything? Anything?"

"I have nothing to offer but a diagnosis," Grant finally said.

"Anything."

He moved to the window and peered out into the deepening night. "Your friend is correct that ordinary machine doctors will be of no use here. Her soul has separated from her body. Katja is out there, now, somewhere. Drifting on the winds. If she doesn't return soon, her body may die and condemn her to wander forever as a street spirit."

"This is bullshit, Shay," the Professor whispered, prompting Kelroy to grab his arm and lead him forcefully out of the room, slamming the door behind him.

"Then what can we do?"

The High Lurker sighed. "If the situation were different, we might attempt a projection, but Kelroy is right. We have no choice but the contact the family immediately. Every moment we delay will worsen the...." He trailed off and squinted down. A small sound from the window had interrupted him – a squeak that echoed between the bricks out there.

"What is it?"

When she went to the window she saw Cass down there in the last light, standing with her small fists balled at her sides. She shouted up again three times, unintelligibly, and ran off into the shadows.

"I think she was calling your name," said Grant.

Shayna ran into the hall of pillars and bolted for the front door, hoping to catch the child on the sidewalk before she disappeared forever – but she already stood inside, as motionless as the poles that rose around her.

"Come on, Cass," Shayna said. She wiped her eyes and knelt down to take her hand. "We have to take your sister home now. You and me."

Cass shook her head and then barked again, making Shayna jump. "Shtay!" she yelled. "Shtay! Shtay!"

"Call the family," Grant said.

"Wait," Shayna said.

Cass fell silent again before darting between the pillars. They followed her back to the bed where her sister lay, her glassy eyes still staring straight upward. "Shtay," she repeated, to both of them in turn, to Kelroy when he entered.

"*Stay*," Shayna said. "She wants us to stay here. Or she wants me to."

Cass put her hands on the sides of Katja's face and rocked back and forth, as if to nod.

Grant furrowed his brows and rubbed his chin.

"We can't allow it," Kelroy murmured.

"Please," Shayna said.

The High Lurker muttered: "So be it, if the young prophet says. But you must deliver them both to their family tomorrow morning. You alone. You must solemnly agree never reveal that she stayed here tonight."

She nodded. "I'll take them home."

Kelroy sighed his disapproval and shut the door behind him.

"Oh God," Shayna said. "What can I do? Isn't there anything we can do?"

"You're right that Cass seems to want you to stay here in vigil," Grant said as he slid through the door. "She's more powerful than she may appear to you. You should trust her."

Hearing her name, Cass's attention was called away from her fingers in her mouth. She turned suddenly around and reached upward, and Shayna felt the small hand, damp with saliva, lay softly on her forehead and slide down, as if to shut her eyelids.

"Sweeping," said the child.

"Sleeping is the last thing in the world I can do right now," Shayna responded – but she realized as the words dribbled from her mouth that, against her writhing anxiety, she was exhausted. She was still tired from the Swatter and the Tower. She was tired of fearing for Katja's life here and now, and for her own life back in Greentowne. She shifted from her kneeling position to slump against the side of the bed. She leaned her head back against Katja's lifeless hand, and felt new tears crawling along her cheeks as her consciousness began to dim.

"Wheelgo," the child was saying. "Wheelgo guitar."

She opened her eyes onto a pitch black room. A faint dusting of reddish light covered everything. It took her a moment to recognize her surroundings.

It was the same room, but she was laying on the bed instead of Katja. Katja was nowhere.

In a jolt she was on her feet. She scanned the tiled ground and started feeling her way to the door. When she plugged her phone into the wall, it said it was still before midnight.

"Katja?" she called into the black that was there when she pulled it open. "Katja!"

She heard a door, then footsteps hurrying for her.

"She insisted on not waking you, but she's gone," Kelroy said. "You succeeded."

"I what? I succeeded at what?"

"You projected. You found her street spirit and brought it back."

"I… don't understand. But she's awake? She's all right?"

"Embodied again. She'll be fine. You, however, should sleep." With that, he recoiled again into the void.

She tried.

"Do you remember anything?" Kelroy asked quietly. "From the dreaming."

"No," Shayna lied.

"Nonetheless, the ease with which you restored her is quite notable," said Grant. "You may have an aptitude."

"Katja really left without waking me? You let me sleep through that?"

"She insisted."

Shayna rubbed her eyes and sighed. "By the way, what are you guys doing?"

The three Urbanologers were perched there on a couch facing a television. The room was totally dark outside the blue-gray glow of its garbled static. It was still the middle of the night, and the noise of muffled, fragmented commercial jingles was echoing between the dark stone walls. Grant, Kelroy and Gomad exchanged glances.

"The majority of all sorcery is that of perception," Kelroy confided. "The cosmic powers avail themselves above all to those with ears to listen."

"You've said that, but what do you listen to?"

"To the voice of the Tropolis. Its divine and secret language. With which it is constantly and ubiquitously speaking to us all, in ways very few men are wise enough to grasp."

"And it speaks through the television static?"

The Urbanologers glared disapprovingly.

"It's much too complicated for you to understand," Grant said.

The foggy image of a line of sausages flashed across the screen for a moment before lapsing back into vertical scroll.

She sat with them for some time, sinking into the white noise.

"I can't sleep," she said.

Gomad glanced at her, then back into the screen. He raised a finger to his silent lips. She realized the others were meditating again.

A horribly distorted female voice was coming through the speaker, saying:

"...stole Brad's baby. But not Tiffany's. Who's the mother? I am! There is no mother...."

The signal turned back into noise.

10

Halfway out of her dreams, Shayna saw morning's long shadows climbing like curls of yellow smoke up the wall behind the dead television. She found her eyes aching and the joints of her clothes warm with sweat, and the monks were gone like the night.

Her thought was to fall asleep again if she could, but one glance at her phone and insomnia returned like the click of a lock. The screen showed one missed call from Katja. With a sigh she forced herself to hear the message.

She took its suggestion and headed for the Metro.

The power lines and grunting wheels carried her Inward, following main drags that joined one by one, gaining lanes, until the outer Tropolis's thin veins of neon color engorged into the wider deltas of activity that ringed the outskirts of Greentowne and basked in its stray glitter. Streets here coursed with the great commercial pulse. Signs sold the sleaziness of Outsider life as a form of weird glamour. The strip joints ran for miles.

It dawned on Shayna, as she pressed through the pink glass doors, that she had never seen Katja at work before. She'd never even really imagined it. Idling now on that shiny sales floor, already sick from all the looks her substandard style was getting her, the moment she somehow recognized her friend among the shelves was the last surreal straw. The Katja by the cash register was like anybody who had walked straight out of a holographic billboard, a liquor commercial, a full-page glossy magazine ad. Her legs were inhumanly long under her skirt, her curves inhumanly circular, and every inch of clothed flesh shone ominously in the skintight black metal material. She turned and fixed Shayna in her expertly painted gaze. Then she made the hand sign for 'smoke break' to a piece of one-way glass in the ceiling.

Shayna followed her into the alley behind the store. A lot of things were waiting to be moved. One side was lined with the ivory bodies of mannequins, the other with endless racks full of empty chrome hangars that chimed in the soft wind.

They sat on the concrete step. For a while they shared no words and did not smoke.

"I'm sorry I left last night without waking you," Katja said. "I can't explain myself. I just…. When I woke up, I didn't want to be seen. I didn't want you to see me like that at all. It was the same way when I went to Fish after the tower. Just feeling so wrong, so dirty, like I could never get clean again." She hesitated. "I took Cass home. Told my family we just got separated in the storm and I had to find her before I came back. Something like that. Nobody's in trouble."

"God," Shayna muttered. "I'm sorry I didn't take you straight to your family. I don't know what I was thinking. Maybe I let Fish talk me out of it. I won't let him do that again."

"He's right that they would have grounded me forever."

Shayna said nothing.

"Becker is all right," Katja said. "He's back in school now. Listening to his mother. We probably won't see him again." She went through the motions of finding a cigarette, but just stared at it unlit. "I keep thinking about the look Float gave me. I can't get it out of my head. Because it wasn't hateful. It wasn't anything. It was just...."

Her head dropped down between her glittering knees. Her long fingernail extensions stabbed into her hair.

Shayna held her, leaning over her. Her face rested against the rubbery film stretched thin over Katja's shoulderblades. She heard the breath heaving through her friend's lungs. She saw the sheen of her own tears dripping down the plastic curves of Katja's back, and sighed.

Katja whispered "I barely even knew him. And pretty soon I'll lose you, too. I don't know how to deal with it. I can't. How do you do it? How do you go on?"

The metal hangers played their haunting music. The noise of the street was far away.

"I don't," Shayna answered.

"I never would have come back. I would've stayed up there forever. I know I would've. But they said you brought me back." She swallowed and said "Do you remember anything? Do you remember doing that?"

Shayna sat wordless.

"Me neither," Katja said. She sat up and composed herself as much as she could manage. She tried to rub out the dark rivers of her ruined makeup.

"I'm also sorry I told Carl about your blight. I know it was a secret. I was so far gone I could've told him anything. I don't think I told anybody else."

"Forget it." They let go of each other.

Katja turned briefly and whispered: "I didn't tell Tom, anyway."

Tom, Shayna thought, and bit her tongue.

Katja said "I'm sorry, but I have to fix my face and get back to work before they kill me."

She opened her hand, revealing the crumpled corpse of her unburnt cigarette. Then she stood up and carefully restored her absurd outfit to its original condition. When she had finished, the two of them stood still there among the glossy mannequins, staring with cool blankness into each others' eyes.

There was something very strange about this moment, Shayna realized. Something about Katja. She seemed so naked, standing there, still faintly trembling. Naked in a way that her costume alone could never account for. She wondered whether this was the same nakedness that Shayna had always felt before Katja, as if everything had reversed.

"I'll see you later?" Katja said.

Shayna nodded and watched her disappear back into the glittering darkness of the store.

It was the bustling part of town, and it wasn't long before things started to grate on the senses. The sweet smells were too strong. Holograms spewed from every storefront and joined a street-wide brawl for visual superiority, luminous projections that altered their sex and build for every passerby. Shayna kept her head down, but there suddenly appeared before her an ethereal simulacrum of herself, leaning demurely against the bricks. The projection wore a mirrored plastic top over a chest that made her flinch and recede into her coat.

Her fingers turned The Metro Pass in her pocket and felt the itch to just board the next bus to anywhere, but it looked like all the busses around here were only running even further Inward. There was nothing to do but keep walking, in whatever direction looked right. Today she didn't mind having some time to think.

She had been past knowing or caring where she was for over an hour when happened upon the waiting line. She even followed its course for a while, not realizing where it led, but when the great gray walls of the Charity Center rose up over the next hill, she winced, reached for her cigarettes, and wished she'd never come this way.

She climbed to the top of the hill to get a good look, figuring what the hell. The line was as long as everyone said. Longer. Thousands of people, mostly parents and children (and interspersed among them, the lone hopelessly old ones who must have known they were waiting for nothing), stood nearly still in groaning air. Down there at the line's distant end, walled by comps and chainlink fences and concrete parapets, everyone was sorted out at the points of clipboards and pens and bioscanners. Finally the children were sorted from their parents and taken through the big doors and into the gigantic structure.

Tom was the only person Shayna knew to have been inside the fortress itself. He'd told her the story once of how he'd gotten sick when he was six. He remembered standing in line for days – and how, once inside, they'd shown him pictures of the blight growing within him, somewhere below and to the left of his navel. He'd been taken through halls of white light and foggy glass and then put back out on the street, no longer in pain, never knowing what they'd done to him.

Shayna read the date on the screen of her phone. *Thirteen days*, she calculated – *if I'd come here thirteen days ago, they would have taken me in and cured me. None of this would have happened. I would've been saved.*

Looking up the armored walls of Charity, she felt her hands make fists. The cure was real. It was being given to hundreds of people at that moment. The cure for blight was somewhere behind those fences and comps and clipboards, less than a hundred feet away, and they wouldn't give it to her. Too old.

The urge was strange but unmistakable: she wanted something to be destroyed now. She didn't care what it was or what the consequences would be. She just wanted to see fire. But everyone here was already braced for another riot.

Everyone, that is, except that ragged, long-bearded creature making its way down the line, speaking in whispers to everyone in turn. Scribbling notes on a pad. As Shayna peered through the squinting sun, presently the old man slowly turned, looked over his shoulder at her, nodded once, and returned to his mysterious task.

Nemo's Source, she thought. Doctor Kingsford. The oldest man in the Tropolis.

She kept walking.

It was later in the afternoon when she started to notice the pressure behind her eyes.

She had been walking for hours now, having long since drifted instinctively into the dead neighborhoods – taking refuge from hologram country and the echoes of the Power Elite. Out there in the ruins she could sing to herself where no one would listen. She hadn't thought to turn back toward civilization until the day had turned hot and dry, and thirst was an ache in the bottom of her throat. But as she walked along, chasing the din, the thirst changed into something else. She had nearly fainted before she realized it was a thirst for air.

She found herself collapsing onto a step at the bottom of a ruined flight. She leaned there against the sagging wood and fought to push breath through her chest. The hands she stared down at were clutching each other and buzzing electrically, and everything was suddenly burning hot.

No, she thought. *No, this isn't it. This can't be it.*

Two weeks, she hissed to herself in her mind. *That's what the nurse said. Two weeks. No symptoms for two weeks. I have one more week at least. This can't be it.*

The sound of her own blood rushed in slow waves. Stars swirled behind her eyelids. Then they were all gone.

Her breath returned to normal, and there was nothing but the faint rawness in the back of her throat. Her thirst was ordinary again. She opened and closed her hands many times, but nothing buzzed. Nothing ached any worse than it usually did.

Not knowing what else to do, she got up and went on along the empty street as if nothing had happened.

A few feathers drifted in the lifeless wind.

"Where's Grant?" she asked, pushing irreverently through the great big doors.

Gomad was applying something to one of the big pillars in the middle of the space. He opened his mouth.

"In the garden," Kelroy said from where he was lighting candles on an altar. At the top of the altar was an instant photograph of the departed, and aligned all around it were rows of candy bars.

The garden was small. It looked like just a regular room whose roof had either collapsed or been removed. The floor was raised up on a wooden platform so the tan brick walls wouldn't snuff out all the light. At the top of seven steps she found the High Lurker in his black robe, scratching at his stubbled scalp, surrounded on all sides by rows of troughs. She realized there were only dandelions in all those troughs – nothing but dandelions.

"What is it," Grant said quietly, glancing briefly over his robed shoulder.

"You said you'd help me."

"So you want my help now?"

"Y-yes!"

"Then I want something from you." His back was still turned. "I need you to be serious. About saving your life."

"Serious?" she yelled. "Now you think I'm not serious?"

"I think you haven't entirely made up your own mind as to whether or not you want to live at all. If you expect any aid from me, let alone the City, you must know exactly what you are asking for – and you must be ready to go to whatever length you are asked to, no matter how fearsome or uncomfortable. Do you understand?"

"Yes!"

"Are you *sure* you understand."

"Yes, I'm serious," she said, shaking the flowers. "With the ghost of Our Departed High Lurker as my witness—!"

"Enough."

The dandelion petals settled in the silence.

"You said you people knew something about the cure. How do I find it? What do I do? Where do I go? What do I look for? How to I even start?"

"Consult the divine. I have nothing to tell you."

"Nothing?" She was fuming.

The High Lurker finally turned to face her. His look was pristine and unfazed, bright with the afternoon, and he was both infuriating and strangely calming to behold, surrounded by the flowers.

"Things I know about the blight," he said. "The blight is a very mysterious ailment. It takes many different forms. Killing slowly, killing quickly, affecting both people and animals. No one is contagious. No one is immune. No one can say what causes it, where it comes from, why it strikes some as children and others as elders, and all of us if we live long enough. It is chaos."

"Yes, yes. I know all that."

"I know of a rat that came to suffer the blight. A bulge grew on its spine until it was half the size of the rat itself. No one expected the animal to survive – but one day it simply turned its head around and began to gnaw away at its own sick flesh, eating itself. Finally it had devoured the entire blight. The empty wound healed, and the sickness never returned. The rat is alive and intact as we speak."

Shayna winced into the hazy sky. Her anger faded into the blankness.

"What is the name of your blight?" Grant asked. "How do you know you have it?"

"There was a woman. From the Inner Ring."

"What did she tell you of your fate?"

"She told me how long I had."

"And did she tell you the name?"

Shayna stared into the tiny yellow petals and tried to remember.

"Names are sacred," said Grant, returning to the flowers. "Names grant power over the named, and each species of blight has a name of its own. You must learn the name of your death."

"You're saying I need to talk to her."

The High Lurker said nothing.

Rising onto the tips of her boots, Shayna squinted out over the top of the wall. The dull beige Tropolis stretched into infinity.

For a while she lay back on the ratty covers of the bed the Urbanologers had given her, trying to think of how she would find the woman. It was as dire as it was hopeless. She had nothing to go on, and nothing to do but lie there in the half-dozing ache of thought.

She checked her phone clock and saw that it was still early enough for Tom to be safely detained at the Heaps. The goddamned spare apartment key was still there in her pocket, and it was as good a time as any.

She took a moment and a cigarette to prepare herself as she stepped off the bus. *Just get it done,* she thought. *Just don't think about the smell.* But it was already on the wind. When she finally threw down the dead filter and headed for the front door, she lowered her goggles over her eyes, as if for protection.

Tom's door was unlocked with no one was inside. The bunks were tidy. The clock above the stove ticked away for nothing but her suitcase and her pink electric bass, collected neatly in the center of the floor. She took them up in a hurry. She reclaimed her money wad from the back of the freezer. On her way out she noticed that the sink was full of half-written crumpled notes, but she didn't stop for one word. She just kept holding every breath as long as she could stand, hiding from his venomous aroma, until the door was locked behind her and she was flicking the key into the back of the mousehole in the hall. Just like he had expected from day one.

Perched again at the Metro stop, she realized from her own humming that the idiotic love song was stuck in her head again. Phantom clove smoke wafted through her nose with every throbbing note in the melody.

It wasn't long before the solution dawned on her. She chuckled deviously, took her bass off her back and started playing the song. It only took her a few tries to find the key that transformed it from cool and bubbly to dissonant and grotesque, and she kept hammering away at the mutilated notes until they finally dissolved from her head. When she looked up again, the bus doors were hissing open for her. She took her seat in the back.

The song was gone, but the psychosomatic smoke lingered faintly – that, and little flashes of red light in her mind's eye, which she struggled to snuff out. It was all far worse than she'd realized, this contamination.

I should've left a note, she thought.

Dear Tom: hope I never see you again in my whole week of remaining life.

Tom: fuck off and die.

Tom:

She stared out the window, looking for the barely-visible icy peak of the Cology in the haze, and tried to redirect her mind to some other impossible thing, until her phone buzzed merciful distraction against her hip.

"Hi Carl," she said.

"How are you doing?" his voice asked, with a twinge of hesitation when he realized it was a stupid question.

She found herself wanting to give him an answer anyway. She needed to tell someone. For better or worse, he knew her secret – and the more time passed since their awkward conversation, the more she found herself ironically relieved that she didn't have to keep it from him anymore. She said "I need to know something and there's no way I'm ever going to find it out."

"What do you need?" he asked instantly.

"The name of a nurse. The one who diagnosed me that day at the factory as part of the 'population forecast'. I thought maybe Katja mentioned—"

"She didn't."

Shayna thought aloud: "I guess I could just ask Larry. I'm sure he'd just tell me." *Maybe if I pointed my gun at him*, she thought. *I guess that's not a bad idea. If I can only figure out a good escape route.*

"Who's Larry?"

"My old boss," she said, and told him about everything that had happened, and all the work-related felonies she was wanted for now. Carl just listened in perfect silence to the whole tale – but the moment she finished, he suddenly said "All right" and hung up.

She rolled her eyes and dropped the phone back into her coat.

A while later she had leapt off the bus and was pushing through the monastery doors for the second time that afternoon.

The gun was there under the corner of the mattress, as fully loaded as ever, if not more so. She took a moment to sit and think. Grant's words rang through her head – something he'd said about the lengths she was prepared to go.

Her phone and the sunlight told her there was still an hour or so left in the workday. So there was a good chance the bus wouldn't get her to the factory in time – but she had to prepare herself for the possibility that she would.

So she would arrive at the fabric plant before Larry went home for the day. She visualized the little chain-linked lot around the far side of the building, opposite the hordes. That was where he would come out, she figured. Even if she got there in time, there was a good chance she'd only be waiting in vain while he escaped by some other route – but she had to be prepared for the chance that she would intercept him.

So she would see Larry, and point her gun at him, and ask to know the nurse's name. If he didn't know, she'd march him back to his office to dig through his files and find out. There was a good chance that he would do everything she asked – but she had to be prepared for the possibility that he would try to resist, maybe even try to overpower her.

There was a good chance she could prove her point with a warning shot, but she had to be prepared for—

Her phone buzzed.

"Janet Wallace," Carl said.

"Who? What?"

Carl cleared his throat and said: "Janet Wallace, Unified Company Health, attached to Tropolitan Industrial Safety and Onco... um. Oncological Socio-biometrics. Whatever the hell that means."

Shayna's jaw dropped.

"I have her home address here, too," Carl added. "Does that help?"

"How did you find it?"

Carl cleared his throat at length, and then a voice rumbled through the speaker – a voice whose enunciation was perfect, whose syllables were as sharp as knives, and whose sound was as deep and harsh and full of authority as an onrushing mag-train. The voice said:

"*This is Grover Jarvis Aldman calling on behalf of the Central Office of Corporate Security. I am obliged to notify you that pursuant to various enquiries implicating your facility we have immediate requisition of the following information pertaining to the population forecast survey administrated to your staff on April the third of the current fiscal—*"

Shayna was already out of breath and struggling to stay upright in her laughter. When she managed to put the phone back to her ear, he was still rattling off:

"*—should be aware that failure to immediately disseminate this data may invoke an immediate chapter thirty-eight violation and possibly expulsion and subsequent litigation for management personnel including but not limited to—*"

"Carl!" she said between breaths. "Stop!"

"So you like my Insider accent? I've been practicing."

"He really bought it?"

"Every time he started to sound suspicious I just said the word 'litigation'. That's what you do when you talk to these assholes."

"What is *litigation?*"

"That's where they cut your leg muscles."

Shayna was dumbfounded. "Carl, you're a miracle!"

"Okay. So I'll give you her address."

She rooted through her pockets for a pen, rolled up her sleeve and said "All right."

"No, I mean, I'll give it to you in person."

"Give it to me now."

"I mean, I'll give you the address, if.... If you kiss me."

She chuckled, but the line just sighed nervously.

"Are you drunk?" she said.

"It's not a lot to ask. I just did you a miracle."

"Carl, give me the address. I need that address."

"I *need* you to kiss me."

"No."

"Well..." Carl said, and hung up.

She gritted her molars and waited a moment to call him back.

"Changed your mind?" he asked.

"Give me the address," she said, slowly, "Or I swear I'm going to litigate you."

Back to Greentowne, she thought darkly when the numbers were inscribed on her forearm and the phone was dead. Not just Greentowne – the Inner Ring. The street number was just a single disconcerting digit: ninth street. This woman lived just nine blocks from the crystal walls, closer by far than Shayna had ever been to the Cology. This wouldn't be easy. People from the outer Tropolis didn't just walk into the Inner Ring.

The door started to open. She managed to bury the gun in the folds of her coat just in time for Grant's fresh-shaved head to lean inside and peer at her with its cool, haunting eyes.

"Well, I found her," she said tiredly. "I found the nurse who knows the name."

"I see. Then you have it?"

"I know where she is. Now all I need is invisibility."

Grant's eyes were thoughtful, his head cocked very slightly to one side.

Shayna laughed. "I guess you don't have another artifact in your case for that. Turning invisible."

"We may."

She stared at him.

"Tomorrow," he said, and backed away.

She jumped up from the bed and hurried after him into the central chamber, calling "Wait. This isn't some kind of stupid test, is it? I swear I'm serious. If you really have something I can—"

"It is too late now. You'd be returning here by Metro after nightfall. It wouldn't be safe, and I won't allow it."

"I ride the Metro at night all the time."

"You'll understand tomorrow," he said, and moved along. Over his shoulder he said "You look as if you should rest."

She was tired. Very tired. But sleep was the last thing she wanted now.

"Let's get hammered, but not at the Green Room," she said into her phone when Katja picked up.

"Why not at the Green Room?"

"Carl is being a creep, I never want to see Tom again, and I hate Fish's guts. Or whatever he calls himself now."

"Don't worry. The old crowd kind of dissolved after you left that night. I haven't seen Tom since. Carl only comes to check if you're around, and he's given up now. And as for Fish, please don't hate his guts. Not because of me."

"We'll talk about it. After we get hammered."

"Okay," said Katja.

"How are those whacky monks treating you?" Katja asked on the bus. She looked human again.

"Good, I guess."

"I could never figure them out. It upset me a lot at first, that they treated Cass's syndrome like it was a super power or something. Told her all kinds of things. They made her proud of it."

Floating down, Shayna thought compulsively, but bit her tongue.

"But I guess I'm thankful for it, really. That she has somewhere she gets respect and attention. It's a lot better than she'd get in the schools, even if they hadn't rejected her."

A freak swell of rain was hammering on the bus window and splashing under the wheels in the long-shadowed light.

Katja said "We asked the school administrators how we'd take care of her all day, when they said she couldn't go to school anymore. Since our parents work. They just told us to lock all the doors and windows when we left in the morning."

The two hopped off the bus and hurried along under the thinning rain. The clouds up there were passing in a hurry, looking nervous. Then they were gone.

"Boys are stupid," Shayna said between her cigarette and her tin can full of gin, reiterating the theme of the night's conversation.

"I guess, yeah," Katja said. She seemed to be having trouble focusing her eyes. "At least the ones we know. Except Carl's not exactly stupid, he's just.... And Tom—"

"Don't even talk about Tom. Fucking Tom. I never want to hear Tom's fucking name again."

Katja rolled her eyes.

Shayna considered pressing the point, but her phone buzzed. It was Tom.

She held the phone to her ear.

"Shay?" his voice said meekly.

"I can't talk right now," she said. That last gulp of gin just wouldn't stop burning. That's what it was.

"Can we meet? I want, need, to talk to you. Just for a moment. Maybe before work tomorrow. Like around seven-thirty. Maybe at the rail hub. That's close to your place, isn't it?"

No fucking way in fucking hell she thought, and said "Fine. See you there."

"Okay."

She hung up.

Katja stared with expectant curiosity.

"Fuck," Shayna said, and took the rest of what was still in the can.

"Indeed," said a familiar voice over the chatter of the Green Room.

Shayna glanced up and saw Fish, the Professor, whatever—

"What *is* your name now?" she asked.

"Alice," he said as he joined their table.

"Alice is a girl's name."

Alice combed his fingers through the rather spectacular blue wig he had on. There was more: the shirt he was wearing had a sawed-off low neckline and short sleeves that emphasized the skinniness of his arms, while the skirt he'd draped over his too-tight jeans perfectly masked his plumbing. In the smoky darkness of the space, it was shocking how convincing an Alice he was making.

"You're saying I'm not," he said, acquiring a shot glass from the neon haze.

"That eyeliner looks really great on you," said Katja, kissing his cheek. "You should take my job. Please."

"I don't understand," Shayna said.

"Of course you don't. You're wrongly assuming that just because you've identified me as a guy, I must identify myself the same way."

"So you identify as a girl?"

"No," he said with a girlish shake of his head, and said no more about it.

The gin hit Shayna hard then, and she could no longer think of a reason not to just go ahead and say: "You know, Alice, I hate your guts."

"Don't hate Alice's guts," said Katja.

Alice was unfazed. He swallowed his booze unflinchingly and then settled into a sort of weirdly prim pose in his seat.

"Why shouldn't I?" Shayna asked Katja. "He almost killed you."

"He just helped me... almost maybe die, if you hadn't saved me," she corrected, uneasily. "*Maybe.*"

"Shay," said Alice, re-hanging a strand of his metallic blue hair above his ear. "It's important to me that you stop hating my guts."

"But I *hate* your guts," she said, and squinted coldly.

"It's important that you understand what I am really about. Because what I am about is not bad. It's not evil. All I do is give people power over themselves. That's all."

"For a price," Shayna accused.

"A really affordable price," Katja insisted.

"It's not about the price," said Alice. "I do it to empower people. Over what's inside of them. What they do with that power can be good or evil. It's entirely up to them."

"Yeah," said Katja.

"Why can't you just *not* empower people so much?"

"I want to introduce you to some friends of mine," said the dealer. "I want to show you something."

She followed to the far end of the intoxicated human tunnel, where she found him in a raised section of the space. He indicated six black-clad human shadows gathered in a circular booth. They all stared coldly out from under their stocking caps.

"Who are they?" Shayna asked.

"You're into the Smurge, right? Smurge songs are all about revolution, smashing the Company, breaking the Machine, freeing the People, right?"

"Mainly."

"These people are revolutionaries. They're my clients."

It was then she noticed the little spark that shone and dimmed as it moved between the stocking-capped shadows. A joint. One of the revolutionaries waved Alice over, and he dragged Shayna with him.

"You guys, this is my friend Shay," Alice said. "She hates the Machine too."

"My codename is Blue Dog," said the revolutionary. "Black Faction. You said your name is Shay?"

"Yeah."

Blue Dog nodded his head slowly while the circular blood-red lenses covering his eyes reflected the light of the joint. It was with a small smirk that he echoed the name. The others smirked too.

Shayna said "Wait, you people are Black Faction?"

"You sound surprised."

"I guess I thought you were, you know... black."

Blue Dog frowned slightly.

She asked him "So you put up all the flyers in the bathroom stalls?"

"We put them in other places too. They get torn down."

"So, what are your ideals? And who is this Rocoz person you're always quoting on the flyers?"

"*Rokosz*," he enunciated.

"So who is *Rokosz?*"

"You say you hate the Machine, but you don't know Rokosz?" Blue Dog shook his head and grinned sadly. "We can't even discuss our methods until you've read the treatise." When the joint was passed back to him he offered it to her.

She shrugged and accepted it. Her toke was shallow and short, a friendship gesture. The smoke had a bitter twinge to it.

Alice was watching her. The revolutionaries were watching her.

It hit her in a wave: the watering in her eyes, the quivering in her lips, the throbbing tightness in her throat. It was sadness, purer and stronger than any emotion she could remember ever feeling, and it had no object or reason. It was as if absolute withering sorrow had somehow been triple distilled, abstracted from any particular cause or situation, and crystallized into a sadness liqueur more perfect and gut-wrenching than nature would ever have allowed. For no conscious reason at all, she wanted to lie down on the crowded floor and bawl. She wanted to cease to exist. Then in only a few long seconds it had faded.

Meanwhile, the revolutionaries continued wordlessly passing it around. Their drags were reckless and deep.

"I have a joint for every basic emotion," Alice said. "Although the only one people seem to ask for is sadness. Sometimes rage, but I don't let them smoke it around me."

"What the fuck is the point of that?"

"We smoke this in solidarity," said Blue Dog, through a half-stifled sob, "with those who know *only* sadness. The Thirty Percent. The true Underclass. The incarcerated."

Shayna stood speechless. She turned to Alice and demanded, through a clearing head: "Why did you show me this? Was this supposed to prove that you're doing some kind of valuable service?"

"Not valuable," said Blue Dog. "*In*-valuable." He sniffled, and a shining tear escaped the bottom of his glasses.

"I just thought you'd think it was pretty cool," said the dealer, twirling a lock of his wig around his finger. It was only then that she noticed his heels.

9

Her decision not to set any alarm for the meeting with Tom was somewhere between on purpose and accidental. She trusted the drinking to be her scapegoat – but when she found herself awake at dawn, the room around her had never looked so sober and sleepless. For half an hour she shut her eyes and rolled onto her side and watched oblivion never come back.

Six-thirty AM, breaking through the cracks in the wooden shutter, found her swearing into her boots and putting them on anyway. *Fuck it*, she muttered to the army coat and the Metro seat she slumped down into. The world on the way to the transit hub at Union Station dribbled damply past the window, both too slow and too fast, charged with both boredom and anxiety. She stuffed down her dread with the reminder that there were bigger things to think about today – that if she could just get this stupid chore done, it was on to Greentowne and the nurse and the name of death. Important things. Things that mattered. She stuffed everything down with that mission. That, and a vision of kicking Tom's groin, replayed in her mind over and over to infinity.

It was a whole ten minutes early that the bus dumped her with a hiss out onto the marble tiles, tired and sleepless, empty and without appetite – left with no option but to doggedly follow the thought of water through the lines of dusty glass and into the station.

He was early too. Her eyes had picked him instantly out of the vast distance full of strangers, as if by a sixth sense. It became like electricity switching on; a sharp jolt that gave way to a steady fizzling burn in her furrowing brow, her entrails, the acid in the back of her throat and the skin behind her ears. She shook out the bristling and walked.

He sat on the shore of an island of sagging benches, lapped by the square sea of scuffed marble, hunched over with his long fingers clasped in front of him like the turnstiles. A faceless blur of people flowed around him in slow motion, murmuring to itself in every language of the Tropolis. The lighted numbers flickering across the boards were just empty symbols, without meaning. In the station, the garbageman alone was clear and real, and the light in the towering windows fell down on him like lazy snow.

He glanced up from her boots when she stopped in front of him – for only a moment. His eyes hurried to nowhere and stayed there as she hesitantly slumped down next to him.

Neither of them breathed a word. The voice from above echoed about comings and goings.

Tom said into space: "You scared me. You just went out there. Into the superstorm, in the middle of the night, and never came back. I saw the ice form on the window. I must have called you dozens of times that night and you never picked up."

"The storm killed the network."

"That was the worst thing that ever happened to me," he said, emotionlessly. "You running out there, and all of us not knowing whether you were alive, or hurt, or what. I was afraid to call again after the storm. I didn't even know until Monday. I had to find it out from Carl. That you were okay."

Shayna said nothing. *He doesn't even know*, she realized. *He still doesn't know I'm doomed.*

Tom kept staring away into the flickering numbers. He said: "Carl really seems to hate my guts now. So do you."

Words caught in her throat, and she couldn't unstick them. She sat her head in her hand and felt the faint wind of the passing strangers over her closed eyelids.

"I didn't mean to hurt you," he said. "I'm sorry I came off like I was committing to something – and, I mean, I wanted to. I'm just weird. I warned you I was weird. I told you I have this thing, that I don't really like, um, being physical. With people. Usually."

She smiled helplessly and stared into the back of his head.

"No," he interrupted himself. "I mean. What do I mean?"

You mean unless you're drunk, Shayna thought, but the words stuck in her throat.

He said "Only with people I don't know. And won't ever see again. And, um, only when I'm drunk. That's why I could never – I mean, that's why I didn't do that with you. Because you mean a lot to me. We've been friends for so long and that means so much to me. That girl, she— she's just some person. That's the only reason I could even think of doing...."

He shook his head and almost managed to make eye contact for a moment. The voice above spoke of final destinations.

"I grew up in this house down in Dexter, across from this synthetic hormone factory," he said. "I think that's why. Why I have this thing. And some other things, but that's not important. It doesn't even matter."

Shayna sighed.

"It's because I love you that I can't be with you," he said. "I hope – I wish there was some way you could understand." He leaned back into the bench and stared into his knitted hands. He said "But you must hate my guts."

Something in her said "I don't really."

The garbageman finally turned to meet her eyes.

"I don't hate you," she whispered, and rubbed her face.

"You mean it?"

"Yeah," she said, and knew with a sigh that it was nowhere near the whole truth, but it was still the only true thing she could think of. The snowflake light turned brighter for a moment. The voice from above was echoing down a language she couldn't recognize, but it was musical. She decided it was better that she couldn't understand it, as she looked into his cool eyes and thought: *God damn.*

They sat together in awkward silence for half an hour.

"I have to get to work," Tom said, rising meekly to his feet.

She nodded mutely. She raised her hand to wave goodbye, but his back was already turned, his buzzed head hunched over in the direction of the lines of dusty glass. In a moment he was gone.

She refused to slouch and she buried the water in her eyes. She just got up and marched for the Metro, meeting no one's gaze.

This is pathetic, she thought. *This is stupid.* With burning eyes and clenched fists she trudged down into the puddles, and only on the teeming sidewalk did she let it wash over her:

She had never loved him more than she did now.

"Let's get on with it," she was already hissing under her breath as she pushed through the heavy monastery door, but she stepped into a pristine and suffocating silence, alone between the pillars. The candles had all burned down and the photographs and trinkets were rooted in puddles of hard wax. She moved deeper into the space, but not even the random nameless acolytes were there to be seen. The graffiti loomed ominously.

Something shuffled on the stone ground behind her. She whipped around to find Gomad stepping uncertainly through the door and approaching her, looking apologetic for her shock. He had something tucked under his arm.

"Where is Grant?" she asked. "Oh, never mind. Sorry. I know you can't—"

"They're in Wednesday service now."

She stared at him in shock. "Did you just break your vow of silence?"

"I never took any vow of silence. I'm not a eunuch either. Did they tell you I was a eunuch? They tell that to people sometimes."

"What's a—?"

"Never mind." He turned red and added: "They'll be in the service for an hour at least. Do you want to go somewhere?"

"Go where?"

"Well, we don't know yet." When he saw her confusion he shook his head and said "Sorry, I'm not very good at explaining these things. I don't know where to begin. I have an aptitude. Just like maybe you have an aptitude for what we call *projection*, with me it's something we call *observantism*. In a sense, you could say that the Tropolis speaks to me through small objects."

"Small objects?"

"I mean… I'm able to find things, and I can help other people find things. Things the Tropolis wants them to have. I was the one who found the Metro Pass. I've found many other blessed artifacts. Maybe I can help you."

"How?"

From under his arm he took out a roll of paper, ancient and thickly creased. He knelt and spread it out on the floor before them, revealing what she realized was a crudely-fashioned but intricately detailed map of Angelis. The angular white shape of the Cology was there in the middle, radiating the flyways like rusty spokes, outward into concentric rings whose poverty and decrepitude deepened with every mile from the center. She could recognize some features, but she could also tell that it wasn't a normal street map. The thousands of fine lines and curves were none of the streets she knew; their angles and shapes were strange to her, if not totally random.

Gomad sat there with his legs folded and motioned for her to do the same. When she did, he produced from the folds of his robe a small paper bag, full of fine sand. He poured it onto the smooth floor between her and the map and spent some time carefully spreading it into a thin, even circle.

"What's that?"

"You'll see. You're searching for something."

"A cure for blight."

"No. I mean, if you can, don't think about that. Observantism only works if you're not focusing on any particular thing. If the Tropolis gives you something, it will be what you need, not necessarily what you ask for."

She stared at him. "What could I possibly *need* more than a cure for blight?"

The monk looked sheepishly away and only said "If you want to try this, start by clearing your mind of all thought. Relax as deeply as you can. Straighten your back and take deep, slow breaths, like me. Close your eyes."

She sighed, rolled her eyes, tried to set aside the fact that he seemed to be contradicting what Grant had said earlier, and followed Gomad's instructions. In spite of herself, as the long breaths entered and exited her lungs, she felt a blank peace begin to wash over her. She could hear the background drone of anxiety that had been in her head since all this began; with every deep exhale it seemed to dissolve a little further. She had almost forgotten that Gomad was there with her when he said:

"Now let shapes come to you. Draw them in the sand at your feet."

"What kind of shapes?"

"Any kind. Don't think about it or discriminate. Just draw what comes into your mind when it's completely empty."

She opened her eyes and looked down at the circle of sand. With a sigh she carved out a line with her finger. Then a wide, jagged curve with her thumb. A small spiral. Another line, bisecting a circle, with a dot for punctuation. It was nothing; it reminded her of the random patterns she'd drawn in the margins while dying of boredom in school. She shrugged at Gomad, but he was studying the sand doodle intently. He started combing over the map, looking back and forth between it and the sand.

"I know that's a map of the Tropolis," she said. "But what are all the lines? They're not streets."

"No. They're lines of force, in a sense. It's hard to explain. This is a map of the other world that overlays our own. The Dreaming. I'm sorry it might take me a moment to find your shape. I don't have the map memorized yet." He kept combing over the old paper for several minutes, going outward in a spiral from the center. He pinned his finger in one place and kept scanning until he'd scoured the entire map. Then he squinted closely at both the map and the pattern in the sand, triple-checking. "Found it."

She looked at the map where he was pointing. In that one place, hidden amid that vast tangle, the weird formless lines came together to make a shape a lot like what she'd drawn. In fact it was almost exactly the same. But surely on such a large map, with so many random lines and shapes, that same combination of squiggles was bound to happen many times. She started looking.

"It only occurs once in the entire map," Gomad said, noticing her skepticism as he unfurled a Metro route guide. "You can look for yourself, but you drew a strong shape. Usually the querent draws something that occurs in numerous places." He smiled briefly and said "Perhaps the City has a strong feeling about you."

She kept looking for another random instance. They worked together to find the same point on the regular map and pick the right bus.

"But what are we expecting to find?" Shayna asked. "You don't have any idea? You really have no expectations?"

"I try not to," the monk responded, distantly. From where he sat by the window, he barely seemed to register her presence. He'd barely spoken since they left the monastery, and it struck Shayna how his silence made him, if anything, even more imposing than Kelroy or Grant. Those two were strange enough in their own way – a way through which visible traces of melodramatic effort had peeked once or twice – but Gomad was unearthly in a way that went beyond them. Every small movement he made was unearthly in and of itself, as if each muscle was individually willed.

She was about to light her cigarette when it occurred to her to make a gesture of friendship. She held the pack toward him.

"I'd rather not. They destroy the lungs."

"But these are Balmic style. They're good for you. See?" She pointed to the notice on the box.

"They don't really clean the smog out. It's just a ploy."

She threw up her hands and put the pack away. "Right. *Just a ploy*, says the guy who…." She cut herself off and looked apologetically away when he finally stirred from his trance and looked at her. "I'm sorry. I didn't mean that."

"You think what we're doing is ridiculous?" His voice was still so ethereally calm. "You think the Church of the Tropolis is ridiculous."

"I'm trying to keep an open mind. I promise."

"I'm not Grant. You can be honest."

She bit her tongue, but his eerie coolness had a way of putting her at ease. "It's just— this is all frustrating. Ever since I came to the Monastery you've all been telling me that the cure is just *out there* somewhere for me to find. I don't mean to be so impatient, but I'm running out of time. I don't have much longer to spend looking."

Gomad seemed to stir this in his head. "It *is* a bit ridiculous."

She gave him a double-take.

"Grant and Kelroy can be a bit dogmatic sometimes," he said. "It makes them poorer listeners than they could be. Not just to people, but to the voice of the Tropolis, if it has a voice. But they are wise men."

"*If* it has a voice?"

"Yes."

"But you're wearing those robes. You're a certified Lurker, aren't you? Aren't you supposed to be certain about these things?"

"Certainty tends to be the enemy of truth. If I am a certified Lurker, then…." He trailed off. "In honesty, I sense you're not a spiritual person. Are you? Would you say you dismiss notions of the divine or supernatural sort?"

"Basically."

"Did Cass foretell your friend's death?"

Shayna hesitated. "I'm not sure anymore. Maybe that's just how I took her words after the fact."

"Did you save Katja last night?"

She said nothing.

Gomad said "I've felt and experienced many things that can't be accounted for too simply. I know it's more sensible to believe that the universe is chaotic, and yet I keep seeing an order. One that rational thought, common sense and machine science all say should not be there. You see an order, don't you?"

Shayna thought about this.

He said "I've seen you see it, I think. As for me, I have small glimpses of it. I have strange intuitions. One day I knew I wanted to devote my life to the study of that order. The teachings of Urbanology seemed to offer the best framework for doing it. I do believe the teachings – but foremost among them is that it's more important to listen than to speak. That's what I try to do. It's how I find objects." He looked out the window and checked his map one more time and said "This is our stop."

She looked out the window and winced. "What stop?"

Gomad went to the front of the bus, where it took him some time to convince the driver to let them out in the middle of the route. The machine finally lurched to a halt, and they stepped down into a neighborhood that wasn't just lifeless but deep-dead. Shayna guessed that the nearest powered street lamp was at least five miles away. By night this place would be pitch black, and there'd be too many stars to count on both hands. It was hard to estimate how long it had been since any human being had set foot here.

The monk perched at the curb, looking at his map and compass and scratching his naked scalp as the bus rolled away on its black fumes. His cool gaze surveyed the hollow ruins in long, slow sweeps, as if skimming a text.

"I think the place you drew is somewhere in there," he said, pointing down the most debris-strewn street in sight. "Perhaps a quarter mile."

She scrutinized the map herself and nodded uneasily.

"I'll be looking out," he said. "I'll keep my senses open and let you know if an object speaks to me."

She bit her tongue and followed uncertainly after him. Within half a block they were doing more climbing than walking. The path was jammed with the rust-red corpses of cars, downed street lamps, fallen walls, the occasional artifacts of old televisions and appliances. In places the street itself had started to cave in, revealing the black chambers below. Sometimes the sound of running water rose from those depths, making her cringe – but unlike the last sewer she'd been in, there were no smells here. In fact it was strange to her how clean the air tasted and felt in her lungs. No traffic here. No trash that hadn't long ago decayed as far as it could. Everything that could flavor the air had weathered completely away by now.

There were sections of street where the rubble was piled so high, and spread so evenly, that it almost seemed as if it had been put that way intentionally. As if someone had tried to build a wall out of the ruins – but what was there out here to seal in or seal out?

Her curiosity pushed her on into the crumbling remains after Gomad's clambering tangle of black robes, but as they probed deeper into the dead section, her anxiety began to seep in. When she looked back, the chaos of rust and concrete was too thick to make out the street where they'd stepped off the bus.

"Any intuitions yet about what we're here to find?" she asked.

"Nope." He tripped hard when a heap of bricks gave way under him, but dusted himself off and kept climbing over and down the other side.

“Are you sure we’ll be able to find our way back if we keep going like this?”

He looked over his shoulder and rubbed his chin. “Eventually. Sometimes one gets a little lost when searching. Sometimes it’s a necessary part of the search.”

Shayna pursed her lips and swallowed her misgivings – but ten creeping blocks later, they came to ledge. The desiccated city was suddenly cracked open into a gigantic rift, fifty feet wide and nearly as deep, carved out of old dirt and the protruding rusty bones of rebar and concrete. They stopped to catch their breath and look down.

“It must have been an earthquake,” he said. “Or something eroded the ground underneath the concrete. It must have happened years ago, whatever it was.”

“Are we going around it?” She tried to look down its length, but she couldn’t make out whether there was any intact bridge to the other side.

Gomad was already climbing down into the rift, using some rebar as hand and foot holds.

“Wait,” she called down. “How are you going to climb up the other side? I don’t see any way to get up on that side.”

“Not up. Through. That passage must lead back to the surface at some point.” He pointed to a black hole on the opposite bank of the rift. Some underground corridor buried three stories deep, probably a sewer, had been cut open and exposed by the rift.

She climbed down after him and ran to catch up as he ducked into the tunnel and disappeared. She stopped at the entrance, looking inward.

“Can you see anything in there?” she asked.

“Not really. But I can feel my way, I think. You have a cigarette lighter, don’t you?”

She looked over her shoulder and sighed. “Let’s go back, Gomad.”

His voice echoed in the dark. “Are you sure? I feel like it’s not much farther. I think I can see something glittering.”

She squinted in there long enough to see it for herself, but she said “I’m not going down into another sewer. I’d hate to tell you why.” She briefly remembered that the necklace of teeth was still in her pocket.

“Okay,” he said, and they headed back for the Metro route. “The High Lurker will be ready to see you soon anyway. Better not to keep him waiting.”

“Invisibility is one of the simpler powers,” said Grant to Shayna as she hurried after him. “The complication is that each *place* has its own art of invisibility – its own range of effect, outside of which it will act the opposite. Are you listening?”

Kelroy looked over his shoulder to scrutinize her closely as they walked, too fast.

"Yeah," said Shayna, irritably. "I don't understand what the hell you're *talking* about, but I'm listening to every word."

"Good." Bad smooth music echoed from somewhere, underlying Grant's words. "I am speaking of the mystic art of Camoumancy, a kind of magic that is vital to moving and interacting within distant parts of the Tropolis. I will now instruct you in the Camoumancy of the Inner Ring. It is one of the most difficult kinds, and it will require your complete application."

"Fine. Let's get on with it."

The thrift store spread its buzzing-lighted aisles far and wide around them. The easy listening was momentarily cut open by a garbled, ear-splitting voice from the checkout stands, unintelligible and full of shrieking feedback. Shayna squinted out in its direction.

She crashed into Kelroy's back when the monks stopped short.

"Here," said Grant. He took a hanger from the rack and held it up to her, judging its dimensions. "Yes. This seems proper."

It looked like something that had fallen out of a television or a magazine and spent some time in a real-life gutter: a gray dress made out of some dull, metallic fabric, with only a few stains and split seams. It was small and thin. She felt the blood rising in her face.

"I haven't worn a dress since I was eight years old," Shayna said. "And I never wore one like that."

Maybe I should call Alice for advice, she thought smugly.

"Take it to the dressing room," said Grant. "The fit must be perfect."

"Can't you just sprinkle me in pixie dust? Couldn't you just give me a magic invisibility ring or something?"

The monks snorted their disapproval.

Back at the monastery, Kelroy sat hunched in the corner, furiously sewing away at the dress with a magnifier clenched in his sweating eye socket. Gomad was shining the shoes. Grant was whispering mantras and studying some torn-out bits of glossy magazines as if he were consulting a holy text, while Shayna slumped on a stool in the corner, dripping dry, hand planted despairingly on her forehead.

"Sit down here," Grant said, manifesting the makeup - but when she did, the cases stayed closed. He only held the candle closer to her until she squinted, and looked very long and hard into her eyes.

"What?" she demanded.

"Your eyes. Do you know where they're from?" He called Kelroy over with a wave of his hand, and then both of them were staring at her.

"My mother? What do you mean 'where'?"

"It's subtle," said Kelroy. "It will only be a problem if someone gets close to her."

"We can't take that chance," Grant said. "I'll have to mask them somehow. With the eyeliner."

"Sunglasses," said Kelroy. "Large ones, close-fitting."

"What the hell are you two talking about?" Shayna asked.

"You're not of Inner Ring stock," Grant told her, providing a small mirror. "Most of your features will pass well enough. This foundation will lighten your skin sufficiently. But your eyes would betray you for an Outer Tropolitan. Their shape."

Shayna looked at her own dimly-lit eyes in the circle of the tiny mirror. "What's wrong with their shape?"

"Nothing," Kelroy said as he rooted through a collection of glasses. "Not out here. But there are no Asians in the Inner Ring."

"I'm Asian?"

"Aren't you?" Grant asked.

She shrugged.

"One of your ancestors, then. A family member."

"I never had much family," she said, putting on the wine-colored lenses Kelroy handed to her.

Just remember the mission, Shayna whispered to herself. *The mission. I'm on a mission.*

"Hurry up," Grant said through the door.

"Are you sure there's no other way to do this?"

"Yes."

"Shit," she sighed, and pushed meekly out of the room.

Gomad averted his eyes instantly. The other two looked her over in methodical, pensive judgment.

"I don't feel like I have this thing on right," she said, fighting the urge to tug at the fabric again. "It doesn't fit right—"

"Unfold your arms," Grant commanded.

"It fits," Kelroy appraised.

"Like a condom," Shayna said. She felt claustrophobic at the same time as she felt more naked and exposed than she could remember ever being. Flickers of excitement and twinges of hysterical laughter were swirling within her too – what Outsider girl never once feverishly dreamed of the absurd Insider-style femininity that sang from all the billboards and bus ads and televisions and storefronts and food packages and magazines and posters and aerial holograms and everything else? – but she hadn't expected that excitement to be drowned out by such a sense of nudity. She kept reaching reflexively for her army coat.

"The stain I couldn't get out is there on your side, to the left of your n-navel," Kelroy said, clearing his throat, "So that's where, as much as possible, you should hold this." He handed her a silvered plastic hexagon about the breadth of a hand.

"What the heck is it?" Shayna asked, grabbing it, and the strap fell down. "A purse? But it's so small. Where am I going to put my switchblade?"

"Women don't carry knives in Greentowne. They carry cyanide jets, but we don't have any here."

"Well what am I going to do then?"

"Lurker Gomad will ride Inward with you as far as he can," Grant said uneasily. "You should be safe on the streets from there. You can meet him again on your way back to the monastery."

Shayna sighed and dared to look herself over again. She felt her own anxious breath on the makeup-caked tops of her breasts, and her shaved and stocking-clad legs itched and burned in ways they never had before.

"Let's get on with it," she said angrily, and started for the door. Only on her way down did she grasp the complexity of walking in heels that high. Gomad caught her awkwardly. Her powdered arm scratched a creamy mark across his black robe.

"As for the matter of walking, I found a magazine article that seems to explain," Grant said. "I put it in the purse. Study it. Intuit its secrets. Perhaps you would prefer to stay here and practice until—"

"No, damnit. I've got a mission to do. There's no time to waste. Let's go, Gomad."

He followed at her side through the columned hall, his arms always a little spread and ready.

Only twenty minutes down the line it was already the strangest Metro ride Shayna had ever taken. The off looks intensified as the bus filled up. Her knees ached from keeping her legs crossed for so long. She kept the wine-colored lenses close and tried to stay focused on the rushing scenery.

"How will you find this woman?" Gomad asked in his muttering way.

"I have her home address."

"Won't she be at work now?"

"Probably. So I wrote a note. I'll put it under her door or something, if that's the best I can do." She opened her purse to check that it was still there.

Gomad peeked in at the thick fold of pages. "That whole note is only you asking her for the name?"

She closed the purse and answered sheepishly: "Not just that. Everything. I wrote down everything I could think of to say at all. Everything that's happened to me. I started writing and I couldn't stop. I hope it's not too long, or too gushy – but this might be the only chance I get. Didn't make sense to hold anything back."

"You could have just sent it through the mail," the Lurker said – and then, after a smirking pause, added "But that would never satisfy you. You had to go there yourself. To the true source."

She looked at him through her big glasses.

The bus climbed down from the flyway as the first visible fringes of Greentowne were spreading out across the front windows. When the doors hissed open at the next stop, the few Outer Tropolitans who remained blew away like cellophane wrappers. By the stop after that, the bus was full again – with Them. People with buttons and briefcases. People whose hair was straight and clean, and Shayna forgot that this time so was hers.

The looks she'd been getting before were one thing, pure and lecherous – but the looks she was getting now were something else entirely. These eyes were so opposite from the ones that had burned into her the day Carl had rescued her. They burned cool now. As much as she tried to ignore them, she was entranced by them, unable to stop wondering what those traces of illegible expression were standing for.

"I've practiced Camoumancy too," Gomad whispered in her ear. "I know what you're thinking. What shocks you: suddenly they aren't afraid of you."

"Yes. But it's more than—"

"They also think you're farther In than they are. They envy you."

"Envy," she mouthed to herself. She wondered if anyone had ever envied her before. She couldn't think of anything quite like the faces of all those silver-earringed women, each taking her brass ones for gold.

"It'll be over in a few more stops," he said. "This is as far as I can go." His voice, like the rest of him, was recoiling into timid oblivion with every street that passed, and she could see the glares that fixed on him, too. One creased and crusty suit at the front wouldn't look away. When the doors hissed open and Gomad stood to leave, she looked at him over the tops of her glasses and swallowed hard.

He said "Remember. Catch this bus, the number 2. I'll be here. The stop at Holiday street. Stay safe."

Shayna raised a few shy fingers in parting. Then he was gone and it was a different man's ass slumped in the worn vinyl beside her – an older man whose face pointed forward, but whose left eye peered eerily down and sideways into the depths of her exaggerated curves. Ignoring Kelroy's advice, she covered her neckline with the silvered hexagon and forgot about the stain.

The scenery decayed in reverse as she penetrated deeper and deeper into the heart of lightness. All the steel lost the vibrancy of its rust, the concrete lost its lichen and its lime, and all the tags and murals were muted by armies of mismatched squares and rectangles and finally made into nothing but ghosts. There was something ghostly everywhere now; she pulled away the glasses for a moment to see that the light out there really was increasing. It seemed to come from inside of everything. In another few blocks the shadows were bleached completely away, and the luminance that filled their space was dull and colorless, not like sunlight, not like any earthly light. It covered everything like a powder, blurring it all together, half-erasing it. Only when she got up and made her way through the suddenly near-empty bus and perched by the front windows did she see that it was all reflecting down, raining from the white crystal walls rising ludicrously high at the end of that road. She was on the other side of it now, between it and the afternoon sun. She was out of its shadow – and she was so close now that it looked like a whole sky in itself.

"Last stop," grunted the driver.

Shayna squinted out the window. The street number was 30.

She swiped The Pass. "Where can I catch a bus farther Inward?"

"Inner thirty streets, car traffic only," said the driver, slowly and condescendingly.

The glass panes pried themselves shut as soon as she was through them. Then she was standing there in those stupid heels, hands on her hips, squinting even through the wine-colored lenses down twenty-one blocks of powdered sugar and silvered glass.

There was nothing to say or do. She smoked and walked.

Everything that passed was ominously quiet. The cars had silencers. The pedestrians were only a handful, and they spoke only into phones and only in whispers. Some walked on silenced shoes, and the eerie, narrow sidewalks beneath them were seamless and polished smooth. No gum. No tan tufts of weeds or blowing trash. No shit. There weren't even utility poles or surveillance cameras; the sidewalks had no features except for weird, inert metallic bubbles at every corner.

She wondered how she would tell anyone about this. She tried and failed to imagine the lives of the men and women who slipped past her by wide margins – in whose wakes swirled no human scents, but only faint and strange perfumes.

She took her time and tried not to trip. She stopped a few times to air out the blisters – standing at the curb, ridiculous shoes in hand, pretending not to notice anyone who noticed her, pretending she was waiting for something specific. Then she went on.

There it was. She read the number in burning silver leaf on a white marble arch, just where it was supposed to be. The building was only a few stories in height, but every story and its tinted windows loomed abnormally tall.

Leaning against the smooth stone by the entrance, she decided to take a moment. She looked up into the searing luminance of the Cology above, trying pointlessly to make out the shapes of its sides, but all she saw were vast white polygons etched into half of an overcast sky. She tried to take this bizarre scene in, knowing—

"I say it *is* up for *fucking* discussion," shouted a voice from above. It was a man's voice with a slight Insider accent. Something about the way it said *fucking* made it clear that it never used that word, and its harshness made Shayna shiver.

There was another voice. A woman's, breathing indecipherable words between little puffs of cigarette smoke coming from a half-open window directly above. Shayna stared up and began to bite her long false nails; it was the nurse's voice.

"—believe I told you to *fucking* quit it!" the male voice shrieked.

"Oh, what's the damn difference anyway?"

"How many years have we all been telling you? How long, Janet?"

"You don't see what I see."

"I'm taking—" he shouted, then the soundproof window whirred shut and all was dead silent again.

Shayna waited a while. When nothing happened, she took a deep breath and started up the white marble steps. She followed them to a glass door that wouldn't open, and a short line of glittering mailboxes. She took the note from her purse and examined it.

Suddenly a tall man was throwing the soundproof glass door open and barreling through it. The neck of a clear plastic bag was twisted in his fist, and in the bag were a dozen cartons of cigarettes.

A shot of blood hit Shayna's head. She panicked and thoughtlessly shoved the note into the slot.

The man stopped. His icy eyes darted back and forth between her and the mailboxes. Hurriedly she put the purse over the stain, but she knew he saw. She knew he was looking at the stitches.

"Who are you?" he demanded. "Exactly what are you doing here?" His free hand swept over a smooth lacquered shell of brown hair.

"I—" she stammered. "Just. Note for Janet."

He passed his hand over the mailbox and it popped open by itself. He reached in and grabbed the note. He unfolded it with a whip of his hand.

Shayna bit her tongue and watched the wrinkles in his brow deepen by the moment.

He crumpled the paper in his palm and shoved it into the plastic bag.

"Get out of here," he said.

She pulled the glasses off of her face and said "I have to talk to her. I need to speak to Janet Wallace."

"There's no one here by that name. Get out." He hurried down the stairs and onto the luminous, silent street.

"You don't understand. I just need—"

"My wife isn't accepting visitors at this time. Get out of here."

"Wait!"

She followed him to one of the shining metal bubbles in the pavement. He passed his fingers over it and a black hole formed, leading down into oblivion. He fixed his harsh eyes on her as he threw the bag down. It echoed in the void. The hole sealed itself.

"I'm notifying the police now," he said, reaching for something in his pocket. "I'll notify them if I ever see you again. Now, get the *fuck* out of here."

It made her jump when he said it – but she made a point of taking a long look around and trying to think of an alternative, before stepping out of her shoes and turning her back on him. This was too dangerous a place to try anything.

Nothing to do, she thought as she marched sorely back into the eerie blankness, heels in hand – *nothing to do but get out of these fucking clothes*.

Leaving the Inner Ring, she watched the world return to ordinary dimness. Surfaces sagged and rusted and took on soot in the right direction, and something in the back of her throat relaxed to see it happen – even as it occurred to her to liken the decay out there to what would inevitably unfold, maybe was already unfolding, inside of herself. For half a second she thought of her own cells one by one rusting into the ground like the blocks just past the window. The bus rumbled onward into the sun.

People pressed through the hissing doors and began to fill up the space, and the rising drizzle of probing looks turned her attention outward to the street names. She watched them in nervous anticipation, burning the word *Holiday* into her mind.

The street arrived with a hydraulic grunt. She was sure this was where Gomad had stepped off – but there amid the sparse, sulking, stumbling masses, his bald head was nowhere to see.

She half-stood and searched the opposite side of windows. Panicking, she muscled through the clogged aisle and leapt down onto the sidewalk of middle Greentowne. She whipped off the wine-colored lenses and searched the whole scene, but there was no one waiting for her here – save one overbuilt shirt and tie, his head veins glistening in the yellow afternoon, his jaw clamping and unclamping on something, his sweaty eyes fixed tightly on Shayna but missing her eyes by twelve vertical inches. She heard the hissing of the doors behind her and leapt back up into the sweaty space, muttering profanely.

She realized one of those absurd shoes hadn't made it back inside. She watched in horror as the shirt and tie stepped forward, picked it up and held it high with a leering, cud-chewing smile, shouting: "Cinderella!" The light changed and the bus crawled mercifully away.

She stopped caring whose glares said what. Within a few stops they were all gone anyway, along with the last of the silvered windows and ferns in concrete boxes. Then there was just the outer Tropolis, rushing by like television static, sprawled out into infinity just past the flyway divider. She settled uneasily into a window seat in the back and took out the last cigarette she'd been able to fit into the silver hexagon. She lifted up her foot to brace against the armrest of the nearby seat, like she always did, but halfway into the motion she hurriedly put it back down and refolded her legs. No one had been looking, but her hand was lightly shaking when she flicked the lighter. The familiar landscape turned menacing and strange.

From here to the monastery, she judged, would take maybe an hour. She sighed and pressed the sunglasses back over her eyes. She tried to get comfortable. Before she could, her phone rang in her pocket, but the screen listed all zeroes as the incoming number. Uncertainly she answered: "Hello?"

It wasn't a commercial. On the other side there was faint wind. Slow breathing.

"Who's there?" Shayna asked.

The call ended.

"Great," she sighed.

After a while she just pretended to be half-asleep. It stopped people from asking her if she was lost, even if it didn't stop the snickering. She kept the purse cracked open with one hand planted half-inside, as if keeping her cyanide jet ready. *And thank God for the makeup*, she thought, thick enough to hide the shades of red she knew she was turning – and the glasses, dark and big enough to hide whatever twisted fear she felt rising in her own eyes. Thank the whacky monks.

Through the red vision of the sunglasses, however, she watched as the younger ones with hungry grins and hopes at most for their own vicious amusement were one by one repelled by the encroaching energy field of something even more sinister. She felt its approach like the thickening air in front of a storm. It took the form of an old man, pushing forty by the looks of him, with a hunching back and irises that to different degrees were as overcast as the sky. Every time a seat opened closer to her, she watched him get up and move, always reaching ahead of himself in just less than total blindness. He moved in these increments for half an hour. Finally he was there, sitting directly across from her and staring. She dared not meet his eyes. Even the dark and thin-worn flesh that framed them was hard to look at. She found herself hoping and telling herself that these fat sunglasses had some magic to them too, some form of protection, even if Kelroy had just dug them out of that big plastic bag. *Magic in the Tropolis is inconspicuous*, Grant had said. *Magic in the Tropolis is—*

Some sound welled itself up from the depths of the stranger's gaunt, stubbled throat, scattering her thoughts. She pretended not to hear it, but it came again, louder:

"You are one of them," said the stranger.

"One what?" she asked quietly.

"Insider."

"No."

"I hear the lie in your voice." His bottom lip trembled in the corner of her red vision. His voice rumbled: "You are one of them."

If you could only see my teeth, she thought, but the electrical charge in the air was too thick to speak through. She sat still and kept her mouth shut, and kept her focus on the hollow rushing street – but in the corner of her eyes she knew nonetheless that his milky pupils were burning even hotter, and the bony fingers in his lap were clenching into withered fists.

"You know what your house is made of?"

She didn't answer.

"Blood," he said. "Your house is made of blood."

Out there, the street numbers were getting high enough. In the distance she saw the crownless tower rising up above the broken bricks. She was close.

Then the stranger growled:

"Fallon's Field."

That was all.

A few minutes of nothingness ticked by between them. Then it was her stop. She got off in a hurry and felt that energy field pushing her through the hissing doors.

She survived the hundred-foot shoe-in-hand walk from the Metro to the monastery and heaved panting relief when she slammed the door to her lonely quarters behind her.

Grant's voice called through the door: "You made it back. Did you learn the name?"

"No," Shayna shouted as she stripped. Fighting her way back into her own clothes, she yelled: "Now I have three questions. First: what the hell is Fallon's Field?"

"I don't know."

"Two," Shayna yelled as, fastening her belt, she caught a glimpse of herself in the mirror she'd left sitting on the bed. "Where can I wash this stuff off my face?"

"Down the hall."

Relishing her return to the shelter of her army coat, she said: "Three: what the hell happened to Gomad?"

"He's been arrested."

Her goggles hesitated in her hands. Grant was there, as monolithic as ever, gazing stoically down when she pressed the door open.

"What?" she gasped.

"He called here from the detention center. Company security took him on a vagrancy charge while he was waiting for you. He traveled too far Inward."

Shayna twisted the rubber straps in her hands and said "Well, what are we going to do?"

Grant sighed as he turned away: "Keep it among our prayers that incarceration is merciful to him."

She rushed after him. "That's it? They're sending him straight to the community service camps? There's nothing we can do?"

"What would you suggest?"

The back of his bald head receded into the scrawled poles and shafts of light.

"Thank you," Carl said as they walked along under the hot sun.

"For what?" Shayna asked through the flame of her lighter. "For agreeing to meet you here? I have soft spot for desperate, begging messages."

"For letting me say sorry in person," he said miserably. "I'm sorry, okay? It was wrong of me to ask."

"I'm not going to kiss you, Carl. Blackmail or no. I'd get that through your head now if I were you." Something about being fully clothed again (and armed), she decided, was making her feel newly invincible. Certainly towards the likes of Carl.

"F-fine." He fixed his eyes bitterly on the sidewalk ahead of them. "Anyway, don't flatter yourself. You couldn't *pay* me to kiss you."

She smoked and walked without a word.

"With all the tail I catch with the Chickmobile, I don't have the time *or* attention to waste on a girl like you. I've already got a mountain of pussy. Any time I want. So don't flatter yourself thinking you could pay me a billion bucks to kiss you. Got it?"

Shayna bit her tongue.

They walked in silence for a while, following the steel-clutched confluences of power lines all humming softly in the baking light.

"How have you been?" Carl asked.

"Almost got arrested again today."

"Oh."

"How's work at the Regulator plant?" she asked, steering the conversation away from his other job and the Chickmobile, she hoped.

"Crazy. The stuff I overhear from the whitecoats. I mean, do you actually know what the Regulator does?"

"It shoots sulfur up into the sky, right?"

"Yeah, but do you know *why* it shoots sulfur? I didn't even know. I've been working there for two years, and I only overheard yesterday. What it's actually for."

"I guess I don't know."

Carl narrated excitedly: "So there used to be, like hundreds of years ago, this natural layer of the atmosphere that bounced some sunlight back into space so the world didn't get too hot. But it was destroyed somehow, so they had to make up for it artificially, with the Regulator. It basically cools the entire planet down. If all the Regulators stopped working, the ocean would boil. Boil straight up."

"Hmm."

"They just have to make sure they don't put too much up there, or it'll freeze the world and cause more superstorms. Plus, you know, that's why there's that huge area East of the Regulator that had to be abandoned. Fire Alley. The whole ruined neighborhood there."

"I thought nobody lives in Fire Alley because there was, you know, a *fire* there," Shayna said acidly.

"No, no. Go there on a rainy day and you'll see. It burns your skin. It eats metal."

The end of the road appeared before them as two tall chainlink gates. Beyond it stood a geometric forest of green steel pylons, gigantic cylindrical stacks of wavy metal plates, and a thousand separate power lines all weaving together into one vast buzzing knot.

The two left the road and followed where a narrow path was etched into the brown grass along the fence, until they came to a dusty, half-constructed hill. From the top they looked down into the depths of the metal forest, and out along the endless lines that reached for every corner of the urban horizon on towering legs of steel. In the hazy distances of those lines they could see more chainlink-bounded forests, more pylons and plates, seeming to go on forever.

"What is all this stuff?" Shayna asked, gazing down into the machinery. "What is it for? Do you know? Does anybody?"

Carl scratched his head and said "Have you ever really looked at a circuit board? Like in a busted television or a broken phone. All those chips, the capacitors and the transistors, all the microscopic parts. The Tropolis looks just the same from high up. The streets and buildings and power lines and things."

Shayna exhaled the last of her cigarette and squinted into his glowing passion.

"It's like the whole Tropolis is just one great big machine," he said, reaching out across the singing pylons. "And all of this, and everything we can see, and maybe even you and me, are all just parts on the circuit board."

She sighed and thought of what the monks had told her. She said "But what is it all for? What does the whole machine do?"

Carl stared thoughtfully into the infinite sprawl and said "Fuck if I know."

"Just like that," Shayna said to the luminous surface tension. "He was gone. They took him. While he was waiting for me."

Katja leaned back into a pensive silence. Carl was there too, pausing with his shot. Tom was there, still meek and sober, huddled on the sidelines. Shayna was spending all her concentration pretending he wasn't.

"I feel responsible," she said. "It wouldn't have happened if.... He was only there to watch out for me."

"You can't blame yourself," Katja said.

"I know. But, shit, *he* never even *did* any felonies. I'm the one who—"

Her friends were watching her. The crowd of smoking silhouettes behind them loomed ominously or lay in wait, one phone call away from an arrest commission.

She cleared her throat, readjusted her goggles on her forehead and said "I mean, he just didn't do anything wrong."

"'Vagrancy'," Tom said. "What does that even mean?"

Carl said "That's when people think you're ugly. So ugly that it's a crime."

"You must get that a lot," Katja said.

Carl narrowed his eyes and huffed.

"This is serious," Shayna said sharply.

In the corner of her eye she saw Katja nodding and looking away with reddened cheeks fading into shadow. She saw Carl draw a slow breath and look at her.

Tom took a wheezing gulp of booze and asked "What were you even doing in the Inner Ring? I must have missed that part of the story."

"Nothing." She put her chin in her palm and stared into the luminous smoke. "Anyway, I just wish there was something I could do about it. I wish I could help him."

As she stared aimlessly into the hazy space the silhouettes miraculously parted – and there at the end of it all was Black Faction in their matching stocking caps, slumped around the same ratty booth seat.

She got up and muscled her way through to them. They weren't smoking anything this time, but they all looked even more sullen as before. Their mouths stayed shut when she stepped up to their table. They just watched her.

("Where did you go?" Carl's yell echoed. She ignored it.)

"You're revolutionaries, right?" she said. "Black Faction."

"Who's asking?" muttered the ring leader – Blue Dog, she remembered. He didn't seem to remember her.

Her liquor-numbed lips improvised: "Maybe I'm a revolutionary too. We met last night."

"Shay." Again there was that quiet grin that crossed him, and the faint difference in the way he pronounced her name; the way they all pronounced it to each other and grinned the same quiet grin.

"That's a special name," said one of the women. "How did you get it?"

"I don't know what you mean. Listen. You were talking about the prisons last night. Well, friend of mine was just arrested today. He's probably already on his way to the community service camps."

"We all have friends among the Thirty Percent," said Blue Dog. "Some of us have brothers among the institutionalized. Sisters. Parents. Some have children."

"What if I want to do something about it?"

One of them cleared a seat for her on the booth. She quietly took it.

"Like what?" said Blue Dog. "Maybe you want to bust him out?"

"Maybe."

"No." He shook his head dismissively.

"You think I'm not serious?" she whispered hatefully, reading him the same way she had read Grant in the dandelion garden. "Maybe you think I'm not willing to do what it takes. But I'm ready. I'm fucking *ready*, even—"

"You can be as serious as you want. It doesn't matter."

"Why not?"

"Because even if you succeed it wouldn't make any difference. Not only would the comps just find someone else to fill up their arrest quota. Not only would your friend have suffered civic death even as a free man. It would be superficial. It would have no impact on the fundamental problem. The problem is not one man imprisoned. The problem is not even one in three men and women in the entire Tropolis imprisoned. The fundamental problem is an insidious entanglement of socio-economic power structures which exist to exploit human beings to the maximum monetary benefit of its architects. Rokosz explains all of this."

"What the hell are you talking about?" she demanded.

"The disease. While you're just talking about symptoms. We aren't interested in symptoms. We are only interested in the disease itself, and curing it. That's the only thing that will make any meaningful difference in this world."

A few solemn nods passed among the rest of the black stocking caps.

"There's no point in even discussing this until you've read the treatise," he added.

She rolled her eyes. "Symptoms, disease. Fine, I get it. But if you don't care about the symptoms, what are you doing about the disease?"

Blue Dog cracked a chuckling smile which spread among his comrades. "We're not participating."

Shayna studied him in quizzical contempt.

"We don't have to do anything to hasten it," he continued. "The revolution is inevitable. The system is going to overturn itself by the very intensity of its flaws. It's totally unsustainable. There will come a tipping point. When that happens, we'll be there. We'll be prepared. Psychologically.

To do what has to be done." He reached into his coat pocket and withdrew a virgin joint. "That's what else this is for."

She watched the revolutionary find a silver lighter within himself, and when he flicked it the flame came out in an erratic crooked sliver of red light, shooting off small sparks. She stared hypnotically into the drug's ignition with eyes unfocused. There in the blur of smoke and ember and darkness, she thought of the Heaps.

She thought: *your house is made of blood.*

"What is Fallon's Field?" she asked, lost.

Blue Dog shook his head and shrugged as he bitterly inhaled. The green neon clock behind him ticked toward midnight.

It wasn't until she saw the heads around her turning upward that she noticed the rising noise. Something weird and muffled and mechanical. Something buzzing.

"And what is that sound?"

"Oh fuck," choked Blue Dog. "Black Helicopters."

The stoned and schnockered masses gravitated away from the bar and left their seats of ragged vinyl. They began to trickle up the stairs and bunch around the few slit windows, squinting up in anxious curiosity at the pulsating fury of sound and light. Now there was another noise, rising slightly above the din of what were now unmistakably the whirling rapid-fire blades of the Black Helicopters: the mangled crackling of a high-power megaphone.

"Shay!" Carl shouted above the crowd, but she ignored him. With a slight duck of her head she turned invisible within the gathered crowd. Meanwhile the megaphone voice was barking a lot of short sentences, mostly unintelligible, except that they all began with the same two repeating words. Somebody's name.

"Don Malt," the megaphone squeaked.

"Don... Malt?" somebody echoed.

Through the cracks in the dirty glass she thought she saw the last of the helicopters touching down in the vacant lot down the block. More of the megaphone's words managed to squeeze through the slowing blades.

"—all guilty of felony trespass," it said. "Don Malt is the titular and rightful owner of these premises. Don Malt has never granted fair use of these premises to you or to anyone. Don Malt requires you to vacate these premises immediately and submit to possible detention for your contempt of his lawful property rights—"

"Who the *fuck* is Don Malt?" somebody asked.

People continued to drift up the stairs as the curiosity in their faces congealed into blank paralysis. The electric voice kept repeating itself.

Shayna shook herself out of her trance and remembered the hidden door. She muscled through the crowd and darted for it, but she heard the black blades chopping on the other side of the plywood. One squint through the gap confirmed her fear: a gigantic mechanical shadow was looming through the cracks in the dome. She could see the comps now, silhouetted against their own gray flashlights which fluttered across the crumbling walls, cracking their boots into the vertical plaster as they slid down on black arachnoid tethers.

"Vacate immediately," barked the noise from above. "Or you will be incarcerated."

The population of the Green Room had thinned, but she found Black Faction hanging around by the bottom of the stairs, straightening their stocking caps and watching the rest of the shuffling drunks.

"What do we do?" she asked anxiously, though it crossed her mind that they were probably the last ones to ask.

"They'll only take a small portion of the crowd. We should escape as long as we don't emerge at the front of the line. Or the end."

"How do you know? What the hell is even going on?"

"This is what happened to our last three meeting places. Mr. Malt is probably an Insider. He may legally own hundreds or thousands of condemned, inhabited buildings like this one."

"I don't get it," she said. "If he owns the Green Room—"

"To him there is no Green Room. Just a building full of trespassers."

The revolutionaries gauged the crowd one last time and then joined its upward flow. Shayna shoved her way onto the first step. Then there was no going back. Against her uncertainty, she was lifted upward, out of the green-lit smoke, until the sidewalk was under her feet and the spotlights were burning in her eyes. The drizzle was falling in glowing sheets.

"Don Malt would like to remind you..." crackled the megaphone, a bit hesitantly, "that you should all be going to work tomorrow morning with clear heads. Don Malt reminds you that industrial inefficiency is a criminal—"

"You," barked a voice from up ahead in what Shayna dizzily realized was a wide shuffling line, walled by rain-glistening body armor and stun prods. "You," the voice barked again, and again, regularly. She stretched on the tips of her toes and tried to see above the solemn flow of shoulders and heads, and by the time she saw the black armored glove she had arrived directly before it.

"You," the lead comp barked from behind the impenetrable visor of his black metal helmet. She froze solid, but the armored hand that shot out from that wall of carapace didn't reach for her. It swung instead for the muscular figure in front of her in line – and it was blocked and then responded to with a lightning kick directly into the comp's un-armored groin.

Fifty stun prods shrieked instantly to life and everyone around her bolted for the gaps in the human wall.

She lost any clear sense of what was happening. Everything erupted into a head-knocking frenzy of shouting and shoving and megaphone chatter and electricity that jumped gaps between electrodes and teeth and convulsing bodies. The fray wore rapidly thinner. She tried to see a way out, but before she could she hit the side of her face on something that knocked hollowly, and when she turned she saw a silver badge burning white hot in the spotlights.

Her mind frenzied and blank, she felt her hand diving into the gun's pocket as the black carapace rushed at her. Suddenly it stopped. The comp froze as if hit with its own stun prod. Then it flipped up its visor. The shocked, wide-eyed face that had been hidden there gasped:

"*Shay?*"

"Balboa?" she yelled.

The strike came from behind.

8

She startled out of a singing white light and into a darker one. It flickered from above, grayish and dim, down onto the blurry forms spread around her: what resolved itself into medical machines, plastic cabinets, collapsible beds draped in plastic. When she leaned upward the ache crackled through the back of her head like lightning.

She took a wincing look around and found herself alone. Her goggles were on the bed beside her. Something clinked when she put her boots on the floor – when she looked down and lifted her foot she made out the metallic glint of a scalpel. When she reached instinctively for the ache in the back of her head, the first thing her fingers touched was a piece of gauze, and beneath it the tips of buzz-cut hairs, and then the raised flesh and the stitches. The sealed wound she cautiously traced was about an inch long, surrounded by a fat patch of scalp that had been reduced to fuzz, and the flesh there was still fizzling with anesthetic.

There was a window meshed in crosshatched wire. Two figures stood on the other side, peering occasionally in at her. Now one shook its head dismissively and walked off down the hall, and the other turned the steel knob on the steel door. Slowly, with his palms open toward her as if to prove they were empty, Balboa approached the bed. His comp boots squeaked on the plastic tiles. His frame, even with his armor stripped down to the glove-like underlayer, was ominous and huge and as featureless as shadow under the dim artificial light. He sat on the edge of the bed across from her. He hung his bulbous head and sighed.

"I'm sorry," he said.

She swallowed hard. She could feel that the hard weight of the gun in her pocket was gone.

"Don't tell me, don't—" she stuttered. "Don't tell me I'm...."

"No." He shook his head. "No, you're not arrested. You're not in any trouble."

"Did they run my ID card?"

"No," he said unsurely. "Why?"

"Doesn't matter."

"Shay, I'm sorry. I'm real sorry this happened. Like I can't tell you."

"My head."

"You'll be okay. I was afraid for you. I thought Joseph – thought he'd cracked your skull, a hit like that. I took you back to the chopper and made them bring you here. Docs said there was nothing serious. Just a cut. I'm sorry about the hair. But I'm so glad you're okay."

The other figure walked past the far side of the caged glass again, pausing a moment to glower inward. She saw the glinting metal on his uniform before he moved along.

"You're the one who's in trouble, aren't you?"

He looked brokenly at her and said "Don't matter."

The splitting ache fizzled through her head again, making her wince. She bent her head down into her hands and breathed deeply. The tiles between her fingers flickered sickeningly.

"We have a lot to talk about," he whispered sadly.

She said "And nowhere to drink."

Balboa left and returned in the same old stitched-up denim jacket and shorts that he still wore in Shayna's rusty memory of him; the clothes of a simple punk kid. Then they went ahead together, through the long corridors of gray and blue, past comps who were adjusting their armor or washing off their batons or gulping down their coffee – all of them in turn looking up from their tasks to shine their raw glances like flashlights in her face. Pressing through the glass doors and clambering down the wet concrete ramps was a tangible decompression.

The 3 AM darkness was moist and cool, but the drizzle had passed. She didn't notice herself lighting the cigarette until the smoke hit her tongue. There was too much to keep track of. *Where was the fucking gun? Fallen out somewhere at the scene of the riot?*

As soon as the blue lights were small dim enough behind them, she said "So you're one of them now. A Company Man."

He nodded uneasily and stared into the deep space of wet bricks and street lamp stars.

"What the fuck?" she said. "Let's start there. First question."

"I know."

"What the fuck?"

"I know. But listen. You need to listen. Just give me a chance to explain myself."

"Okay. Explain."

He met her stare and snorted a steaming breath. "No."

"What?"

"I won't explain. Because I can tell you're not going to give me a real chance. Because you can't see through it. I can see the hate in your eyes."

She bit her tongue and looked ahead.

"You see me like I've become part of everything we were against," he said. "Like I betrayed you. But I never did, and I'll tell you what I hated, Shay. I'll tell you."

"What did you hate?"

A bus rolled up to the stop and the bright doors hissed apart. Shayna started up the stairs, but Balboa was back on the sidewalk, motioning into the soggy dark.

"I'll tell you," he said.

She sighed a wisp of gray smoke and stepped down.

In the next alley he unchained a bicycle from a hissing pipe. He patted the rear rack, an overbuilt makeshift thing with a pair of rebar foot pegs. She put her goggles down onto her eyes and took the seat and they rolled among the night puddles. She was still too shell-shocked to ask where he was taking her. She just held on and smoked.

"Did I ever tell you about my name?" Balboa said over his shoulder. "I probably never did."

"What about it?"

"It's a last name. Not a first. Didn't you never notice that?"

It was the only name she'd ever known him by. She said "What's your first name then?"

"I don't have one. Not anymore."

"How did you lose it?"

"When I realized it didn't matter anymore. When I knew I only needed one name."

"Your last name?"

"The name of my family."

Balboa steered the bike around a corner, through an intersection and up into a steep incline, but somehow the pedals didn't slow at all. She watched the undulating hulks of his calves as the slanted blocks zoomed along. Even with her weight behind him, he wasn't even breathing harder.

"It's true, isn't it?" she asked him quietly, "What they say. About all the comps having to take steroids. About... all those things being done to them. Chemically. Surgically."

His bald head nodded. He said "Some of it is true."

"What have they done to you?"

He sighed and answered "Enough."

Shayna flicked her cigarette stump into the night and just watched the streets roll by over the crest of the hill. She couldn't decide whether to she was exhausted or inhumanly awake. Her head still ached.

"I wish I could make you understand why I became a comp. I wish anybody could understand. Tom, Katja, Carl, I wish they could all understand. But I know none of them could. You won't. Nobody will."

The bicycle started to pick up speed. At first it didn't bother her, but soon they were climbing the hill as fast as she had ever sped down one, and still accelerating. The wheels began to whine.

"Balboa," she said. "Maybe you should slow—"

"Fuck. I have not one friend in the entire world anymore. Not since I joined the academy. Not since I left the Green Room the last time. But I had to. I *had* to."

"Slow down!" she yelled. She had to raise her voice above the wind now. The rack and the rebar were shaking fiercely enough that her bones ached to hold on. The last working street lamp flew by at forty miles an hour and plunged her into the pitch black.

"I don't know anybody anymore," he said, and the pistons of his calves fired still harder. "Not one person. I don't know anybody."

"Me neither," she said, swallowing down the fear of the black pavement now rushing like a flooding canal just past the tips of her shoes. She could see the bolts buckling on the rack beneath her, but she didn't tell him to slow down again. She put her hand on his heaving dark denim back and said over the wind: "I left too. The same time you did. I left them all behind and I hid out in my shithole apartment alone and I stopped knowing anybody, talking to anybody, anything, and I only just got back, but I still feel like a stranger to them, like an alien, like I'm not there. No one knows me either."

The bike made a terrifying lurch when he took one hand off the bars to wipe his eyes, but it did not fall. In the blurry vortex of speeding night, she felt the wheels mercifully die down into a coast.

"I'm not friends with any of the other comps," he said. "I'm not like them, and I know it, and they know it. We don't get along real well. Maybe I shouldn't have joined. But it was all I could think to do."

"Then explain it to me. I'll listen. I'll try."

"You promise?"

"Yes. Just slow down!"

The brakes hesitantly began to groan against the bent rims.

"Sorry," he said with a sigh. "We're almost there."

The bike skidded to a halt in the middle of a lightless street. The glow of the dirty red sky trickled very faintly down on the hollow buildings, but Shayna could barely make out her hand in front of her face.

"Oh, crap," Balboa said. "I forgot you don't have my nightvision augment."

"Your what?"

"Just follow me. I'll make us some light."

The blocks around them were completely vacant. Not even the little fires of squatters defied the featureless void of sagging bricks. The sky's reflection in the damp street made the ruins into islands of vertical symmetry, like a vast black-on-red ink blot test.

"This place looks like it's been dead for a long time," she observed.

"I saw a map of the Tropolis once, at comp central. The whole sector, all of it, all hundreds of miles across, down to every tiny block, showing which ones are dead and which ones have squatters and which ones are legally lived-in. Most people never realize how much of it is dead, but it's like a great big spider's web – an old one, full of holes, with just a few live threads left, barely holding together. Do you ever think back into the past?"

"How far past?" She tripped over an invisible curb.

"Not just your own past. The past way before you. History."

"I guess not much."

His dim shadow shook its head at her. "Nobody does! Not many people anyway. But I think about it. I can't stop thinking about it. Like when I saw that map. You know that somebody built all these buildings, and somebody lived in them and used them, once. The entire Tropolis had to be full of people once, with no dead neighborhoods at all. It had to be, right?"

"Yeah, I guess."

"There are a lot less people in the world today than there were, maybe, fifty years ago. My grandfather told me there were twice as many people when he was born as there are now."

Shayna said nothing. From where she stood on the edge of the sidewalk, she dimly perceived Balboa taking slow and reverent steps on his holey punk shoes toward the blank concrete wall before him. She saw his head bowed.

"*A world like this*," he said quietly. "My grandfather said to me that a world like this only ever happened because good people stood around and did nothing."

A cigarette lighter flicked within his silhouette, until the damp wick of a candle sputtered uncertainly to life. Then another, and another, until Shayna could see them all in a line resting along a little rain-worn ledge in the concrete wall. At the center of the empty altar, six small letters were carved into the stone.

"What is this?" she asked.

"My family cemetery."

She took a step back into the street.

"There used to be a real cemetery here," he said, "A hundred years ago. It was paved over and this building was made here – but my ancestor from back then remembered exactly where it had been, and he waited for the neighborhood to die, and he made sure he was buried here with his kin when he could be. Down under the basement. My grandfather is buried down there too, like his father and grandfather before him. I hope I'll be buried here too, when that time comes. If there are Balboas left after me."

She stared into the red clouds reflected in the pavement between her boots, and shivered. Something scraped in the ruins somewhere behind her – whether wind or ghost or bird, she couldn't tell, but she shoved her hands into her pockets and wanted to leave and wished she knew where that stupid pistol had gone.

"Do you know the word *legacy?*" Balboa asked.

"The whiskey brand."

"It was a word before that. It means something you leave behind. Something bigger than you that outlasts you through more generations. Goes beyond you."

She stared into his black outline against the candles and sighed.

"Balboa is legacy. My grandfather received it from his father, and his father before him. It goes back centuries. From before the Tropolis. From before the Company and the comps and everything we know, me and you and everybody, as the way things are – but the legacy is the same, like our name. The legacy is a fight."

"Fight who?"

"Not who. There's no one who, no one what. There's a *for*. An idea. For my grandfather, it was.... Have you ever heard of the Unionists?"

"Maybe, once."

"My grandfather was a Unionist. Back when there were still a lot of them. There were things called unions back then. They were like groups of employees who would join together to get the Company to listen to them and treat them better. There were a lot of them, the unions, back all those years ago, but the Company got fed up with them, wanted them all destroyed. So the Unionists came together to resist."

"How did they fight? You mean they fought with comps?"

"Kind of, or... No. That wasn't the idea. They rallied together and protested and refused to work. They talked to the people and got organized, because that's all it takes to change everything. That's the only way, in the end. If people listen and work together. It doesn't take physical fighting. But the comps fought them, oh yeah. My Grandfather got hit in his spine with a rubber bullet. Pop! Straight between two bones, below his heart. He never walked again, and he was almost blind for the rest of his life, from the riot gas. Blinded and crippled. He sat by the window in our living room for the rest of his days, and nobody listened to him. Except me."

She heard the shake in his voice and the breath he was catching. She wanted to ignore the ache crackling through her skull and ringing in her ears; she wanted to do something to comfort him, but she knew all she could do was listen.

"One day it just hit me," he said, "that it was time for me to do something. To find a way to join the fight any way I could. One day I woke up and I couldn't *go on* doing nothing. I couldn't! And I guess I thought this—" he took his badge from his breast pocket and considered it in the flickering light "—was the way I could make the most difference. It's a way to become a leader. It's the *one* way for Outsiders like me and you, the way it seems like. No matter where you come from, as a comp, if you stay on long enough and survive long enough and work hard, you move up. You become a District Commander in a little while. You can make a big difference from up there, commanding all the comps in the whole district. Or you can make a difference just as one comp. Just for one person. Just by doing the right thing for once. By being the right guy in the wrong place. That's what I... what I would have thought."

"Now you think differently?"

"Doesn't matter." His shadow shook its head. "Doesn't matter if I think it's the worst mistake I've made in my whole stupid life. I made a choice, and I swore to take everything that was coming from it."

She shivered in the dark and wrapped the army coat tighter. The candles fizzled in the damp air.

"Maybe you can't respect that. I don't care if you can't. It's okay."

"No," she said somberly. "No. I can. I do."

A moment of silence passed over the sidewalk cemetery.

"Then thank you," was all he said. His silhouette turned back to the candles and bowed its head again.

"It's still hard for me to...." She trailed off.

"Hard for you to what?"

She squinted up into the fast clouds and said "To think it all really happened like this. To think of you out there bashing people's skulls in—" She winced "—or being the one comp who isn't hoping to bash one in, I mean. You were just a punk with a drum set. You were just a shy quiet kid like me. We used to hang out in your family's basement. It all seems like a different universe now."

The shadow of Balboa began to extinguish the candles with its fingertips.

"It's just hard to wrap my head around," she said.

"I never wanted to push anybody away. I didn't want to sacrifice our friendship. Not yours or anybody's. I wish I could tell them all that."

She nodded.

"You still living in the Unfinished District?" he asked as they rolled along through the liquid dark, heading for the cold glow of living electricity.

"No." Shayna sighed and straightened her goggles. "There are these whacky monks I'm staying with now."

The shape of Balboa's head half-turned against the brown sky. "Where can I take you?"

"The monastery is out by the old, um, King Tower. Northwest of the Cology, kind of Rosewood area. Where are we?"

"Far. We're due East here. The busses won't be going at this time of night, either."

No words and half an hour later they were creeping stealthily through a front yard she recognized. The paint had peeled and the weeds grown slightly taller, but the Balboa house looming in the soggy night was just as she had left it. They parked the bike behind a bush and crept up into the small porch while Balboa picked through his keys. By then the curtains of mist were starting to fall down again, making the dark-eyed window frames cry into the thorny flowerbeds. She knew the rest of the family was asleep. She knew to be quiet.

When she pressed through the door there was a moment in which the atmosphere blinded her. The house had a faint smell, something she had never consciously noticed in all the time she'd spent here before, but stepping back into it now sent waves of memory washing through her brain. A year of jumbled image and sense and feeling hung in the air here like faint and muffled music coming from the next lightless room. He led her among the shadows and down into the basement, where it was strongest.

The ceiling light was still a flickering and sickly shade of yellow. The rest of the room's old glory had faded; the drums lay stacked in the corner among boxes of nothing. The scratchy amps and forests of empty beer cans had all gone, leaving the concrete floor naked and cold.

"Give me a moment to clear stuff off," Balboa said.

Her phone rang. *At this hour?* she thought.

"Hold on," she whispered. She squinted at the screen. All zeroes again. By the time she pressed the answer key she'd already missed it. She swore under her breath.

"I would give you the bed, but I can't fit on the couch anymore."

"It's okay." She dropped her phone back into her coat with a sigh. "God I'm tired."

The first gray light of dawn was trickling through the slits of foggy glass at the top of the wall when Balboa killed the ceiling light. She collapsed onto the ratty orange cushions of the couch and started to lapse into aching unconsciousness, but she made out his dark mass still perched upright on the corner of his mattress. It said "Listen, I'm sorry about the head."

"I know," she murmured.

"I'm really sorry. So, we'll say I owe you one. Remember that. If you need anything. If I can do anything to help you, anything to make us square."

She nodded half-consciously.

"Joseph—" Balboa said hesitantly. "The guy who hit you. He told me that you were reaching for a firearm. He told me that's what made him react that way."

Shayna sat up.

"The mind can play tricks, I guess," the hunched shadow said. "In the heat of the moment. When chaos breaks out like that. That's something they teach you – that adrenaline can make you see things that aren't really there. I know you would never really do something like that."

Some metal reflected the eerie twilight in his hand.

After a while, she took the gun he passed back to her. She wanted to say something. Instead she lay back and waited as the world dissolved.

This time the dream was waiting just on the other side of consciousness, as if it had never left. The white void was now brighter than it had ever been; it seemed to burn her mind's eye and throb in the gash behind her head. The sound when it rang out was more grating and shrill – and when the white space split open, it wasn't the blue behind it, but the cracked window behind Balboa's standing shadow. He pulled his coat on and started for the stairs, but first he knelt down by the couch, met her dazed and half-conscious eyes and asked "Is there anything else I can do for you? Anything you need?"

She was in a trance, half-believing she was still dreaming, when she said "Tell me what Fallon's Field is."

His face clenched like a fist.

"Fallon's Field," he said. His voice was concrete. There was something she couldn't read held tight in the edges of his eyes.

She gripped the wool blanket tighter.

"*Fallon's Field*," he repeated. "Is that what you said?"

She nodded and her mouth said "What is it?"

Balboa rubbed his vast hand across his vast face as if to muzzle himself a moment. He raised up and went to a desk against the wall to lean heavily upon it. A pencil scratched something and then he returned to slip a rolled-up scrap of paper between her fore and middle fingers. Then he vanished into a ray of daylight.

It was mid-afternoon light that finally opened her eyes and raised her up, aching and angry at the loss of the whole day. She hurled the blanket into the wall above Balboa's empty bed. The rush of air stirred the rolled-up paper across the cold stone floor. Wincing from the rush of blood, morbidly feeling over the stitches with her other hand, she picked it up and unrolled it. *Fallon's Field* said the note. There was a long set of directions, which she only skimmed, and a small scrawl of a map. The words in larger print at the bottom said *bring light.*

She left the basement behind with a touch of regret. The careful tiptoeing of her boots found the Balboa house empty. She got on the first bus she figured would take her back to the monastery.

Back among the pillars of paper and felt pen scrawls, adjusting her eyes to the glow only of candles and television static, she confronted the back of the High Lurker's freshly-mowed dome of scalp.

"Do you have a flashlight I can borrow?"

Grant turned. His eyes under one raised brow betrayed how far off guard he'd been caught.

"What is it?" she asked his weird look.

"You've been gone a long time," he muttered as he stumbled for the storage room.

"Oh, you missed me? Afraid I wasn't coming back?"

"On the contrary, I assume you just won't appear one of these days," he responded in a thoughtless tone. "Since you don't seem to be making much progress in your search for a cure. Just make sure you return The Pass to us before it happens."

She stopped on the cracked tiles. The flashlight he finally produced fell into her unmoving hands, and then he drifted off without a word, leaving her alone between the dead columns.

She slammed the door to the bunk room behind her and fell onto the crummy mattress. The gun pressed painfully against her pelvis until she turned on her side. The rolled-up note was still held tight in her palm, soggy with her sweat.

Fallon's Field, said the memory of the gnarled old stranger on the bus. *What is Fallon's Field?* asked her memory of herself.

No point, she answered. *No fucking point in it.*

God I'm tired, she thought. *And it's so late already. Nothing to do but sleep.*

But every time she opened her eyes for a moment she saw the ceiling spinning a little faster, and there was a heat now turning noticeable in the center of her chest and sparkles seeping into the edges of her vision. She sat up with her head in her hands, chanting to herself: *Not yet. Not yet.* The room spun harder.

Is ignorance bliss? says the nurse. She says *between fifteen and twenty-three*. She says *fifty million*.

Her memory was boiling into a sickening cacophony. She thought of red light and Tom and kissing him in the darkness of the top bunk. She thought of a crack in the back of the head and the sound of drums and the hiss of the Metro brakes and the chugging of Printing Station 117. Her memory was rushing in her face. It was deafening. It all moved together in slow surging waves, like the hard rushing of blood against her eardrums, but it sounded like pulsating wind. Like the flapping of wings as big as—

"Shay?" something said. "Shay, you there?"

She realized her phone had been ringing and she'd answered it reflexively.

"Carl," she croaked. "Carl."

"Shay! Shay!"

It snapped her out of something. The sparkling hot waves softly receded. "Yeah." She took a slow breath and shook her head clear.

"Are you all right?"

"Fine." She hauled herself up.

"We're all going to the new place – this new place further down the street from where the Green Room used to be. You're invited." His voice was weak, almost whimpering.

"I'll come around a little later. There's somewhere else I need to go first. It shouldn't take long."

She took the awkward silence that followed as her cue to hang up.

The phone's luminous screen listed twelve missed calls. One was from the mystery number, the zeroes. The other eleven were all from him.

"Oh, Carl," she murmured – and, summoning her courage against the residual sparks still swarming restlessly in her eyes and guts, she forced herself onto her feet. "Fallon's Field," she told the pressure in her head and the horrible sloshing of her vision. She said it to the heavy wooden doors and the sidewalk and the Metro's diesel breath. She knew it was gibberish. It was only two meaningless words given to her by a bum on a bus – but it was a question needing an answer. With every whispered repetition, the world spun a little slower, and the deadweight of exhaustion untangled itself a little from her limbs.

She held the flashlight tightly. Fifty blocks down, the bus was swallowed by the darkness – and some indistinct length of time and space after that, following the instructions on Balboa's note, she talked the driver into stopping in the middle of the route. She stepped off far from any vestige of the inhabited city, and started out into the wreckage of old buildings and caved-in streets.

It wasn't until the great fissure spread out before her that she realized she had been here before, and the realization stopped her dead in her tracks. Everything looked different after dark, but here she stood, in exactly the same spot on the jagged ledge, looking down into that gaping wound in the earth where only days before Gomad had stood and squinted back up at her. Now her dim light under the last blue glow of day traced the edges of that sliced-open tunnel entrance where she hadn't dared to go. This time her heart was pounding many times harder. This time she entered – and when she felt her way through the pitch black, she saw for herself the strange glimmer of white light that Gomad had seen, almost too tiny to make out. It was a tiny shard of glass, catching the light of the full moon through the gaping ceiling.

When she took the glass and looked up through that hole, there was a skull that looked down on her. It was ten feet tall and painted on concrete. Stuffing down her fear, she climbed up through the rubble, back to the surface, and saw everything.

The smoke was rising out of the new pit. A hundred combined exhales of burning herbs turned bright and opaque in the street lamps three blocks from the boarded-up corpse of the old theatre, swirling around the shadow of Carl – who, making out Shayna's own brand of shuffle over the gum-caked sidewalk, scurried back underground. When she came to the door she found only Fish, or the Professor, or Alice—

"What's your name tonight?" she asked the drug dealer perching on the top of the dumpster and leaning over the top of the door.

"Call me Jesus," he said.

– she found Jesus, using the claw of a hammer to scratch a few familiar words into the concrete there. Abandon all hope.

She climbed down into the new pit with its new smoke, and everything was the same. The floor plan was different and some of the lights still needed to be draped in green plastic, but nothing else had changed. (She wondered suddenly: how many times had this history repeated itself now? How many Green Rooms had there been?)

Her friends were all gathered around in a new corner that was just like the old one. Carl pretended not to have been standing out there waiting for her as he and Katja and Tom all trailed off their sentences and watched silently as she stepped down into their stuffy space. She met all their eyes except Tom's. She picked up a shot glass as she sat.

An awkward pause stretched out between them.

"You told Carl you were going somewhere," Katja said. "And now... are you okay? You look like—"

"Just give me a moment to catch my breath," Shayna said and took the shot. "Don't let me interrupt."

Awkwardness swirled on the winds of glowing smoke.

Tom turned hesitantly back to Carl and said "Anyway, your poem. I was going to say that I read it."

"Which one? 'The Wind Storm'?" Carl asked.

"Yeah."

"Well?"

"If you want my opinion, honestly...."

"What the hell else would I want?"

Tom stuck out his lower lip a moment and then answered: "It was kind of melodramatic, okay?"

"Okay," Carl said. "Go on."

Katja listened intently.

Tom said: "It's just so heavy-handed, you know? Everything is really gushy and over-the-top and super-serious. It's like getting hit in the face."

"Maybe I *wanted* it to be like getting hit in the face. Maybe that's what I was expressing."

"Okay."

"I don't get to read your poetry anymore?" Katja asked.

"You'll just tell me it blows."

"So does Tom."

"I never said that – that it blows," Tom protested.

"That's not what he said," said Carl.

Shayna watched them through her empty glass. They were talking to each other but their attention was on her. She found herself now expecting to wake up a week and a half ago to find that this had all been a dream; that they were all still just the regular friends they'd been right before she came back to them; that they were not each visibly anxious about her for their own separate reasons.

"Come on, Shay," Katja said with a nervous chuckle. "Tell us what's going on."

The first of the booze washed over her brain in a wave of warmth. Her lungs filled up with the gray smoke and released it with a hiss, and she felt the mad thundering of her heart when she finally dredged up the strength to look at Tom, who quickly looked at his feet.

She said "There's a place called Fallon's Field. It's an old bunch of factories, deep in a dead zone, miles from the nearest actual Metro stop. You have to climb over blocks of debris and down through a tunnel to get there. Most of it has collapsed or been demolished, but there are still some walls standing. There's this one wall.

"I went there tonight. Somebody told me to go there, to this one wall. It's the last remaining side of a warehouse. It's two stories high and a whole block wide, and it's completely covered. In graffiti. I mean, in writing, with murals and illustrations. You know I can't read very well. I'm really slow, but I shone my flashlight up on it and walked along, taking as long as I had to. There was something pulling on me, it felt like. It felt important for me to read all of it. So I did.

"Years ago, there was a battle there. The wall tells the whole story of it, in words and paintings. All the workers there – the workers in a factory where dozens of people had been hurt or killed by problems with the machines – the workers all walked out one day, just refused to keep working until the Company fixed things. They blocked off the street and shut everything down. They stayed there together.

"The comps came. They ordered everyone to get back to work, but they wouldn't. The next day they told the workers they were all fired and ordered them to go home, but they stayed, they wouldn't leave. Thousands of people. Children, women, men, everyone. All the workers in the whole complex. They locked their arms together and wouldn't leave.

"The comps started with riot gas, but it wasn't working. So they started with rubber bullets, but the crowd was so big and so determined that those didn't work either. So at the end of the third day they loaded their guns with real bullets. By the end, a thousand people were dead. They were left in the street."

"A *thousand?*" Carl gaped.

"That's what the wall says. Their names are all written there. Every name."

"How is that possible? How could that have happened without anybody knowing about it? I never heard of any such place as Fallon's Field."

"If it was decades ago—" Katja began.

"It shouldn't make a difference if it was a hundred years ago!" Carl hissed. "I would've heard about it. You would. We all would've."

"If you don't believe me I'll take you there to see it for yourself," Shayna said dispassionately. Her second shot was waiting in her hand – but it was her other hand, locked in a tight fist, that she was looking at. It was something in her palm that she was turning over now and then, thoughtfully.

"It's not that hard to believe," Tom said quietly. "After last night. After how lucky all of us were to make it out of there."

Everyone was visibly unsettled by this statement.

Shayna put down the glass and leaned her face down onto her folded arms against her knees.

"My God—" Katja shouted. "What the hell happened to your head?"

"Nothing," Shayna said, sitting hurriedly up again. "Nothing. It's fine."

"Bullshit!"

"*I said it's fine*," she hissed, more viciously than she realized until she saw it reflected in Katja's retreat and the dead silence that followed. Amidst another wave of alcoholic warmth she found a cigarette in her pocket and set it on fire, full of regret, ignoring all their eyes.

Jesus the drug dealer dropped out of the tendrils of haze and managed to disrupt the tension with some witty banter; Shayna didn't listen to a word he said. She couldn't focus clearly. Safe in the shadow of all the attention he was taking up, she retrieved from her pocket the thing she'd been turning over in her palm for hours, and dared to look at it again. Even then, surrounded by the darkness and the smoke and the sickly green glow, it shone pure eerie white. Lunar white.

"What is that?" Tom asked. She hadn't noticed him sliding onto the couch next to her – keeping an awkwardly careful distance between their hips.

She sighed and opened her fingers wider to stare down into the pearly surfaces of the glass shard. *Hypnotize me*, she thought to its mesmerizing inner glow. *Wipe my mind all away*. It said nothing in response. She dropped it back into her pocket and answered: "Something I found there. Just a piece of broken glass. They were glass factories."

In the corners of her down-turned eyes she saw him picking nervously at the holes in the couch. "Do you want to get some air?" he finally asked.

She made herself look up.

They misinterpreted other's body language and started walking a circle of the block. The sky was clear and cool between long veins of troubled reddish cirrus clouds. She kept waiting for him to say something, but whenever she really looked at him she only saw him waiting back. He opened his mouth a moment and shut it. They jerkily passed the door and started their second lap of the building.

"What are we doing?" she asked with a chuckle.

"Getting air?"

She sighed and stared away at the distant blur of white light.

"How have you been, uh, doing?" he mumbled.

"Wonderful," she said, but the sarcasm was too subtle.

"Good, that's good."

She turned to give him a frustrated glare, but something in the resonance of his voice, or the renewed burning of her hate for his guts, as if shaking her suddenly awake, stopped her dead on the sidewalk and found her looking straight into his eyes.

God damn, she wanted to say. *God damn this. I'm wanted by the comps. I've narrowly escaped death more than a few times and I'm dying of the blight anyway. I've seen craziness and chaos and I've just come from a wall that bears the names of one thousand people murdered by the Company, but God damn, Tom. You... This... Standing right here—*

"What?" he asked squeamishly.

She let herself imagine kissing him. By force, she thought – pulling herself up the zippers of his coat, with a foothold on his belt or in the concavity of his chest if necessary – if necessary reaching up and grabbing onto those floppy ears like handles for his greasy face. She thought this and her teeth began to ache and her hands made fists full of the ratty wool lining of her coat. *After everything I've been through,* she thought at him – *everything you don't know anything about. And all the more for all of it. You're still all I can think about.*

His Adam's apple swam restlessly beneath the stubbly skin of his long neck.

"I'm sorry," he mumbled. His eyes quivered faintly in the orange shadows.

It was without much thought that she simply turned and headed for the stairs. She felt the coldness she'd left in her wake, and decided it was just cold enough. The next liquid ounce scalded away the lump in her throat, and she thought to herself: *all those thoughts were lies.* But, rubbing the roughness of her sleeve into the welling dampness of her eyes, and meeting the angry, tongue-biting gaze of Carl on the couches, she knew it was useless; she knew her teeth still ached.

The table was slick with a spilled drink. Katja was working to mop it up using some sheets of paper that were strewn around the floor. Shayna watched the booze soaking through one, blurring the cheap copy ink in mesmerizing patterns. The page read:

BLACK FACTION

"It is absolutely certain that no two people agree about everything. It is also relatively certain that no one thing, no matter how apparently self-evident ("two plus two makes four"), is agreed upon by absolutely everyone. But it is even likely that, were we to fully interrogate the understandings in question, we might discover that no two people truly agree about anything at all. The simplest idea in the world is transformed in the moment it touches a new brain.

"By implication, all systems (if we proceed with the thought that a system is a sort of tentative agreement) exist in a state of permanent collapse, somewhere between the subtle and explosive. Nonetheless, without a new agreement (if only the agreement that the old agreement is null) a reigning system can be as boundlessly chaotic, as violently conflicted and as hopelessly ineffective as it likes, and it will never fall. This is because human beings need to agree, and not merely for practical considerations.

"The Company principals have long justified a sociopathic governance through various ideological claims that the drive to transcend and dominate our peers is the most universal and fundamental force within the human condition. Though we should not deny the existence of such a force, the very history of the Company's evolution from constituent parts is a testament to the existence of a contrary and much more fundamental drive. It may in fact be the case that there is nothing that the human animal craves with more basic and desperate passion, than to agree."

— *Rokosz*

There came the inevitable reverse of the alcoholic tide, when euphoria began to ebb and regular drowsy sickness started to flow, and the passing drinks could only do so much. But there was something else. The pressure on the backs of her eyeballs was building again. She looked around and couldn't decide how many of the sparkles in her vision could be blamed on the strobe lights or the wafting of other people's chemicals. Without thinking she had receded from the conversation around her; without much thought she had started to press the glass shard harder into her palm. When she looked again the skin was close to breaking.

"Shay!" Carl shouted.

"What?" she asked bitterly, looking suddenly up.

"Are you—?"

"I'm fine. What are you looking like that for?"

"I was just sitting here shouting your name," he said shakily. "I was just sitting here making a fucking dipshit of myself, sitting here and shouting your name over and over again, and you weren't noticing at all."

"You weren't shouting my name."

"Yes he was," Katja said. She looked crushed. Her makeup was already smeared and getting smeareder. Her usual solar system of suitors had been pushed completely away into the buzzing crowd and her bare shoulders were the loneliest Shayna could remember ever seeing them.

"I'm fine." She forced herself upright and looked casually around the space.

"It's started, hasn't it?"

"Don't," Shayna hissed. "Don't do that! You had no right to tell everyone!"

"It's just us here! Tom and Fish are upstairs and they're the only ones who don't know. And for fuck's sake why don't you tell them already?"

"Because of this!" Shayna yelled, loud enough to turn anonymous heads even against the thundering bass line. "Because of you two sitting there and staring at me like that. It's like you're already saying your fucking goodbyes!"

"It's not—!"

"I told you I don't want any of your pity. You can mourn for me when I'm dead." As she spoke she knew regretfully that she'd had too much to drink – and yet also not nearly enough.

"I'm sorry!" Katja cried. "I can't help it!" In a blur of motion she had risen from the crummy vinyl and collapsed around Shayna, holding her tightly, and Shayna felt their tears running together between their pressed faces.

"*I love you,*" Katja sobbed in a whisper, and then her lips pressed a hard kiss into side of Shayna's face. "I'm sorry. I'm sorry."

Shayna hovered on the verge of returning the hug, but a painful rigidness spread through her face and down her body, constricting her throat, making fists of her hands. She pushed Katja away and started taking slow steps backwards into the crowd.

"No—" cried the tear-blurred ghost of Katja in the neon haze. "No, not again!"

But Shayna had already bolted halfway up the stairs. She was knocking her collarbone against the doorframe as she flew out into the alley and past all of the suggestions carved into the brickwork by Jesus' hammer. She was blinded by water, out of awareness, no longer knowing or caring what was going on in her own head. She yearned only to bury herself in the darkest streets she could make out – until she was sunk down and out of breath behind another dumpster.

She struggled for a while to shake the booze out of her swimming head before she got up, dusted herself off, shoved the pistol back into her pocket, sniffled her nose clear and finally headed back for the dull orange glow of the sidewalk. There was no one in sight. Within the din there was no sound but her boots beneath her.

She looked back in the direction of the new Green Room, but only sighed. *Just need to clear my head*, she thought. *Just need to take a walk*. If only she could summon the same composure her mother had been able to in the face of her imminent end. A cigarette helped. It helped to focus on breathing.

It was as beautiful a night as the Tropolis ever had. The haze layer was thin, the clouds sparse, the sky very dark between the roofs and walls. She found herself looking upward, at first without even knowing why. And then, two blocks down, the moon hit her. It was full and gigantic, and the color of blazing gold.

A mangled growling cry sounded from behind. "*Wa—it!*" it screamed.

She turned around to see Carl barreling over the dandelion heads, or doing what passed for barreling for a Carl as drunk and exhausted as this one. He arrived at her feet, barely able to stand, panting heavily. He kept trying to talk between his asthmatic breaths.

"It's okay," she said, patting him limply on the back, unsure of what else to do. "I'm sorry I've been this way."

"Stop. Don't... run away again!"

"I'm not going anywhere."

He looked at her with straining eyes, caught somewhere between despair and confusion and holding back tears. He hugged her mutely and hard, and she sighed and hugged him back apologetically. His mouth behind her ear was mumbling an incoherent stream of syllables.

She stepped back from him and said: "What is it?"

"*What can I do?*" he shouted in drunken agony.

"Nothing," she said.

"What can I do? I can't—I can't take this! I.... I would do anything! I would do *anything* if it would help you! Don't you understand that?"

She sighed sadly and met his pleading gaze.

"There has to be something," he said. "There has to *be* something!"

"I don't know. I mean, the Urbanologers seemed like... they tell me there's a cure. Something I could just magically find. But to do that I need to know the name of my death, and there's only one person who would know it, and I can't talk to her. I tried."

"Didn't the nurse say anything? About a treatment?"

"She said..." The memory replayed itself in her head, and something skipped. "Fifty million."

"What?"

"Fifty million dollars. When she diagnosed me, the nurse told me you can buy the cure. It costs fifty million dollars." She said gravely: "You said you would do anything. Anything to help me."

He nodded between still heaving breaths.

"Then let's go," she said, and started walking.

"Wait!" he yelped. "Where are we going?"

She flipped the gun open just to look at the bullets and let him see it too. Then she spun the chamber, snapped it shut and said "Christmas shopping."

The two figures huddled in the orange electric shadow of a utility pole as if it somehow gave them cover. Shayna spit into her goggles and rubbed the lenses clean on her shirt. The tan full moon was blazing down onto the lifeless concrete, as bright as a streetlamp. The all-night corner store shone with creepy greenish radiance through its windows of chain-linked glass.

"*Shit!*" Carl hissed again under his breath. "*Shit!*"

"Carl. If you don't want to go on this mission, I'm giving you the opportunity to get out right now. I won't think any less of you."

"Do you have any idea the kind of firepower these corner store clerks pack?"

"They have guns?"

"They've got fucking *comp-issue assault shotguns*. I mean that's what I heard. That's what my friend told me, and he knows professional robbers."

"So we'll be careful."

"We could get shot. Or incarcerated. The security systems in some of these places are—"

"*Listen* to me," she said, too loudly for his comfort. "I've already got a notice out for my incarceration. And I'm good as dead anyway if I don't do something." She paused – she said to herself: "The High Lurker is always questioning whether I'm serious. Whether I'm willing to do what it takes to save myself. Maybe this is what he means. And here I am."

"The *what* said you're—?"

"This is my mission," she interrupted. "If you're not willing to risk your life and your freedom with me, that's fine. I don't have a lot to lose."

Hearing this, his face hardened. He swallowed, took a deep breath and finally said "Neither do I. Let's go."

'Neither do I?' she thought. She could tell when she looked her accomplice in the eyes that something strange was going on behind them, but there wasn't time to question it here and now. She nodded and took one final breath before starting across the street.

"Wait," he hissed, and ran for the alley. She heard the clang of the dumpster. When he emerged back into the light he was struggling to tear a strip out of the side of a paper bag.

"What the hell are you doing?"

"If the cameras get a positive faceprint on us we're dead meat." He pulled back his overgrown hair and pulled the greasy bag over his head. It just fit. His eyes squinted out through the uneven rips, and his breath flapped noisily against the paper in the moonlight.

Shayna pulled her goggles down. She dug her bandana out of the bottom of her coat pocket and tied it over the bridge of her nose.

They were only halfway across the street when they made out the clerk squinting curiously through the glass at them

"He's seen us!" Carl yelled. "Run! Before he can reach under the counter!"

She had already jumped the curb with lunatic swiftness. She leapt up and aimed both her feet in a flying kick straight into the front door, which flew halfway off its hinges and slammed thunderously against the counter. She got miraculously back onto her feet with the pistol already stretched out and aiming straight into the neck of the weathered man hunched over by the register. Without her saying anything he raised both hands.

"Don't move!" she shouted, automatically. "Right! Get your hands up! Good idea!"

Carl rushed in, shut the door behind him and then stood in the snack aisle, panicking, looking back and forth between her and the clerk through the hole in his paper bag.

"The cash register," she remembered, then shouted "I mean the fucking cash register! Open it! Now!"

The hunched-over man just sighed and kept his hands up.

"Open it or I'll— I'll, um, blow you in half!" Shayna yelled, in what she imagined was the right tone.

"I'm, um, I'm keeping watch," Carl said shakily, running to the window. "Shit! Tell me what to do!"

"Hey!" she shouted at the Clerk, but he still didn't move. He just stared straight at her.

How could he be so calm? she wondered. But at every spark of hesitation she chanted in her mind: *This is for my life. My life or my death.*

She turned to Carl and said "Convince him."

"How? I don't have a gun! Give me that one."

"No. Get something else."

Carl looked around desperately. "Oh Christ," he said, and pulled a bicycle pump off the shelf. He ran around the counter. Squinting desperately, he gave Shayna one last look of agonizing hesitation before he swung it at the clerk's upper arm.

The old man groaned and stumbled to the register. He turned the key that had been in the lock all along. The money drawer clicked open.

Shayna leapt up and slid over the counter to the lines of crumpled flattened bills. She dug her hand into the biggest green number she saw.

A small, crumpled voice echoed faintly between the cigarette cases. They realized it had come from the clerk.

"We have no insurance," he said. "Whatever you take from me, you take food from the mouth of my two sons."

Shayna looked down the gun at his heart. Only when she looked at the wad of cash in her other hand did she realize that they were only thousand-dollar bills, and there were less than ten of them. She turned and lifted the money drawer out completely and emptied it onto the counter.

"What are you doing?" Carl yelled. The bicycle pump was shaking in his raised hand.

"This isn't.... There can't be more than twenty or thirty grand here. We couldn't buy cold medicine with this."

"What were you expecting?" the clerk asked emotionlessly.

"Well," Carl yelled. "What, uh, what now? What should I do?"

"The safe!" To the clerk she yelled "All right! Where's the safe?"

"We live day to day. We have no safe."

"That's what they all say!" she yelled – but one good look at him and the store made her realize that it was true. Stars danced sickeningly across her vision. When they cleared, and when she found herself hearing only the sound of her own breath and the whirring of the ice cream case, and when she mentally calculated the number of corner stores she would need to rob, all the pent-up surreality of the moment washed over her at once. Her shooting arm sank slowly.

"It's not that I can't do this," she said.

"What do I *do?*" Carl shouted.

Shayna sighed. She climbed back over the counter and stood by the door, looking both ways.

"Come on," she told Carl. "Quick."

"Sorry," he whimpered as he dropped the bike pump and ran.

She waited until he was through the door. Then she backed through it herself.

They stopped running and settled into a fast walk when their breath ran out and enough corners had been turned. They looked back many times, but the red and blue lights painting the building sides were only the afterimages of their paranoia. There was no flutter of jackboots, no explosion of shotgun shells. There were only the remains of Carl's paper bag mask, flapping listlessly in the streetlamps some long way back.

Carl was strangely wordless long after they had caught their breaths. He just kept walking along at Shayna's side, ignoring her in every other way besides that. The furrows in his brow were impossible to read, leaving her to wonder what to feel toward him now – and, if guilty, how guilty. For blocks she tried to think of anything worth saying. She wanted anything but the silence in whose suffocating thickness she had started to feel she'd taken some horrible advantage of him, their friendship, his strange attraction to her, whatever it really meant or amounted to.

"I know alcohol impairs judgment," she said, mostly to herself, "but so does knowing you don't have long to live, doesn't it? When has my judgment ever not been impaired by something?"

Carl didn't seem to hear.

At the end they came to a place where a chainlink fence lay fallen and rusty and half-sunk in the congealed mud of a low hillside – and climbing to the top, they looked out across the long black mirror of a reservoir. The burning yellow moon was balancing in its center, perturbed and tinged in rainbows of oil.

"I could have done it," said the last of Shayna's dwindling intoxication. "It's insane but I know I could have shot him."

Carl just peered down into the water, as blank as before she'd said it. "You're drunk."

"But it's not just that. It's more than that. I could feel the trigger, how close it was. I felt like I was holding his whole life."

Carl only sighed.

"Does that make me evil? That I know I could do it? I didn't expect to ever have a thought like that – to know I had the ability to kill someone. Some innocent bystander. Just because he was between me and what I needed. I thought good people didn't have that in them, and evil people did, and that's what separated them. But now I think...."

Carl looked at her, then quickly away.

"I could've done it. But I wouldn't. Even if that was all I had to do to get the cure. If all I had to do to save my life is kill one innocent clerk. I could do it, I know I could. But I wouldn't. I wouldn't choose to. If it was just trading somebody else's life for saving mine."

"If all it took to save you—" Carl began.

"Because what is my life worth?" she interrupted, and each word made her shiver. "What is my life really *worth?* Do you get what I'm saying?"

"If all it took to save your life was killing a random person, *I* would do it."

She stopped talking and her eyes turned back down to the sickly light riding on the thin black waves. The first purple of dawn was staining through now.

After a while longer she turned and headed back for the Metro without a glance or a word, and this time he didn't follow. She looked over her shoulder only once, to see him still standing on the top of the hill, perched on the horizon next to the darkening cigarette-burn moon – and somehow, from half a block away, it was the moon that looked within reach and it was Carl who looked like he was floating in dead outer space. And the cold bit into her, and her breath was thin, and for a moment in the perfect blackness between dead buildings even her footsteps were silenced.

7

It was her phone that woke her. It was late in the afternoon but the smog layer lay heavy, the light already like night outside the window by her the narrow slab of monastery bed. The zeroes were glowing on the screen as before.

"What," Shayna answered groggily.

Dead silence.

"Well, fuck you, whoever you are," she said.

"Shayna," said a woman's voice, faintly. It was familiar, but from the single soft-spoken word she couldn't place it.

"Who—?"

"I found a message from you. Mixed in with my cigarettes."

Shayna's hand froze around the phone. She sat up in a jolt.

The voice said: "1001 Union Circuit, number 206. Six PM."

"Janet Wallace?" Shayna whispered.

The nurse hung up.

"Very well," the High Lurker said irritably, "I'll get the clothes. We may have a left shoe in storage to replace the one you lost. In the mean time, the shower is through that door. I'll bring you a razor, but—"

"No time," Shayna said with anxious distaste. "No time to shave legs. She said six. Six!"

Grant peered sternly down at her and said "I hope you're thinking this through. Even if you manage to reach the Inner Ring – which even in itself would require the spiritual favor of the Metro—"

"Remember she has the Pass," Kelroy said, stepping up behind him.

Cass followed after Kelroy, holding onto his robe with one hand while gnashing the other lightly between her teeth.

Grant continued, "Even if you get there in time, and even if all Greentowne doesn't immediately see through the shoddy and irreverent kind of Camoumancy you're proposing to practice – not even a shower! – that leaves a very narrow margin of possibility for you to make it back before nightfall. You're taking a grave risk."

"If that's what it takes."

Cass looked up and met her eyes gravely.

Grant said "You don't even know what the nurse meant in saying this to you. A place and a time. There are any number of ways to interpret—"

"Get the dress," she said, fighting her way out of her boots. "Go get the dress and the shoes or watch me get on an Inward bus in my regular clothes and go straight into the back of a comp car. I'm sure you'll get the spiritual favor of Our Departed High Lurker that way. I'm going. I have to go. You know I have to."

Grant stood there in his monolithic way, but this time he did not scowl. He looked down with eyes that for almost the first time were more thoughtful than cold. Then he walked quickly for the storage room.

"Ormay beewee," Cass was now mumbling rhythmically. "Ormay bewee, ormay bewee."

Shayna knelt down to her. "What are you trying to warn me about now? 'Or, maybe, we'? Or maybe we what?"

Cass just gazed back at her. Another incomprehensible prophecy, useless until it happened.

Ten minutes later she stood at the bus stop, looking like a poor excuse for a Greentowner. Her hair was still in its usual greasy tangles. Her makeup was insufficient and asymmetrical. One shoe bore the marks of scissor-point alteration and the toe was crammed with newspaper to make it stay on her foot, but it would all have to do.

The bus hissed up to the stop and flung its doors open.

"Tropolis keep you," Kelroy said with one reassuring squeeze of her shoulder.

Grant handed her the purse. She took it and climbed up.

"Thank you," she said, and felt all at once the back interest with which she owed it. The wind of the doors made her naked shoulders shiver – and then, watching the child and the two black-robed bald men recede in the rear window with their hands all raised in solemn farewell, she thought ominously that there was something final about this moment.

The flyway was different this time. From the middle back seat, everything seemed to be moving faster than it ever had before, the cars reduced to smears of color, the sun falling straight down through the skylights. The frozen knifelike clouds were blowing due East out of the corona, straight Outward from the endless walls of geodesic ice that swelled by the moment in the front windows. Greentowne and its mirrored monoliths swallowed the bus like a mouthful of metal teeth with twenty lanes of dirty concrete for a tongue. She had no idea what was going to happen at six o'clock or what lay in wait at the end of this line. She only knew the seconds were racing by in the cheap electronic digits of her telephone screen, and everything pointed to this.

The bus ground to a hydraulic halt, and for a moment so did her heart. She had arrived, but the building looming over her wasn't the kind she had imagined. It was a hospital.

Climbing the concrete ramp, she released the thought: *am I here to be cured? Is that why she brought me?* But something already told her otherwise. Something did not fill her with hope or curiosity as she stepped into the shadow of the vast tower of slit-windowed concrete. Something kept her blood running cold. She breathed the number of the room to a face behind a front desk and was pointed wordlessly down the hall.

Mechanical panes of semi-opaque glass parted, one after another, leading into the dim glow at the end of a long corridor whose walls were lined endlessly with doors. Each door was lined with lights that blinked in different rhythms and colors, all of them chirping shallowly, and the chirps sang in a chorus against the metronome ticking of those stupid rigid heels against the plastic floor. With every step it grew louder in her mind: the sense that she should not be here; that somehow these alien walls were seeing through her disguise.

She stopped and stared at it. Door 206. The soft lights glowing on the panel's surface were red and unsteady, and there was a single alien word printed there – EUTH – fading in and out. *Youth?* she thought.

She reached into her purse and touched the teeth – and, calling up all the strength she had on her, she touched the door and watched it slide open. It was a beige light that spilled out, and when she stepped into it, and the door slid quietly shut, there was suddenly no other light or sound.

She drifted deeper into the small, low-ceilinged space, and somewhere in the blur of cream light there appeared a bed. An androgynous human figure in a medical uniform stood there. The figure was holding a mask over the mouth of the woman sitting up in the bed. She drew three deep and slow breaths through it.

The medic took the mask back and said "It's done. It will also stop the coughing."

"Thank you," said Janet Wallace.

The figure in the uniform moved past Shayna and vanished through the sliding door. Then there was only the bed, and the woman wrapped in the sheets, and Shayna, quivering in the naked and unbearable stillness. A pale hand lifted up and waved her closer.

"Well, come on," said the woman, with half-suppressed anger. "This visit might be cut short."

"I'm sorry I'm late."

"You're right on time."

"I know I shouldn't be here."

"No you don't. You wanted to talk to me. Badly enough to come all the way to my house and hide a note in my trash. Imagine my surprise when I went to fish my cigarettes out."

"I still feel like I shouldn't be here."

"I wanted you here."

Shayna finally stepped closer and asked: "Why?"

The woman drew a shallow breath and ignored the question. "You wanted to ask me something."

"Doctor Wallace—"

"There's no need for that bullshit anymore. My name is just Janet. It was always just Janet. What did you want to ask?"

"I wanted to know—" She swallowed hard. "I wanted to know if you remembered the name."

"What name?"

"Of my blight."

Janet's frail lips spread into a partial smile. Her voice crackled: "Do you know what my job is, darling? Do you understand that I have spent every day of the past twelve years of my life performing blight screenings on people like you? Collecting data. At Charity Centers. At factories and shipping centers and refineries and what-have-you. I'm sure that I have personally screened more than ten thousand terminal cases of this blight. And you have the balls to ask me, now of all times, for the minute details of your one specific diagnosis?"

Shayna lowered her head and stepped back from the bed – but Janet said: "And that's just it. I *do* remember. I remember every single one, by name, by face. I'm sure my teachers at the crèche never imagined that my memory augmentations would be so horribly misused in the end. Yes, Shayna Faith Newman, born April the second. I do remember. The answer to your question is Subtype M-9 Hyperacute Myelogenous Leukemia. But why? What does it matter to you?"

Shayna whispered the name to herself, repeating it, trying to memorize it.

"You want me to write it down for you? Here's another one while you're at it. Metastatic Small Cell Lung Carcinoma. That's mine. If you were curious."

"I'm sorry."

The woman in the bed drew a sigh and squinted her eyes as she relaxed a little, and when her voice returned it was softer.

"No, no. I'm sorry. Don't leave just yet. If you would just wait here a while longer, I'd appreciate it. I would prefer not to be alone." Her eyes, wreathed now with a deepening tiredness, fixed on her.

Shayna returned to the bed. Her spit tasted sour. Was there something in her eyes, or was the beige light dimming very slightly with each moment? She managed to say "Why? Why did you want me to come here?"

Janet dismissed the question with a shake of her head. "What does it matter to you what the name is?"

"Names are sacred. Names grant power over the named. Someone told me that."

The nurse said nothing.

Shayna thought of explaining more. She thought of saying she was searching for the cure – but standing there in the cream light, beginning to comprehend what she was seeing, she could not.

"That's it? You just wanted to ask me what kind you have?"

"I guess there's— there's a lot I want to ask you. But I don't know where to begin."

"Of course you don't. I bet you don't even know what the blight is. Tell me. What do you think it really is?"

"It's a disease. Fatal disease."

"Then just how do you think you acquired it?"

"What do you mean? It's a mystery. No one knows what causes it."

The woman in the bed gave off a dry, sad chuckle. "Oh, we know. People have known for centuries."

"You know? Then what causes it?"

The woman paused and then let out a stream of alien language: "Nitrosamine, dioxin, benzene, polycyclic aromatic hydrocarbons, polychlorinated biphenyls, phthalate esters, alkylphenols, asbestos, vinyl chloride, arsenic, mercury, heavy metals, radiological byproducts, solar radiation unmitigated by the presence of any ozone layer. Mutagens, teratogens, carcinogens. The Tropolis."

"I don't understand."

"Everything around you. Food, water, clothes. Cigarettes. That milky crap you were soaked with when I screened you that day. Even the fucking air you breathe. All of it. It's poison. You don't even know it's poison. Because it's gotten so bad now that they can't afford for you to know. Oh, the hell they'd have if you people only knew *why* the mean life expectancy for Outsiders is thirty-one years."

Shayna stood still and listened as well as she could, but she was distracted by the sense that each passing word was a little softer than the last. Each blink of those ancient eyes was slowing.

"Oh, what does it matter. I'm sorry. Waste of breath." Janet glanced sluggishly between Shayna and the ceiling for a while, then finally said: "I wanted so much to look Inside. I never even asked to *live* in the Cology. I just wanted to see what it's like on the other side of all that white glass, even just for a moment. Don't you wonder?"

The woman's hand grabbed Shayna's and held it. The thumb rubbed softly at the skin of the back of her hand.

"Y-yes," Shayna said uncomfortably. "Everyone does."

"But it doesn't matter. You have to live in the moment."

Shayna nodded mutely.

This time the woman opened her eyes and looked at her, unblinkingly. "Have you ever been present? Were you ever there in that moment? When someone passed away. I'm sorry. I don't mean to frighten you."

Shayna's throat tightened. She thought of Float, of Ravenly, of her mother. She said: "I've been close by. But never actually...."

"It changed me. Every single time, it changed me. Better watch closely."

"W-what?"

"It must be an experience to die naturally. Slowly, skipping nothing. In my work I've met so many. For twelve years I've been there, bearing witness. I always wondered how they did it. How they learned to accept what was happening to them. How one can... accept death. That's the real secret, you know. Maybe I could learn it too if I really tried, but I'm not that strong. I'm just some broken down old woman, who wonders whether ignorance might be all the bliss we get in this life."

Her hand's grip was weakening. Her eyes drifted away to the ceiling.

"Why did you ask me to come here?" Shayna said. Her voice sounded angry in her throat. The tears were filling up her eyes as she held the fading hand as tightly as she could, shaking it, trying to keep it awake. "I'm just a stranger. I'm just empty-headed trash from the outer Tropolis. You said that."

The woman in the bed snorted a soft breath and said nothing.

"Why me? Why not people you know? Why not your husband?"

She grimaced. "I pushed all of them away. They hate me for doing this to myself. It sounds so cruel, but I couldn't stand to see them anymore. None of them less than Bill. After all the years we spent pretending to know each other, we just don't. And I guess it... it tortures me to look at them, and understand that. The more I love them, the more it tortures me."

Shayna tried not to think about her own friends, but she did. She found herself asking: "How do you not know them?"

The nurse's face was knotted in anxiety. "But you understand, don't you? Oh my. It's close."

Shayna failed to speak.

Janet said "Those people and I, we've all known each other our whole lives. Worked together, studied together. We all learned the same science. We all saw the same types of patients and we all watched them die. But that's just it. The more everyone else saw, the less they wanted to smoke one cigarette as long as they lived. The more I saw, the more I had to smoke."

The beige light was sinking fast, deepening into orange. Shayna found herself stepping involuntarily back toward the door. Their held hands strained against each other.

"You understand," the nurse pleaded. "You know how that feels."

Shayna stopped. She nodded. She did.

The old woman shut her eyes and released a deep sigh. The anxiety vanished from the lines in her face. "Then stay a moment longer."

"But I'm no one."

Janet looked as if she were about to speak again, but her mouth only spread into a worn and wrinkled smile.

"Why me?" Shayna whispered. "I'm no one."

"Maybe," whispered Janet. "Maybe you are no one. Or maybe we...."

The wrinkles around the dying woman's eyes shone like gutters full of rain. Her other hand raised up in a limp, labored motion and placed itself on the side of Shayna's damp face, and the two of them stayed there in that position, sharing no words. The woman's breath moved in slow rasping tides for a long time, each ebb just deeper than the flow that followed, until in one fluttering second she felt the last energy fade out of those hands.

PART 3:

SKY

7

The haze was rolling in thick on the western horizon and casting premature darkness over the whole breadth of the Tropolis. Past the rooftops and between the lesser monoliths, the Cology's crystal walls burned gold against the leathery brown sky. At the bus stop she could feel and hear and smell the onset of Greentowne's Friday night rush hour and feel it quickening like a pulse. Blocks and miles passed indifferently. Passengers stepped on and off in a windy blur. This time, between only a few pensive glances, the whole Inner Tropolis had passed away and left the bus empty except for her.

There was some thought here she tried to bring into focus but couldn't. There was something she knew she was missing as it all accelerated into a meaningless blur past the panes of scratched glass.

"This has all been more than I can take," she imagined herself saying. Maybe to Tom. In her mind she told him: "It's all too much. More things have happened to me in the past two weeks than I could really accept and let sink in if I had a year to sit with it all. But I have a week."

"I'm sorry," she imagined him saying.

"I love you," she whispered as the bus stopped at a light.

An electric jolt ran through her. Something had been outside the window for a moment, then gone. Some angular shadow, the shadow of something huge – and in her brief memory, it had moved upward. She scanned the rooftops and the deepening sky, but there was nothing. *Nothing*, she thought angrily – angry at herself. *Nothing.*

When the adrenaline waned, she felt much more tired than before. Weakness was creeping over her now. Her limbs felt heavy. Before she could worry about missing her stop, she was already laying back and nodding off.

She awoke, or thought she did, stirred awake by some sound. A short metallic boom. She left her head leaning against the glass, opened her eyes and peered down the aisle. After a while, she saw it: a depression in the thin sheet-metal ceiling, down towards the front. Like somebody standing up there. *What the hell?*

She tried to lean up straighter, but her entire body was dead weight. She found herself glued in place – and in the moment this knowledge hit her, there came a second metal boom, followed by a blood-curdling scratch. Now that weight was in the middle of the bus's length. No human could jump that far. Now she made out, along the edges of that dent, two pairs of four sharpened divots.

It jumped again, and this boom came from directly above her. She couldn't move her head to look at it even if she'd wanted to, but now she could hear its breath. Its talons were ticking softly on the steel. She screamed and heard nothing but a trickle of a squeak, and paralysis held her more tightly than before.

Her heart was hammering on her ears as the motors fell silent at a stop. Another dent banged into existence above the rear door and she saw, vaguely, a formless black peeking through the slits of glass. The tip of an ebony beak began to pry between the rubber strips.

You're not real, she thought at it. *I'm dreaming this. This is not real. I will shut my eyes now, and when I open them, you'll be gone. I will shut my eyes and wake up.*

Another squeak left her mute lips when she heard the crack of the forced doors, followed by a giant thud on the floor. She could feel its heavy steps between the seats, making the whole bus faintly shudder.

She opened her eyes. Outside the windows, the bus was rolling toward a tunnel. Inside, directly before her, the thing stood. It had no features or substance; it was a pitch-black hole in space, carved in the shape of a bird that loomed over her, six and a half feet tall. As she looked at it, it kept almost perfectly still.

All at once its wings opened and flapped madly. They spread across her whole vision until they became a bottomless pit, and she was falling down into it.

Something caught her, hard. Strong and bony hands clutched at her stubbled armpits, lifting her, and she raised up partway to consciousness. Everything was buzzing and prickling.

"Hey," barked a voice, somewhere in the swirl of dirty vinyl and steel. "Hey!"

"She's with us," said Kelroy's voice. "She needs our help."

It must have been him, Kelroy, who hoisted her up, laying her over his shoulder and carrying her out. She wanted to move, to groan, but exhaustion held her like a vise. With all her strength she turned her head and squinted one eye down the length of the bus. She only made out the driver, reluctantly standing aside, glaring down his flared nostrils at this scene and trying to decide whether something about all this was illegal.

The electricity was shining yellow above the bunk they laid her down in. The cracks in the ceiling were getting more familiar. A hand lifted the back of her head toward a jar of water and she managed to reach up to touch it, if not hold it all the way up. Her fingers brushed against stale bread.

"What can we do?" Kelroy asked.

Cass whimpered anxiously from somewhere by the door.

"Summon the sister, and get another blanket," said Grant, rubbing his scalp. He approached the bed and the others parted around him. His scalp eclipsed the ceiling light as he solemnly leaned over and said: "Did you find the name?"

6

She came awake under a heavy membrane of rough old green wool. She wasn't alone.

"How do you feel?" Katja asked.

The light on the window resembled early morning.

"Hot," Shayna groaned. She leaned up and threw the wool off, but her skin was still burning, particularly under the dress's absurd shoulder straps. The sparkles washed immediately across her eyes again. "So goddamn tired."

Katja's mouth wavered on the edge of speaking. Instead she flipped her phone open and dialed.

"Who are you calling?" Shayna groaned.

"Jesus."

"Why?"

"To tell him to hurry up and get here. So he can help you."

"I don't want his help. I've seen his fucking help."

"No. This is different."

"I'm here, I'm here already," said the dealer, pushing through the door.

Shayna sank helplessly back against the wall and held her head, trying to stop it spinning.

"You must have something that will help," Katja told him. "Something to help with the tiredness."

"Maybe. But like I told you on the phone—"

"No one can help me," Shayna croaked.

"You said you had a million things that cure tiredness," Katja said, ignoring her.

"Yes. But without knowing what's causing it—"

"The blight is causing it."

"What am I, a doctor? I could give her speed or spark or swatter but it might not *do* anything! Ordinary lethargy is one thing. Sleep deprivation, exhaustion, depression – fine. Clinical lethargy is a completely different—"

"*No one* can help me!" Shayna shouted with all the volume she could manage.

The room went deaf.

"I appreciate that you want to help, but do you know where I've just come from?" she said. "I've just come back from the Inner Ring, where I was talking to the woman who told me I had this. I watched her die. She was a doctor, an actual professional, and rich, and she knew everything about the blight – and she couldn't do a thing to save herself. Not a god damned thing."

Jesus folded his arms and leaned against the wall. Katja sighed and wiped her eyes.

"No one can help me," Shayna repeated.

"The name," rumbled a voice from the door. The High Lurker stood there, a solid wall of darkness capped with a dome of shiny flesh.

"What does it matter?"

"Do you have the name?"

She swallowed. She leaned over and rested her forehead against her knees and clenched her jaw against the ache behind her eyes and said "Subtype M-9 Hyperacute Myelogenous Leukemia."

Everyone recoiled lightly into themselves as if a strong wind had just blown through the room.

"You have the key," Grant said solemnly. "Now find the lock."

Shayna squinted up and said "What is that supposed to—"

He was already gone.

"My ears are ringing," she said as her swimming head sank back onto her knees. "It doesn't fucking stop. But it's not really... it's not *ringing*. It's something more. Something familiar."

Katja moved onto the bunk beside Shayna and lay arms across her back. "What can I do?"

"Find my cigarettes." But when Katja put the pack and lighter in her hand, she just stared at them.

"What's wrong?" Katja asked.

"It's all a lie."

"What is?"

"The Balmic brand. It doesn't mean shit. They kill you just like any cigarettes. Don't they?"

"Yes."

Shayna sighed and threw the pack away. She said "Then just help me get out of this dress."

Jesus received a few motions from Katja and retreated backward through the door, closing it behind him. The wood sagged a little where he leaned on it from the other side.

"I'm not talking about a cure," Katja said quietly as she helped Shayna incrementally peel up the sweat-darkened fabric. "Just something that could help. Something to make you feel better at all. There has to be something."

Shayna shivered as her head cleared the bottom of the dress. She looked away and groped for the holey jeans Katja handed her. It took all her energy to put them back on.

"Something that can make you less tired."

Jesus said through the door: "I'm telling you I don't know. I'm just a provider. You need an expert."

"Damnit, Jesus!" Katja yelped.

"That's not my name," said his wood-muffled voice.

"*She* was an expert," Shayna interrupted. "For all the good it did her, and I don't know any other...." She trailed off. "Except."

"Except what? Except who?"

"Nobody," Shayna whispered as she pulled the shirt over her head.

"Bullshit."

"It doesn't matter, okay? He can't help me. I already asked him about it, and he couldn't before. So forget about it, okay?"

Katja held her close. Placing a hand softly on Shayna's head behind her ear, she whispered "I know you want me to forget this. I know you just want it to be like normal, with me, with everybody. And I know that you hate it, when I ask how I can help you with this. So do this one last thing for me. Just let me try to help you this one last time, really let me, and I'll stop asking. I promise. And if you don't, I'll keep asking, and keep trying to help you, forever, and I promise that too."

Shayna sighed. She felt the coat's reassuring weight, twisted in her hands, bulky with all the things inside it. Her switchblade. The last straggling bills of a once proud wad of cash. That damned pistol. A stolen pair of goggles. A shard of broken glass, which she grasped in the pocket and pressed hard into the clammy skin of her palm.

"I love you," Katja whispered close.

Shayna drew as deep a breath as she could and let it go.

"Okay," Shayna said. "But there's somewhere I need to go first."

"Anywhere."

The voice through the door said "I've got an appointment to keep, ladies."

"Tough shit," Katja yelled. "Bring the motorcycle around front." She turned to her friend and said softly: "You ready to get up?"

Shayna nodded and won the fight with gravity. Katja lifted the coat up onto her shoulders. It felt good to have it back. It had always been her armor.

"One more thing," she said. She moved wincingly to where the pink electric bass leaned. With effort she hung it over her back.

"You really need to bring that thing?"

"Yes."

"Why?"

"I don't know yet."

Somewhere outside, the drug dealer's engine revved to earsplitting life.

On Deckard Avenue little white sparks of sun danced inside the silvered wrappers swirling on the wind. The sky was clear and purple, and the thin-stretched clouds all pointed over her shoulder, back toward the apartment building, back toward Tom. She tried not to look that way. She focused on the bars on the mildewy windows in front of her as she raised herself up out of the sidecar.

"You sure you don't want me to come in with you?" Katja asked.

The drug dealer, still yet to announce his latest name, silently put a cigarette in his mouth and fumbled his outer pockets for a light.

"I won't be long." She wrapped her fingers around the pistol in her pocket, heaved a breath, and pressed on through the doors of the pawn shop.

He was there, just as he had been, propped up in the corner with only the red glow of his cigarillo showing. Nemo said "You. Shit."

"Problem?" Shayna asked as her eyes struggled against the sparkles and the darkness.

"Nothing. What do you want? More bullets, huh?"

"No." She crept closer to the counter.

The shadow leaned slowly forward on its creaking chair. The burning light dimmed.

"What, then?"

She pulled the gun out of her pocket. She considered it in her hand. Then she lay it down on the glass.

"Trade back," she said.

"This ain't no school lunchroom, little girl."

"I never fired it."

The fire glowed hot as he took a pull that was lost in thought. "Never?" he said, incredulously. "Not one bullet? Not one?"

"Not one."

His hands materialized in the dim upward glow of the display case. He flipped the chamber open and let the bullets fall down into his massive palm, and then he sifted them with his fingers, looking over each one in turn. He sighed quietly and smoked again.

She waited. She looked into the glass case and saw the velvet blood-red under a dusting of cigarillo ash. She saw a three-prong dinner fork made of gold.

Finally he said grudgingly: "You better understand, I don't do returns. I've never done one stinking return. Never a one, in all my years. But love me or hate me, at the end of the day I am an honorable businessman, so I will make this one exception, and never another. Understand?"

Shayna said nothing.

Nemo's hands lifted the snubnose 38 special back into the void from whence it had come. His silhouette turned away – she heard the opening and closing of an invisible drawer – and then, with overwhelming hesitation, there clinked down onto the glass a shining ring. But....

"That's not mine."

"This is a solid fucking gold ring, little girl."

"I don't care what it's made out of! I want the one I gave you. The silver one. The same one I gave you."

"You dumbshit," said the shadow through a luminous puff. "It *is* the same one. It was never silver, tarnished silver, like you told me it was. That sooty black crap wasn't tarnish. I dunno what it was, but I scraped it off and, fuck me, it was solid fucking gold underneath."

Shayna reached uncertainly for the ring and picked it up. The metal was beautiful. It looked innocent. She'd never seen that color before.

"Solid fucking gold?" she whispered.

Nemo snorted smoke. "And that's the only reason. I'm an honorable businessman. The contract was under false pretenses." He broke into a short fit of coughing, and when he finished he said "I'll give you ten thousand for it. Market rate. Final offer."

"No," Shayna said as she turned back for the light of day, "but thank you."

"Hell," said Nemo.

That was the last she saw of him.

The motorcycle roared to a sharp stop at the broken curb and a backfire blew the pigeons off their branches, falling upward in panicking waves and disappearing into the hollows of the crumbling old school building. In the morning sun the play field was dead and full of dust.

"We're here," Katja said, when Shayna didn't raise up her head right away. "Don't be afraid. The birds are gone."

"It's not that," she said, although the flapping had brought acid to the bottom of her throat. "My ears."

"What's wrong?"

"My ears are still ringing. But it's not just...."

"Where is this guy, this expert?" asked the dealer, squinting around apprehensively. "You sure this is the place?"

"He was here."

"Show me," said Katja, helping her up.

The dealer leaned his head down against his speed gauge and sighed.

Katja said "You. Fish. Whatever. Come on."

"My name is Nick."

More fences had been put up since the last time, blocking them and confusing the map in Shayna's memory. The chainlinks were new and shiny and naked of rust. It occurred to her that chainlinks didn't really come from anywhere; they just grew and spread like roots through the dirty meat of the Tropolis. She wriggled between the frayed steel edges and felt her way through into mountains of plastic bags, towers of rotten newspapers, the darkness of a narrow alley where concrete steps sank down to a wrought-iron door.

For a moment she'd doubted it would still be there. The three of them beheld it silently. Then She stepped down, wrapped her fingers around the rusty latch, and pulled. It rang a low, mournful gong sound, but budged no further. Locked from within. She rubbed at the television static in her eyes and slumped down on the steps.

"What now?" Nick asked, checking the time on his phone in annoyance.

Katja stepped down and gave the door a hard kick. It rang again, louder, briefly filling the whole alley with the noise and sending specks of dirt filtering down.

"Fuck," Shayna said, suddenly cringing, holding her ears. "That ringing."

"What ringing?" Katja asked.

"It's... it's almost like that one note. Oh God. It *is* that note."

"I can't do anything about a ringing in the ears, okay?" Nick growled. "I don't have a fucking thing that helps a *ringing in the ears!* Nothing! No thing! Now you girls are keeping me from an extremely important—"

Shayna shushed them both. She had swung her bass around before her and was plucking in deep and uncertain concentration at different notes.

"What are you doing?" Katja asked anxiously.

"Trying to find it."

"Find *what?*"

"The tone of the ringing."

"What the hell will that accomplish?" Nick barked.

"I want you to hear it."

"It's not real. It's just in your head. What the hell does it matter that we hear it?"

"I want you to fucking *hear it!*" Shayna shouted.

The alley fell silent.

"Sorry. Just be quiet for a moment and let me concentrate."

The quiet experimental notes continued.

"I'm getting out of here," Nick announced. "I'm really keeping the wrong people waiting right now, understand?"

"Stop—" Katja yelled.

"I can't—!" Nick yelled.

The steel strings rang out.

Shayna gasped: "Found it!"

At that same moment the door screeched. A crudely-sawed slot clanked open, and from the darkness within came the low rumbling voice she remembered.

"What," it said.

She swallowed hard and peered wordlessly into the iron-framed void. She leaned up onto her feet.

"Speak!" bellowed the slot.

"I came to ask for your help."

"You followed me here?" the slot accused.

"I was here before."

They eyes still struck her when they appeared; they were so old, so weathered, so blue. They furrowed in uncertainty and squinted down at the three intruders and finally said "Leave, leave me alone."

"Please," Katja said. "We know its name!" She grabbed Shayna's shoulder and whispered "*Say its name.*"

Shayna closed her eyes and did.

A dead silence passed between the plastic bags and newspapers.

"You know I can't cure it," grumbled the ancient. "I don't have that power."

"I know," Shayna said.

When she looked up, the eyes were sinking back into the void, but they stopped. A gnarled, antique nose remained on the edge of the light and a ponderously wrinkled hand rubbed at the face and the beard around it.

"Then come in." They heard the squeak of the latch.

The gong of the door was low and steady as it leaned open. They saw only the ragged threads of his poncho, trailing along the concrete and disappearing. Shayna followed first.

The television static swarmed her vision in the dark of the tunnel. It unfolded now, falling into limitless crystalline formations, spiraling like galaxies of glittering stars that caught and went out a thousand times a second. Green, purple, white, getting brighter. The pins and needles were biting deeper. Dim blue light sliced the nebulae open as she guided herself down the stairs and among the cluttered rows of glass and machines.

"I presume you are past the initial onset of symptoms."

"Yes," She answered.

Behind her, Katja and the dealer stepped down hesitantly.

Shayna told them: "This is Kingsford. Doctor Kingsford." She turned to him. "This is my friend Katja. And my, um, drug dealer. Nick."

Kingsford glimpsed up momentarily from the drawer he was sifting through, then abandoned it for the bookshelf behind him. Shayna thought she heard him mutter "Damned figures."

"You're that bum," said Nick. "You're him. The one who hangs around Charity Center. I've heard of you."

"That bum," the doctor muttered, taking down a heavy black notebook.

"How old are you? They say... they say you're over—"

"Fever," the ancient interrupted, loudly, leafing through a spiral of tortured pages. "Lightheadedness. Fatigue. These effects can be suppressed by way of an archaic chemical treatment. Methyl-oxylithate. Five hundred milligrams, every eight hours, orally administered."

"Oxy... what?" said Nick.

"Methyloxylithate."

"You have it?" Shayna asked. "Was there some in with the stuff we brought back from the Heaps that night? Those—"

"No. The drug hasn't been commercially produced in more than ninety years. I have here... enough for a few days. But I will synthesize more if you supply me with certain chemical precursors." He tore out a corner of a page and started scratching a note.

"What precursors?" Nick asked.

"Nothing a man of your profession would have difficulty in acquiring. They are used in the Arctor Process of amphetamine production."

Nick scratched his head and gingerly accepted the list he was handed, though he didn't dare to meet the coldness in the weathered eyes that fixed on him. He skimmed the list. He winced a few times.

"Look, I'll see what I can do," he said as he started up the stairs. "But I gotta run. Now."

"Nick!" Katja protested, stomping one foot. She ran halfway up the stairs and looked back, torn between them.

"Let me talk with the doctor alone," Shayna said. "Go with Nick. Bring back the chemicals."

Katja wavered on the stairs. She ran down and between the spires of glass tubing, held Shayna's face and hissed her forehead. Then she left.

Shayna turned and watched those ponderously wrinkled hands produce a glass vial full of gray pills. The doctor slid it grimly across the table toward her

"That's it?" Shayna asked. "I just take one of these and I'll feel fine again?"

"No," rumbled the voice from within that endless white beard. "First, understand that nothing has changed. You are still dying. You will quickly develop a tolerance to this treatment. It will become useless."

Shayna nodded.

"Second, understand that this drug, particularly at the purities attainable with my limited equipment, is assuredly as lethal as your blight."

"What difference does that make?"

The ancient gazed down at the gnarled black notebook and murmured "Many of the blighted whom I have met are hopeful, through their last moments, that they may yet survive. They wait in the line at Charity, or they resort to the spiritual. They have heard of the sudden and miraculous recovery. Indeed, such recoveries are known to occur, few and far between though they may be."

Shayna said nothing.

"If you select this course of treatment," he said, "you will be abandoning that hope. You will live better in the time you have. But you must be resigned to what will happen."

She wiped her eyes and said "I am resigned. Completely."

"When did you come to this decision?"

"Yesterday."

The doctor handed her the bottle – and when she took it, and felt the thinness of the skin of his hand, she shivered, and she could not help whispering:

"How old *are* you?"

His face twitched underneath the edge of his long beard. He turned away and hobbled among his instruments. "You have what you came for. Return with the precursors when you require more of the drug." He lowered his eyes into a microscope, as if for no reason but to hide them from her.

"I won't tell anybody. You can trust me. I'll take your secret with me."

"I share that particular secret with no one." He still didn't look up. His voice was creaking. With shocking agitation he said "Now go!"

Shayna stepped back reflexively. She turned toward the stairs, but at the last moment she stopped and faced him again. "Why can't you tell anyone?"

Virgil Kingsford left the microscope and leaned against the shelf, his back turned to her. There beneath the scraggly, matted tendrils of silver hair and the ragged rust-colored yarns of the poncho, his lungs heaved. Then his voice came back different, broken.

"Some day soon they'll come to tear this neighborhood down. Even though I own it. Finally. After all of this time, it's finally stopped mattering to them. I'll have nothing to do but walk the streets, then. Uselessly. But if it's the divine will, let it be."

"What do you mean?"

"Shame. I can't tell anyone my age because I am ashamed of it."

The silence lay heavy between the glass tubes. She went to him on silent feet and, both fearfully and reflexively, lay her hand cautiously on the ragged fibers of his back.

"How old are you?" she whispered.

"My name is Virgil Louis Kingsford. I was born in the Angelis Arcology, on the tenth of October, one hundred and sixty-eight years ago."

The number replayed in her mind and her mouth many times before she grasped it – and when she believed it, her hand recoiled reflexively. She couldn't put it back. She could hardly look at him.

"You're an Insider?"

"*No,*" he said instantly. "Not anymore. I'm not one of them. But... neither am I one of you. I can never be. This too is an element of my atonement."

"You committed some crime? They sent you into exile out here?"

At this he turned gradually around and gave off a short, sad laugh – one sneer just wide enough for Shayna to know that she had seen, with direct eyes, the ominous glow of perfectly white teeth from beyond the veil of his beard.

"It's no law of theirs that I violated. I left of my own will. One hundred and thirty-two years ago."

The number hit her like a fist and she gasped "*How is that possible?* How could you have lived that long?"

"It's... difficult to explain." He crumpled slightly and shuffled off down the rows of glass and machines. She didn't know how she hadn't seen it before: that shame. It weighed him down in every small thing he did or said – as if the ragged, trailing threads of that poncho had been made of wrought iron. As dazed as she was by all this information, as ironic as she knew it was, she knew that the tightness now rising in her throat was not for herself but for him. She felt sorry for him.

"Maybe you'd feel better if you told me," she said.

He responded shakily, but with ascending violence: "We are—I was genetically modified. I mean that my... my life, my organs and cells were... patched, corrected. You probably believe that Insiders are cured of the blight when they contract it. Insiders are not even susceptible to most of what you call the blight. Nor to any other malady that can be reasonably expected to eventually kill you, Shayna, and everyone you have ever known. My flesh is invulnerable to virtually any toxicity or infection, or even the natural progression of age. I have already lived out nine of your lifetimes and I have no idea how many more will pass before my life finally and mercifully stops. Understand that I say none of this to *feel better*. It's not for me to feel better. It's my province to serve out the term of my sentence. To atone as best I can. That and nothing else."

"One hundred and sixty-eight years is a long sentence."

"It is."

Though he kept his back turned to her, she saw the violent shaking of the hand he held in front of himself – subdued in tune with his breathing to a perfect stillness.

"Why did you leave the Cology? Why come here? What was your crime?"

The ancient shook his head.

"Please. Tell me."

"I cannot tell you. Only because it would be a separate crime for me to ask of you that you keep that particular secret, and it must be kept for now."

Shayna tried and failed to think of a response. Meanwhile her fatigue was returning in force. Her hand as she finally reached for the jar of crude gray tablets was already becoming sluggish and hard to lift. So she sank onto a metal stool and stared through the heavy glass. She didn't even hear the ancient shuffle along the rows, to appear at her side with a broken-handled mug of water and eyes that wouldn't meet hers. She accepted it. She dropped one gray pill into the quivering, prickling palm of her hand and managed to push it through her lips – and it tasted sickeningly bitter and metallic until she washed it down.

Katja was wreathed in smoke, perched on the steps in the daylight at the end of the tunnel. Traces of tears were painted in mascara along the curves of her cheek. For a while Shayna stood concealed in the dark of the passageway, studying her friend's down-turned eyes and the anxious movements of her smoking. She thought of the nurse on her deathbed. She looked at Katja and thought: *I love you. But do I know you?*

Finally she stepped out into the light. She squinted and said "I thought you were going with him. You've been waiting here all this time?"

Katja looked down and mashed out the fire of her cigarette where a second butt lay. "You took it? How do you feel?"

"Better. Maybe."

"You still have a fever?"

Shayna touched her forehead and was surprised to wipe off a few heavy beads of sweat, but she said "I don't feel hot. I guess I still am. But I'm not tired or dizzy anymore."

"Are your ears still ringing?"

"Yes. But I know what I have to do about it now." The latch squeaked closed on the iron door behind her. Somewhere a crow cawed. "Let's get out of here."

"Do you still carry that flask?" Shayna asked. They were bouncing with the potholes in the bus's back corner.

Katja handed it to her.

"No, I don't think I'm tired at all anymore." She filled her mouth with the fire and swallowed. "There's still some pain, but nothing I can't dull."

"Good," Katja said with a crooked smile, and took the flask back.

"Maybe the monks are right. Maybe there is some magical cure, somewhere out there. It's a strange enough world. But I don't have time, and maybe there's something even more important anyway. More important than just living."

"What could possibly be more important than that?"

"Lots of things. I started to realize that when Carl and I almost killed the clerk."

"You almost *what?*"

Shayna sighed. "I'll tell you later."

The factories and warehouses lay flat for miles, their smoke plumes rising straight and thin like blades of dry grass in the yellow sky. In her hand Shayna turned the white shard over and over again, pressing the tips of her fingers against the cutting edges.

"I'm still waiting to hear what happened to your head," Katja said, squinting at the stitches and buzz-cut hairs.

Shayna almost answered, but she only sighed and readjusted the strap of her goggles to cover the stitches better.

"But I know you're not going to tell me."

Shayna just stared into the white shard in her palm. "You remember when we met. Don't you?"

"Yeah, of course."

"And when we still had our band."

Katja smirked and nodded.

"Things were really different then," Shayna said. "I mean, *we* were different."

"I guess."

Shayna's phone rang. She glanced at the screen and dropped it back into her pocket.

"Who is it?"

"Carl."

"God, you should talk to him."

"Why?"

"Because he's really messed up. I mean, we all are, but him especially. He was at the Green Room last night. He...."

"He what?"

"Well, he just sulked alone by the stairs most of the night, waiting. And then at about ten, when I guess he figured you weren't going to show up, he just started pounding it. I mean, he was delirious. I've never seen somebody make himself that sick that fast. We had to carry him out. Twice. And he threw a bottle at Tom's head."

Shayna sighed absently.

"He really cares about you," Katja said. "We all do, I mean. But Carl...."

"You all want a way to help me."

"Yes." Katja took her hand and held it tightly.

"Well, I thought of something."

"What is it?"

"I know what the ringing in my ears is. I think I know what to do about it. To do that thing, though, I'll have to ask everyone for a special kind of favor, and it's something you probably wouldn't do otherwise. It's not a small thing."

"Just say the word."

"Okay," Shayna said, and exhaled.

"Okay."

Shayna nodded to herself and returned the grip of Katja's hand. She turned the shard over in her other palm, deep in thought.

"Okay – what?" Katja said impatiently. "What's the favor?"

Shayna squinted into the sun and said "We get the band back together."

Walking alone from the bus stop, it dawned on Shayna that Katja hadn't asked what the plan was beyond that, or whether there was a plan at all, or whether she believed it had a chance. She'd just listened and nodded and promised unquestioningly to do the part Shayna asked of her – and in the wake of this memory, Shayna sighed and let her feet linger on the sidewalk. Quiet love wafted in the warm wind with the salty aroma of the Smarty's down the street.

She made her turn and the same breeze turned rottenly sulfuric and hot, spraying up out of the exhaust pipes below Tom's apartment. She moved out of their way as best she could and tried to get a good angle, peering upward at the cracked window she knew was his. She could see the bend in the curtain rod, the water-stained ceiling tiles.

The hammering of her pulse was too strong, humiliating in and of itself. It told her she should have given Katja this half of the errands instead of the other one. She wiped the sweat from the goggles on her forehead, and dialed.

His phone picked up on the first ring, but there was no sound.

"Hello?" she said. "Tom?"

"Yeah."

"I need a favor. Are you at your place?"

His bony figure appeared up there in a swirl of clove smoke, naked save his beige underpants, leaning heavily against the window frame and squinting into the afternoon.

"No," he said. Then he looked down.

Their eyes met. They both took down their phones from their faces and stared emptily at each other.

Time passed.

They raised their phones again.

"I'm coming down," he whispered in the thick static.

There was another voice beneath his, faint and unintelligible. Feminine.

Shayna's jaw clenched hard.

"Don't let me interrupt if you're busy," she said. Her phone snapped shut in her hand. She turned her back and started walking, but she heard his window wrenching open, and she half-turned to see his burning cigarette fall two stories to the puddles below. Even from down there she could see his hands shaking on the sill.

"Never mind," she yelled up. She turned the corner.

"You're dying," his voice yelled.

She hesitated, drifted backward, stared up into the throbbing clouds.

"Shay!" he cried out, scattering the pigeons from the eaves.

Tom found her there in the same place a minute later when he came stumbling down the front steps. His shoes were half-tied and his pants wouldn't stay up while he struggled to loop the belt. She was leaning back into the bricks at the mouth of the alley, her fingers picking idly or nervously at the mortar in between.

"Want to go ride bikes?" he said.

She exhaled and said emotionlessly "I threw my bike into a canal that night."

"Which night? —Oh."

She raised her eyes to give him a cold look, but instead she accidentally saw just how broken he really was. His eyes were red, his nose sniffling back watery snot. Her look didn't go as planned.

"Well, we should go somewhere," he said, wiping the crust of an old tear. "We should talk along the way. Want to take a bus ride?"

"I'm tired of the bus."

"Then we'll just walk."

They walked straight down along the main drag, headed nowhere in particular but hurrying anyway until Shayna wasn't sure anymore of who was trying to outpace who.

"I only came to ask a favor," she said. "Your amps. I want to borrow them if I can."

"The amplifiers? Why do—?" He sniffled, then said "Yes, of course. Take them."

"Thanks. I appreciate it."

"Are you playing a show?" He looked at her bass.

"Not a show. Just one song."

"Which song?"

"Machinery Anthem."

"Oh."

"I'm putting the band back together."

His feet hesitated for a step. "Do you want me to play?"

"I've got Carl. It can be played okay with only one guitar."

"So you don't want me there."

"Not anymore."

"Why not?"

"Don't you have some girlfriend you'd rather be fooling around with?"

"She's not my—"

Only then was she sure she'd heard that voice on the line. She shuddered and felt the ache in the roots of her teeth flare to new life.

"She's just someone who..." he said through his quivering face. "She just helps me feel better when I feel like shit the way I have since yesterday, okay?"

Shayna scowled straight ahead and said "Poor Tom. What's wrong? Did I hurt your feelings?"

"Why didn't you tell me?" he stammered. "Would you *ever* have told me?"

"What does it matter."

They came to a crosswalk and stopped dead, encased in noise and exhaust.

"It *matters* because—" he rasped. "God damnit, yes, it matters!"

"Why?"

"I l-love you. Just because I don't necessarily love you in the exact same way that—"

Tires screeched somewhere in the street, cutting him off.

"You love me?" she said, over blaring horns. "Well I'm *in* love with you, you asshole!"

Tom sank to his knees on the hard concrete, fists clenched into the sidewalk, and the little scream he let out was mostly drowned out by echoes from down the street: the crunching of metal and glass, the exchange of profanity, the burning of rubber. Then the lights finished changing. The street subsided.

She stood there a while before stepping forward and letting him lean the side of his face into her stomach. She lay her hands awkwardly on his head and held it – and his skin, like everything else she touched with those hands, felt burning hot and charged with static.

"I'm sorry," she whispered. "I take it back. It doesn't matter."

Tom was upright and walking again. It was strange the way he could apparently recompose himself.

"How long do you have?" he asked with some effort.

"I'm not sure. Days now. A week. Something like that. It'll be fast."

He flinched, and quickly turned his head to stare away down the lines of dusty lots, the yards of rusting trucks and barrels and scrap, his neighborhood. He stopped. They had come to the desiccated remains of a burger outlet. There were plastic tables attached to benches for ghost kids. There were two adjacent metal slides with tiny steps to climb up.

"Maybe I can help," he said, perching on one.

She started up the other and said "It's the blight, and I'm too old to go to Charity."

"I don't mean that kind of help. I wish I did." With some struggle he squeezed his legs around the tiny railing and sat there at the top, looking down the slide. At the bottom there was a wide puddle of featureless black ooze, just something else boiling up from under the old lots.

"So what then?"

"I have a lot more money than I usually let on," he said uneasily. "From my side job. Running Heap salvage. I've really saved up a lot."

"How much?"

"Enough." He stared away into the glowing yellow sky. "Enough for a sort of retirement. When the time came, I thought – when I get the blight myself, or when my father or brother or his wife do. I mean, I've been investing. In a house."

"A house?"

Tom's gaze lost itself in the dry wind. "Way out there in the Sierras. Up into the mountain tops. Where the Tropolis doesn't even go. At a certain altitude, the blocks just end. Have you ever been out that far?"

Shayna shook her head and pulled her hair out of her eyes. "I didn't know there was such a place." Everything was baking in the sudden sunny warmth. The light seemed to make her ears ring louder with the phantom sound.

"I've only been out that far once, when I was a child. The house is near where I went that time. It's why I chose it."

She turned and stared into his profile, nodded into the breeze, backdropped by the ocean of tar and concrete and cargo containers.

"What is it like there?" she asked.

"The sky is a different color. It's green, kind of turquoise on clear days. And at night it's black, really black. The stars and the moon are the whitest white. Just like you said to me that night on the Heaps."

Shayna sighed into herself and squelched a grin. "I didn't think you were listening to me."

"It's way out there. I haven't even seen it in person yet. I don't have a car to get up there. But I have enough to buy one if I have to. I mean, I could take you up there if you want. If you want that to be where...."

Shayna smirked.

"Where you spend the time you've got left," he finished. "It's the most beautiful place I've ever been. I think you would like it."

"Probably."

The hollowed plastic signs around them rattled in a hot gust.

"You don't have to decide now," he said.

"It sounds nice, but I think there's something I have to do here."

They sat together at the tops of their slides, watching the passing black plume of a faraway truck. She felt something brush her fingertips, then encase them. She glanced at their held hands. Then she stared down into the black goo and exhaled.

"You don't feel that way about me, remember?"

"I know," he murmured.

She held his hand back tightly.

"Can I bum one of your foul-ass cigarettes?" she asked him.

He produced two of the cloves, lit them in his mouth, and meekly passed one to her with his free hand. She breathed as deeply and slowly as she could stand to. She felt the hairs on the backs of his fingers. She pictured the unknown girl who probably, even now, lay in his bed. She let everything roll over her like the smoke she let bleed out of her lips, and everything buzzed and burned and rang in her ears all over again.

"This'll all be over pretty soon," she said.

"D-don't say—" he began, but trailed off when he saw that she was smiling.

Nobody on the sidewalk knew anything, but Shayna pretended that they all did; she pretended that her walk toward the old Green Room held for every turned head a long-awaited and deeply epic significance. She hid her eyes under her goggles so she was free to study their faces: all the kids who stopped poking at their cat carcass to look up; all the ruffled men and women just now awakening from the last night's debauchery, gazing down from narrow windows in quiet, smoking wonder; and all the vendors and street urchins who fumbled key words in their speeches as they watched the three hobble or march down the street in a delta formation, Shayna bearing her pink bass, Tom and Carl behind her armed with their electric guitars and doggedly lugging one battered amplifier each.

"Are you sure about this?" Carl asked, surprising her. His face was turning colors from the lifting.

"Never more sure." She flicked a smoking stump to the concrete.

"But the comps—" Tom said nervously.

"No comps," she said, and lifted her goggles to look back incredulously at their worries.

"But how are we going to break in through all that?" Carl asked.

The three paused at the mouth of the familiar alley, peering in at the entrance to the Green Room – the original Green Room. Now that door was covered in a big plate of metal and laced with luminous lines of orange tape. There were exhaustive lists of everything that couldn't be done and warnings of incarceration. There were the numbered names of Company directives.

"Through the front door of course," Shayna answered, and led them in halting steps past the alley altogether. Then they were standing, for the first time, under the vast brass hulk of the dead marquee itself. There were no seals or signs here. The doors hung open on their broken hinges as they always had.

"We've been in the green room long enough," she declared. So she marched into the lobby, and broke through the big splintered doors at the end, and opened her eyes wide to adjust to the dimness of the main theatre under the cracked gold-leaf dome. There at the distant end, past the lines of shattered chairs and crumbs of plaster and the black holes in the floor, the old stage lay in wait. There was Katja, standing up, waving.

Shayna went down to the lacquered wood, breathing the place in as she walked. The smell of the ruin. The smell of that moment. The boys lumbered along after her, panting heavily.

"You get the stuff?" she asked Katja.

"Microphone," she replied, swinging it on its ragged cord and setting it back on its broom-handle-fashioned stand, "and power." The car batteries were stacked at her feet.

"Perfect."

"Then we're all here," Katja said through the end of her cigarette.

"Not yet," Shayna said, and at that moment they heard the echo from the lobby. Everyone turned and froze. The amplifier slipped out of Carl's hands and crashed to the floor, and then the whole vast space was dead.

The gigantic figure stood there in the open double doors, pitch black against the dusty daylight behind him, perfectly still and monolithic. Gel glistened in his obsidian hair for one eternal anxious moment. Then he reached his massive arms down and lifted up, by a web of ropes, an entire set of drums.

Shayna hopped down from the stage and met Balboa half way. She reached as far around his denim-clad trunk as she could and hugged him tightly. The drums knocked against each other in his grasp.

"Thank you for coming," she whispered to him.

"You sure I should've?" He peered uncertainly at the stage, and the stage peered blankly back. Nobody moved. "You weren't there when I told them I was going to academy. You don't know how it ended between us."

She grabbed his shoulder. "I've got you." She faced the stage and shouted "What are you all just standing around for? We've got a song to play."

Carl and Tom and Katja looked at her and at each other. Hesitantly they went back to plugging everything in. Balboa and Shayna went to them – but it was Balboa alone who was left to lift his drums one by one up onto the stage and set them in their place. Everybody else stood back and watched.

Katja pulled Shayna hurriedly aside, through the holes in the huge weathered curtain and into the shadows of the backstage. "Did I not tell you about Balboa?" she hissed.

Tom and Carl crept around the side of the curtain to spectate.

Shayna said "He's been your friend for as far back as I have. You know him. You know he's one of us and he won't do anything to hurt us."

"And he could arrest every one of our punk asses just for standing here," Katja whispered frantically. Her voice was shaking. "Do you fucking realize that? The moment he remembers he's working for Don Malt, we're all headed straight into community service."

Shayna exhaled. She opened her mouth to speak.

Katja cut her off. "Think of Tom! With everything Balboa knows about his side job, he'd die in prison. That's if a bunch of them aren't lying in wait to break our skulls right here and right now! Maybe you don't even realize. Maybe you haven't had to deal with comps the way I have."

Shayna felt the wound in her scalp and stifled a grin. She said "Will you think about what you're saying? Nobody is going to fucking ambush us here! Balboa's had a long time now to turn Tom in for the arrest commission. If he wanted us in prison, we'd be there. But we're not. Because he's our friend, and has been since the beginning. And I trust him."

"You're staking all our lives on your trust. Maybe, maybe you only trust him because you don't have any life left to stake on it." As soon as she said it she froze solid. Even her breathing seemed pause.

The sound of Balboa setting up went dead on the other side of the curtain. Tom and Carl receded a step into the dusty shadows and turned down their eyes.

"Maybe it is easier for me," Shayna said, as calmly as she could. "But we need him, and I know we can trust him."

Katja bit her lip and looked away. "I'm sorry, but I can't do this. I can't."

She started to back away – but Shayna ran to her. On an unexpected reflex, she put her hands on the sides of Katja's head, and something strange happened. As Katja requited the motion, a different kind of electric tingle spread through her limbs. It was a cool wind.

The horizon is a ring of gold around the haze-choked horizon. Long clouds streak silently by. Shayna looks far down and sees the city blocks pass as an endless and shifting desert of rusty circuitry, all details too small to make out.

"Where are we?" Katja's voice asks.

Shayna sees her there – she sees herself and Katja both from outside. They're both floating, arms spread, facing down.

"This is how it was," Katja says. "When you saved me, that night. I remember now. This is where you found me, isn't it?"

"This is what I dreamed," Shayna answers. "I was looking for you. Calling your name."

"And I said 'I'm here.' You said—"

"'You have to come back! Come back down!'"

"'Why?'"

"'You'll be lost up here forever if you don't.'"

"But I didn't care. I *wanted* to stay up here forever. There's too much bullshit down there." Katja peers down into the rush of dirty blocks. "There's just hurt and fear, for everyone, on and on. It never stops. Up here at least it all looks so small."

The two of them drift. The windy distance between them ebbs and flows. The long clouds make a noise as they pass, odd words indistinctly whispered.

"How did you ever convince me to come back from this?" Katja says.

"You asked me something."

"I asked, 'How do you do it? How do you go on?'"

Shayna doesn't know anymore whether she's seeing the present or her memory of the old dream. She drifts closer to her friend and responds "'Angry. I go on, more angry than I can tell you. I hate all the ways I've screwed up by always being so afraid of screwing up. All the things I could have done if only I hadn't been telling myself I had all the time in the world to do them. Everything I missed by living like I'd live forever.'"

She reaches out to Katja. Their fingers dangle in the empty air, just apart.

In her memory, in the present, she continues: "'Since all this happened, I've been seeing what a small part of our lives we actually manage not to waste. Any of us. And the more I think about it, the more I see there's only one thing, only one single solitary fucking thing in the whole world, that isn't a complete waste of everything.'"

"'What is that?'"

Their fingers meet then. They steady themselves, and the distance ceases to ebb and flow. They pull closer in their soft freefall, until their foreheads lean together and their hands clasp on the sides of their faces. They hold each other tightly.

"'This,'" Shayna answers. "'Now come down.'"

"And I did," Katja whispered.

The daylight dimmed on the other side of Shayna's eyelids, and she knew she was back in the dust and the darkness behind the stage.

"Trust me," she said. "Trust me like you did then."

Katja shivered and wiped her eyes. "All right."

The boys watched awkwardly. Now Shayna turned to them, doing her best not to betray her lightheadedness. She said to all of them:

"Look. Maybe I did this wrong. Maybe I should've warned you. But here we are. Here we all are for the first time in so long. Don't you see that?"

Carl shifted uneasily. Tom scratched his head. Balboa's drums started rattling again. Shayna knew he could have heard everything even without his inhumanly enhanced senses.

When nobody said anything, she said "Look, I'm feeling something. I feel something incredible, just standing here with all of you. I can't explain it. I don't know how to begin, how to say it, but I feel like everything in my entire life, everything has been by accident until now."

She tried to look at them, but it was hard. She knew they could see the beads of sweat on her forehead. She knew her heat-racked skin was looking pale.

"Look, I don't know if I can do this," Tom said quietly, stepping through the ragged velvet and meekly grasping his electric guitar where it leaned.

Shayna told him "If you're angry, or anxious, put it into the music. The song calls for it."

"It's not that. It's been forever since I touched this thing. I don't think I know the chords anymore. I don't think I know how to play at all."

"M-me too," Carl said as he climbed through. His face was red with embarrassment. "I don't think I could do this if I tried."

"Same here," Katja said emptily from the gap in the curtain. "I can't remember *Machinery Anthem* worth a damn and my bass hasn't had an E-string in seven months. I'm sorry, Shay. Really, I am. But I don't see how we can really do this. Not like we used to."

Carl sighed bitterly and slumped his head into his fist. His guitar fell over and slammed into the uneven floorboards.

Shayna's own bass lay heavy in her hands. The scuffed pink plastic was dripping sweat under the buzzing flesh of her fingers.

"Balboa?" she said, rubbing at her eyes.

He sat wreathed in silent drums, only gazing stoically back at her.

She turned out to face the dead theatre. Their dust and cigarette smoke had risen to the height of the broken dome, making the daylight into a thin yellow laser beam that shot down onto the edge of the stage.

"Not like we used to?" she said. "You forget. We could never play worth shit in the first place."

She lay her fingers on the strings in the dead quiet.

It was very softly that she played the first part of the melody. The amplifier was breathing more static than tone, and some of the notes slipped into silence all together. She stopped short of the refrain and started over. Then again. She kept her eyes closed and her back turned to all of them – and she listened anxiously, against her despair, for the sound of somebody packing up and leaving. But the first sound she finally heard was like the thud of a heartbeat, and it didn't stop. It matched her rhythm. It grew very faintly louder, slightly stronger, and so did her strings.

A short eternity passed.

Carl played a loud chord and then aborted it. She heard him plucking very quietly at the guitar again, twisting the knobs, grunting his embarrassment. "Fuck it," she heard him whisper, and then he was playing the melody too. He was noticeably out of tune and far from the rhythm, but his rhythm got better each time he tried and trailed off and swore under his breath and tried again. The three of them grew louder together with every fresh start short of the refrain. Balboa added his snare with a militaristic marching sound.

This went on for some time.

The second guitar snuck into the melody with a shyness that befitted its player, but it was perfectly in tune and synch. Shayna could hear all the money in that shiny thing. She heard him get all the chords right on the second try and she raised her volume again, not to hear herself but to force him louder.

She let herself turn around and look. She saw Katja, eyes still stuck to the floor, nonetheless finally coming all the way through the curtain and swinging the busted strap of her busted bass over her head and picking up the notes she could. She stepped up to the microphone. They were coming up on the refrain again.

"Don't worry," Shayna said to them. "Just hold on."

Nobody needed a cue. They all fell into it at once. In one breath the meek electrified strings had all turned acidic and deafeningly hot, and Balboa's drums became a line of automatic rifles. Tom was struggling to be loud enough, Carl was fighting to make any coherent noise at all, Katja was working hard to play even the notes she had strings for – but it was happening, it was all stuttering up into to violent and unsteady life, and there was no stopping or starting over now. The drums were flawless; they held the cacophony together in a vice grip and they hammered in Shayna's buzzing entrails and forced even her racing heart to fall into the rhythm of the song. She looked at Balboa and saw his head lowered and his face glaring straight ahead, the way it had that night on the bike ride to his grandfather's grave. She looked at Tom and Carl and saw their panic and their self-loathing over every mistake they were making, but every red-faced rise in that hatred only pushed the song louder and more fully into its own real spirit. Soon all the missed notes had stopped taking anything away. Soon the dissonance was layered on so thickly as to be perfect and pristine – and there, she felt it, it was all starting to cohere. With every decibel it gained, the ringing in her head was rising too. It was shaking in the weathered floorboards. It was raining plaster crumbs from the towering walls. Her sickness and her song were based on the same note, and every measure brought the two more perfectly into synch.

She didn't realize she'd been singing the words until her throat was already aching and rough. She hadn't known whether she still knew any of them. She and Katja were singing together, shouting into each others' faces with the microphone trapped between them. The words themselves were lost to any comprehensibility. Everything was oblivionized between all the weird screaming singing metal and the hail of sonic bullets and artillery shells coming from Balboa – and before she could remember where in the song she was anymore, and what was coming next, it was rolling over her, and this one thing they all executed with total fidelity. Balboa's percussion exploded to its peak and then dropped into nothing. The final chord blasted out into the vastness of the space, roaring through Shayna's every cell when she bent her head down to the speaker. Her head filled up with light, and then there inside the sound – the perfection of the sound that had been ringing in her ears for two straight days, and in her dreams for longer, now lanced by their singing steel and rupturing like a gigantic blister on her brain – there inside a note, she thought she ceased to exist. As the white light in her head split wide open, she remembered.

In one moment she is one lone hopeless girl. In the next she is five black silhouettes towering above the earth.

She comes straight from the factory to get in line. It's the first warm night in an unseasonably frigid year, and the last night in which The Smurge will exist. She shows up four and a half hours early for a ticket, ready to sacrifice every dollar she has to her name, though she already knows it won't be enough. She pleads at the front gates until the last seat sells, then pleads to the scalpers, though she knows they'll show no mercy. As most of the other thwarted stragglers bleed away with the last daylight, she smokes brokenly against the wall. The first distant echo of the music over the stadium walls makes her sob.

She feels something wet on her head and looks up to see the old rain dripping off the edge of the wall. It isn't so high – and there at the top, she knows, she'd be able to see them directly, and the music would be more than a muffled echo. A rusty drainpipe clings feebly to the concrete. She contemplates it nervously, calculating whether it will hold her weight and whether she'll be seen.

Somebody has beat her to it. He's an unlikely climber, struggling very hard for every foot he hauls himself up, his coveralls and high-tops fiercely scraping the concrete – but his mad dedication glistens on his bared teeth.

"Hey!" a voice booms from behind her head, making her jump. The massive armor-plated creature pushes her hard aside as it moves for the drainpipe climber, already brandishing a stun prod.

The climber freezes in wide-eyed terror.

"Hey yourself!" shouts another voice from behind as a small stone ricochets hollowly off the back of the comp's plastic helmet. Shayna turns in time to see the black-haired girl bare her pierced tongue before the comp bolts for her and she vanishes into an alley.

The climber slips off the pipe, falls hard on his ass and takes off in the opposite direction. Shayna doesn't know why she instinctively takes off after him. She will never ask herself why.

She catches up with him only a block down, where he ducks into an alley and sags against the side of a dumpster, panting heavily and barely holding himself upright. She stares at him. He stares at her.

"They're coming," says a voice from behind. The boy she finds at her side is older, tall and narrow. A deep green army coat is draped over his shoulders.

"Shit!" says the fallen climber. In panic he flips up the lid on the dumpster and tries to haul himself up over the edge, but he can't find the strength.

A third bystander, stocky with long black hair, rushes abruptly to him and pushes his legs up over the dumpster's lip. The tall boy quietly shuts the lid just as three comps and their prods barrel into the mouth of the alley.

"Where did that zit-faced turd go off to?" one bellows.

"That way," Shayna and the two boys all say in perfect unison, pointing down the alley and then parting for the thunder of jackboots that follows.

In the comps' wake, a grate in the alley lifts up and a girl pulls herself up into daylight. Her hands and knees are covered in oily muck. The rock thrower. And when the climber peeks up out of the dumpster, and all five pairs of eyes meet for the first time, something moves tangibly through the air between them. They are all accomplices.

"Follow me," says the tall one.

He leads them across the street and far from the evaporating crowds. He takes them to a black hole in the towering cinderblock foundation of a hollowed-out and chainlinked set of ruins, a place no one else knows, and helps them one by one up a crumbled and lightless staircase on the other side. Through a gap in the fallen walls, in the beginning of a soft warm rain that catches the light of the street lamps, Shayna first makes out the silhouette of the high dirt mound.

Echoing from the street they can hear the beating of helicopter blades and an electric voice booming down: "All tickets are sold out. You have no reason to be here. Leave the area."

"Thank you," pants the climber to the girl with the rock.

"I'm Katja," she says, wiping her hands.

"Carl," he says, rubbing at his pimpled nose.

"Tom," says the tall one in the army coat.

"Just call me Balboa," says the stout one whose long and messy hair looks like crow feathers in the night glow.

"Shay," says Shayna.

In single file, each steadying the one ahead when the ground gives way, they ascend the gigantic muddy slope of displaced construction dirt. With each step they climb, the ground is a little firmer, anchored by the roots of dandelions and gathering blades of grass. As they rise, the music is less muffled, more direct and clear and unechoing, until at the very summit they all turn to look down over the stadium's walls, over the cluttered bleachers, all the way to the luminous stage where all the searchlight beams begin.

No word is spoken between them for hours. The drizzle comes and goes and soaks their shoulders and the past day's muggy warmth never lets up. The grass beneath them is the rare kind, thick and alive, still young and unscorched by the summer to come, and the grooves it leaves in Shayna's palms are full of its vibrant green blood. In the warmth and the dampness and the urban night wind, its smell breathes over all of them like nothing else in the universe.

Only when the last song ends do they begin to talk. They go to work piecing together the unspoken pact that already exists between them. They stay on the hill all night, leaving only to shoplift two six-packs and then climb up again, until sunrise finds them all splayed out unconscious in the grass, exhausted from six straight hours of music-drunken conversation; six hours of bitter conspiracy theories to account for the breakup of the greatest band in human history; hours of mad declarations of the glory of those songs and all the resonance of their ideals of subversion and sedition; passionate vows to keep their sound and their spirit alive with every act and thought and breath the five accomplices will have from then on. They take oaths with their hands grabbed together in a pentagon. They lay the plan for their tribute band. In the rising light, they climb down from the grassy mound and, finally parting, cast their salutes to a newborn revolution and the ultimate demise of the Company and the comps and the Cology.

Balboa will supply his family's basement, couches to sleep on, and a television. He will never tell them why he only has a last name. He'll buy a set of drums with every dollar left by all his dead relatives combined, and sleep to recordings of The Bomber's drum solos until he can replicate them in his dreams.

Carl will spend a full day glaring in silence and angrily theorizing conspiracies for every member of the Smurge that dies of a drug overdose, until the last one does. In a moment of passion he'll cut a small scar into his chin to make it match that of lead guitarist Bruce Fain, but his face will never be capable of the same beard.

Katja will perfect her impression of Clara Ruthless's bass-playing stance, clothing style and personal mannerisms, and spend two years trying to imitate her singing tone before she realizes her own voice sounds better. By then, no one will be talking anymore about performing for an audience.

Tom will be the one to try to instruct everyone else in the basic principles of music, of which they know nothing. He will bring cheese shards and cans of fizz to every gathering and never be paid back. He will never tell anyone that his guitar was once played by the real Jon Manderlay, and is worth more money than the rest of them make in two years.

Shayna, though cherishing the secret hope that she too could make a good Clara Ruthless, will always be the fifth member of a four-person group – until, one day, she leaves them and goes back to her apartment in the unfinished district, tacitly expecting never to return.

That will almost be the entire life of their band.

The final note of *Machinery Anthem* began to fade, but the new color still filled her vision. It had become a waking dream. That blue resonated in eerie synesthesia with the note still buzzing in the amplifier's grating, ever more vibrant the more she concentrated on it. She felt the weight of the bass in her arms, and as she looked up into that burning field of light, she realized: *This is the part of the dream I'd forgotten. This is how it always was. With me, standing here with my bass. I play the note that cracks everything open and sets the blue free.*

She laughed. They all laughed. Then she twisted her finger in each ear.

"That was insane," Balboa said. "That was beautiful."

"Yeah," said Carl, wiping his brow. "Not bad."

"Which one next?" Balboa asked.

"Whoa, whoa," said Tom. "At least let me go look up the actual notes somewhere before we—"

"This was just the beginning," Shayna interrupted. "That was nothing. Just a song."

"Huh?" Balboa asked.

"I didn't just bring you all here to play music. I brought you here to put the band back together. Like it was meant to be from the start."

Everyone looked at her, not getting it.

"I mean, what were all those songs about?" she said. "What made them mean so much to us? Were they just pretty words and sounds? Did they just sound nice to us, or did they... or did they say something we all wanted to hear, and say for ourselves? Did they talk about doing something we all needed to do?"

"What do you mean?" Katja asked.

"I mean starting the revolution. The one the Smurge sang about. The one implied by the lyrics of the song we just played."

"Whoa, now—"

"I'm talking about overthrowing the Company and tearing down the Cology. All the Cologies. Dissolving the comps. Closing all the Community Service Camps and setting all the prisoners free. Smashing Corporate power and replacing it with a new constitutional government of equals, a public government by and for the people. All the people, both Outsiders and Insiders."

Tom knitted his brows and rubbed his open mouth.

Katja's eyes seemed to search the ground for something that had fallen.

Balboa looked worriedly at everyone else.

Carl scratched his head and asked: "The five of us?"

"Yes," she declared.

The last of the gold flakes reached the ground.

"And if you won't join me, I'll do it alone. Or die trying." She smirked.

"Uh, Shay," Balboa began.

"I'm going to go get some air now. I'll let you all discuss it among yourselves. If you think you're with me, come find me in the back at the new Green Room tonight after dark." She unplugged her bass and returned it to its place against her back. As she hopped down from the stage and started quickly up the aisle, she called over her shoulder "Oh, right – and would somebody please tell Balboa for me? About my blight and all that."

Daylight stung her eyes when she pressed back into it, and she found her hands trembling at her sides.

Yeah, some air, she thought, *and some time to walk off these shakes.*

She stared far down the endless main drag, to the tiny blur of whiteness at the end, and, spitting out a sigh, thought:

And some hours to work out how exactly one stages a revolution.

She left the warmth of daylight for the chilled shadows of the monastery, crushed by tiredness, savoring the silence behind her ears now. All along the way back she tried to think of something, anything to tell them when (or if) they actually showed up a few hours from now. All she could really think of was sleep. Just an hour, she thought. Maybe two. Clear the head. Something would come to her then.

She lay back on the tough, moth-eaten bunk. The stains on the ceiling bore down on her. Her mind drifted along the verge of unconsciousness.

Small shivers came and passed. The cold sweat welled up and wiped away on the back of her hand. The numbered names of minutes fluttered indistinctly through the luminous screen of her phone, and the darkness in the cracks and the ceiling had gradually started to foam up at the edges with sparks of glittering purple – still subtle, but returning, pulsing inside her pulse.

The glass shard turned in her palm in her pocket, getting sweatier.

"Unbreakable my ass," she said, forcing herself up. She took the white shard over to the window. She examined it at different angles in the light. She scraped it against the sill. When nothing happened she scraped harder and harder, until a fine white dust began to build up under the rising ache in her fingers. "Hah!" she said, but when she blew on the shard and looked again she realized that it was exactly the same; the white dust was concrete dust, and there was a deep groove in the sill.

She set it on the cold stone floor by the corner of the bed. She wrapped her fingers around the heavy steel frame and lifted it up, while the toe of her boot pushed the shard squarely under the leg. With all her might she threw the bed down. She shut her eyes to the sound of that glass shooting up and ricocheting around the room – and she found it in the far corner, perfectly intact, its every sharpened ridge and hairline fracture exactly the same as it had been.

She took her lighter and lit the candle on the splintering desk by the door. A quick search of her pockets produced the tweezers with which she held the shard within the flame, as close as she could without snuffing it out, so that the fire licked up both sides. She let long minutes pass while her hands got sweaty and sick of gripping those tweezers. But the unearthly white glass did not burn. It didn't melt or crack. It didn't even pick up the soot of the flame.

Enraged, she dropped it onto the floor and stomped on it. She lifted her foot to stomp again – but it had vanished.

"What—?" she said, squinting across the floor. She smelled something. Then she looked on the bottom of the boot and found the shard there, melting the sole between two treads amid wisps of burning rubber smoke. She pried it out with the tweezers and kicked it away.

She lay down and tried to sleep again.

Her phone rang with a number she didn't know. She answered.

"Yeah," she said.

"I got the stuff," the phone said.

"Who is this?"

"Nick."

"Nick who? Oh. Right."

"I got you the things the old man wanted. They're in a red bag in the alley behind the monastery."

Shayna pushed the window open and squinted out. Between the walls out there she could see the black rear wheel of his motorcycle perched at the curb, rattling with the engine.

"Well, thanks," she said.

"This is the last favor I'm doing anybody for a while. Understand?"

"Okay," she said, and heard him hang up. The wheel out there turned itself into black smoke.

She went down to the alley and found the red plastic shopping bag. Inside were three cans of bug spray, a box of rusty batteries, and a small glass jar full of translucent pink sand.

She yanked the cord when the crumbling silos rumbled into view outside the bus window.

"Hey," the driver's voice crackled through the speaker, "I'll make it this time, but you better know they eliminated this stop from the route today."

"Okay," Shayna said and shrugged as she stepped off – and realized what he'd actually meant. The air was thick with diesel and the roar of engines and hydraulics, and the bricks were covered with men and machines. New chainlinks were spreading out right before her eyes. At first with a hydraulic whimper and then in rolling thunderous bangs, the old brick schoolhouse fell completely inward, and the gigantic yellow steel insect behind it shifted the shadows of its weight in the gray dust that rose up. She saw it inching now toward the building, *his* building. Its scuffed steel claws were already chewing on the edge of the roof.

She ran past the chainlinks and far down the block, desperately envisioning a back way into that alley. She found it, running up a hill of trash that let her climb up onto a one-story roof and then back down a loose drain pipe. A cinderblock crashed out of the sky and exploded a yard away as she leapt down to the steel door and pounded it with her fists, then her boot. On the third kick it bounced open, unlatched. She dove into the black as more cinderblocks started down.

Everything was rattling down there in the basement laboratory. The blue-white screens were flickering unsteadily. The test tubes clinked in their holders. Bits of dust trickled in waves from the moving ceiling. She ran among the lines of counters, looking for him. The plastic bag cut into her hand until she dropped it to the concrete floor.

"Doctor Kingsford!" she shouted over the crashing from above. There at the far side of the space she made out a trickle of a different color of light. She rushed past beakers that shattered on the floor and stepped up to the open door.

Three candles burned on a small table by a perfectly made bed, where the old man knelt on his knees with his back to her, his hands clasped in prayer on the far side of that matted web of sandy silver hair. Sensing her, he turned and sighed.

"We have to get out of here!"

"Of course," he said. Slowly, quietly, he stood up and moved to the bookshelf by the door.

"Hurry!" she yelled.

His hands found a tall jar full of gray caplets and placed it in her hands.

"I was able to make due with the supplies I had on hand," he said, raising his voice above the rumbling. "This is much more than you'll need."

"Fine, but—"

"There's no more use I can be of to you. I've done everything I can."

Some dust fell between them. Something else shattered in the lab.

"We have to get out of here, now! They're tearing this place down!"

"I know. I've waited a long time for this."

"You'll be killed!" she yelled.

The ancient simply turned and moved back to the bed. He knelt down again, clasped his hands, and nodded his head into them. The candles on his table flickered their light across the uneven bricks, a sink, a solitary wooden cross hanging and lightly rattling against the wall.

Shayna stood frozen in the doorway, staring into the jar. She could hear the whining hydraulics and the crashes getting closer, now directly above. The machine sound fell silent for a moment. She started for the stairs, then shoved the jar into her pocket and rushed back to the old man, grabbed at the threads of his poncho and pulled. Kingsford fell back and stumbled reflexively to his feet, and in that moment the ceiling opened and belched a waterfall of bricks onto the bed, snapping it in half before burying it completely. She saw a piece of concrete hit the old man in the head before the dust exploded in her face.

Summoning every ounce of panicked and drug-fueled strength, she gripped his armpits and dragged him through the lab and up the stairs. His eyes were open and blinking. For a moment he even seemed to try to break free of her grip, but he was dazed. In the dying light of the blue-white screens she saw the ceiling giving way at the far corner, bending inward like soggy cardboard and crushing everything. Another surge of bricks cascaded through and the dust scattered the test tubes and blew the notebooks off their shelves.

By the time they reached the dark tunnel above the stairs he was awake and writhing fiercely in her grip, but her strength was still surging to even more inhuman intensities. She hauled him past the iron door and back into the dust-choked daylight, tripping over the remains of the alley. There was nowhere to run but straight into the fray, past the grinding wheels of the yellow steel insect as it devoured the black iron door behind them. She pulled him through a last open gap in the destruction as the last chainlink fence rolled out across it, and only then did he stop fighting. He stood on the sidewalk, half-crumpled, wheezing heavily and staring into the swirling dust. A small trickle of blood streaked the side of his face, but he ignored it even as he seemed to return fully to consciousness.

He muttered softly: "No, no, no, no. What have you done? What have you done?"

Shayna leaned unsteadily against a utility box and tried to catch her breath. She struggled to rub the dust out of her eyes. Her head was swimming.

"Why?" he demanded, his old fists now clenched at his sides. "Why did you do that?"

She stared wordlessly at him and tried to meet his burning eyes.

"If you knew," he said. "By God, if you only knew, you would never have done that."

"If I knew what? What do you mean?"

He sank down. He fell onto the sidewalk and sat, propped up on one hand. He rubbed his face, wiped away the dust-caked blood, and stared ahead. Hidden in billowing dust, the walls went on crashing down under the jaws of the machine.

She stumbled to his side and said "Hey, are you all right?"

"I've waited," he muttered just-audibly, his deep-wrinkled blue eyes fixed on the crumbling. "All these years I've waited."

"Come on. We should get your head cleaned up. I know a place we can go."

He resisted only limply when she helped him up. He followed her, dead-eyed, to the nearest bus back to the monastery. She steered him into the window seat and searched his expression for a clue about what was happening behind the deep furrows of that forehead, but he just stared out at the passing streets in paralyzed bewilderment.

Just once, she thought she heard him speak.

"I killed you," he seemed to whisper.

"What?"

He didn't answer.

The last yellow light of day burnt down into red embers of smog, and then there was only gray dusty shadows and green neon. Somebody's flavored smoke wafted over the booth where Shayna slouched and waited. She hoped Black Faction would show up early, before the band. Assuming the band ever showed up. Assuming it was a band.

There they were, the six in black, drifting in single file through the thickening crowd, Blue Dog leading. Shayna straightened her goggles and approached him.

"You said you were just waiting," she told him, "for the system to start to break down. You were waiting to stage your revolution."

Blue Dog examined her distrustfully through his circular sunglasses.

"Do you seriously not remember me?" Shayna said. "We've met. Twice."

"Oh. Yes. But we're not *just* waiting. You misunderstand."

She followed them. She sat down with them.

"We're blight in the entrails of the system," explained the tall woman in the group.

Shayna winced at the metaphor and bit her tongue.

"We're bringing it down just by being," a second woman added. Her black lipstick gave her the look of having sipped crude oil.

"But you did say you were waiting," Shayna said. "You mentioned a tipping point."

Blue Dog nodded solemnly and started drinking.

"Well, how would you know it if you saw it?" she asked.

The stocking caps passed a glance among each other.

"You're accusing us of missing it," Blue Dog growled. "You're suggesting the tipping point has already come and gone. But you don't even know what we mean by that."

"No. I'm just curious. What would the tipping point look like to you? Whatever it is. What would be the signs?"

"Well." Blue Dog's blood red lenses pointed into space. The other stocking caps watched in silence as more rum disappeared into their leader. "There would be a dissolution of the Company's credibility. The masses would see that the existing power structures were incapable not only of providing for the common good, but even of protecting their own dominion. The Company would lose the legitimacy of its intimidation, as it long ago lost the legitimacy of popularity."

Shayna nodded. In a glance over her shoulder she made out a massive looming shape that could only be Balboa, pressing through the door. Her pulse quickened.

"What are you thinking?" Blue Dog said.

"Wait. Wait and see."

She turned and hopped down in the direction of the shadowy grotto into which Balboa was moving, but everything blurred in the sudden motion. The stars gathered and overwhelmed. She managed to grab a pipe in the wall and brace herself against the rolling of the floor. It had been almost eight hours since the first pill, she realized. So she rattled a second formless gray tablet out of the bottle and, for want of any other liquid within her reach, washed it down with a sip of what she realized was pure grain alcohol.

At first she felt nothing – not even the expected chemical burn in her mouth and throat. Then there was something like an audible sound, a fizzling crack in the center of her head. She blinked hard, and when she looked around she saw the whole room and everything in it standing translucent and luminous and glistening wet. A room of gossamer membranes was swaying, jiggling, shivering biologically around her. As if an effigy of the Green Room had been sculpted from some sea creature's flesh. Or maybe this was not the effigy, she thought – maybe she had been seeing the effigy before, and now for the first time she was seeing the room in its real truth: the throbbing entrails of a gigantic creature.

In a blink the soft gooey shapes snapped back into hard green-lit focus, and her throat was raw. What had been a low ethereal hum lapsed into the heavy metal buzz from whence it had come.

And they were there in the grotto, watching her. The entire band.

"What we need is a symbol," she told them.

The big plastic table between them glowed greenly from within, seemingly radioactive. She knew it was lighting her own face like a weird bonfire from below.

"A symbol of what?" Balboa asked nervously.

"How many people do you know who *like* the Company? Who approve of what it does or the way it operates? Who would side with it in any fight?"

Katja took an apprehensive breath through the hookah tube. The others were studying their hands.

"The Company exists because of our fear," Shayna said.

Balboa nodded slowly. "You're right."

She snuffed out her surprise as well as she could.

"That's something you learn, at the academy," he continued, between anxious swallows and looks away from the looks that fixed on him. "You learn that the purpose of the comps is not really to stop crimes that are already going on. That's not the main thing. The main thing is prevent crimes by making a show of force. It's—"

He shut up suddenly.

"No, go on," Shayna said.

He turned awkwardly to the others and said: "How many civilians do you think there are for every one comp in the Tropolis? What do you think the ratio is? Guess."

Nobody guessed.

"How many?" Shayna asked.

"For every one comp, there are two thousand people. Maybe more. Maybe even three thousand."

"How is that possible?" Katja asked. "How could one comp keep three thousand people in check all at once? It'd never work."

"Like I said, it's about the show of force. When we – they make a move, when they go anywhere, they all go at once. Like you all saw that night when they raided the old Green Room. Remember those choppers? There were eight of them. And we – they, only have ten of them for the entire sector. For all the comps in Angelis. Ten helicopters."

"It's the same reason they wear the full body armor and carry their rifles even when they're just walking around the block," Shayna guessed with an air of knowing.

"Yeah, yeah. Same reason they stage a full-scale operation like that one, maybe two or three times a night. Mobilize the entire force. Take lots of prisoners. It keeps people thinking they're everywhere. But they're nowhere. They can't even be in two places at once. Not in force anyway."

"So it's simple," Shayna said. "If you want to bring down the Company, you just have to expose its weakness. You just show everyone the truth: that there's nothing to be afraid of."

"Sounds like you're talking about embarrassment."

"Humiliation," Shayna said. "Humiliating the comps."

Balboa shifted uneasily in his seat.

"So, how?" Tom asked.

"That's easy," she said. "We cause trouble."

"What kind of trouble?" Carl asked.

"I'll tell you what trouble," She said, and took a long, slow sip from her drink.

The band watched her silently. She tried to ignore it.

She said "What we need is a symbol to attack. It should be a symbol of the Company' power. And what symbolizes power, better than, you know, power?" She shifted her voice fast into a rhetorical tone and said "Where does the Cology get electrical power from?"

"That fission station?" Carl said cautiously. "You mean that fission reactor in Midtown? I heard it only powers the Cology. No one in the Tropolis gets that power."

"Exactly," Shayna said.

"You want to attack a nuclear power plant?" Tom whispered. "Wouldn't that—?"

"No, no." She chuckled anxiously. "Not the plant itself. Obviously. No, we won't have to. All we have to do is break the connection—" She trailed off and turned to Carl. Everyone else looked at Carl too.

He stared at invisible things in the air above his head and said "You're talking about… disrupting the dedicated power nodes that feed to the Cology grid out of the Midtown station."

"Exactly. Can it be done?"

Carl lifted his drink and took a long, slow sip. He said "I think so."

"That's it then. Let's make the Cology flicker. Let's turn it out like a light!"

"Wait a minute," Carl protested. "I mean, I need some time to figure this out."

"How long do you need?"

"A while," he stammered.

"An hour. Take one hour. Then let's do it. Let's do it all tonight. Before sunrise."

Everyone looked at her, dead silent until Katja's glass slipped and exploded on the concrete floor. They all gazed at Shayna, and their gazes were full of emotion, but she wouldn't read them. She cut their silence off, saying:

"It's a Saturday night. What else do you have to do? Sleep? Get wasted? Crash on these couches? Kill more time? Will you ever even remember the night you'll have if you just sit around here, or will it just become another piece of lost life? We can all do something in the next eight hours that none of us will forget! Maybe the whole world will remember it! Maybe—"

She stopped. She let herself glance very briefly down to her side, to check that the bottle of gray tablets was safely hidden in her pocket. Apparently they were stronger than they felt.

"Right," she finished, and sat down, and leaned back with an anxious sigh into the cushions.

Finally Carl said "Okay. I'm in."

"Carl's in. And he *works* on Sundays. He has to get up tomorrow after we burn down the Machine. The rest of you have no excuse."

She cleared her throat and bit her tongue. Then she jumped up onto her feet again.

"You all right?" Katja asked quietly, rising and moving close to her. "I mean—sorry. I have to stop asking that."

"I will be once I get some air," Shayna said and headed for the door. Katja followed, and the boys followed her, in single file, in order of height, in steps that locked – and when Shayna led them past the booth seats where Black Faction still perched, she turned to watch them. She watched their drinks pause, half-lifted. She saw one of the leader's eyebrows slide quietly upward, and, staring into those mirrored lenses, she touched the rims of her goggles and smirked.

"Here," Carl murmured faintly, toward his shoes on the rumbling rubber floor of the bus. He sighed and wiped the fluorescence out of the corners of his eyes.

"This?" Shayna said, squinting through the black mirror windows. "This isn't—"

"This is were I work," Carl said over the hiss of the brakes. "First things first. We need a getaway van, right?"

They pressed after him through the diesel fumes and onto the cracked cement shoulder. There were chainlinks around a parking lot, tall lights of the searing bluish kind. Everything had ten sharp shadows; everything flickered sixty times a second. There it was, through a card-swipe gate, two rows down:

"The Chickmobile?" Shayna asked. "How long until somebody notices it's missing?"

"Does that matter?" he said stiffly. He threw open the back doors and snapped on a light inside, revealing the toolboxes, the man-sized spools of wire. "All right. Everybody pile in. I think there's room You want to ride up front with me, Shay?"

She watched him not wait for an answer. He turned his back and climbed up into the driver's seat, and from down there she could see it in everything he did, every switch he flipped, every look he gave to his whitening knuckles on the steering wheel: he knew he was going to get busted for this, and he was doing it anyway.

She watched Tom and Katja and Balboa climb up into the back. She helped them shut the door behind them and never dared to read the looks in their faces. Hesitantly she went around and climbed into the passenger seat just as Carl gunned the engine. The third time was the charm – but when the van's acceleration first hit her, she was suddenly gripped by fear.

"I feel like something's going to happen," she said. "Something big."

"Like what?"

"I've been having this dream. It's the same one ever time, but I've always forgotten parts of it. I could never remember the entire thing until we played Machinery Anthem. It all came back to me then. I've dreamed of this infinite white space, and I'm standing there inside it. And when I play this one sound on my bass, all of it splits wide open, and behind it is...." She shook her head.

"What? What do you think is going to happen?"

She hesitated. "I don't know. Nothing."

"If you don't want to tell me, fine," he said as they rumbled out through the mechanical gate. "Just tell me one thing."

"Okay."

He looked over his shoulder as if to check the thickness of the wall between them and the back compartment. He stared ahead down the black road and said "Are you making this whole thing up as you go along?"

She swallowed hard. "Yes."

She wanted to ask how obvious it was. Instead she tried to take comfort in the fact that he'd had to ask at all.

"Do you really know anything about the power station?" she asked him. "The dedicated power feeding into the Cology grid? Those things you said."

"Straight out of my ass."

"Then why are you doing this?"

He looked hard at her.

"I mean, what if Katja's right?" she said, holding her voice together as well as she could manage. "What if I'm only taking all these risks because I have nothing left to lose? You still have a lot to lose."

"No." He looked straight ahead. "No, I don't."

"Nothing?"

He shook his head.

"Well, *they* still have a lot to lose," she muttered, motioning through the wall behind them. Potholes darted at her through the van's headlights. The seat rocked softly with the uneven street. She started to bite her fingers.

"Don't second guess this now," Carl said.

She looked anxiously at him. "Yeah?"

"Because you know better than to do that. I know better, and they know better. You have to trust that they're not stupid. They've already put themselves in danger of incarceration just by *talking* about this plan. They know exactly what they're getting into. They're here anyway, and you have to trust them, just like they're trusting *you* to lead them. They're counting on you to embody what they know is right."

Shayna sighed and said "You don't think they're just doing it for me? Out of pity?"

"No. They're not."

"What about you? Are you just doing this for me?"

He shook his head. She saw his throat gulp.

The van ground to a halt at the last intersection before the flyway. She could hear it breathing and see its light on the clouds.

He turned and told her: "You know why you're doing this. That's the only thing you need, and don't let it out of your mind. Don't second guess the mission. Don't be that kind of asshole. Because nothing could screw this up more. Nothing could hurt us more than that. Got it?"

"All right." She nodded. "All right."

"Got it?" he demanded.

Shayna found the white shard in her pocket and closed it tight in her palm. "I got it."

"Then let's go," he said, and the engine roared.

The lights from the plant rested their halo on the tops of the houses, fading the red night sky into pale gray in the gaps. The five crept among the alleys, the trash cans and fenced backyards and sleeping dogs on chains. They heard the snoring of old men from behind cracked and taped-up windows. A block later they were ducking down behind the lips of rusty yellow oil drums that were strangely hot to the touch, to perch at the mouth of a street that ran straight on into the chainlinks and buzzing concrete domes and power lines. Carl took something out of his pocket.

"What's that?" Shayna asked, squinting in the shadows.

"Hand telescope. Have a look." The brass glowed in the far off electricity as he passed it around.

"Stalkervision," Katja whispered, squinting into the eyepiece.

"I don't— I'm not a stalker," Carl protested.

"Then why do you have stalkervision?"

Tom asked "What's our move? Where are those dedicated power lines you mentioned?" He gulped.

From the dark came some weird plastic squeaking sound.

"I can't tell from here," Carl murmured. "Which ones they are, I mean. We need to get closer."

More squeaking.

"And then? What do we do once we find them?"

"Well, they must have off switches."

"Off switches?" Katja chuckled.

"Every machine has an off switch," Carl said defensively. "Of some kind."

More rustling of plastic. Tom squinted his confusion at it in the dim light.

"We'll pull any switches we find," Shayna said. "I'm sure one of them will do the trick. Are we ready?"

"Hold it," Balboa whispered. "Everybody take one of these."

Shayna accepted from his shadow a torn-off strip of black plastic bag with two hand-poked eyeholes. Experimentally she lifted it to her face.

"These will screw up the face scanners, if they have them," he said. "It doesn't take much."

"Brilliant." In the darkness she grabbed his hand and squeezed it, and the darkness smiled shyly.

"I must look ridiculous," Katja said, tying it behind her head.

Shayna said "*We*, Katja. *We* must look ridiculous."

She and Katja stood up together, raising their faces above the hot barrels and into the burning glow.

"We're really doing this," Tom said, rising to his own feet and squinting into the light of the plant.

"Yes," Balboa said darkly.

"What the hell are we getting ourselves into?"

"Let's find out," Shayna said, and ran for it.

They arrived one by one, panting heavily, at the chainlinks surrounding the front entrance. The electricity was loud here. The buzzing echoed in Shayna's bones and made her shudder; she thought she caught it stirring the sand on the concrete. She stepped up to the fence and peered through at the blank walls and machinery beyond.

"It's electrified," Katja said, reading the signs on the fence. She was right - everything in sight was covered in block letters screaming about high voltage.

"Well we need to get through it somehow," Shayna said, raising her voice over the buzz.

Carl squinted. "Maybe it's not really electric. Maybe the signs are just for show. Why put all that razor wire on the top of a fence that's going to kill you just to touch it?"

"Let's not find out the hard way," Tom said.

"I agree," Shayna said. "Let's—"

Past Tom, maybe ten feet from where Shayna stood, a gaunt and bearded man in a gray work uniform was wheeling an oil drum along on a hand truck, then pausing. For a moment he just stood there scratching his jaw and staring down through thick glasses at a clipboard. Then he looked up.

The masked revolutionaries stared at him. Everyone stood still on the light-bleached concrete.

The man took one step back and everyone ran at him at once. He fell flat on his face on his first stride. Before he could stand they were all standing in a circle over him.

"Get his walkie talkie!" Katja yelled. Carl was already ripping it off his belt.

"What the hell are we doing, guys?" Tom yelped.

"We can't let him go!" Shayna shouted. "He's seen us! He'll bring security!"

The revolutionaries looked at one another in panic.

"Who the fuck?" said the man on the ground, squinting up, shielding his eyes from the lights behind their silhouettes. "What is this? Who are you?"

"We're...." Carl trailed off.

Shayna looked anxiously around again. This time she saw a concrete wall. Some words were stenciled there. "Who are we?" she said to the man on the ground. "We're The Loiterers. That's all you need to know."

"What do you want?" he whimpered through the ragged tendrils of a long moustache.

"To turn the Cology out like a light," she said.

"What?" he rasped.

"We're here to strike a blow against Insider power," she narrated. "We want to tear the Cology down and disband the comps, by force if we have to. We're going to smash the Company and replace it with a public government of equals. By and for the people. We are Outsider power."

"What?" he repeated, reaching a shaking hand up to dust off his thick glasses.

"Where are all the off-switches?" Carl bellowed. "Tell us where they are!"

"Off-switches?" He winced.

"Tell us!" Carl reached into his pocket and brandished a pair of needle-nose pliers. "Tell us or I'll cut your toes off."

"Don't! Don't hurt me! I don't know a thing about any off switches, okay? I'm just a grunt! I just move the barrels, that's all, I swear to God. I don't know anything!"

Everyone looked anxiously at Carl.

"Jesus, Carl," Katja said. "You will not."

"Don't say our real names!" Balboa whispered.

"Oh crap," Katja whispered.

Carl ignored them and told the man on the ground "You better be telling the truth."

"I swear to God, man."

"Who's got the rope?" Shayna asked.

No one responded.

She looked at Balboa.

"Why would I have rope? I don't have rope."

"Over there. Drag him over there."

They escorted the stranger, more shoving than dragging, to the darkness of the nearest alley. They opened a dumpster there and helped him climb inside. When it shut, Carl picked up a stray brick and placed it on the lid for some reason.

"Don't come out of there," Shayna yelled inside. "If you try to run and call for help, we'll have to litigate you."

"Swear to God, ma'am," said the man in the dumpster.

They ran back to the stinging light and chainlinks and buzzing.

"Shit," Shayna said. "Shit! We're out of time. We have to get through that fence, now!"

Carl said "I don't think it's really electrified. I'm testing it."

"Don't!" Katja yelled.

He brushed the fence with the back of his hand.

"See!" He grabbed it, again and again. "I told you! I'll just cut us a gap in the razor wire."

"Careful," Shayna said, readjusting her plastic bag mask.

"Don't you see it's all just like Balboa says?" Carl called over his shoulder as he hauled himself up. "All this security. It's just like the comps."

They all watched him in nervous silence.

Grabbing hold of the top of the fence post, he pulled out his pliers again and positioned the cutting part around the razor wire. He yelled down over his shoulder: "Just like the comps, it's not about reality. It's all just the spectacle! It only works because of our fear!"

He made the first snip and the whole line of fences exploded in red lights and the blaring of sirens. Carl screamed and dropped back into the gravel, only half caught by Balboa, and Katja and Shayna and Tom had already bolted for the getaway van. The whole dark street was throbbing in the waves of ruby light. Their feet pounded and skittered on the dusty pavement.

Shayna heard Carl's voice from far behind her: "Wait! Wait for me!"

"For God's sake, hurry up!" she yelled, and slammed into Tom's back, nearly knocking him over. He and Katja and Balboa scrambled madly into the back compartment and struggled to shut it. Shayna helped Carl into the driver's seat and then strapped herself in just in time for the van to shoot like a bullet into the unlit streets, ricocheting back and forth across the centerline and screaming amid the stench of burning rubber. He gripped the wheel for dear life, panting heavily, a mangled expletive in each exhale. He kept squinting into the rear-view mirrors.

"Is anyone following us?" Shayna demanded, craning her neck against the window. "Did anyone see us?"

"No," Carl said. "There was nobody there. Just alarms."

She looked at him.

"Scared the living crap out of me," he said.

5

The dark maroon sky was rising into lavender pre-dawn and the street was dead silent. Shayna sat slumped on a stray traffic divider at the Metro stop, watching it. She heard a rock move two blocks away while the stillness burned behind her ears, and she was as tired as she could remember ever being. Tired and still insomniac. Probably embarrassed more than anything else. A can of cheep beer had done nothing for any of these conditions. Neither had another gray pill.

The mission had been total failure, but at least nobody had been caught. Not yet. At least Carl said he'd dealt with the Chickmobile and covered his tracks. Rationally, it could've gone worse. But emotionally?

She swore under her breath and climbed aboard the first bus of dawn.

Even the softly rocking vinyl seats wouldn't let her sleep, but the blocks all blended together like dreams fading in memory. Time was indistinct. She was hopping off and pushing through the monastery's heavy wooden door. She was standing in her stone-floored bunk room, looking down on the ruffled wool covers of the empty bed, consumed with the feeling of missing something she couldn't bring to mind. Then it hit her. The Ancient.

"Where is he?" she asked Kelroy as he stepped out from the pillars.

"You should never have brought him here," Kelroy hissed with shocking harshness.

Shayna stepped back. "What happened?"

"Our Departed High Lurker's bond was with you. It extended to no one else. This is holy ground!"

"What could I do? His home was just destroyed. I had to help him, and I need his help too, okay? I didn't know it would be such a huge problem for you, just for him to even *set foot* here—"

"He did not just set foot here. He defiled. He desecrated. He violated the sanctity of this monastery."

"What? How?"

"With Heresy," said Grant, stepping slowly among the pillars toward them. Every word he spoke hung coldly in the air for a moment afterward. "You should not have brought him here. That lone transgression, however, we could have forgiven. What is unforgivable is his spoken contradictions of the divine truth."

Shayna hesitated and asked "What did he say?"

"I won't repeat his heresy."

"He said the Cology was unholy," Kelroy growled. "He characterized it as demonic."

He and Grant blinked and stiffened. In unison they made a sign with their hands.

"So the Cology is...?" Shayna said carefully.

"The Kingdom of Heaven," Grant said. He could have been addressing a toddler.

Shayna sighed and stifled all the words that came to her. Finally she said "Well, I need to find him. I think he could be suic—" Her throat contracted around the word. She sighed and said "He could be in trouble, okay?"

"He's left. Never to return here. I neither care nor have any idea where he went."

Her hands turned into fists. She had no more restraint. She said: "So heaven is just for rich people? Is that what you think?"

"Those blessed by the Tropolis," Kelroy answered, his tiny hairs visibly bristling. "Those who ascended the ladder of reincarnation through walking the path and earning the favor of the City."

"No more questions," Grant snapped. He glared until she looked away from him, then said "I'll hear no more blasphemous questions from you."

She watched his shiny head turn and pass back into shafts of light between the scrawled posts. She let out a hard sigh and started collecting her things from under the bed. Most of them she just left there in the suitcase; there was no point.

"Leaving?" Kelroy demanded.

She looked at him wordlessly as she hung the bass strap on her shoulder.

"You have something that belongs to us," he said, laying his hand out. She fixated on it, hanging there in the middle of the room, like a ledge, like a wooden slat.

She moved past him through the doorway, saying "I'll be done with it in a few days."

Grant's voice was ringing out through the space as she pressed against the heavy wooden door. She hesitated and turned to see the lurkers and disciples gathering around him at one of the altars.

He said "—Dispel the venom of falsity to which some of you were exposed, earlier, with the balm of truth. Listen, and I will explain to you what the Cology really is.

"In the beginning there was the Tropolis. And the Tropolis was then, at the dawn of time, much as it is now, as we approach the end of time. The world was dim, and the Immortals kept the Light in their own possession, in their kingdom. And in those days anyone, man or robot or beast, was permitted to enter the kingdom of heaven freely, so long as they obeyed one simple law: they were not to touch the box in which Light was kept. The Light was for the Immortals, and them alone.

"Now the people, and the creatures of the world, still grew envious of the Light and wanted it for themselves. And no one was more envious than Crow – and Crow, in those days, was not black but white, and his voice was the most beautiful sound in the world. So he, in his envy, conceived a plan. Practicing the most exquisite Camoumancy, he made himself invisible. He flew Inward, to the very center of the Tropolis, and passed stealthily into the warehouse of the Immortals, until he found the box. He opened it, and all the Light escaped and spread across the whole world – and the entire world was full of it. The entire world was brighter than you or I can now imagine. There was no night, and no shadow, and all was beautiful and full of blessing.

"But the Immortals were very displeased. First they punished Crow by burning him to a cinder and condemning him to go on living, his once musical voice now turned by the smoke into a bitter rasping cough. They meant his suffering to be a reminder to the people of the price of defying their order – the price of hubris. The Immortals were content to let the Light remain where it was, so long as the people remained true to the law. But the people were too happy, too busy reveling in infinite prosperity amid the all-surrounding light of heaven, and as time went on they only grew more unruly, more self-absorbed and self-righteous. They forgot the order of things and broke other of the divine laws.

"So the Immortals took back the Light. They traveled to every corner of the world and re-collected it, piece by piece. And when they had it all, this time they built all around the borders of their kingdom an impenetrable wall, so high that no thing could ever cross over, and so strong that no blow could ever weaken it. So the world was dim once again, and the golden age of Man flickered to its end, and the Light was in its coveted place. It is only for us to see, shining through. Never again to touch."

She closed the door behind her.

The Tropolis had never seemed so vast and anonymous and desperately empty as when Shayna searched for the old man. She thought about the look she'd left on his heavily wrinkled face, the last words he'd mumbled to her on the bus to the monastery, or the last ones by the wrecking ball. She cased the surrounding streets in ever widening and less systematic spirals, and hopelessness washed over her like the sweaty heat of daylight. Her despair thickened as the tar liquefied at the bases of the lamp posts.

Time was blurring again, moments and hours running together, swirling like colors in puddle oil. She had been staring at the pavement passing in front of her for four hours by the time she thought to check the time on her phone, and by then she had no idea where she was. Still near the monastery, she guessed, but the Tower or any other landmark was missing, either too far away or ducked behind the buildings. It was a dead street, fully overshadowed by enormous ruins whose remaining glass overwrote the shade with weird bubbles of light. Her thirst was incredible.

"I've waited so long," he'd muttered, covered in the dust.

"Don't kill yourself," she said to the empty street.

"Why not?" said the image in her mind.

"There's so much I still don't understand. If I don't find you soon, I never will."

"However much I may know, I do not think I could answer any of your real questions."

"Maybe not," she sighed. "Maybe that's not the real reason I need to find you."

"Then what? What's left?" asked the apparition. "What are you doing?"

She was climbing into the nearest ruin, looking for water. The pipes were all dry, but the concrete was dark in telltale spots. She followed them to remnants of the last rain in an old tin can at the bottom of the stairs. In the yellow light creeping through the wall, she skimmed off the oil and tipped it back just far enough to sip, taking care not to stir up or swallow what had settled to the bottom.

"Like this, see?" Ruth says to her daughter, and watches her duplicate the motion. "No, stop. Spit it out! Spit it out!"

Shayna spits and wipes her twelve-year-old wrist across her frowning mouth.

"See?" Ruth says, pointing to the water and distillate on the pavement. "You were about to drink those little pieces of metal. That muddy stuff that settled. You never drink the mud. You have to let the water settle, and skim off the rainbow, and then you just drink the clear part. No matter how thirsty you are."

"Why can't we just use a pay fountain?" Shayna protests.

Ruth bends down to look into her daughter's eyes and says "Because you have to learn this. Someday you might not have money for a pay fountain, or you might be far away from one. Ruin water could save your life."

Shayna sighs and folds her arms.

"Come on," says Ruth. "I'll teach you to hotwire a car."

"Why do you have to give me all these lessons all of a sudden?"

Later, they sit down together at the bus stop, sipping fizzes.

Ruth tells her daughter, "Remember, really listen close today. It's more important than all that bullshit they force-feed you in school. Don't forget anything. Do you promise to do that?"

Shayna nods.

Ruth sighs into her bottle and says, more quietly, "It's the same lessons my mom gave to me when I was about your age, so that my life would be better than hers. She wanted mine to be better. She loved me, just like I love you. She'll always be with me, just like I'll always be with you. Do you know that?"

Shayna stares into the street and says nothing. She feels her mother's arms wrap around her.

"I want your life to be better," Ruth says. "I know it will be. Because I know you won't make the same shitty mistakes your mom made. You're smart enough to stay above it. Strong enough inside. Don't listen to the allocators at school. Fuck them in their big ugly faces. You are beautiful, my daughter, inside and out. Something beautiful's going to come from you. I know it."

Shayna feels something damp on the side of her face.

"Stop crying," she tells her mother.

She found herself tipped over with her cheek in the edge of a shallow puddle, and her phone was ringing in her hand. Katja. She answered it.

"Shay! Where are you?"

"Nowhere."

"Are you near a TV?"

"No."

"Can you get to one?"

"No. Why?"

"You haven't been watching the news?"

Shayna fished the vial out of her coat pocket and struggled to pick out another gray pill. "Who the hell actually watches the news? And why?"

"We're on it," Katja's voice whispered excitedly. "We're on TV. We're on half the channels."

The sun was sinking by the time Shayna reached the Green Room. She swept through the doors to find her friends all clustered around Carl's phone on the ratty couch. A dead TV sat in the corner.

"Why aren't you watching it on that?" Shayna asked.

"They pulled the footage from the network," Katja answered. "They stopped the reporting altogether, a few hours ago. They don't even have the same newscasters anymore. The news channels are acting like they never mentioned it in the first place, but Carl made a recording before that. Look!"

Shayna looked. It was the man on the ground, the man they'd put in the dumpster.

"They were here, man, and I saw them myself," said his inch-tall image from between the rough pixels of the phone. "Ten of them, man – nine, ten really big guys decked out in black, armed to the teeth, with these black bands over their eyes, like old-timey bandits, man, swear to God. They said they were going to blow up the Cology, starting by cutting the electricity. It's about Outsider Power, that's what they said. Talking about public government. Shit, man. These were some highly trained professionals, like, complete demolition experts. You gotta know there are more of them out there, like a whole underground, man. They called themselves *The Loiterers*. A whole secret society. A secret army. I know it. I wouldn't doubt it for a split second."

Shayna's jaw dropped.

"It was fucking *intense*," the man finished.

The video cut away to the anchors, repeating, paraphrasing, saying the comps wouldn't comment, saying the Energy Section wouldn't comment on whether the reactors might at that very moment be melting down.

"The Loiterers," Shayna echoed in awe.

"You couldn't think of a better name?" Carl said, biting his knuckle.

"Holy shit! But they stopped the reporting? They pulled the footage?"

"You could guess why," Balboa said. "Some suit in Company Public Relations is getting spanked with a stun prod right now. Probably thought it would get him ratings to air that story. Probably right about that. But it worked, Shay. It's a humiliation."

"For the Energy Section," Tom said. "Like they can't keep their facilities secure worth a damn. For the comps, like they've got some kind of giant rebellion stirring up right under their noses."

"For the whole Company," Katja said. "They stopped broadcasting it, but people saw first. Lots of people made their own recordings, and now they're talking about it. Everywhere. It's all spreading like crazy, and the whole story just gets bigger and crazier every time it's retold again by someone else."

"And what are they saying?" Shayna asked. "How are people taking it? What do they think?"

A glance passed between the five of them, unanswered. Katja shrugged.

"I think nobody knows yet," Balboa said. "Everyone's waiting to make up their minds."

Shayna grinned and said "You mean they want to see more."

They all looked uneasily at her.

"So let's not disappoint them," she said. "And I know exactly how not to disappoint them." She backed away from the couch and headed into the smoking crowd.

"Wait, where are you going?" Tom asked.

"Be right back."

A moment later she found the booth she wanted. She put her hands on the table and leaned heavily over it. She eyed each of the booth's occupants in turn, and they eyed her back.

"You're either in or you're out," she said.

Blue Dog coughed suddenly, and the spray of liquor caught the green light.

"Shay," said the stocking-capped woman at his side, lowering her mirrored sunglasses for the first time – and Shayna heard, again, that weird difference in how they had always pronounced her name. It was subtle enough to mistake for an error or an accent, muted enough in the noisy space, but this time she heard it clearly: the 'sh' made partway into a 'ch'.

The name breathed among the stocking caps, their whispers full of fear and secret and excitement. One by one, except for Blue Dog himself, they took off their shades. They looked at her.

"You can't have done it," said the leader, pushing his sunglasses back up the bridge of his nose. "You can't be *them*. I don't believe it."

"I'll ask you one more time. In or out?"

The eyebrows over those blood-red lenses were knitted hard. He sighed through his nose. With labored hesitation he grasped the frame above his ear and took it slowly down. His bare eyes squinted in the dim smoky light.

Shayna grinned. "Follow me."

The walls rumbled from the bass, but only faint echoes of conversation penetrated the back room. The air was quiet, almost lightless, throbbing with nervous energy. The eleven of them sat among four broken couches arranged in a square – the band of five regarding Black Faction in muted apprehension.

"And them?" Carl muttered, tilting his head toward them. "What's their group called?"

"Same as ours," Shayna said. "There's only one group here. The Loiterers."

"I don't know about this."

"That's natural. But you know we need people. If this thing is going to go anywhere, we need all the people we can get. We're going to need the entire Tropolis, sooner or later, and eleven is a lot closer to that than five."

Blue Dog leaned forward on the squeaky vinyl and told Carl: "Exclusivity and elitism are the anathema of transformative insurgency."

Carl squinted. "What?"

"Me?" Balboa responded shyly.

"Yes," Shayna said. "I want to know what you think."

He blew a sigh through his lips and looked aside. He said "I can tell you what I *don't* like."

"Then tell me," she said evenly.

"You're talking about going to practically the one place in the entire Tropolis where comps are actually certain to be. A serious number of them."

"Tom said they're spread pretty thin. Their guard posts only have a few guys each."

"Don't hold me to that," Tom warned.

"Forget about winning by numbers," Balboa said. "You won't. Surprise is the one thing you'll have going for you. They're used to people making a run for it. Little escapes happen all the time. Nothing like what you're talking about. They're advised not to resort to lethal methods, and they'll be sluggish to respond. But when they do, we better have our shit together."

"We," Shayna said. "I guess that means you're in."

Balboa lay back in the creaking couch. The others waited in uncertain suspense.

"I better be," he finally grumbled. "For your sake."

Shayna tried not to show her relief.

"Tonight," she said.

"No point. In doing it at night, I mean. A comp can see just as clearly in pitch black as in the middle of the day. You'll just give them the advantage. Broad daylight is better."

Shayna nodded. "Tomorrow."

"So it's just the matter of the gas masks," Shayna said.

"Forget them," Tom said. "Nobody wears them in that section. The air is horrible, but it won't kill you. Respirators would just slow you down."

"Fine by me," she said, though she saw the others grimace. "Anything else you think we need?"

Tom stiffened. He looked at the ground and shook his head. He hesitantly lifted something out of one of his deeper pockets. Everybody's eyes widened.

"Holy—!" she gasped. "You have a *hand grenade?*"

Balboa grabbed it out of his hand. "Riot gas," he said, inspecting it. "Where the hell did you get this?"

"There was a box of them in the Heaps one day."

"If anybody finds out you have them...."

"I know, okay?" Tom said bitterly, grabbing it back. "If anybody finds out *lots* of things, we're dead."

"How many do you have?" Shayna asked.

"Three."

"Bring them. The rest of you know the drill. Bolt cutters. Good running shoes."

"Is that it?" said Blue Dog. "No weapons? No guns? Nothing?"

Shayna sighed toward the ground and regarded him icily. The stocking caps exchanged glances.

"This is your secret army?" he said. "This is what you're calling a revolution?"

All eyes fixed on Shayna, and she met them all in brief succession – except for Carl's, whose look she read and understood. She drew a breath and said "The revolution isn't just us. It's in the hearts of everyone who's watching now, waiting to see what we'll do next. It's just a spark right now, and nothing will snuff it out faster than *shooting at comps.*"

Blue Dog rubbed his mouth.

She continued, "And the only thing more stupid than labeling ourselves comp-killers would be giving them any extra excuse to kill *us*. They outnumber us, they're stronger and more heavily armed than we could ever be, they're experts at shooting, experts at fighting, and they're almost totally bulletproof anyway. Eventually we'll need them on our side if we want to win this. No weapons. No guns."

Even the bass rumbling in the walls seemed to have shut up.

"And one more thing," Shayna said, calming her voice, "I asked you whether you were in or out, and you said in. That means you work with the team from now on. You don't get to just sit there and talk shit about what we're doing. Is that understood?"

Blue Dog pursed his lips and raised his eyebrows above the rims of his shades. "Yep."

"All right," she said. "Tomorrow."

"What time?" Tom asked.

"Dawn. Say, six AM sharp."

Tom nodded. The others sat in brooding pensivity.

"If you want to back out of the mission, speak up. Last chance."

A few glances circulated. No one spoke.

"Then get some sleep. I'll see you all at the rally point."

She stood and left, taking the back exit into the alley and heading for the nearest Metro. Everything was still draped in the day's last soft purple twilight. Maybe there was still time.

The waning three-quarter moon passed behind a road sign, and it was only by a faint subliminal tingling that she noticed the graffiti there on the metal. It was a photocopied sticker, one she'd never seen before, freshly applied. It was a hand in a fist, but with pointer and thumb extended at right angles. Like a gun pointed straight up.

Forming the letter L.

It was everywhere.

She had to hold her hopes down as she rode the Metro toward Charity center. She kicked herself for not going there earlier in search of the old man; it was so obvious. It was the only other place he ever went as far as she knew. It was the one place anyone else might know him. But as she made her second futile lap around the whole waiting line that zigzagged through the steel railings and bored comps, she remembered that all this hope depended on the chance that he was still alive at all. How intent had he been to be buried alive in that basement? How long had it already been since she'd lost him?

As for the people in the waiting line: they knew of him, but nothing about him. Some had learned their specific fates by his diagnosis, and there were others who told stories of miraculous healing at his hands – if only for one of overlapping sicknesses, if only temporarily. Not even those people knew him by name; not one out of the dozen or so Shayna spoke to before the colors of blotchy skin, the frailness of bones, the gathering tumors were too much to press on through.

She sat on a curb under the first moment of night and thought about the cigarettes she didn't have. She searched through every pocket in her coat and came up with the very last remains of the old cash wad: enough for one more pack, if that. Maybe one last morsel of sustenance. *But it doesn't matter*, she thought. *I don't experience hunger anymore. I don't sleep anymore. I've run out of needs.*

She thought at his ghost out there in the night: *Why do I need to find you? Could I ever find you now even if I kept trying? And what good would it do if I did?*

A cart squeaked past her in the street: the day's last food vendor, done with trawling the dying throngs, now shuffling away into the orange lamps. The dented front wheel thudded and screeched in a regular rhythm.

I have so much more to think about, she thought. *I have a revolution to stage in eight hours. They're all depending on me. I shouldn't even have come here. Shouldn't have wasted the time.*

But I have to find you.

I have to find you.

She thought this, and it must have been that the rhythm of the broken wheel caught the cadence of the words in her head. Sounds started to cohere. The chord she'd played against the walls of the old theatre. The ringing in her ears and the burning blue color of her dreams. Words that had been stuck playing in her mind all this time. Parts of conversations or half-remembered dreams. All these things, one by one, began to crawl between her vertebrae and fall into place.

She found her bass still slung over her back. She took it in her hands and went to work.

When she looked up again, it was into the first eerie glow of dawn. Her phone confirmed the inconceivable passing of time. She took her raw fingertips off the strings, put the bass behind her, and ran swearing for the Metro.

4

The assault on the Southside Community Service Center began at dawn.

They met under the sign that called it that – tipped over, jutting out of the sludge, today congealed hard as concrete and cracking like plates under all their boots, though mainly Balboa's. One by one they showed up and stood around in the long shadows, underslept and overanxious, struggling to stand the rancid air, experimentally snipping their bolt cutters – smoking cigarettes that, or so they muttered under their exhales, might be their last. There were other things they said that way: things they said facetiously even though they were true. By six o'clock there were five of them.

By six-twenty, Carl said "Where the fuck are those assholes?"

"Can we go in without them?" Tom said.

"Maybe they betrayed us to the comps. Maybe there's an ambush waiting for us."

"Listen," Balboa said. "There's something coming."

Everybody ducked under the broken sign, and a moment later watched the car roll up to the curb. It was a black convertible with luminous chrome hub caps. Three stocking caps piled out of it and stepped uncertainly toward the broken sign.

"You're late," Shayna said, coming out. She thought: *you have a car?*

Blue Dog sighed and kicked the dust.

"Where are the others?" she demanded.

"Can't make it. Sorry." He straightened his glasses. The other two stocking caps, slender women in black jeans and tank tops, looked at the ground.

"Why not?"

"They have work today."

"So do all of us," Katja said.

"You do? Oh."

Carl moved toward him, squinting bitterly, bolt cutters swinging at his side.

"We don't have time for this," Shayna said, rushing between them. "Remember the mission!"

Carl stood where he was. Finally he backed away with a snort and a shake of his head.

"Remember the plan," she said, "One of us sticks around here. Watch our escape route and lay down the spikes, and be ready to answer your phone. Any volunteers?" She looked at Carl.

"Me," Katja said. "I'll stay here. You want me to hold on to your bass for you?"

Shayna had forgotten it was still strapped to her back, as if it had become a part of her. "I'll keep it," something in her said, though she knew it would only slow her down and endanger the mission. It was when she readjusted the strap, and felt the baggy twill of the coat rustling around her, a different instinct welled up. She took the bass down momentarily to peel off the coat. She emptied its pockets of what few things she still needed: the golden ring and the necklace of teeth, which she put on; the white glass shard and the last of her money, which she fit into the pockets of her jeans; the riot gas grenades, which she hung on her belt. She looked at the wad of worn green fabric that she'd relied on for invisibility through all these years, and what had always been her cloak and armor were suddenly only a dessicated husk. Standing before the rest of the Loiterers with nothing to fully obscure the shape of her body anymore, she felt new. Everything felt different.

She lay the coat in the ditch and returned the bass to her back. She took one last look into the warm and glowing sky and said "Anything else?"

No one spoke.

"Then let's go."

Katja retreated into the yellow sun and the rest of them ran. Their bounding feet hammered on the broken ground and blew up the stray dust in explosive clouds of foulness. In a moment they were cutting through the first set of chainlinks, seven cuts at a time, until it all rustled wide open and they were peeling the fence all the way back to its posts.

"Next one!" Shayna shouted, and they bolted out into the true no-man's-land beyond. For the second or third time that morning she realized that this was really happening. The stinky wind flying through her hair as she strode ahead, the sinking of one foot and then another into the soft and disgusting terrain, the orange Pacific clouds rising against the lavender sky between the translucent black streamers of smoke from underground fires. The criminality. The danger. The six others at her side. All of this was real. The terrain ahead of them lifted up into the perfectly symmetric barrier mounds, and at the top and knelt down to look over.

The haze was much thicker down there, and it took a moment to make out the features of the compound. At first she could only make out the poles and security cameras. Then the blocks of portable buildings. Only through a break in the smoke did she make out the sparse antlike forms of human beings wading through the opaque atmosphere – and then the bulbous, black-clad comps.

"Where are all the prisoners?" she asked. "That can't be all of them."

"Here," said Carl, handing her Stalkervision – but she had already realized.

They were almost invisible in their brown coveralls, but there were thousands of them. They gathered in huge clusters or walked in long, slow lines. She saw them crossing a point and disappearing – and through a passing break in the haze she first saw the gigantic pit. It was hundreds of feet wide and lined with metal stairways and ladders. From where she perched, it looked bottomless.

"What are they doing?" asked one of the Black Faction women.

"Digging," Tom said. "Digging out the new trash pit."

"Isn't there a machine to do that?"

"All the pits are excavated by hand. There are never enough machines, but there's always convicts to spare."

"People who snuck outside candy into movie theaters," Katja said. "People who cut a few days of work. People who copied songs from a friend's music player."

"People who were just in the wrong place at the wrong time," Shayna said. "Who stood at the wrong street corner. People who were in the Green Room that night. That could've been any of us."

"Such a waste," said Blue Dog.

The stink blowing up from within the compound was much heavier than what blew along outside. Everyone kept breathing through their mouths long after they caught their breath.

"There," Shayna said, pointing down at a point along the fence, near to the biggest part of the crowd of brown coveralls. "That's where we'll open the main hole. What do you think?"

"Might as well," Balboa said.

"Two teams. Team A cuts the big hole in the fence while team B creates the diversion." She scanned the perimeter with the telescope and pointed to a place much farther down the fence line, near a tiny portable building where the shadows of comps stuck out of the haze. "There, that's where we'll divert them to."

No one responded this time.

She went on anyway: "Team A needs more fence cutting power, and the decoy's job is more dangerous, so it should be smaller. I'll be on team B. I'll take two other people."

Balboa raised his hand.

"Decoy," Blue Dog chimed in.

Carl sighed and closed his mouth.

"All right," Shayna said. "The rest of you sneak down there as close to the fence as you can, and get ready to make the cut. I'll call you when it's time. One of you has your phone on you, right?"

"Got it," Carl said.

"All right." Shayna shivered inexplicably. "Then let's break some people out of this hellhole. As many as we can. Team B move out!"

Hurriedly at first, but with dwindling energy, she led their creeping path along the top of the dirt mounds toward the diversion point.

The haze thickened and cleared in slow waves. The dust sifted into their boots and caked in the sweat under their plastic masks. Balboa sank deep with every unbalanced step. Every time they peeked over the top of the mounds to gauge their position, Shayna realized it was a lot farther away than she'd thought – but the farther the better. All the more distance for the comps to run, she told herself. With every exhausted step, she focused on that.

Her boot caught on something and she fell flat into the billowing dust.

"Oh God," she shrieked, and jumped to her feet when she saw the bones she'd tripped on. A femur. A pair of ribs pulled partway out of the dirt. The faint edges of others were there in the imprints of her boots. She backed into Balboa.

"This is the Heaps," he said, letting her lean into him. "You knew you'd see this."

"Yeah."

"A reminder of why we're here," Blue Dog said darkly. "Just keep your mind on that."

"Damn right." She cut off the tears and kept walking, one foot in front of the other.

Soon they were starting over the top of the mound and creeping carefully down into the shadows and the rancid haze, toward the last line of fences.

"It won't be like this anymore," Blue Dog said, looking over his shoulder at the bones. "Just remember that we're erecting a world that won't be like this at all. Some day, years from now, you'll look back on these atrocities. All this squandering of human life and resources."

Shayna squinted ahead and sighed.

"It'll all be so different when we're in the Cology," he said.

The fences loomed fifty feet ahead. Shayna stopped. "What did you say?"

"I said it will all be different once we're in power."

"In power? In the *Cology?*"

Balboa crouched anxiously, looking back and forth between them and the fences. The silhouettes of body armor and stun batons wavered in the thinning tendrils of haze.

Blue Dog said "Surely you don't mean—? You actually meant what you supposedly told that guy at the power plant? You actually intend to destroy the Cology?" He snorted. "So you're an anarchist?"

"Guys," Balboa whispered. "Quiet!"

"Not anarchy," she said. "Democracy."

Blue Dog shook his head. "You actually mean anarchy."

"I mean democracy! One person one vote! A government of equals!"

"You need to study some real history. There's no such thing as that. The historical examples of the forms of governments you're referencing – what you call 'public government' – were almost as corrupt and inhumane as our current power structure. It's all in the treatise. There were just more gradations between—"

"What the hell does any of that—?" she hissed, then quieted down and said exasperatedly "Then how do *you* say we should make an equal society?"

"Guys!" Balboa whispered. "Now's not the time—"

"The human animal is inherently hierarchical," Blue Dog said. "And most people are just stupid. There will never be an equal society. The problem with the Company is not that it exists, but in how it's run. The problem with the Cology is simply the problem of the wrong people, with the wrong values, controlling society."

"No. That's not—"

"Just listen. The primary purpose of our corporate government, and the purpose that has thereby been perversely assigned to all of our lives under it, is to produce the maximum monetary benefit for the principals at the top. What if we replaced that sole motive with something like, I don't know, raising the standard of living? Very soon we'd all be living to be fifty years old. Maybe even older."

"No, no, no!"

"Why not? What's wrong with that?"

"Because you're missing the point," she struggled.

"The point of what?"

"Everybody shut up!" Balboa hissed.

They shut up. The haze swirled around them.

"Remember how good their hearing is," he whispered.

Shayna bit her tongue.

"Remember what we're here for." Balboa reached out and held her arm firmly. "We can argue about the details later. Right now we need to stick together."

"Right," Shayna whispered to both of them.

They crept all the way down to the fence on slow feet. The ground was riddled with plastic bags that crumpled faintly underfoot, making her cringe with adrenaline. Finally they arrived to kneel down at the edge of the fence. From there, in the air's clearer moments, she could see the comps inside that cardboard box of a building. Their silhouettes through a glassless window looked like they might be playing cards.

Shayna lifted the grenades off of her belt, one by one, by their rings. The dark green metal gleamed evilly in the dirty light. She passed one to each of her accomplices and then was left to her own. She felt its smooth weight in her hand. Two solid pounds of aerosolized pain.

She looked at Balboa, and he looked back. They stared into each other's eyes for a long time amid the fine haze.

"This is it," whispered Blue Dog, just above the wind. "Realize. This is the match point of a revolution that will shake the Tropolis to its core. This is where everything begins. Everything will change."

"Are you ready?" she whispered to Balboa.

"I want to throw the first one," whispered Blue Dog.

Shayna eyed them both. "I don't know. Balboa has more experience."

"We'll all throw at once," Balboa whispered.

Shayna nodded. She opened her phone and prepared the text message to Carl. "Ready," she mouthed, her thumb resting on the send key.

Balboa shut his eyes tight and held his hands in prayer, rolling the grenade between his muscular palms.

Shayna swallowed hard and said "For the Thirty Percent."

"For Balboa," said Balboa.

"For the future," said Blue Dog.

The sickly haze wafted down over them.

She pressed the key on her phone and read the writing on the screen:

NOW

The three of them stood up. Two pins ripped from fuses. One grenade arced over the fence and flew straight through the window of the guard post.

Shayna kept fighting with her grenade, but the pin was stuck.

"Fuck!" Blue Dog shouted and ran to pick up his from where it had bounced back down from the fence. "Ow, fuck! Hot! Hot!" He threw it again. It clinked in the barbed wire and dropped a few feet away on the other side. The white gas blew directly back at him and he stumbled away, coughing and screaming.

Suddenly Shayna's eyes caught on fire. She shut them tightly and rushed half-blindly back up the hill. Instinctively she ripped off the plastic bag mask and lowered her goggles, and when she looked back down she saw Balboa still standing there unfazed, engulfed in the gas from Blue Dog's grenade.

He yelled "Crap! You guys, these are just harmless smoke grenades! They're not riot gas at all. Or— are they?"

"Oh God," Shayna shouted through her burning lips, "You're immune!"

"I am? Then so are—"

The first gunshot rang out between the dirt mounds.

They ran.

The individual shots turned to explosive bursts of automatic fire and the encrusted muck all around started to pop up jets of dust where the bullets hit. The sound was deafening. The fire in Shayna's eyes seemed to spread to her heart as she flew like the wind toward the crest of the hill and the safety of the other side. Something punched her in the back.

When her senses returned to her, she had just finished rolling down the far slope of the muck hill. The gunfire was muted there. Balboa was struggling frantically to help her up, and then they were running again, balancing on each other when their feet sank into the ground, scrambling after Blue Dog who was still coughing uncontrollably. His glasses had fallen off and he was breathless halfway to unconsciousness when they passed him and yanked him along.

"Damnit!" Shayna shouted as soon as she could. "I thought they only used lethal force as a last resort!"

"It's more a guideline than a rule," Balboa panted.

Stumbling as quickly as possible over one more lump in the terrain, about two hundred yards away, they could see the peeled-open section of the outer fence and the abandoned blocks beyond, the rising sun glaring through the silhouettes of windows. They could see Blue Dog's convertible there, gleaming like a silver pill.

Something else was running into the sun. Three black-clad human figures, too small to be comps, too far away to recognize their gaits. *Shit*, she thought – *only three?* She hit her speed dial and welled up as much breath to speak as she could.

"Are you all right?" Katja asked.

"What about Team A?"

"Carl's calling again. I don't have three-way calling. I need to put you on hold—"

"*What happened to Team A?* Who did they lose? What happened?"

"Comp car coming," Katja's voice buzzed.

Shayna took the phone down from her face. "Wait!" she told Balboa and Blue Dog. They stopped running and bent over to catch their wheezing breath.

Past the edge of the fence, far down to the North of them, they saw the police van flying on a tail of dust. The three human shadows were getting close to the gap in the fence. Shayna counted down the blocks between them and the speeding van as it came: *eleven... ten... nine?*

She lifted the phone again and shouted into it: "Katja? Katja!"

Her voice crackled to life in the speaker: "Where the fuck are you? Get out! Now!"

"Did you put out the barbed wire?"

"They rolled right over the barbed wire. Didn't slow down. Oh, shit! Shit!"

The three running shadows cleared the gap in the fence just as the police van passed the two block point. The siren screamed out over no-man's-land.

"We're running," Katja said, and the line went dead.

"We're fucked," said Blue Dog.

"Follow me," said Balboa.

He led them across the terrain, alternately ducking down and crawling on their stomachs, taking what cover could be taken behind the elongated mounds of knee-high slag or down in the muck-filled ditches.

"I can't breathe," said Blue Dog between labored inhales and heavy coughs – but still he kept breathing, just enough. The whites of his eyes were stained blood red. Shayna's still burned, but her vision was finally clearing.

"Hurry now," said Balboa.

They crept along parallel to the fence until the black van was five blocks down, and there was nothing but the wall of chainlinks between them and the outside streets.

"Ready?" Balboa asked.

"Let me catch my breath," Blue Dog wheezed.

"We should get farther from the van," Shayna said.

"We're dead once the choppers get here," Balboa said. "We're out of time."

Blue Dog ripped off his plastic mask and stocking cap and rubbed madly at his eyes, groaning, yelping in quiet agony. Finally he pulled the bolt cutters out of his backpack.

They got up and ran, blind from exhaustion and chemicals, hammering their feet into the cracked ground. The snapped the links in the fence with shaking hands, every movement desperately uncoordinated, cutting anything they found in front of them until the random breaks added up to something Balboa could tear open with his bare hands. They didn't spare a glance to see if the van was charging at them. They didn't look back at all. They just dove across the street and into the dark alleys on the other side. They stopped only long enough to breathe and ditch the bolt cutters, and kept running until they reached the Metro.

They sat down in the back seats and stared blankly at the blocks outside until the shock began to wear off.

Shayna held the pink bass, feeling over its surface with madly shivering hands. There were three dark pits in it. She turned it over and found the three marble-sized glimmers of bullet copper shining through the raised cracks in the plastic body.

Blue Dog bent down and held his face in his hands. "Oh God," he murmured. "My car. They have my car."

Balboa rubbed his mouth in dire apprehension and just looked out at the passing pavement.

They have one of us. Shayna thought mutely. *Or else one of us is—*

She called Tom.

No answer.

She called again.

The plan had always been to split up for the day, not meeting again until the evening, but she couldn't do anything else. She went straight to the rendezvous point in the Green Room's storage closet and perched on the couch and knitted her fingers until they ached. Then she picked at the upholstery until the orange foam made a pile at her feet, and made unanswered phone calls until the battery was dead. The shivers slowly died out but the pressure remained like a clamp on her entrails as the time passed.

She held the bass in her hands. At first it was impossible to play. Then it was impossible not to.

"*I have to find you*," she sang, very low, with notes just loud enough to hear at all. The lyrics and the melody began to string together, one after another.

"It's not safe here," said a voice through the cracked door to the alley, startling Shayna out of her trance.

"Carl? Where's Tom? Was anyone hurt?"

The door slammed on its spring. She burst through it and ran after him down the alley. The sky had the beige color of late afternoon. The heat out there was incredible.

Carl was covered in an ridiculous, oversized gray coat. When he paused at the corner long enough for her to catch up to him, he only barely turned to whisper: "So you haven't seen the TV."

"No."

"This way."

She couldn't bring herself to ask a second time. She followed him mutely down the sidewalks nobody used, ducking behind anything that was there, watching his eyes feverishly scan the baking street and the windows and the rooftops. He led her to a back door and knocked a rhythm on it. Finally they crept through into dim light.

When she saw Tom, she couldn't hold back. She hugged him tightly and felt her eyes making damp circles in his shirt. His hands only lightly hugged back.

"For a moment I thought you...." she said into his chest, but trailed off. She backed away and looked around. Balboa was pacing the floor heavily, Katja was hunched over in a plastic chair in front of a television and Carl was hitting his face against the brick wall.

"Everybody's okay?" she asked. "Who did we lose?"

"Look for yourself," Katja said. Her eyes just stared into the flickering screen.

Even through the static, even with the collar turned up on her prison coveralls, the bruises were clear around the girl's neck. Her eyes had no shades now; they stared ahead with no emotion. She looked like something that had been smashed to pieces and then hastily glued back together.

Her voice buzzed through the static, "—my confession that the purpose of our group, The Loiterers, was to free the underworld crime lord and mass murderer Hector Cuchillo from the Southside Community Service Center, and ultimately to incite a royalist coup—"

"What the—?" Shayna gaped. "Hector Cuchillo?"

"That's what they're saying," Katja muttered.

"The TV is saying it. What are real people saying?"

The pale image in the static continued, "—I was deeply disturbed, both mentally and physically abused by members of the group, but now that I have been rescued, I am cooperating fully with Corporate authority and I ask to be forgiven for my crimes—"

"This is insane," Shayna said. "A *royalist coup?* Who could believe this shit?"

"Just watch them."

"They broke her," Balboa said. "They did it in hours. But they let her live. Because she's a Greentowner. All those kids with the black hats are."

"I know." Shayna sank down into a plastic chair.

"They got her, which means they'll get to the rest of them – and they'll spill everything under torture. Whatever they know about the rest of us. What we look like. Our names. Where they met us. The Green Room is probably under heavy surveillance already."

"But does Black Faction know any of our names? Besides mine? Did we ever use them?"

"We'll find out soon, won't we?" Katja murmured.

Carl shook his head and said "I *knew* we couldn't trust them. The black hats were in on it all along. This was all an elaborate trap. This was an ambush."

"Wait a sec—"

"There was no fucking *ambush*, Carl!" Tom shouted with shocking violence.

The room went silent except for the television.

"This is what real revolution looks like," he said, leaning heavily against a pipe and staring down into the bruised flesh on the screen. "This is it. But we're not revolutionaries. We're a joke. We're a tribute band. Get that through your head."

Shayna stared at his back. The walls seemed to be moving in closer. Her heartbeat was in her ears again, rising.

"What are we going to do?" Katja whimpered.

Balboa said "We stay away from the Green Room. Stay away from each other. Don't let anyone see any of us together. There's nothing else we can do but forget it ever happened, and pray they don't find us. Any of us. Because none of us can hold up against what they'll do."

"Just lie low and act normal," Tom echoed. "That's all we can do."

The television said "If you provide information leading to the arrest of these individuals, a commission of one hundred thousand—"

Katja switched it off, leaned her head into her knees and began to sob.

"Does anyone else know about us?" Balboa asked Shayna.

"What?"

"Did you *tell* anyone about us?"

"No, I did not fucking tell anyone!" she shouted back.

They all looked at her.

She turned around and shoved through the door, not hearing whatever they were yelling. She just walked, eyes turned down, bitterly swearing at every spraypainted L-hand that passed.

Another gray pill rolled through the glass neck. She swallowed its disgusting bitterness and tried again to figure out how long it had been since the last one. The schedule had broken down – but it didn't matter, she realized, because their effect was getting weaker every time. She'd been doing her best to ignore the creeping stars and the welling fatigue.

Of course she was feeling fatigue. She hadn't slept or eaten in more than fifty hours now. With a sigh she cinched up her belt again and leaned her face into the glass of the bus window.

Close now, she thought.

She thought, *I tried. At least I tried. But what did I finally accomplish? Besides fucking over everyone I know. Besides getting all of them arrested sooner or later. That'll be my fucking legacy. Everything I added up to.*

Whenever she closed her eyes now she could only see the bruises on the stocking cap's neck, the scrolling static of the television replaced by the throbbing static in her head – so she left her eyes open. She just stared straight ahead and wiped the tears off when she needed to.

The lurkers she knew were nowhere in the main hall of the monastery. She heard their mass chants rumbling through doors at the far side of the scrawled pillars, and there was no other sound. The sun was so beautiful then, shooting through the slits in the ceiling, cutting bands in the heavy dust motes, painting its gold light up and down the poles thick with paper and paste and indecipherable glyphs of black felt tip pen. What had they said about tags? That they were magic spells. That they were wishes. And there it was again: the L-hand symbol. She wanted to tear it off, but monks were watching.

At the curb she collapsed, sobbing uncontrollably. A convoy of garbage trucks was passing by, one by one grunting their diesel breath in her face, deafening her with their noise. The old man, she thought. Even now she couldn't stop thinking about the old man.

She put her hands together in front of her, knitting the fingers until the joints cracked, and leaned her face into the knuckles. She couldn't hear a word she was saying, but she said anyway:

Tropolis,

I've never been very religious, or spiritual, or anything. I know I haven't been the most faithful believer. I don't know if you exist the way they say you do. I don't know if you can hear me now. But if you can....

I've never prayed for anything. I've never asked you for anything before. Soon I'll be dead, and I won't have anything left to pray for then anyway. So if you are there, if you can hear me, if you can hear prayers at all....

Just let me find him. I know it won't make any difference. I know it doesn't matter. So it's not a lot to ask, right? Just let me know he's alive and okay. Tropolis, just let me find him.

Just let me find him.

The last garbage truck turned the corner and left the street dead in its wake. She opened her wet eyes and looked up, and he was there.

"I hoped I could locate you here," said Kingsford, making another cut.

Shayna just looked down at him in a daze – too dazed even to feel relief yet. It was still too surreal. They were in the empty parking lot across the street from the monastery, sitting on plastic crates. She was holding up a mirrored hub cap. He was sawing away at his beard with a rusty pair of scissors. The matted hair was piling up in the gravel between his soot-blackened sneakers.

"It's been one hundred and thirty years since I shaved," he said, emotionlessly.

"You were looking for me?" she asked him.

"Yes."

"Why?"

His beard was hideously asymmetric now, but he dropped the scissors in the gravel and pushed down the hub cap in her hands. He looked at her. "It's you, in the news. You're the one they're talking about."

She swallowed hard and looked down.

"They have your name," he said. "Told to them by the one who was captured."

Shayna nodded.

The ancient closed his eyes. A smile showed through the holes in his beard. And then there was a sound welling up from deep within that profound throat. Laughter. The deepest, oldest laughter she had ever heard. It sounded wicked.

"Loiterers," he said.

"There are no Loiterers. There's no secret army. Never was."

"It doesn't matter. You are enough. And now you and I...." He trailed off, looked into the hair at his feet, sighed through his white-toothed smile. He said: "All these years of my exile. For one hundred and thirty-two years I waited for my absolution in death. I was angry at you for taking that from me, yes, but I seen now that it was His will. You and I. We'll have something for ourselves better than mere absolution. We'll have vengeance."

She couldn't meet his eyes. "What do you mean?"

He extended a time-withered hand toward her, palm up.

"You have something," his voice rumbled. "A piece of glass. I've seen you holding it."

She hesitantly reached into her pocket and produced the white shard. She placed it among the lines of his palm.

"Why do you carry this?" he asked.

"It's Cology Glass, isn't it? The factories at Fallon's Field manufactured the Cology Glass."

He nodded. His crystal blue eyes bore into her.

She said "I keep it to remind me. That even it can somehow be broken."

"Yes," said the ancient. "It can."

She sat back on her plastic crate. Stars swam through her vision.

Kingsford had fixed the shard between two toothed clips, above the blue jet of a gas torch. They were in a storage locker not far from the remains of his laboratory, stacked up to the ceiling with cardboard boxes, notebooks, bottles, old machines. He had mixed a series of unknowable substances together and was now swirling them very carefully in a beaker while the blue flame burned.

"Can the glass be melted?" she asked.

"By no heat on earth." He was peering carefully into the beaker. The stuff inside had turned gooey, transparent, full of microscopic bubbles. "At least, not heat alone. Now observe."

Shayna wiped the sweat from her face and watched carefully as he took an eyedropper of the stuff and held it above the shard in the flame. One glittering bead of liquid grew and fell.

The white glass exploded into tiny fragments and scattered across the concrete floor. The dust it had become was glowing down there in the dim light, like stars.

"How did you do that?"

"At one time I was a doctor, an engineer, and a chemist. I myself was briefly involved in designing the modern variant of Cology Wall. We realized its weakness, but of course the production of this—" he held up the beaker "—was considered too advanced for Outsiders to credibly master."

"What is it?"

"A chemical relative to the glass itself. It's the only practical way. The crystalline structure of the wall is too perfect, too redundantly bonded, to respond to virtually any physical shock, heat or corrosion. But once that chemical structure is compromised in any one point, once some of the polymer chains are re-bonded to the relative, it becomes possible for the entire crystal to unravel."

"You're saying this could make a hole in the Cology's wall?"

"No. The glass does not comprise merely its walls. It is the principal material comprising the entire substructure. Every endoskeletal crosshatch. Every support column. Every load-bearing element is fashioned from it."

Shayna held her breath.

"Together," the ancient said, "we will destroy the Cology."

Every successive thing to leave the old man's mouth as Shayna hurried after him was even more incomprehensible or unthinkable than the last – but it was all beginning to process. That he meant everything he was saying. That, even if he was crazy, he had all the clarity of mind he needed in order to do what he was talking about. The longer she spent listening to the mad passion in his voice, the more her initial amazement was wearing down into uncertainty and dread.

"The synthesis is uncomplicated," he said. They were carrying more boxes into the nearest empty building. "I believe I have everything I need to produce a significant quantity of the agent. The precursors can be distilled from commercial cleaning products." He winced and gripped his head, apparently conjuring the shopping list from memory as he scribbled it down. "From these four products, we'll extract the seven chemical precursors. The difficulty will be the explosive. It must burn hot. The polymerizing reaction will be inhibited at any temperature below 800 Kelvin."

He lapsed momentarily into rambling chemical language that Shayna could not understand. He tore off a box's cardboard flap and started scrawling formulae and diagrams on it under the white hot glare of a work lamp, the only light in the room.

"Look at it," he said. "Like a long snake of sequenced molecules, biting its own tail. How my mind burned when I first beheld this shape. So infatuated with my own intellect in those days. This is what we will make now."

Shayna held the ink-smeared cardboard in her hands. It felt unusually heavy. The lettered elements and connecting lines stared back at her, seeming to hypnotize her until she shook her head and said "Okay, but first things first. I mean, we need to figure some things out."

Kingsford closed his eyes and rubbed the sides of his head. "Indeed. The temperature is a problem. Unless, yes. Unless the relative itself is also the charge. With only slight modification it could be hybridized...."

"I don't mean the technical details. We need to think about—"

"A kind of crude thermal plastique might be appended to it, without destroying its reactive properties to the glass. Eureka. And the ingredients and the synthesis process will still be very simple. I'll teach it to you as we go."

"Doctor Kingsford—"

"The only thing we're missing then is a fuse or a detonator of some kind. Unfortunately, it should be industrial grade. It must detonate reliably and at high temperature, and it should have a few seconds of delay."

In her pocket, Shayna had been holding the grenade, turning it slowly in her hand, but she froze when she heard these words. She let it sink softly to the bottom of the pocket and folded her arms in front of her. “Listen. We need a plan.”

“Plan. We construct the device tonight and use it tomorrow at dawn.”

“That’s it? We’re not even going to issue a warning? No demands? No ultimatum?”

His hand stopped scribbling and his eyes rose slowly from the formulae. He stared blankly at her.

Fighting the coldness of his gaze, she said “Shouldn’t actually *using* the bomb be our very last resort after everything else fails? We can use it to make demands. We can open some kind of negotiation with the Insiders, to share power. If we try it that way first, maybe more people will side with us when—”

“Insiders will never honestly *negotiate* with your kind. Even if they did, they excel at nothing so much as manipulating and confusing public opinion. At most they would stall just long enough to relocate or erect some new defense. They would only leverage the....” He stopped himself. “There’s no point in even discussing this.”

“Even if it could save lives? If we show them we’re reasonable human beings—”

“The Principals would gladly scorch the whole of the Earth before ceding control of any part of it to Outsiders. Nothing will make them see you as human beings. Now listen. You may be the leader of a secret army, according to the television. You are not the leader here. This is my endeavor and you are merely assisting me.”

She cleared her throat fearfully. “Then I don’t think I can do this.”

The old man sighed and closed his eyes in frustration. “You fear capture and interrogation.”

She shook her head.

“Then what?”

“How many people die if the Cology collapses?” she asked.

“Perhaps one thousand.”

“A *thousand* people?”

“Yes. Roughly.”

Water dripped slowly somewhere in the decrepit wooden void.

She swallowed and said “I don’t want that.”

“Understand. They are Insiders. They’re not like you. I know them. You do not.”

“I still won’t kill a thousand people just like that. Never.”

He seemed to grow larger as he stood upright. She’d never realized how tall he was until he said “You’re merely eighteen years old and nearly at the end of your life. Men and women behind those walls have already lived more than *two hundred years*, and they may *never* die. They inhabit a gilt palace of earthly delight while you toil in the factories and drink from the sewers. Don't you feel envy? Don't you feel hatred?"

"It doesn't matter," she said quietly, stepping back from him. "Even if I did hate them. I still can't do that."

"No, no. I misspoke when I suggested that revenge is the issue. It goes further. It may be beyond your grasp, but you must believe me when I say that the Cology and its people are not merely wealthy. They are even as we speak perpetrating a crime larger than you can imagine. They must be stopped at any cost."

"I can't judge them all together. I can't sentence them all to death."

"Only because you don't know what they've done!" he bellowed, his fists shaking at his sides.

"Then *what?* What have they done? What did *you* do? What is this crime you keep talking about?"

Kingsford stopped. His fists and his gaze sank down and he went back to unpacking the box in front of him, his movements now eerily serene. He drew a long breath and said darkly:

"I am committed to this action. Your help would be valuable but not necessary. If you don't intend to participate... will you attempt to stop me?"

Shayna saw his hands waver out of sight behind the lip of the box, maybe holding something. She couldn't tell, and her switchblade lay back with her coat in the ditch. She thought of the door behind her, but she didn't run. She told the truth. "I don't know."

He leaned his head down and nodded. After a while he looked up and said "One of the greatest monsters ever incarnated as man once said: the death of one person is a tragedy, but the death of millions is a statistic." The words echoed through the space. The ancient's hands raised, empty, from the box. "Blight is a generic term, used informally in the outer Tropolis to describe any of over three thousand differentiable, chiefly terminal illnesses – all of which share only one pathophysiological commonality: the uncontrolled replication of cells whose genetic data has been corrupted by chemical or radiological contamination."

"I don't understand."

"I'm telling you my crime," he whispered. He closed his eyes and began to pace back and forth as he continued: "In the Cology. Where I was born, where I was raised, educated. In that society, that culture, there is a commonly held or perhaps universally agreed worldview. It's how they read the narrative of human history, past, present, future. It's how I was taught. But, no, no, I do not mean to excuse myself from this. I was taught to think this way, yes, but I elaborated. I advanced it far beyond what was given to me. I conspired in the plan. I helped conceive it myself. I was at the forefront. It was me. It was mine."

His hands were shaking again. His voice was shaking. Shayna didn't know whether to try to comfort him or to get out while she could.

He continued, seemingly not even aware of her presence anymore: "The view that there is a question. The question of Outsiders. There were Outsiders, Shayna – there were Outsiders and Insiders long before anything such as the Cology was even an inkling in Men's wildest dreams. Thousands of years ago. What *they* would call stupid people. The rabble. The masses. The writhing and miserable bulk of the species, the off races, fornicating like rabbits, multiplying their bacterial numbers across the face of the Earth, every once in one million iterations managing by blind probability to recombine their feeble genetic material to produce one of *us*, the real kind, those with the innate strength and intellect and will to power to rise above the sea of our insapient peers. The Kings. The leaders by any means. The demonstrated engines of their own success. That is how we saw ourselves. That to which we attributed our lives in the Cology, apart from yours, on those rare occasions we subjected ourselves to looking outward at all. At the dregs of the species. The stooped, mindless wallowers, the unestablished, the defective, the unemployed, feeding off the teat of the public good. Exploiting the weakness of the old State and its prescriptive compassion. Until we did away with all that."

She thought she saw his spit foaming at the corners of his mouth. His hands were rapidly making and unmaking fists. Then he seemed to struggle to calm himself down and his voice tranquilized again.

"But that was only the beginning," he said. "Of the answer to the question of Outsiders. Once we had established our enclosed paradise, there was still everything outside it: a planet already depleted, ravaged by industrialization, sustained only by crude stopgap measures such as stratospheric sulfur dioxide injection – its human carrying capacity far, far overextended. The world was overpopulated. By who? By your kind, we deluded ourselves into thinking. The mindless rabble.

"I believed this. My teachers, my peers, they led me toward it, yes, but it was I, *I* who committed myself to it. With others. A secret society. A group at once kept hidden from the majority of Insiders, and yet also the direct application of what they all believed. Our project was to accelerate the extinction. There were countless methods. First the dismantling of all legal restraint and regulation. The subsumation of the old national governments first by the Trusts, then the Consortium, and finally the Company. We initiated the anti-terraforming. What we made look like negligence was secret intention. Carefully executed increases in ambient radiation. Chemical releases. Small acts of industrial sabotage, subtle enough to go undetected. The declines in birth rate and life expectancy were exactingly planned and correlated to the development of technologies that could automate the labor of Outsiders by degrees, until, theoretically, a functioning industrial base could exist without human workers at all. A fully cybernetic society.

"We aspired to poison to death a world we had already deemed terminally ill – so that we, the fittest, the cream of mankind, the overmen, rendered immune to all of our own contrivances, could one day inherit it from you. It would be a blank slate for us. The outer Tropolis and all its refuse could be covered over with fresh earth. The oceans would retreat again, the glaciers swell. The whole of the planet would be rendered a pastoral playground for superior minds, superior bodies. We did not invent the blight. We only sought to leverage it to realize a perverse vision of grandeur. It was my vision. It was what I worked toward. Confidently. Skillfully. Without hesitation. But eventually the dreams began.

"I couldn't stop them, my peers. I tried. I *tried*, but I couldn't destroy the group or the mindset that created it. I tried until none could look at me anymore. Then I could only leave. But by that time, I had already killed you. I had killed thousands. Millions. I have tried to calculate the number. God in His omniscience would be hard pressed to finish the calculations I have begun –but He will, in His time, and in proportion to that number I will surely burn. For you, Shayna. For the seven generations I watched die before you. For everyone else. So understand that proportionately the deaths of one thousand Insiders is of no consequence to me, nor should it be for you – because I swear to you, I *swear* to you, as long as the Cologies exist, the world itself is only one more thing slated for demolition. Angelis must be brought down."

When the last echoes of his rumbling voice had died out, Shayna heard the drumbeat of rain starting against the metal roof.

The grenade was in her hand. She set it in front of him.

The ancient unscrewed the fuse and held it to the light.

The rain soaked down toward her sweating skin as the minutes passed on the edge of the bed at the monastery. Her phone was in her hands, charged and ready, waiting. The heat was deliriously intense now; whether it was in the air or in her blood or in her mind, she couldn't tell. She just stared down at the phone resting across the bars of her fingers.

"Don't be that kind of asshole," she echoed. Finally she lifted it up and made the call.

She went to the hideout past the Green Room and found Carl already there, waiting.

"You got here fast," she said.

"You said it was an emergency."

"Yes," she answered distantly. "An emergency meeting."

Carl stared at her, then looked quickly away when she said

"What are you looking at?"

"You don't look so good."

"I don't feel so good either."

"How do you feel?"

She hesitated and said "You're asking me how it feels?"

Carl looked at his hands and shrugged limply.

"It feels like dying."

Carl looked anxiously at his feet.

She sighed and said "Just hot. Prickly. Tired. But it'll pass."

"Still no way I can help?"

She bit her lip in thought. She leaned up and said "Alcohol?"

When the door shut behind him, she pulled from her pocket the folded up chemical diagram the Ancient had given her, and found it only more laden with weird magnetism than before. It was strange to think that somewhere within these inert smears of ink was the power to level something so unimaginably large. To think that of a white crystal one mile tall and five miles to a side, and somehow these glyphs could shatter it. Somehow they would tomorrow.

She read the strange names scrawled around each of the different parts of the complete agent – the things he'd called the precursors. She touched one and felt a shiver when she whispered it aloud: *cyclopentane*.

The pipes all abruptly stopped clanking. An eerie stillness breathed through the room.

"Back," Carl said, pushing through the squeaking door.

Shayna quickly hid the cardboard and tried not to show that he'd scared the shit out of her. She picked the wrapper off the high-class gin he handed her. Hunching over it as if it were a crutch, she sighed and asked him:

"Have you ever not known whether you were physically ill, or whether something was just bothering you? Has something ever bothered you that much?"

"Yes."

"Good thing this works on both," she said, unscrewing the cap.

He stared at her through the bottle she tipped back. He opened his mouth to speak but fell silent as the door opened, and one by one they all stepped down.

When she finished explaining the mission, no one moved. They all passed anxious looks amongst themselves – not at her. Katja leaned her head down against her crossed forearms.

"Any concerns?" Shayna asked her authoritatively.

"You said it was an emergency," Tom said quietly. "We all came because we thought maybe you were in trouble. We thought you needed our help."

"I'm asking for your help. Did you hear anything I just said? The mission—"

"Do you understand what's happened?" Balboa said. "Do you really understand that we are all hunted now? We shouldn't even be associating with each other. Our only hope is to not get seen together. We can't go on any mission."

"Not *any* mission. *The* mission! I'm talking about the entire revolution fought and won in one strike! I am talking about destroying the entire Cology!"

"With one single gas grenade fuse," Tom said.

She stared at him. Her fingers ached until she forced her fists back open.

"You don't believe me? I saw it. He showed me. He broke the glass right in front of me."

"You have to admit, Shay," Carl said, scratching his head, clearing his throat, trailing off.

"I saw it!"

Balboa rubbed his eyes. Katja glanced only briefly up from her arms. No one spoke.

"Who's with me?" Shayna asked, summoning into her voice all the force she had left.

"No," Balboa said. "Don't ask us to do this."

"It's only everything the Smurge ever sang to us about," Shayna yelled. "It's only everything we ever dreamed of. Only everything *Balboa* ever fought for."

"Don't," he said, his face hardening, his back straightening. "Don't."

"You said you owed me a favor once."

"I already did you that favor."

"When?"

Balboa hesitated. "The night of our first mission. The power plant. No one...."

"None of us would have done it," Tom said. "We were all going to back out. Balboa talked to us when you were out. He convinced us it was safe enough. He convinced us all to go."

"So be convinced one more time."

"This is completely different. Everything is different now. We can't do this. You know we can't. No matter how much we...."

"We love you," Katja said softly, leaning upright. "We all love you, Shay."

"Yes, we do," said Tom, sadly.

Shayna stood up and the wooden chair clattered on the floor.

"Prove it," she said. "Fucking prove it."

"Shay—" Carl began.

"I'll do it without you. Go and hide. See if I give a shit. I'll go in without any of you."

"No," Tom said, shaking his head.

"*No?*"

"You can't— None of us can—" he struggled. "You can't risk getting caught. You most of all out of any of us. The comps know your name. They have your photo. It's all over TV now. People can recognize you. If they get to you they'll—"

"Let them," she said.

"If you're captured, *all* of us are dead," Balboa said. "You'll lead them to us. You won't be able to help it."

"Because they'll what, *torture* me?" She pounded the top of her chest and screamed "*This* is torture! *I* am torture! Right now! You think they have something worse? Worse than this? Worse than the blight? My blood is poison. They'd have to cure me before they could torture me."

Katja was sobbing.

"You're all dying too," Shayna yelled. "You're all dying. You're all just letting yourself forget it."

Balboa leaned his forehead into his fist. Tom tried limply to hold Katja's heaving back. Carl perched on the edge of his chair, the only one still meeting her eyes.

"You're *all* dying," she said. "And you'll die as nothing. You were born into this piece of shit world, and you'll float on through it for ten or twenty years longer than me, and leave it exactly the way you found it, as if you were never even here. Nothing to show for it. And I'll die tomorrow morning. And I'll die changing *everything*."

She grabbed the gin bottle by its neck and pointed it threateningly at all of them before throwing the door against its hinges as she left. There was a large soggy cardboard box by the dumpster in the alley; she lifted it up and crouched underneath. From through the cardboard walls she listened to them run after her, desperately yell her name a few times, and recede into the distance.

She sighed and rubbed her eyes. The meeting hadn't gone as planned.

She thought of how she'd felt on the night this all began. Nothing had been more terrifying then than the thought of sleeping alone on her last night – and now that this night had come, all she could think about was how surprisingly good it felt to sit there in the cardboard darkness with her palms pressed to the oily pavement. It was restful, holding herself, watching the purple stars blow through the pitch black. She stayed there a while, anticipating the crushing dizziness that she knew would come when she tried to stand again.

The ancient picked up without a word when she called.

"Change of plans," she said. "It's just you and me."

"I understand," came the gravelly voice.

"See you tomorrow," she said, and hung up.

At the corner of two lifeless streets, she paused and waited for the shakes to pass. She stared down along the lines of street lamps, into the waning and logo-scarred moon at the very end. She wiped the water out of her face and drank.

3

The breath of the Tropolis was shallow on the last morning. The rain came back and left for good an hour before dawn, leaving the streets and blocks darkened but dry. At first light, the corpses of the storm clouds were stretched into only a few shimmering fingers of cirrus, and the sky behind them was clear and pink.

She leaned up off of the bed where she'd been lying sleepless for a few hours. She'd been letting her mind digest whatever it could in the time left. Building her strength. She looked into the light outside and was amazed at the lightness of her hangover. She looked down on her knees, her boots, her hands spreading and closing in front of her, and thought to them: *almost there. Just give me two hours and all the energy you have left. It's all I need. Then we can sleep.*

Her phone rang the moment she stood up, and Carl's name was on the screen. She answered without speaking.

"I'm in," his voice crackled quietly.

"Do you mean that?"

"I'm in."

She sighed. "I'm at the monastery."

"I'm already on my way. Five minutes."

Her suitcase was re-packed and on the bed, but it was only more dead weight now. She straightened her goggles on her forehead, cleaned the Memento Mori on her shirt before putting it back on her finger, and straightenned necklace of teeth behind her neck. The bass, bullet holes and badly tuned strings and all, went on last. When it was all in place, she knelt at the window sill. She closed her eyes and held her hands together in front of her.

"Do you believe now?"

She looked up. Kelroy stood behind the doorframe, bald head and black robe banded in the sunlight.

"In something," she said. "Maybe."

"It answers those who'll only listen."

She reached into her pocket and lifted out the Metro Pass. Rising achingly from the floor, she placed it in his hand. She was about to leave, but when she met his eyes there was something there.

"What, you're sad to see me go now?" she asked.

He seemed about to speak, but nothing came.

"Thank you for your help," she said.

"Good luck."

She nodded sadly and went to wait at the curb.

It was unbelievably bright out there – whether by itself or just through her eyes, she didn't know. It was as if the whole world was overexposed.

"What changed your mind?" she asked Carl as the Chickmobile roared into high gear.

"I just realized you were right." There was redness in his eyes and sweat in his creases. He'd been up all night. His voice had the sound of holding back, but what else was new.

"Right about what?" she asked distantly.

He stared stoically ahead, lit his cigarette, and said "Everything."

The cars out there rumbled and whirred for a long time while the Chickmobile's cab was steeped in anxious silence. The distant white hulk of the Cology passed between the buildings.

"I can barely even remember what I said," she murmured.

"What you said about having something to show for having lived."

She nodded mutely.

"About having nothing left to lose," he said through his smoke, and squinted up into the yellow haze, showing no emotion.

She turned reflexively away from him, into the window. She chewed on her knuckle until she tasted the blood.

Virgil Kingsford stood at the curb with the bomb in the broad daylight, as if it was nothing. At first she didn't think he was the same man. With his beard cut completely down to only a few bits of sandy stubble, and his long hair tied back, his inhumanly deep wrinkles and his blue eyes were the only way to recognize him. His Persian rug poncho was gone, and the body that had all along been hidden underneath now showed itself muscular and lean in a black tank and work pants.

The bomb swung at his side, suspended from a nylon rope that coiled around his other arm. It was little more than a glass jar the size of a human head, with the grenade fuse sealed into the metal lid. The Cology-killing goo was inside, viscous and slow, bluish and nearly opaque.

When she rolled down her window and Carl braked, Kingsford looked at the two of them in turn and said "I thought you were alone."

Shayna squinted into the light. "He's just getting us there."

"I've wired this for contact detonation. No delay. There will be no time to escape the probable radius of the avalanche."

Shayna swallowed hard.

"Understood," Carl said before she could speak.

"So be it." The old man climbed up to the side door of the cab.

"There's room in the back compartment."

"No," said Kingsford as he slid onto the bench seat, forcing Shayna to make room for him. He said simply "We go."

Carl looked apprehensively at his hands and finally put the machine in gear. The Chickmobile made its grunting way up the nearest onramp and lurched up to flyway speed, barreling down the Inward route amid a swirl of black exhaust. Only then did he clear his throat and announce "I'm not just getting you there. I said I'm in. I meant all the way."

Kingsford only stared indifferently ahead.

"Do you understand what he just said, Carl?" Shayna said. "Once the bomb hits the Cology wall, that's it. It's all coming down."

"I know."

"There won't be any time to get away."

"I *know*."

"Then why?"

"I want to be there," he said coldly into the rush of traffic. "I need to be there to give you any help I can. I want to be part of it. I told you, you were right last night."

Shayna bit her lip and squinted ahead. Her voice caught in her throat while miles ticked by and the Cology assumed more and more of its whole unimaginable size.

"What if I was wrong?" she said.

The ancient's eye shot her a sidelong glance from between its wrinkles.

"About what?" Carl murmured.

"About your life being worthless. About those extra twenty years being worthless."

Carl only stared ahead.

Angelis was swelling faster now. The breadth of the sky was increasingly assimilated into its formless white silhouette.

"I *was* wrong. You shouldn't die today, Carl. You can't."

"But you can?"

"I don't have anything left to lose."

"Neither do I."

She looked hard at him. She tried to read through his expression but every muscle was bolted in its blank place.

"You keep saying that," she said. "But I don't understand. You have everything to lose. Why do you keep saying you've got nothing to lose?"

Carl twisted his fists on the wheel again but said nothing.

"Answer me," she said.

One red-eyed glance. Nothing more. The mirrored spires of Greentowne rose up and shot by on the other side of his stubbled chin.

"This exit," Kingsford grumbled.

Carl obeyed. The offramp walls spiraled sickeningly down and then it spread out before them: one straight street running inevitably into the walls of ice. A mile of stoplights was all that held them back now from the surface of the pure bright void that had replaced the whole sky, and everything was painted in the weird colorless luminance of the glass.

It hit her in a wave. The ringing in her ears abruptly resurged to full volume.

"Oh my God," she murmured as she stared ahead into the field of white. "This is it. This was my dream."

"You were right," Carl interrupted. "This isn't about life being worthless. It's about *making* our lives have value, by being part of something bigger. Something worth remembering us for."

"Remembering us for," Shayna echoed as the waves of sudden nausea hit her. She braced herself against the seat and the white light filled up her eyes. "We can't do this. Stop."

Kingsford sighed and stared dead ahead.

"What?" Carl gasped.

"Stop this thing! Stop it now!"

Carl braked hard. Horns screamed all around.

She grabbed his arm and said "This can't be our legacy. It can't."

"You are certain," rumbled the ancient voice. A low pulse of energy seemed to run through the veins on his muscular arms.

"Yes."

The old man sat still and sighed. Then his movements were too fast for either of them to respond: jolting his long arm across both their laps to crack the driver side door open, bracing himself against his own door and kicking with both feet straight into Shayna's hip. She heard the bass strings shriek horribly against asphalt and then she and Carl were squinting up at the old man as he slammed the cab door and revved the engine.

"No!" Carl screamed. He leapt up and fought with the door handle, but it cracked off in his hand and the door held fast.

The window rolled down to the level of Kingsford's time-weathered mouth. He sat there looking down at them, and they looked back in wordless shock.

"I would have thought, but... never," the ancient said. He squinted away into the light and said "Never but with blood."

Carl tripped backward as the engine roared and the van jolted away in a blast of hot exhaust and tire smoke. He and Shayna stood frozen as it faded into the weird light. Car horns kept blaring behind them until they scrambled to the sidewalk. Only then did she realize how close they were. The nearest cross-street was numbered twenty-three and the luminous void covered almost the entire sky. The déjà vu that washed over her was scalding now.

"Run," She whispered in terror, though she knew there was no hope of making it to the safety of orange sky. Fifty feet of white marble sidewalk flew beneath her in stunted motion, and then she was on the ground. Her head was swimming and the stars returned in force. From somewhere between the cubic forest of crystal and glass there came the wailing of sirens.

"Shay!" Carl screamed.

She propped herself up on her elbows and looked back, Inward. She pulled the bass around in front of her. Her fingers instinctively formed the chord, but she hesitated to play it. Carl reached her just as it happened.

The bomb sounded just one short, fizzling shot. The yellow spark of the explosion left a tiny mark on her vision before the colorless light re-absorbed it, leaving only a brownish wad of rising smoke, distant and small.

She silently counted off the seconds while she held her breath to listen for any sound. She scanned the ominous white for anything. Cars silently slowed and stopped. People hesitated on the sidewalk, squinting Inward at the dark wisps.

Before the faintest rumble, it was the light that shifted. For a split second everything in sight dimmed faintly reddish, and then it became visible above: a rapid and uneven wave of subtle darkness, shuddering upward through the formless white, momentarily betraying the edges of each hexagonal pane as it moved. It appeared again, this time heavier and slower. Only now was there any sound: a terrifying polyphony of screaming glass, descending into an audible range from sounds too high-pitched for any human being to hear. In a moment it had become earsplitting. She wanted to clamp her head between her knees and shut her eyes, but she saw something now.

What looked at first like the cloud from the explosion, Shayna realized was the third rise of the dark wave, stabbing upward in the shape of a sharp curving peak. The panes all dimmed in its wake, assuming different and darker shades of gray. The white sky turned into hundred-foot-wide pixels of television static. Then came the roaring crack.

Carl's hand held hers so tightly that her knuckles ached. The ground shuddered under them. People scattered in a crazed panic, mouths open as if screaming, but everything was silenced by the sound as the sky above Greentowne split open.

She braced herself against Carl and stopped seeing anything but the light changing colors through her eyelids.

Ready? she thought.

The sound began to subside. The screams of Greentowne became audible again – and then even they, bit by bit, hushed down. In a moment there was no sound left but a chorus of faint residual glass sounds, like chimes.

When she opened her eyes, the wall was solid and unchanging. Nothing had fallen and the cracking had stopped; the rows of panes held, only slightly deformed, parted from one another in a long polygonal fissure a thousand feet high and a hundred wide. They hung just open enough to see through to the Inside. And there, inside—

Blue.

A blue sky.

Everyone stood around in sublime awe. A few people drifted unthinkingly down the street toward it. The car engines were all dead, everything standing still under the surreal new light.

"Have you ever seen a color like that?" somebody muttered. "Have you ever seen a sky like that?"

A white cloud passed across the vein of clear air and everyone gasped. Everyone was looking at each other to see whether they were seeing it too. Everyone was gripped by the shock of recognizing, with perfect intuition, something none of them had ever seen before.

"God I'm tired," Shayna murmured.

"Hold on," Carl said. "I said hold on."

She tightened her slipping fingers behind his neck and squinted around again at the walls of the stairwell. The shapes were all vague. "You're not very good at carrying. This is all just an excuse, right?"

"Excuse to do what?" he groaned, mounting another step.

"To stick your hand all inside my knees," she said, kicking one foot.

"Yeah," he said, leaning back into the wall for support. "Just like you being this exhausted is just an excuse to get a free ride up all these fucking stairs. Right?"

"Yeah."

Everything began to fade out again.

"Hold on!" she heard him yell. "Just hold— almost there—"

"Almost."

She felt the bed beneath her, and the covers damp with her sweat. From somewhere came a faint, garbled yapping.

"Carl," she groaned.

"H-hey. It's all over the TV."

She rolled her head from side to side and squinted at the ceiling. "Where's my bass?"

"Right here," he said, moving to somewhere by her head. "It's right against the wall here."

"I'd like it," she said, and a moment later she felt its weight pressing down on her abdomen. The rough edges around one of the bullet holes stabbed into the front of her pelvis. She lifted her hands up and lay them on the strings, and immediately felt some energy return to her.

"This your place?" she asked, squinting around. She saw sun-bleached Smurge posters, water-stains on the plaster, little else. The air was thick and musty, but she imagined she smelled much worse herself.

"Home sweet home. Seemed like the place to go. This way it's just me who gets arrested, if they come for you. But I think we made it here all right. I don't think anybody followed. No one's going to call them on us. Not many people live around here."

She sighed and wiped the sweat off her ungoggled forehead. The electric yapping continued. "What are they saying on TV?"

"They just keep saying 'The Loiterers were not involved,' over and over - but it sounds like the more they say we weren't, the more everyone thinks we were. Some people recognized you. You're getting more famous all the time."

The TV switched off.

"God I'm tired," she said, and closed her eyes.

"Can I get you anything? Alcohol?"

She shook her head and drew another shallow breath. "Tired."

"All right. I'll, um, I'll just let you sleep then."

She heard his feet on the floorboards and then a door clicking closed. As she drifted out of consciousness, she thought for a moment she could hear him weeping.

She opened her eyes and the room was dark. The first light of the street lamps winked on in long lines across the walls.

Carl said "You hungry? Man, I am starving. I could eat ten chickens."

She shook her head. She heard paper bags rustling.

"I went to Smarty's. A whole feast. Ten meals. That's what I've got here."

She shook her head.

"When's the last time you ate?" he asked. "You should eat something."

Three days, she thought, and welled up the energy to say "Sorry. I can't. You go ahead without me."

Carl sighed. "I'm full."

2

When she opened her eyes again, the light on the wall was smeared with rain and she heard it ticking on the window. Carl slumped on the sill, water dripping off the greasy tendrils of his hair, staring at the floor.

"What?" she asked.

"I just talked to the others."

"Are they here?"

"No. We talked over pay phones. Afraid our cells might be tapped."

"What did they say?"

"There's some good news. Katja ran into Blue Dog last night. It turns out his dad's a lawyer, so the comps can't touch him or the other girl, and that leaves no link back to the band. Except you, being all over TV. They're sorry they can't come here, but they're afraid comps might be watching us. They might be waiting to see who else shows up."

"Do you think they are? Shit. What about the Chickmobile? Won't they trace it back to you?"

"Don't worry about that. I reported it stolen after our first mission. Covered my tracks in some other ways. They won't find me that way. If somebody recognized you on our way here, though, there's a seven-digit arrest commission now. The biggest anyone has ever seen."

Still not enough to pay for a cure, Shayna thought.

"The others think they need to keep their distance until things cool down," Carl continued, only half-spitefully. "They say they'll try to visit later, if they think it's safe."

"Oh."

"Fuck it. The jackboots would be on us by now if they had anything. I say *let* them come. They'll never take me alive."

Shayna squinted at this, but shook it off and asked "Did they say anything else? Katja and Balboa and Tom?"

"Just that they're sorry. Sorry they can't visit. And that they were wrong."

She sighed. "Were they wrong?"

"Well, they thought you made it all up," he stuttered. "They didn't think the bomb was real."

"You didn't think it was real either."

He looked aside and cleared his throat.

"But you came anyway. Why?"

He rolled his head around and said nervously: "I figured the important thing was that we'd get shot to pieces whether it was real or not. So I couldn't just let you, you know, hog the whole blaze of glory."

Shayna sighed and turned her head to the wall. "They were still right not to come. I can't believe I even asked that of you. You have to tell them *I'm* sorry. The way I've treated everyone since all this started, it's...."

"There's nothing to apologize for. You've been under a lot of stress." He almost laughed, but only squeaked nervously.

"But the whole mission, it was all a mistake. It was pointless."

"How can you say that?"

She sighed into the wool and said nothing.

"Pointless?" he protested. "But it worked! We opened the wall and everyone saw inside! We proved in front of everyone that it isn't unbreakable at all. That's huge, isn't it? That changes everything! Doesn't it?"

"Is it enough to change everything? No matter what the change is?"

Carl seemed tongue-tied.

"And you don't even know the things he told me," she said. "You don't even know how the old man convinced me to do it. Why he gave his life to do it himself. I know all that, and I still think it was a mistake."

"Then tell me. Explain it to me."

So she did, as well as she could. She told him what the nurse had told her about the blight, and then what Kingsford had said after her. She repeated, as far her own understanding would reach, everything she'd heard about the way the world had come to be the way it was, and what it was still becoming. Carl never spoke, even when she paused to regain her breath between sentences. He sat in uncharacteristic silence, watching either her or the window.

"Even then, even having heard all that," she finished, "I still wish I could take it all back. I wish I'd never been part of it."

Carl looked stricken.

"It's complicated," she added. "The whole thing is. But, I mean.... Even if destroying the Cology, destroying the entire thing, would really change anything. Even if it weren't just revenge. Would that make it right? I don't know. Who am I to know something like that? Who am I to say?"

Carl just kept still, biting his tongue, and Shayna squinted uncertainly at him. She tried to weigh the fire in his down-turned eyes. She looked through him to the clock on the wall, or as much of it as she could make out.

"Don't you have to work?" she asked.

He hesitated and said "I quit my jobs."

"What? All of them? Won't you get arrested for that?"

"I'm not leaving you."

She swallowed hard and looked away.

"I'd do a lot more than that if it would help you," he said.

She stared emptily into the wall, listening to her own pulse. She hesitated and said "Maybe there is something. Can you write music? Do you know how?"

"Completely," he said, finally looking up.

"I've been writing a new song. I just finished it."

"Where is it?"

"Only in my head."

He nodded. He made crashing noises in his closet and returned with an amplifier, which he plugged into the bass on her lap. It hissed static and kept cutting out while he twisted the wires.

She lay her fingers across the strings and felt the sound rise. It sounded awful, but with some effort she put it well enough into tune. She collected her strength and picked the first notes. "Here's how it begins."

She watched him pick up his guitar and listen. She watched his sleepless eyes pass through states of profound concentration and brief moments of subtle rapture, as it all began to come together. They worked for hours without a pause, going through numerous complete repetitions. She lost count.

When Carl had re-transcribed everything in his neatest and most reverent hand, she asked him "Do you think it's any good?"

He smirked for a moment before he looked up and said "I think it's the most beautiful song I've ever heard."

"You're just saying that."

"No. I'm not."

"When you're seeing me like this. I can't ask you to be honest about something like that."

"Shay. Listen. Look at me."

She turned and focused on him as hard as she could. Hard enough to see through her thickening haze that his face was as serious as she'd ever seen it – and yet it wasn't the seriousness he usually had. It wasn't macho or contrived or dramatic. It was quietly shaken. It was tinged with envy and admiration that she couldn't understand.

"This is the most beautiful song I've ever heard," he said, and she knew he meant it.

She looked at the ceiling and sighed.

The short windows of consciousness grew foggier and more disjointed. After it had all happened, she couldn't decide how much had been dream – but there was a time when she opened her eyes to find a child's face perched there at the side of the bed. Squinting hard, she finally recognized her.

"Cass?"

"Hello." The word was clearly enunciated. She wasn't chewing her lip or her fingers as usual. She only stood there, serenely composed.

"Did they come to visit me after all? Is your big sister here? Who else is here?"

Cass shook her head and said "I came here on my own."

Shayna only gradually realized that she wasn't sure the child's mouth had moved when she spoke. She held the covers a little tighter.

Cass said "I am not unintelligent, though my intelligence is estranged from yours. I am here in different spaces. It can be difficult for me to communicate the way you do, but now that you're closer to this end, I can reach you more easily. There are things I need to share with you now. I have things to show you." Her large eyes widened with expectation.

"What things?" Shayna asked, recoiling a bit further into the bed. This felt more surreal with each passing moment.

"Don't be afraid. You did this once before."

Shayna saw the child's hand reach carefully across her vision. She closed her eyes and let the small fingers lay down on her eyelids.

A cool wind blew, and the whole infinite circuit board of the Tropolis was flying far below. The blocks and streets, the fences and utility poles were all microscopic between the cloud edges. Everything glimmered and burned in the light shooting its fingers through the sparse rain, and warm fragments of a storm framed the yellow sun.

She realized she felt no pain now, and the weight of fatigue had been lifted. She felt Cass's small hand holding her own, guiding her into the eerie colorless light which gave away Middle Greentowne even before she perceived the overarching crystalline walls. Only when she traced the full outline of the Cology did she realize just how tiny that fissure really was in proportion to the whole.

"You created this," Cass said.

"No. I tried to stop it."

The faint sliver of blue sky was still showing through the crack. Her vision was drifting toward it amid the rising wind.

"It can be broken," Cass's voice said – whether it was a statement or a question, Shayna couldn't tell.

"Yes. There's a special chemical. The Ancient and I made it. There's a formula for it."

"It can only be broken in the proper way."

The shapes and symbols danced through her mind. She snuffed them out and said: "Do you mean – are you asking me what the formula is? I wouldn't want to know it, even if I did."

The sharp white edges sparkled in the yellow light as Cass said "I can show you the Inside, but you wouldn't understand the things you'd see there. In some ways, it's how the outside world was long ago. In other ways it is different from how human life has ever been."

"The Ancient told me it's evil – that they're all evil in there."

"Evil. Good. Words for everyone. It's true that the ones on the Inside, a long time ago, lost the power to relate to the ones outside. This loss has shaped the world."

She sighed inwardly and said "So would destroying the Cology really have helped anything? Will the crack? It won't help anybody on the Inside *relate* to anyone else. It won't change anybody's mind about anything. Will it?"

Cass was only perceptible by the pressure of her fingers on Shayna's – but somehow she felt as if she was being smiled at. Now the small fingers were on her forehead. The child's voice said "There's music in your head."

Shayna started to ask— but before she could, she heard the first echoes of the sound. It was only a small murmur, too distant and muffled to make out any of the words or identify the instruments, but she recognized it perfectly as her own song. No, it wasn't exactly the same: it was complete. That lost murmur was being played by a group, and it was embellished in small ways she had never imagined herself. The bass and the voice were not her own. They were flawless. They were beautiful.

They were Katja's.

"How is that possible?" she asked. "How could she have learned it already? How can she even have heard it so soon?"

Cass didn't answer, but she didn't need to. The difference was faint but unmistakable: the voice in those echoes was Katja's, but it was also older than the Katja she knew. It was weighed down with multiple years of future smoking.

When Cass's voice finally returned, it was suddenly grim. "You can hear the music. You don't see it."

"No."

"Are you ready to see it?"

"I don't understand. I mean, I know you're warning me about something, but I don't know what." She braced herself and said "Yes. I'm ready."

The shift was too subtle to notice at first. The light began to change; everything dimmed to twilight except the ever-white Cology, and the sun melted back into the width of the sky. At the same time, the infinite maze of streets and buildings half-ignited with the orange of its street lamps. All the cars down there ceased to be cars and became pure veins of red and white fire, their glow softly throbbing like a patchwork of embers in an unsteady wind. For a moment she saw the shape of it all like the concentric and radial creep of a dent in a windshield, or just as Balboa had described it: like a vast spider web, disintegrated down to its last few strands, barely holding together around the Cology at its hub. Before she could study it any longer, she felt Cass guiding her down, out of the soaring winds and in between walls of looming concrete. When they were only a few stories from the street, the blur of colored lights suddenly hardened into perfect focus, and the sound of the music changed sharply. Now it was pounding, hammering, yelling, chanting.

The light in the streets had turned into a vast throng. There were thousands of people. Young and old, female and male. Some wore the sooty and stitched-up fare of the outer Tropolis; some were even enveloped in the angular iridescent gray of Greentowners. All of them were shouting in rhythmic unison. All of them were shouting the song. They were shouting it at a shiny black wall of comps.

"This is the past," Shayna found herself saying, almost pleading. "We're seeing the past and this is Fallon's Field."

"No. You know where we are."

Now she recognized the buildings. It was the same Greentowne intersection in which she'd fallen, and where she'd turned back to see if the whole sky would fall next. When she looked there now, the towering blankness looked back down on her, nearly as perfect and infinite as ever. There was only a fine trace up there where the crack had once been, now sealed up like a scar. The chanting below seemed to echo back down from it, distorted.

"All these people are singing my song?"

"Is it yours? Or did the song sing *you?* But I take what you mean. It is the same one. It has more power than what you have thought yourself capable of harboring. No song will be more heard than what your friends will perform. What Carl will teach your friends. What you teach Carl. It will grow to become anthem. It will be fire for fuel."

"You mean the song did this? It stirred up this crowd?"

"No. An epoch of violence and neglect did those things."

And my friends? Shayna was about to say, but they were already drifting into the center of her disjointed awareness. Three of them stood there at the front of the crowd. Tom was missing. Carl and Katja stood together with their eyes fixed straight ahead, and their faces were older. It was hard to tell how many years they'd gained. Now that she focused more tightly on them, she made out the lines of scars, tangled and thick, rising up the side of Katja's neck and left cheek. She saw her hand clamped tightly onto Carl's. Balboa stood at her other side – and it was when she saw him that her heart, in some other place, seemed to stop. His hair had grown out long. He was missing one arm.

"No," she whispered. "Not like this."

"You already know what happens next," Cass said.

Something crackled, rising above than the human cacophony like one hard beat of a drum. Her vision pushed instinctively away from the direction of that sound; she struggled ever more frantically to look away, to will herself away from this scene and back up into the sky, but she couldn't. The horrible drumbeat grew louder. Its tempo accelerated. The music from the crowd was collapsing into pure shrill noise just as she felt Cass's hand pressing more tightly on her own, until finally they rose up again. The music, the shots and the screaming were all muted, and everything in the streets resumed itself as only a throbbing blur of light. It was throbbing more tensely now as her vision pulled back into the high and chilly winds.

This time she kept willing herself upward until she passed above the Cology, and then still higher, until she was even above the winds. No altitude seemed far enough from that ground. When she finally stopped, every last individual detail of that circuit board was too small to see. From up there, looking down over the entire Tropolis as it rushed through a formless blur of years, decades, generations, she watched the web's last thin strands of living light fade and recoil, dripping back toward the center like water in a drain, until it was all gone.

It was quiet up there. She had never in her life heard a silence so deep.

"You always knew that this world is dying," Cass said. "A long time before you knew you were. Before anyone told you."

"Yes," Shayna whispered in her mind.

The cool wind blew again, and she felt the present rising back to meet her. Back above Greentowne, the thin blue fissure still peeked through the crystal walls, crooked like a question mark, the sun was still burning on the mirror of the ocean.

"And still you are afraid of what could be born from these ashes while there's still fire left in them."

"I'm afraid? Is that what you think?" she replied instantly – but in the hesitation that followed, the question trickled back through her mind. She felt a rising tightness in her face and throat, and her eyes somewhere were watering when she answered: "To be responsible for it? Alone? Of course I'm afraid. I've never been so terrified of anything."

Her voice on the wind said, as if puzzled, "Are you alone?"

The thin clouds blew through Shayna's suddenly silent head. She tried to call Cass's name to the empty air. She looked down and saw the shadow of two people, hands joined, arms spread. But there was some other shadow there too, much larger, bringing itself steadily into focus.

Cass said "It comes."

Shayna turned in the air as something's black weight crashed into her chest and jolted her to consciousness. She found herself drenched in sweat and breathing hard, with only the bass weighing her down. Her head fell back onto the pillow.

"Shay?" Carl gasped, hurrying to the side of the bed.

"Is she here?" she demanded. "Was she?"

"Who?"

She grabbed the pillow and threw it away. "Never mind. Just a fever dream." But she stared at the pages of music stacked there on the table by the bed, and almost said: *burn them. Burn them now.*

"Oh," Carl said, rubbing his face. When he took his hands away, she saw the red in his eyes, ringed by creases, caked with old tears. He looked almost as old already as he had in her vision. She wanted to tell him about it, but the words caught in her throat. She could only whisper sadly:

"You don't need to do this."

"I want to."

"You've done everything you can. You don't have to put yourself through this."

Carl said nothing.

"I think I can finally understand why my mother didn't. Put me through that. I'm finally seeing why she left."

"She left you?"

"She was sick. She got it before I was even born, but somehow she kept herself alive long enough to take care of me. Through my whole childhood. When she knew it was time, when she couldn't hold it off any longer.... She left one night while I was asleep."

"That's horrible," Carl said quietly.

"It's hard to explain." She turned the teeth on their necklace chain, deep in thought. "It's hard, but the closer I get, the less I'm afraid of doing it alone. The more I think maybe I should."

"Don't say that." His head leaned down against the edge of the mattress. "I can't. I can't leave you."

Her hand fell softly on his head. She saw his breath come and go unsteadily through his back.

"You really are in love with me," she whispered.

"I know you always thought I was just some stupid arrogant fat-head. I tried so hard to be that. I thought that was what you wanted. I thought that's what every girl wants. A big, fat-headed asshole like me."

She stroked his sweaty head with her thumb and sighed.

"I'm sorry," she said. She wanted to say something more than that. She wanted to give him words that could actually mean something – but all she could think of was his face as she'd just come from seeing it, and all she could see was the thin stack of paper on the table by the bed.

She barely heard him when he said "If you ask me to leave you alone, I will. But please. Don't ask me that. I want to be here with you."

The horrible drum beat crackled through her memory, making her shut her eyes. "I don't want you to get hurt."

"You can't help that," he whispered.

"What?"

"You can't help hurting me. I just wish you'd trust me. Trust that it's my choice, and that I want to be here."

"Trust you," she echoed, lost in thought. Behind her closed eyes she still saw him, standing with Katja and Balboa at the front of the crowd, lit by fire. His words washed over her in her head in repeating waves, until she said "I have to trust you, don't I? That's it. That's the only way."

When she opened her eyes, she only saw the younger Carl, now squinting slightly and asking "Are we talking about the same thing?"

"There's one last thing we need to add to the song."

In a flash the paper and pen were back in his hands. He cleared his throat and wiped his face. "Ready."

"Before I give it to you, though, you have to make me a promise. It's an unusual promise."

"Anything," he said instantly.

She sighed and said "This one last thing I need to add to the song – I'm not going to tell you what it means. I know you'll figure it out on your own. When you do, you have to promise me you'll keep it a secret. You can't explain it to anyone else. You have to let them figure it out for themselves too. But play the song for them, as many of them as you can."

His brow furrowed slightly, but he replied "I will. I swear."

"There's one deeper layer of notes I want you to add. It should be way in the background, just loud enough for you to notice it there. No chords. Just individual notes. It will sound kind of random and dissonant, but that won't hurt the song."

"What are the notes?"

Shayna closed her eyes and focused her memory. "There will be seven of these extra sequences of notes. Separate them a little and spread them evenly throughout the song. The first section starts with… middle-C."

"Middle-C?"

C for carbon, she thought. "Yeah. Start by hitting it five times. Just five C-notes in succession." *Carbon has six protons. Hydrogen has one, so six minus one…* "Five notes higher than Middle C, that's E. Right?"

"Um… yeah."

"Then follow the five C notes immediately with ten E notes."

"Okay."

Five carbons, ten hydrogens, she thought, and she whispered just under her breath: *Cyclopentane.*

"What?"

"Nothing. That's the first set. Here's the second one."

1

It was there the moment she opened her eyes. Her eyes had stopped focusing properly, but she perceived its shape, perched on the windowsill, icy black against the purple gloaming. The longer she focused on it, the larger it grew. The hooked beak turned.

She looked away, shivering in terror. *Just a dream*, she thought. *Just a sick hallucination.* She forced herself back to sleep – but it was there every time she drifted awake.

"C-Carl," she whispered fearfully as soon as she heard him leaning up out of his sleeping bag on the floor.

He hurried up to her. "What is it?"

"Do you see it?"

"See what?"

"On the windowsill."

He turned and walked toward the window. She heard him unlocking it, sliding it up.

"Don't open it!" she screamed. "Don't let it in!"

He slammed it shut. He closed the blinds until the room was dark.

"I didn't see anything," he said.

She kept her head turned to the wall and swallowed hard. His hand lay down on her forehead for a moment.

"God, you're burning."

He ran to the sink to soak a washcloth.

When his back was turned, she looked again. It was still there. Its monstrous shadow showed through the narrow strips of light between the blinds.

In another blurry interval of consciousness, there was a second shadow in the corner of her eye – smaller and softer. Cass's voice, from within a face whose details were too fuzzy to make out, said: "You changed the song."

"Yes," Shayna whispered back.

"That music I showed you before is gone now. Do you want to see the new music? It's very different. I want you to see how it will go."

Shayna swallowed hard and turned away from the small reaching fingers. "No."

"Why?"

"It was hard for me to make that choice, but I made it. If things turn out differently because of what I've done, even if some things turn out worse, I can't take it back now. I have to live with it."

Cass's foggy outline seemed to consider this a moment before whispering "Then I'll show you just as you cross."

In a blink she was gone again, but the bird remained.

It stayed perched there and did not leave. Once she saw it stretch its wings. Sometimes she thought she heard the clicking of its gigantic talons along the brickwork, or the tap of its beak against the glass. Sometimes, even through the blinds – even when the purple stars had swarmed her vision to the point of near-total blindness – she thought she saw its monstrous eye, always peering inward. But she couldn't stay turned toward the wall forever. She tried to focus on the ceiling. She tried to focus on the bass in her arms, but the ache in her fingers had risen until she couldn't play any more. She held them close to her face and looked. The tips were all red, full of broken capillaries.

"Carl?" she called.

He didn't answer and she couldn't see him, but she knew he was there.

"We've been here three days," she said. "You haven't left this room. You haven't eaten."

"Neither have you," he mumbled back. "You first. I'll eat after you eat."

"I can't."

Somewhere in the fizzling clouds of static, she thought she saw him, hunched over, back to the wall.

"You have to take care of yourself," she said.

"No, I don't."

"Why the hell not?"

He chuckled sadly. She heard him flicking his lighter.

"Because," he said, expelling smoke.

"Because what?"

The window rattled faintly. Beak taps. Sharp points scraping on the bricks.

"Because once you're gone I have nothing. It's over for me. All of it."

She said nothing.

"I knew, that…." he began, and his voice was quivering now. "I knew all along, since the first moment you told me you had the blight. I knew that once this day came, I'd have to die."

"You don't," she protested.

"I have to die," he said, more forcefully. "And that's that."

"You have to play my song."

Carl's breath entered and exited without a word. His foggy outline in the purple stars seemed to shake its head.

"You don't understand," she shouted. She clamped the blanket in her fists and started pushing herself up from the bed. "You have to play it. That's it, Carl. Fuck that dent in the Cology. Fuck all our missions. They were still worthless. They're not the legacy. The song is. Promise—!" She lapsed into breathlessness.

His hands held hers and eased her back down onto the mattress.

"Promise," she said, gripping his arm tightly.

"I swear," he said awkwardly. "I'll do it. I'll play the song."

Gradually she let go of him. She lay back, fighting for breath.

"I would be doing this alone in my concrete box now," she whispered between breaths. "I would've stayed there in Printing Station 117, and none of this would ever have happened. If I'd just said yes instead of no when she asked me."

"When who asked you? Asked you what?"

His hand reached for her face, hovering shakily on the verge of pushing her sweaty hair away from her eyes, but recoiled.

Her own fingers closed around the necklace of teeth and held it tightly. She turned her head and stared into the window.

"Open it," she said.

"Are you sure?"

"I'm done being afraid."

His vague shape stepped back from the bed and regarded her anxiously through the swirling stars. He hesitated. Finally he raised the blinds, flipped the lock, and pulled upward.

The man-sized bird stood there, pitch black against the burning daylight.

"Come on," she said. "What are you waiting for?"

Behind her eyes, everything turns into a harsh white light –

Until, amid a deep and resonant sound, it cracks open.

IF YOU LIKED
THIS BOOK
TELL PEOPLE ABOUT IT

WORD OF MOUTH IS
PROBABLY THE ONLY WAY
ANYONE WILL EVER
KNOW IT EXISTS

COPIES CAN BE ACQUIRED AT
ELBANGS.COM/LOITERERS

Acknowledgments

This book owes its existence to the help of many accomplices, both witting and unwitting.

Foremost among them are all the brave men and women of the *Loiterers Publication Exploratory Committee*: Alice, Bill, Cameron, Carla, Charlie, Dominique, Erin, other Erin, Graham, Isha, Jared, Jennifer, Jessica, Jill, Katheryn, Kirsten, Laura, Mia, Michele, Nora, Oliver, Patrick, Phil, Rachel, Stephen, and Mom and Dad.

Thanks to the three brave Greeners who bore the deeply unfortunate task of working with me on the first version: Brian, Joe and Stephanie. We need not speak of that draft again.

Much is owed to the invaluable assistance of my developmental editors, Beth Stokes and Marta Tanrikulu, without whom this work would be a dim and self-sabotaging shadow of its present self - with thanks also to Barbara Sjoholm and Kyra Freestar for bringing us together.

Thanks to Joshua Ortega for early inspiration.

Thanks to the Bauhaus crew, who supplied me with the horrific quantities of caffeine required to produce this and all my other work.

Thanks to Disturbed Type for their splendid Pistolgrip typeface.

Special thanks are owed to the following people for unspecified reasons: Aaron, Kristin, Laura, Lauren, Michael, Madison.

Incalculable gratitude is owed to my many teachers. I was good friends with most and bitter rivals with some. Without the following in particular, I would be nothing. They are Kathleen Eamon, Norm Hollingshead, Nancy Koppelman, Hersh Mandelman, Tara McBennet, Steve Miranda, Harumi Moruzzi, Lawrence Mosqueda, Dave Robinson, and Stephanie Taylor.

This book could never have been written without the George W. Bush Administration.

Thank you, stranger.

About the Author

~~Elliott~~ ELLY **Bangs** lived in Seattle, Washington, where she was raised on a steady diet of thin but perpetual rain, orange street lamps, new-age cult spirituality, and crumbling neo-classical public schools. Over the years she grew stranger and more obsessive. She became convinced that this first novel was ~~his~~ her best shot - at what, exactly, remains unclear. As soon as it was cursorily edited and self-published, she rolled away on ~~his~~ her bicycle, leaving behind everything and everyone she once knew. She is out there now, somewhere, lodged in cheap motels or roadside ditches, living on gas station food and wild berries.

All profits from the sale of this book go to keeping ~~him~~ her alive and fed. You can learn more, and follow ~~his~~ her progress and mumbled ruminations on ~~his~~ her website, **elbangs.com**.

UPDATE:

SHE SURVIVED

SHE CAME BACK

SHE CHILLED THE FUCK OUT

SHE'S TRANSITIONING FROM MALE TO FEMALE

SHE'LL WRITE YOU A BETTER BOOK NEXT TIME

Made in the USA
Charleston, SC
05 February 2013